"You mean to tell us that the United States has been . . . destroyed?"

The four of them looked at each other in absolute despair. Trask struggled with his emotions as he fought to stifle thoughts of what might have happened to people he knew and loved in the United States. What was it like back there? He thought of the movies he had seen depicting the horrible aftermath of nuclear war and a shiver arose from deep within him. Could it be like what was portrayed in the movies? Probably not, he concluded. It was probably much worse.

"So where does that leave us?" Elverson asked of no one in particular.

Trask shook his head. "In Hell, I guess."

Other Avon Books by
John Campbell

RAID ON TRUMAN

COBRA DANE

DANE

JOHN CAMPBELL

AVON BOOKS ◆ NEW YORK

COBRA DANE is an original publication of Avon Books. This work has never before appeared in book form. This work is a novel. Any similarity to actual persons or events is purely coincidental. Though some names and characters in this book are real, events surrounding them are fictitious.

AVON BOOKS
A division of
The Hearst Corporation
1350 Avenue of the Americas
New York, New York 10019

Copyright © 1995 by John Campbell
Published by arrangement with the author
Library of Congress Catalog Card Number: 94-96257
ISBN: 0-380-77686-3

First Avon Books Printing: February 1995

AVON TRADEMARK REG. U.S. PAT. OFF. AND IN OTHER COUNTRIES, MARCA REGISTRADA, HECHO EN U.S.A.

Printed in the U.S.A.

RA   10   9   8   7   6   5   4   3   2   1

To Mom and Dad
Thanks for everything

Acknowledgments

Many people have come together to make this work possible. My brother, Chris Campbell, helped greatly with research, and Clark Hafer provided a candid early review. My daughter, Christine, also helped research some details, along with Nick Giangiulio, Jerry Dietrich, Stan Reinhold, Rikk Wolfs, Eric Sudano, Chuck Fulton, John Nuttall, and Carol Mittman. LCDR H. V. Ross, U.S. Navy, Naval Air Station, Adak, helped with information on one of our nation's most remote, but not forgotten, naval bases. I am grateful to my agent, Elizabeth Pomada, for handling my works with a great deal of professionalism. I thank my editor, Tom Colgan, for giving this novel the opportunity to get before the public.

To all of these friends, I give my heartfelt thanks.

Author's Note

■ ▪ ■ ▪ ■ ▪ ■

The island of Shemya and the COBRA DANE radar depicted in this novel are real, as is most of the description of the island and its environment. The nuclear power plant and the situation screen in the Space Surveillance Operations Room are fictional.

As an aid to the reader, the time differences among the major locations in the novel, with the island of Shemya serving as the reference point, are as follows:

Moscow—thirteen hours later than Shemya
Washington, D.C.—five hours later than Shemya
NORAD in Colorado—three hours later than Shemya

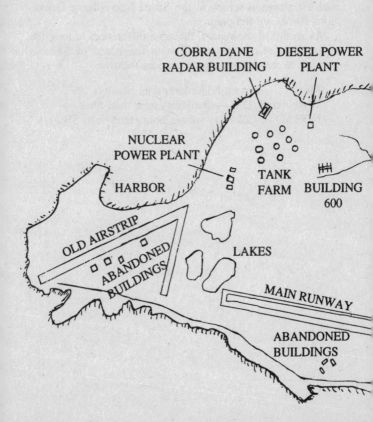

COBRA DANE
RADAR BUILDING

DIESEL POWER
PLANT

NUCLEAR
POWER PLANT

HARBOR

TANK
FARM

BUILDING
600

OLD AIRSTRIP

ABANDONED
BUILDINGS

LAKES

MAIN RUNWAY

ABANDONED
BUILDINGS

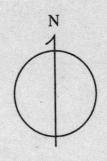

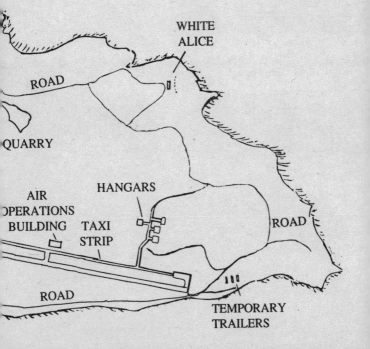

N

WHITE
ALICE

ROAD

QUARRY

HANGARS

AIR
OPERATIONS
BUILDING

TAXI
STRIP

ROAD

ROAD

TEMPORARY
TRAILERS

COBRA DANE

PROLOGUE

His code name was Vulcher.

The safe house he had just entered was at the end of the block with its rear backing up to dense woods. The agents worried about that particular arrangement—it was anything but a coincidence. The SVR, successor to the KGB, had carefully selected this house to provide a means of escape through which no vehicle could follow. Had they cared to investigate, the agents knew that they would find a hidden car, or most likely a van, on the other side of the woods.

CIA counterintelligence agent Nancy Logan peered through the periscope that poked through the roof of the van they were in. She could see the front of the house and a car that was parked in the driveway. Both belonged to Vulcher's control agent.

This particular control was new to the agency, and the CIA agents working on sleeper activities eagerly anticipated discovering who else the control was involved with.

A secret protocol hidden within the aid deal worked out with the former Soviet Union had included the provision that all sleeper agents within the United States were to be deactivated. Accordingly the Commonwealth of Independent States began to recall all sleepers and their control agents, while the U.S. intelligence agencies and the FBI worried whether the Russians would deactivate all of their so-called illegals. The FBI and the CIA launched a massive effort to monitor their deactivation.

Normally the CIA doesn't operate within the United States except under special circumstances and when no U.S.

citizens are involved, but extra agents were needed to ensure that all known agents from intelligence agencies of the former Soviet Union were sent home.

Nancy Logan, leader of Surveillance Team Tollroad, heard the front door open and close through her earphones, and listened to the conversation begin. Agents had hurriedly set up audio equipment to listen in on conversations within the house. Safe houses normally didn't have elaborate countermeasures for eavesdropping equipment. Just their presence was a tip-off that the house was used by the SVR. Logan's surveillance team utilized an old technique of bouncing a laser beam off a window and precisely measuring how the reflection of the laser beam varied in intensity. Conversations caused vibrations in the window glass which varied the angle and hence the intensity of the reflected laser light which was received by a detector in Logan's van. With some signal processing, conversations within the house could be recovered.

The Company didn't know much about Vulcher. Nancy Logan had been tracking him for a few years now, since March of 1991. The Soviet Union was still in existence then, even though it was fatally ill at the time. No pictures of him existed, except a couple of rear shots that Logan herself took two years ago. She had stared at those shots for many an hour while wondering what the man was like. She hated to admit it, but Vulcher had become something of an obsession to her.

Now the end was near, and an anticlimactic one at that. Vulcher's control agent would give him the orders to go home, and off he would go, perhaps never knowing that he had been chased so diligently and for such a long time.

Logan took her eyes away from the periscope eyepiece and glanced at her partner, Tom McCue. He was busy scanning their laser equipment until he caught Nancy's eye. He winked and grinned. She smiled back. There was no stress with this assignment, just monitor, record, and go on to the next set of sleeper agents.

She turned her attention back to the conversation in the safe house. They spoke in Russian, but both Logan and McCue were fluent in the language. The voices would fade

now and then, but she caught most of it. After some des-
ultory talk about nothing in particular, the control got down
to business.

"I have new orders for you," said the control.

"Is it the replace— . . ." The voice faded momentarily.
". . . that we were waiting for?"

Logan winced and pressed the headphones closer to her
ears.

"No. It's not that at all," said the control, and hesitated.
"You're being recalled to Russia."

Logan held her breath and heard only the pounding of
her heart. An angry voice, presumably Vulcher's, responded, but she couldn't make out what he was saying.
So, she thought, he doesn't like the idea. Well, I don't like
the idea of you roaming around all over my country with
orders to do Lord knows what.

"These are orders from . . ." The control's voice faded.
". . . and you will obey them," he concluded matter-of-
factly.

Logan heard no response and strained her ears for any
sound. There was a scraping of a chair and some footsteps.
She wished that they had an X-ray machine to see what
was happening inside the house.

"Oh," said the control. There was surprise in his voice.
"Let's not get melodramatic about this. Put that down and
let's talk about this rationally."

Put *what* down? thought Logan. A gun? "Uh, Tom. I
think we've got a problem," said Logan hastily.

He turned around with his eyebrows raised. "What?"

Logan pointed to her earphones. "I think Vulcher has a
gun on his control."

McCue quickly put on a set of earphones and listened
intently. Suddenly Vulcher's voice came through loud and
clear.

"You're the only one who knows about me, aren't you?
I mean, those idiots in Yasenevo know they have an agent
here, but they really don't know it's me, do they?"

"Look, don't get any ideas—" began the control.

"And they don't know what my next assignment is either, do they?" asked Vulcher. "Only you know that, don't

you? They tell people to replace agents in certain locations, but they don't know exactly who that is."

"For God's sake, it's over!" shouted the control. "Go home. Relax. The war we were preparing for will never happen."

"Are you sure?" said Vulcher. There was a hesitation. "There are many people who would like to see the old ways return."

"Like who?" asked the control. "A few Communists and those stupid nationalists in the Duma?" he retorted, referring to the Russian parliament. "The people will never permit it."

"If you dismantle this network, then . . ." Vulcher's voice faded. ". . . without you, the network will go on."

Uh-oh, thought Logan. She reached inside her thin summer jacket and fingered her weapon in a holster on her hip. Logan yanked out the Beretta 9-mm automatic and took a Knight silencer out of another pocket. She snapped the silencer on the gun barrel and placed it by her side.

Logan gave McCue a sideways glance. His eyes were wider than she had ever seen them, but he took the hint and duplicated her actions. If they had to fire, then the silencers would improve their chances of keeping the action from the surrounding residents.

One last remark was heard over their headsets. It was Vulcher's voice. *"Va fun qulo."* His voice had a menacing tone to it, even while pronouncing the obviously foreign expression, as if he were at an execution.

Logan gave McCue a quizzical look. What does that mean? she mouthed quietly. McCue shrugged and glanced at the reel-to-reel tape recorder, as if to say, We've got it on tape, and we'll analyze it later.

"Do we save him, or what?" asked McCue out loud after a moment.

It was a fair question for Nancy Logan, the leader of the surveillance team. They were under strict orders not to interfere, but could they stand by and listen to a man being murdered?

Logan thought furiously. She had only three units. The unit she was in was to monitor activities inside the house;

there was one unit to cover the streets behind Logan's unit, and one to cover the roads beyond the woods in case they escaped in that direction. If there was any intervention on their part, it would have to be from Logan and McCue— the other two units couldn't get there in time.

The argument between the two SVR agents seemed to wind down, and Logan and McCue began to relax. The voices stopped, but a few seconds later they were replaced by scuffling sounds. They heard the sound of a chair being knocked over.

"Oh, man," said McCue nervously. "They're struggling for the gun."

A loud, powerful sound, like a puff of compressed air, came over the audio link. A silenced gunshot!

"That's it," said Logan in a loud voice as she keyed her microphone. "All units converge on the house. Possible gunfire." She ripped her earphones from her head and looked at McCue. "Let's go!"

They both jumped from the rear door of the van into the murky heat of early summer twilight. Logan and McCue kept their weapons at their sides and inside their jackets in an attempt to hide them from any of the local residents who might look out their windows. They hurried up the street, with McCue taking the rear door that led to the woods and Logan going up to the front windows. Luckily one window was open with only a screen in between her and the inside of the house. She peered in and saw no movement and heard no sound except the constant racket of the crickets in the woods.

Logan forced the screen upward gingerly. It scraped a little, but the din of the crickets swamped the sounds. She got inside quickly and moved quietly through the living room to the short hallway that led to the kitchen.

Another loud puffing sound was suddenly heard in the silent house. Logan's breath caught in her throat. She stopped and leaned against the living room wall and peered cautiously down the hallway. A chair was lying on the floor in the kitchen, and she could see that the rear door was closed.

She sensed sudden movement in the kitchen without actually seeing anyone, and pulled her head back behind the wall. The puffing sounds came to her in rapid succession with the immediate destruction of the wall right behind her. She was thrown away from the wall with a sudden force as if a wrecking ball had slammed into her back. Her left shoulder felt like lead, then pain shot through her as she tumbled to the floor.

Logan groaned out loud. I'm hit, she thought as she faded into unconsciousness.

Tom McCue froze when he heard the gunfire from the silenced automatic emanate from the kitchen. He was uncertain of the origin of the sounds due to the loud noises from the crickets that populated the woods behind the house, and because both the kitchen window and door were closed. More gunfire? he asked himself. He'd have to get in there in a hurry in case Logan was in trouble, but he'd have to be careful doing it.

He slid along the back wall of the house with his weapon pointed toward the kitchen door. McCue got next to the kitchen window and cautiously peered inside. He saw no one, but part of the kitchen was blocked by cabinets on either side of the narrow window. McCue strained his hearing to pick up any additional sounds, but heard nothing.

He ducked below the windowsill and slid toward the kitchen door. The door suddenly opened and a man filled the doorway. McCue's eyes focused immediately on the weapon the stranger had in his hand. The barrel was pointed directly at his head. McCue saw his situation clearly. He was still in a crouch to get by the window, and he had his weapon pointed down at the ground and not at the kitchen door.

McCue yanked his arm upward in a desperate attempt to aim his weapon at the man in the doorway.

A minute and a half later, units Beta and Gamma of Surveillance Team Tollroad arrived, with one unit taking the rear door and the other unit taking the same route through the front window that Logan had taken moments before. Joel Eldridge and his partner in Beta unit found

Logan lying in a pool of blood where she had fallen. She was unconscious, but she would live.

Eldridge examined the wall next to Logan. It had been shredded by several bullets from what looked to be a 9-mm or larger weapon. Recovered bullets from either the wall or Logan herself would tell them many things about the weapon used. Vulcher had apparently just fired through the wallboard and wooden studs to get to Logan as she stood behind the wall for cover.

But why hadn't he come into the living room and finished Logan off? Eldridge asked himself. Gamma unit found the answer.

Gamma unit found McCue dead with two bullets in his head just outside the rear door, and they concluded that McCue must have interrupted Vulcher. The SVR agent had finished off the CIA man and then escaped through the woods.

They also found the SVR control agent dead in the kitchen. Eldridge surveyed the scene with mounting disgust. Couldn't anything go right? Did the damn Russians screw up everything? They had just cost the life of a CIA agent and had wounded another. This incident would be investigated very thoroughly and the search for Vulcher would take on new meaning. Now he was wanted for murder.

Eldridge's partner walked up to him and showed him a pad of paper that had been found in the kitchen. On it, scribbled in capital letters, were two words.

COBRA DANE.

CHAPTER 1

■ · ■ · ■ · ■

In the early hours of Christmas morning Lieutenant Colonel Alan Driscoll received the message he had been waiting for. The message came in the form of a code word uttered in a low voice during a seemingly innocuous phone call. All their preparations were complete. There was nothing to do but wait for the right conditions to complete their mission. Their preparations were thorough, but they had barely enough people to accomplish the task.

There were a few worries, however. The security people could present a problem and the timing of the whole operation had to be just right. One slip . . . He left the thought unfinished. He contented himself with the fact that they were still at DEFCON 4 and that left plenty of time for last-minute adjustments. As the deputy commander of the 16th Surveillance Squadron, his orders weren't likely to be questioned. He'd have to stay right on top of the entire situation, though, right up until the moment of action.

He came out of his reverie as one of the console operators said something about increased activity. He stood up from the table and followed the watch officer over to the console. The console operator, a master sergeant, pointed to some rapidly changing numbers on the screen.

Could this be it? Driscoll turned cold as he realized what the next few moments would require of him. The screen registered a blinking DEFCON 3 indication.

The phone rang. He could hear the two men near him inhale quickly. The ring was continuous and stopped only when the phone was answered. The watch officer hurried over to the telephone and put his hand on the receiver. He hesitated and glanced back at Driscoll with a look that was laced with fear. Driscoll nodded to him. He picked up the receiver, listened for a while and said a few words of acknowledgment. The watch officer hung up and looked straight at Driscoll.

"It's no false alarm. DEFCON 3 is straight from NORAD," he said in a hoarse voice. Driscoll swallowed, but his mouth was dry. He glanced quickly at the other console, which was identical to the one he was standing next to, even to the master sergeant who was the console operator. The indications on its display were the same.

"Let's get the situation screen up," he ordered.

Five seconds later, the screen on the wall facing the consoles began to light up. After a few minutes to get the proper commands into the computer, the screen was set up with the desired displays. The blue-and-yellow emblem of the 16th Surveillance Squadron, or 16 SURS, lit up the screen in much the same manner as NORAD's logo, which is displayed on screens in the North American Defense Command's headquarters in Cheyenne Mountain, Colorado. The emblem depicted the COBRA DANE radar building with lightning bolts radiating from it to a missile and satellites, thereby indicating the radar's dual mission of missile tracking and space object tracking. A huge cobra snake coming out from behind the building overlooked the scene.

A master sergeant typed in another command and the display changed to a map of the United States at the bottom, with Canada and the Aleutians in the middle, and the Kamchatka Peninsula with Siberia beyond at the top of the screen.

It'll begin at the top of the screen, he thought, and he kept his eyes glued there for several seconds.

"Nothing yet," said the watch officer with obvious relief

in his voice. Driscoll began to breathe almost normally as he settled down for a wait. These things sometimes take a while, he thought. He suddenly realized how ridiculous a thought that was. During a drill it sometimes took a while, but this wasn't a drill. As the number two man in 16 SURS, he was briefed on all drills beforehand—there hadn't been any briefings this time. He and his men had orders to swing into action in the absence of any signal from his superiors if the United States went on a war footing. He had better get ready. There wouldn't be much time to correct things if anything went wrong.

Driscoll walked over to his briefcase that was lying on the floor next to the door, picked it up, and brought it over to the table in the middle of the room. The action would afford him a few extra seconds, and he felt better for it. He sat down and thought furiously about each step of the operation, where people were located in this part of the building, and how many there were.

The fifth floor of the COBRA DANE radar building had three main rooms and a corridor interconnecting them. Driscoll was in the Space Surveillance Operations Center, which had the control consoles for the COBRA DANE radar and the situation screen, which provided a command view of the strategic situation between the former Soviet Union and the United States. To Driscoll's right as he faced the situation screen was the Mission Processing Room, which contained analysts who provided NORAD invaluable data on Russian ICBM shots. To Driscoll's left was the Computer Room, which held the massive electronic master of the COBRA DANE radar. The main system console was located there along with arrays of disks that formed the extensive memory of the computer.

There would be three men in the Mission Processing Room; one, possibly two, in the Computer Room; and the three with him in the Operations Center.

He added them up mentally and swore under his breath. If only they could have spared another man. He forced himself to calm down and think about the other locations on the island. A lot depended on the young men in the adjacent building, the Administrative Building. There were a lot of rooms to check with the potential of a lot of scattered personnel. It all would take time, lots of time. He steeled himself for the wait. It wasn't long.

An alarm went off. It was a kind of a warble, a wavering noise that struck terror in the minds of all the military and civilian personnel who attended the radar. The radar changed from a tracking mode to early warning mode, indicated by pie-shaped sectors appearing over a map of Russia on the two consoles. Lieutenant Colonel Driscoll reached for his briefcase.

The phone rang again with its incessant bell.

He unzipped the briefcase.

The watch officer stared in disbelief at the console.

"DEFCON 1!" he gasped.

Driscoll pulled an automatic from the briefcase.

Symbols appeared at the top of the situation screen.

Driscoll flipped off the safety, aimed, and put a bullet into the head of the master sergeant farthest from him. He whirled and with another deafening blast he shot the watch officer in the side. The other master sergeant began to move before the watch officer hit the floor. He got up and ran for the doorway that led to the Processing Room.

Driscoll put a bullet in his back just before he could open the door. The man was lifted off the floor by the force of the bullet entering his body. He pitched forward into the door, and then fell backwards spread-eagled on the floor. The phone continued its awful ring, but now there was no one to pick it up.

Driscoll sprang over the body and rushed through the doorway with one thought frozen on his mind. The next room, the Processing Room, contained air force personnel who also could pick up a phone and foil the whole operation.

The watch officer for the Processing Room was seated at his desk furiously typing into a computer console; he was distinctly whiter in complexion than when Driscoll had seen him last. The other two people in the room were doing much the same thing. Apparently they hadn't heard the commotion that Driscoll had generated in the next room.

He walked quickly up to the watch officer, who didn't

even glance up. Driscoll shot him in the face at point-blank range. Before the watch officer's nearly headless body hit the floor, Driscoll turned and fired at the other two men who stared in amazement. He *missed*. The two began to move in opposite directions. He fired again, hit one of them and sent him writhing and screaming to the floor. The other man ran to the door which led to the corridor beyond. He was through it in a flash, and Driscoll desperately ran to the doorway after him. He looked out and saw that the man was almost to the end of the corridor.

He fired twice rapidly, with less than accurate aim, and managed to hit the fleeing man in the leg. This sent the terrified enlisted man sprawling at the end of the corridor. Driscoll went halfway to him and shot him twice in the head as he tried to crawl to the doorway of the Computer Room. The Computer Room door opened and, in perfect position, Driscoll easily shot the stunned air force captain in the chest.

Driscoll cautiously covered the remaining distance to the Computer Room door and tiptoed over the body of his most recent victim. He paused to listen in the doorway. Hearing nothing, he entered the room and his gaze swept past the bulk of the computer cabinets to the system console and back again. The room was vacant.

COBRA DANE ADMINISTRATIVE BUILDING

Airman First Class Bobby Jensen heard the DEFCON 1 alarm and knew exactly what to do. The boiler room in one corner of the single-story, flat building adjacent to the CO-BRA DANE radar building had concealed his equipment. He wondered if he had the guts to complete his mission, but after the DEFCON signal had come, he had had no time to think about it.

Sergeant Ed McDonough suddenly showed up at his elbow. Jensen jumped at his quiet arrival, and they gave each other a quick shocked look. Is this really happening? they asked each other without a word being spoken. A second later they turned to the business at hand and started to get their gear on. Jensen was responsible for this side of the building. McDonough had the other side.

The gas mask was the first thing they put on, then the sack of tear gas canisters along with their M16s and clip belts. They were weighted down, but they would lighten their loads quickly as they moved throughout the building. Jensen exited the boiler room looking like some alien from another planet rather than the cherubic-faced, clean-cut young man that he was. Sergeant McDonough quickly disappeared up the corridor to get to the other side of the building.

Jensen glanced down the corridor from the boiler room at the offices on either side. This would be his toughest challenge. Most of the rest of the building was for fuel for the backup generators that would power the massive radar in the building next to him if anything happened to the island's nuclear power plant. There were some other offices, but there probably wouldn't be many people in them. The possibility of APs nearby gave him some worries.

Jensen didn't hesitate. He threw three tear gas canisters down the corridor, one to the far end, one in the middle, and one only a few feet from him. He pulled back on the M16's T-shaped cocking bar and boldly walked down the center of the corridor. The gas issued from the canisters with a seeming vengeance, rapidly permeating the hallway and the offices on either side. Most of the office doors were left open, which aided the process immeasurably.

A man came choking out of the manager's office on Jensen's right, tears streaming down his face. He staggered over to the opposite wall and slid to the floor while gurgling in agony. Jensen knew now what was meant by incapacitation. The airman stared at the man, then took aim. He had never killed a man before. Two other men, in much the same state as the first man, came stumbling out of offices up the corridor.

Jensen knew he had to act quickly or the situation would rapidly become uncontrollable. He squeezed the trigger of his M16 twice and put two bullets into the chest of the first man. Orders were orders, Jensen thought.

He walked up to the other two men in the corridor. They

hadn't seen Jensen kill the first man due to the increasing density of the clouds of tear gas that were still being created by the three gas canisters. The two had heard the shots, but in their agony didn't know and didn't care where they came from. The two stricken men fell to their knees and began to crawl toward the end of the corridor and safety. Jensen shot them both cleanly in the back of the head using one shot apiece. It'll be all right, he thought. I'll complete this part of the mission no sweat.

COBRA DANE RADAR BUILDING

Lieutenant Colonel Driscoll reentered the hallway from the Computer Room and began to wonder how many were left in the building when he heard sounds of footsteps on the stairs at the opposite end of the corridor. A second later, two APs appeared with M16s chest high. Driscoll thought about a bluff, but instantly decided there was no time. He snapped off a shot at them, then quickly looked for someplace to go. He was right next to the Operations Room, where it had all started, but the door had a cipher lock. He shifted the gun to his left hand and fired the last two shots in the clip to keep the APs ducking as the fingers on his right hand flew over the keys in a short, instinctive dance.

Driscoll was through the doorway and to relative safety just as the APs opened fire. The burst of automatic weapons fire slammed into the door and shattered most of it in a frenzy of violence. Driscoll flipped the empty clip to the floor and desperately groped in his pocket for a full one. He grabbed the last one and rammed it home. He thumbed the lever that allowed the slide to move forward and pump a bullet into the chamber. With the phone still ringing continually, he retraced his steps and ran back to the Processing Room.

The Processing Room was quiet, with only the humming of the fans in the computer terminals and the sound of a printer spitting out some data on the incoming warheads. The unnerving stillness drilled into him. They were all dead now, but just moments before the room had buzzed with activity. Driscoll commanded himself to think about his situation and the very dangerous Air Policemen just outside the room.

A desperate plan formed in his mind. After crossing the room as quietly as he could, he listened at the door that led to the corridor and the APs. He heard them move past the doorway and down the hallway toward the door they had just destroyed.

Driscoll boldly moved through the doorway and into the corridor. The APs had their backs to him and were moving away from him, only instead of them being side by side as Driscoll had hoped, they were in line, with the lead AP obscured by the trailing one.

Driscoll opened fire, and instantly killed the rear AP but missed the other as his quarry leaped through the shattered doorway and into the Operations Room. Driscoll swore out loud and returned quickly to the Processing Room. He pointed his weapon across the room toward the door that led to the Operations Room and wondered how long it would take the AP to come through the doorway. The doorway was a strategic point in this miniwar, and Driscoll instantly decided to take it.

He leaped across the room and cautiously peered into the Operations Room. There was no movement. His gaze spanned the room, taking in the bodies of the men he had killed, the shattered doorway, tables, consoles . . .

The phone had stopped ringing! He squirmed around until he saw the top of the table where the phone had been. The phone had been moved to one edge of the table and the receiver was off the cradle. His eyes followed the cord to where it disappeared behind one of the consoles. He thought of his men and wondered what was happening on the rest of the island and whether the other units were successful. If they weren't, this one phone call could destroy the entire mission. He looked about in a desperate search for something to throw. He found nothing. An idea hit him and he pulled out his wallet. He gauged the distance and threw the wallet at the smashed doorway.

Driscoll heard the phone drop to the floor, and he jumped into the room as another burst of fire pounded the already mutilated doorway. Driscoll got to the nearest console, peered around the rear of it, and saw the back of the AP in the low light of the room. He lined up the fluorescent dots on the forward and rear sights of his automatic with the AP's back and hesitated until he could calibrate for the pounding of his heart. After a second watching the sights jump up and down, he fired twice, and heard the AP moan in the aftermath of a bullet's impact.

Driscoll started around the front side of the console on his hands and knees, but automatic weapons' fire reduced the console display just above him to fine pieces of glass and metal. It was a wild shot by the wounded AP, but it nearly did the job. Driscoll hit the floor and stretched out flat.

The moaning started again, and Driscoll fired into the gloom in the corner of the room where the AP seemed to be. He heard a metallic clatter of the AP's M16 hitting the floor, and he fervently hoped their battle was over. After listening for a few moments, he decided to crawl toward where the AP was lying.

He cautiously rounded the second console and found the AP on his back with three gaping holes in his body. The young Air Policeman gurgled a bit, rolled his eyes, and died.

Driscoll got to his feet and staggered backwards until reaching a chair, and then sat down quickly. He surveyed the room and was flabbergasted at the death and destruction he had produced in a few short minutes. He hadn't thought it was going to be like this. He had trained all those years, kept his secret and his silence, all for five minutes of extreme violence.

Driscoll lifted his eyes and looked at the situation screen. The symbols on the screen had seemingly multiplied and had advanced more than halfway down the screen. His brain went numb with the meaning of the pointed symbols, their number, and the direction they were heading. He dumbly looked at the numbers on the remaining console. They represented target coordinates inside the United States: ICBM silos, cities, towns.

How many will die?

The phone on the table in the center of the room rang.

Driscoll automatically picked it up. It was his unit on the sixth floor of the radar building, the one above him. That floor contained the second computer for the radar and, more importantly, the communications center for the radar. The excited voice gave him the status of their operation to take over the comm center. It had been successful.

"Listen, Colonel, I'm worried that we might not have gotten everybody. You know, we didn't have the number of people that we really needed," said one of his men.

"It doesn't matter," replied Driscoll in a depressed voice. I only need this charade for another five minutes, he thought.

The voice went on. "We got the stuff from disk going right on schedule. Judging by the message traffic from NORAD, they're buying it." He was ecstatic. "The missile tracking data was intercepted and killed just as we planned. NORAD never knew that COBRA DANE went to an early warning mode."

"Good," mumbled Driscoll. They hung up. Everything was going according to plan. They had labored intensively the past few days on updates to the software modifications that prevented the automatic early warning message from being sent to NORAD from the COBRA DANE computer. Had the message gotten through, it would have blown their entire mission.

He heard a noise and rolled his eyes in its direction. It was the watch officer, the second man he had shot, and he was still alive. Driscoll got up and stood over him.

The young lieutenant was trying to look at the situation screen. Driscoll sat back down, then thought better of it and went back to the wounded man. He grabbed him under the arms, dragged him up to a sitting position, and put a chair behind him to prop him up. The lieutenant's arms hung limply beside him, and he could barely move his head. His eyes wandered up to the situation screen.

Driscoll made sure that the lieutenant wouldn't fall over, then sat down to watch the progress of the war. The white, pointed symbols gradually moved their way down the screen until one by one they hovered over points in the United States. Then, in rapid succession, they each ballooned to over ten times their size until the map of the United States was bathed in white.

The young lieutenant gasped and fell over dead.

Lieutenant Colonel Driscoll broke down and wept.

CHAPTER 2

▬ ▪ ▬ ▪ ▬ ▪ ▬

COBRA DANE ADMINISTRATIVE BUILDING

Airman Jensen had been correct in his assessment. Everything had gone off without a hitch. No APs had shown up, much to his relief. The killing had been only so much target practice.

How many people had he killed? Ten was it? Or eleven? He had lost count. He dumbly realized he had rapidly been transformed from a scared, anxious young man to an accomplished killer in the few moments it took to "clean out" the Administrative Building. With his last two victims he had approached boredom. Could that be the reason he was selected for this particular assignment? Someone had known he had the capacity for this kind of killing?

Jensen walked out into the frigid early morning air and watched Sergeant McDonough head toward the COBRA DANE radar building. He was going to check on how things went in this most important of all buildings. It began to rain Shemya's peculiar version of flying slush that was common in the winter months. The world was still dark— Jensen instinctively looked at his watch in the glow of the light from the building's entrance—even at the relatively late morning hour of 0735. Sunrise on Christmas Day on Shemya only came at about 0800 due to its extreme northern latitude.

He discarded his sack of tear gas canisters and went back to the boiler room in the Administrative Building to retrieve another sack of equipment. This one contained a high-tech,

VHF digital radio. Jensen lugged the sack around the outside of the building until he had a clear view of the sea
and began to set up the radio. It was one of the best ones
the West had produced, small, compact and easily set up
by one man in minutes. He set up the small antenna, a
dipole with reflector, and after consulting a small compass,
pointed it at the correct point on the horizon. A push on
the test button and the stark red glow of the LED confirmed
that the battery still had enough charge in it to do the job.

Jensen connected the radio cables to the antenna and the
power cables to the battery case. He double-checked the
connections and wiped off the slush that had quickly built
up on the antenna, then pushed the button to send the signal.

Airman Jensen sat back and let his radio send its fateful
message over and over.

ABOARD THE KURSOGRAF

Ivan Chelyuskin looked over his electronic equipment for
the ten thousandth time on this cruise. He stifled a bored
yawn. Nothing was ever new, just monitor the COBRA
DANE radar and try to get into a sidelobe of the island's
satellite communications antenna to intercept communications from Shemya's occupants, the U.S. Air Force. The
only trouble was that the uplink frequency was high enough
that the electromagnetic radiation went in a straight line and
did not curve around the earth as the lower frequencies did.

Chelyuskin's ship had to stay just over the horizon to
avoid an incident with the Americans. They knew Russian
intelligence ships were about, and the U.S. Navy kept an
eye on them, even though tensions between their two countries had diminished greatly over recent years. Indeed, their
cruises had come less often and with greater intervals between them as Russia concentrated on its own internal
problems.

And Russia's problems were legion. The attempted coup
in August of 1991 had left everyone wary of the intelligence services, but with the farming and food distribution
failures and obscene inflation levels, people were openly

talking about another revolution, which was just a euphemism for a coup by the intelligence agencies, GRU, and the military. Chelyuskin wondered what he would find when he finally got back home.

"Ivan Mikailovich," said one of his technicians quietly. Chelyuskin's attention wandered over to his subordinate. He yawned in the tech's direction.

"There is a new signal here," said the man, and pointed at the spectrum analyzer screen. Chelyuskin leaned his way out of his chair and walked over to the man. His body felt like a creaky door that had been run over by a truck. He bent over and stared at the bright green lines on the dull green background of the spectrum analyzer screen. The lines, which showed frequency content, varied in height like a semicircular blob that looked like a fuzzy upside-down cup. The entire signal suddenly disappeared. After a few seconds, the lines came back and repeated their short dance on the screen. He looked at the calibrated frequency dials on the analyzer. The signal was around 145 megahertz, and by the appearance of its frequency spectrum on the screen, the modulation on its carrier looked like it was BPSK, or binary phase shift keying.

"Are the recorders on?" he asked as he glanced two consoles down at the large reel-to-reel machines.

"Yes, they automatically went on when the signal appeared," his tech replied with a smile. Chelyuskin returned the smile—it was one of the few times their hardware worked the way it should.

He looked at the spectrum analyzer again. "Data rate is not exactly state-of-the-art," said the tech. He gave another quick smile. "About five kilobits a second."

"Direction and range?" asked Chelyuskin. His ship had two loop antennas mounted at ninety degrees to one another that provided a direction-finding capability. There were two of these dual antennas, one at the top of the forward mast and one on the top of the aft mast. Both sets of antennas gave direction to the signal source, but by virtue of the distance separating them, their angles to the signal source were slightly different. This information was fed into a computer and, using some simple geometry, range to the signal source was calculated.

Chelyuskin's man typed some commands into their computer. In a few seconds the computer gave bearing and range to the transmitter: 035 degrees relative at 31 miles.

Chelyuskin picked up a phone and dialed the bridge. "This is Chelyuskin. Give me bearing and range to Shemya."

A minute later the answer came back. "035 degrees at 31 miles."

Chelyuskin nodded and absentmindedly went back to his desk. He thought for a moment, then pulled out a reference book with international frequency allocations in it. That signal's frequency was in an amateur band. Probably some amateur radio operator on Shemya doing some experimenting. Chelyuskin leaned back in his chair. Yes, that was it. He thought for a moment. But with BPSK?

Chelyuskin yawned again and settled back into his chair. Whatever the signal was, it would be transmitted, along with all the other signals in the area, via low-level radio to the communications station on the Komandorski Islands. They would relay it to Petropavlovsk and it would ultimately be retransmitted back to Moscow.

COMMUNICATIONS STATION AT PETROPAVLOVSK

"Relay from Mednyj Island, sir," said a man behind a console.

His supervisor walked over to the console to peer over the man's shoulder. He knew the relays from Mednyj Island in the Bering Sea were from an intelligence-gathering ship, but had no idea from which one. Only the people at Mednyj Island knew that the signal was ultimately from the *Kursograf*.

The supervisor suddenly bent over the status console next to the relay console. He swore under his breath. "Our new fiber-optic lines from here to Moscow have failed again," he said, and shook his head in disgust. Nothing seemed to work anymore in Russia. The alternatives to the fiber-optic lines were microwave line-of-sight links. The

Americans' ability to intercept them were well known. The advantage of the fiber-optic lines was the inability of any space asset to intercept its signal. Virtually nothing is radiated out of a fiber-optic line, therefore antennas, even optical ones, would receive nothing. The CIA would have to put a tap physically right on the cable itself, which would be a much more difficult task.

The supervisor sighed in resignation. The relays from Mednyj Island were always encrypted by his station, and probably encrypted by Mednyj as well. He wondered if the intelligence ship also had its own encryption. That would be three levels of encryption, enough to keep the Americans at bay.

The supervisor gave orders to send the signal to Moscow via microwave line-of-sight links and went back to his office.

GEOSYNCHRONOUS ORBIT
22,236 MILES ABOVE THE EQUATOR

The ELINT satellite, or electronic intelligence satellite, Magnum, already had its huge antenna pointed in the right direction to intercept the *Kursograf*'s triply encrypted signal as it sped its way from relay station to relay station on its way to Moscow.

The terrestrial microwave signals traveled in straight lines from transmitter to receiver with only a fraction of the total signal energy being intercepted by the ground microwave station's receiving antenna. The rest of the signal energy went straight past the receiving antenna. With nothing to reflect the signal or to impede it, the signal simply kept going straight past the horizon and out into space, where the Magnum satellite was waiting with its large antenna to intercept some of the signal's energy and relay it back to its ground terminal.

Twelve miles southwest of Alice Springs, Australia, at Pine Gap, lay the control center for U.S. ELINT satellites. Its large antennas, enclosed in radomes, received the data from Magnum and quickly relayed the data up to another satellite in geosynchronous orbit, which in turn sent it down to its ground station and ultimately to Magnum's masters at the National Security Agency in Fort Meade, Maryland.

NORAD—NORTH AMERICAN DEFENSE COMMAND POST CHEYENNE MOUNTAIN, COLORADO

General Mark Deneen, USAF, looked down from his "battle station," a large conference room above and behind a host of consoles and their operators who manned the command post. Two of the large screens that covered the wall that faced him were more active than he'd ever seen them. One had incoming ICBM tracks portrayed as ever lengthening lines that stretched over the North Pole and headed inexorably toward the United States. The other screen had a quickly increasing list of impact points and estimated time until detonation.

The sounds of the huge room sent an unceasing chill through him. "This is Crystal Palace. DEFCON 1 is confirmed!" said someone in an astonished and terrified voice. All the other voices floated over to him and produced an ambience of horrified excitement. When the DEFCON 1 alarm had gone off, the tension in the large room had increased to an excruciating level. Beads of sweat broke out on almost every forehead, and voices quivered on the edge of panic. None of these people, including the general, had seen this sort of thing. All wondered if this was the end of civilization as they knew it.

All except the general. His mind was on the extreme left side of the large screen where there were no incoming ICBM traces at all. He quickly took in the rest of the screen. BMEWS, or Ballistic Missile Early Warning System, at Clear, Alaska; Thule, Greenland; and at Fylingdales Moor, England, were providing good tracking data over three quarters of the polar sector, but in the far west there was nothing.

General Deneen turned to an aide who was at the general's elbow. "Get a hold of Shemya and find out what their problem is."

CHAPTER 3

—·—·—·—·—

The sun warmed his back as he luxuriated in a state between sleep and wakefulness. The warmth gradually spread its way throughout his body, thereby sustaining his euphoric, semidream state. He stayed in the same position for a long time, or he thought it was a long time; it was difficult to tell. However long it was, he didn't care.

Instinctively he rolled over onto his other side and the sun obediently began to warm his chest and the tops of his legs. Frank Trask opened his eyes and lethargically gazed at the ribbon of black sand bounded on one side by palm trees and on the other by the stark blue of the sea. The sky was cloudless and nearly perfect, and ranged from a light blue near the horizon to a darker blue at higher elevations.

The dull realization filled him that he had absolutely nothing to do, nowhere to go, no one to see about anything.

He smiled.

He rolled over to his other side, this time a little faster than the first time. She was lying on her back with her eyes closed, perfectly relaxed, perfectly beautiful. He started with her toes and languorously examined every inch of her until he got to the top of her head, then turned around and repeated the process in the opposite direction.

She had blond, shoulder-length hair that was wind blown and always seemed to fall in the most provocative manner. He knew her eyes were blue, even though she had them closed at the moment, and her lips were slightly pursed as if about to give him a kiss. She was tall and slender and wearing a white string bikini which provided an incredibly sexy contrast with her tanned skin. His gaze finally settled on her stomach. He had a thing for flat stomachs. Hers had a slight contour in the middle that made it all the sexier.

His eyes followed the string of her bikini bottom as it traveled from underneath her, up over her hipbones that showed at the tops of her legs, across her front where it widened into a triangle, until it disappeared on the other side of her body. He reached out and put his hand on her stomach as a feeling of excitement ran through him. She stirred and opened her eyes. They were even more shockingly blue than he had remembered. She smiled and he moved toward her.

Her face shifted and changed as a mist seemingly surrounded him. Her skin grew darker and her eyes, now blue-black, widened in fear. The mist faded and he saw that, in an instant, her face had totally changed from a fair, blond, sleepy-eyed beauty to a dark-skinned, high-cheekboned Oriental mask with the unmistakable stamp of horror frozen into her features.

She was standing, stopped in mid-step by the faces she had seen in the jungle, dirty faces with round eyes, their murderous intent etched within square jaws and stern countenances.

He didn't have to gaze about to know that the jungle surrounded him. The scent, humidity, the feeling of leeches and insects bombarded his senses and made his insides quiver with pangs of fear and loathing. The jungle, alive with hellish things, was something he could *feel* as it pressed in on him and took his breath away.

His eyes remained locked with hers for a long instant, then she raised her hand out in front of her as if to fend him off, while bringing her other hand up to her mouth in an instinctive gesture. Trask knew he only had a second, maybe two, and he knew what his job required. In half a heartbeat, he had the crosshairs in the sight trained on the middle of her face. Her horror rushed in at him, seemingly magnified by the telescopic sight, and made him cringe.

The sight of her eyes, as wide open as humanly possible and reflecting an insane horror, made him stop in awe. Her jaw shot downward in the beginnings of a shout.

Pull the trigger.

The sense invaded him that those round-eyed faces in the jungle were staring at him with disapproval. He had let things go too far. There still was time—the faces would approve if he acted *now*.

Pull the trigger.

He gulped the jungle's decaying breath in an effort to settle himself for his impending action. The crosshairs wound up on her cavernous mouth as the rest of her face seemed to disappear.

Kill her! Kill her now!

The command was sent. It was such a simple thing. Move the right index finger a fraction of an inch. It didn't happen.

He lowered the gun barrel in a fury until the crosshairs intersected at her feet. With a reflexive twitch, he sent two bullets into the dirt in front of her.

She screamed.

The faces became livid and panic shot through him.

KILL HER!

He brought the crosshairs up and lost their intersection in the darkness of the woman's open mouth. She was in mid-scream. The faces changed from fury to panic and redirected their attention toward the huts in the clearing.

His heart pumped once, then twice. His finger gave another reflexive twitch as if it were an afterthought, and the woman's scream was lost in the conflagration that enveloped the clearing and the surrounding jungle. The thunder rolled over him, along with the mist, and then the air around him turned into a cold, heavy fog.

The fog slowly lifted and he gradually became aware of his surroundings. He remained still and allowed the full range of feelings into his mind, then, after a few moments of internal debate between his body and his will, he opened one eye. Gray. He saw nothing but gray.

Trask decided on impulse to throw caution to the winds

and opened the other eye. He gauged the effect that the light had on the level of pain within him and decided it was tolerable. The mists slowly faded and his surroundings took on form and substance, with dirty walls encompassing him and a littered floor under him. Meager light came from a half-covered window, causing the edges of the space to fade into varying shades of gloom. A jumble of shadows in one corner gradually took on lines, edges and surfaces, and eventually became a broken chair after some concentration.

He gathered his left hand under him and pushed in order to roll over onto his back. As he rolled, he closed his eyes, afraid of the possible pain, but it seemed acceptable. When he opened his eyes again, he saw a featureless ceiling except for an empty light fixture, then closed them again as he gathered courage for an attempt to sit up. Trask shoved himself up to a sitting position and put his face in his hands while waiting for his stomach and the thundering in his temples to settle down. His mind wrestled listlessly with the question of his exact location, then wandered into analyzing some of the sounds of the place.

There was the unmistakable sound of wind and a muffled pitter-pat of something else. A leak in the roof? The wind gusted and he heard a million little somethings collide with the exterior of the building. Probably slush flying around at fifty knots, he thought. That's the kind of weather we have around here.

He opened his eyes again after anticipating what effect the light would have on the throbbing in his head. The light from the window flickered slightly to confirm his hypothesis of the horizontally flying slush.

Abandoned building. He was in one of the abandoned buildings. He looked around to see the empty liquor bottle, the source of his pain. After dragging himself to his feet, he kicked the bottle into a corner. Now what? When does the first wave of guilt arrive? Trask staggered to the window and looked out. More gray. He licked his lips and grunted at the familiar, dry, fuzzy taste in his mouth. A shiver caught him and he wrapped his coat tighter around him while idly wondering what the temperature was. Lucky he didn't freeze to death. After thinking for a moment about the walk back to Building 600, he finally decided that he could still freeze to death on the way.

He had the vague realization that he had been dreaming, but couldn't remember what the dream was. It was probably about Tahiti, that's all he ever dreamed about nowadays. The flight from reality. He was a bit surprised that he had been dreaming at all. Do drunks dream?

A shudder filled him from some unknown source, and he suspected that it was some forgotten horror in the dream.

Why? The thought flashed through his mind unbidden. The first wave of guilt, he thought. Time enough for that later. He had to get back to Building 600 and his bed, then maybe he could sleep until he felt better.

Trask walked over to the door while gauging his steadiness on his feet. Not too bad. The wind would have to be at least five miles per hour before it knocked me over, he thought sarcastically.

There was nothing to do but try it. He yanked the door open and the blast of wind nearly blew him back into the room, but with an effort of will, he bent over and forced himself into the weather. The snow and slush immediately assailed him and quickly forced him to put up the hood on his parka. He leaned into the wind and struggled to walk in a straight line toward the road leading to Building 600.

Trask walked along the edge of the abandoned runway toward the northern end and looked for the dirt road he must have traveled the night before. As he approached the road, the slush turned to snow and rapidly turned the air around him to a white blur. Visibility grew worse as he slogged along his way. Periodically the gusting wind and the intense snowfall would combine to produce a "whiteout," the total lack of visibility. It was difficult even to see an outstretched hand during a whiteout. Thankfully such conditions would only last for a few moments and the normal poor visibility would return.

He avoided the middle of the road for fear that some air force lunatic would run him over in the low visibility, and walked near the edge while being careful not to wander off into the tundra or to slip into the drainage ditch that lined the road.

His thoughts returned to the previous evening and he felt the same feelings over again. Familiar feelings, they were almost old friends. A kaleidoscope of events rolled past his consciousness, and he found himself in the habit of agonizing over hopeless situations and things long past. Ghosts, he thought suddenly, just like I'll seem to the guys at Building 600 as I walk in out of the snow. He luxuriated in a rare smile.

He puffed and panted his way uphill and lamented the fact that he was no longer eighteen years old. The throbbing in his head grew to a level that wasn't easily ignored, and he stopped for a brief rest as the wind whipped around him. How much longer? He could only hope that he was over halfway there. Trask started out again, grimly determined to get to the relative bliss of his bed as the wind hit him in the face and threatened to pull the hood off his head. He grabbed at it quickly and pulled the drawstrings tightly together so that there was just a small circle lined with fur that exposed him to the outside world. By bending over and looking at the ground, he kept the wind off his face, but periodically he would lift his head and risk an icy blast to see if he could make out the shape of Building 600.

Trask spotted the lines of telephone poles that ran close by Building 600 and knew that when he got past them, he would be very close to his destination. After passing under one set of lines, he looked to his left for the landmark of the multicolored totem pole which was in the parking lot in front of the main entrance to the building. It was a curious and unexpected thing to see on the island, and it provided a stark contrast to the military buildings and severe terrain. He was used to seeing it by now, after eight months on the island, and had used it many times at night for navigational purposes, especially when he had had a few drinks too many.

Building 600's gray color blended in with the flying snow and served to hide the structure from him until he was less than a hundred yards from the main door. He actually spotted its strange, orange-framed windows first, and they seemed to hang disembodied in midair as the snow melted the walls of the building into the gray sky.

Trask gasped from the exertion and grunted in delight at the sight of the multistory building which alternately became clear then faded from view as the snow swirled in front of him. His toes seemed about to lose all feeling, and he had been worrying about frostbite, but with his destination so close at hand, he forgot his worries and concentrated on hurrying his agonizingly slow pace. Fifty yards more and he would be safe and warm . . . and in bed.

He altered his course slightly as he decided to enter by one of the side doors. Security might wonder why he was out in this kind of weather, and he didn't want to answer a lot of questions. He looked up periodically to make midcourse adjustments and to gauge his remaining distance to the door which was in one of the miniwings that extended from the front of the building.

It didn't register all at once even though he saw what was in the doorway through the falling snow. The doors all had automatic closing mechanisms at the top, but this door was held open by a form at the bottom. Trask stared at it as long as he could stand the wind and the snow in his face, and only turned away when his eyes watered to the point of obscuring his vision. The form at the bottom of the doorway was a partially snow-covered man.

Trask briefly wondered how long he had been lying there, then decided it might have been for an hour or two judging by the amount of snow that covered him. Why hadn't Security put him into the drunk tank? Air Force Security had an office in Building 600 and routinely put drunks in an unused freight elevator in the interior of the building. He mentally shrugged, then grinned briefly. There, but for the grace of God, go I.

In a moment he was there and held the door open with his foot, so that he could roll the prostrate individual over. After a few seconds of heaving, he managed to get the man on his side. Trask squinted and took a close look at his face. The man's mouth was open in an interrupted shout, one eye was closed, the other open in an unnerving contortion of facial features. Trask immediately pulled off one of his gloves and felt the man's carotid artery.

He was dead.

Frank Trask straightened slowly while staring at the body at his feet. He looked up quickly and peered into the interior gloom of the building. *There were bodies in the entranceway.*

2230 HOURS, LOCAL TIME, 25 DECEMBER HEADQUARTERS, RUSSIAN FEDERAL AGENCY FOR GOVERNMENT COMMUNICATIONS AND INFORMATION

"Isn't this interesting," mumbled Boris Parchomenko as he looked at the quickly prepared memorandum in front of him. He pushed his intercom talk button without looking up from the memo. "Ivan Timofeyevich, come and see me," he said quietly. When his boss wasn't around, Parchomenko ran what was once the Eighth Chief Directorate of the KGB. Even though it was renamed, the communications agency was still the Russian equivalent of the U.S. National Security Agency, which has the charter of intercepting signals and decrypting messages.

His subordinate, Ivan Timofeyevich Krivitsky, appeared at the office door in less than twenty seconds. Parchomenko finished reading the memo and flipped it face up on his desk. He gazed up at the memo's author, who stood expectantly in front of Parchomenko's austere desk.

"The memo states that these signals were intercepted two hours ago. Is that correct?" asked Parchomenko. His man nodded.

"Based on your preliminary analysis, the American CO-BRA DANE radar went from its spacetrack mode to early warning mode, and this was based on its pulse repetition frequency and deductions about its scan angles. Correct?" stated Parchomenko.

Krivitsky nodded again and a small smile began at the corners of his mouth. It was good work and he knew it.

"Excellent," said Parchomenko quietly. His man

beamed. "Any idea why the radar changed mode?" asked Parchomenko without raising his voice.

His subordinate's smile vanished. "Uh, no sir. A test perhaps?"

Parchomenko rubbed his chin as if in consideration of Krivitsky's suggestion. "Yes, I'll have to check with headquarters."

"Or maybe the other signal that was intercepted will give us a clue," added Krivitsky.

Parchomenko looked down at the memo again. "Yes, that was mentioned in the memo. But you correctly state that the frequency of this other signal is in the amateur band. Could an amateur radio operator's signal provide the key to this mystery?" It was clear that he didn't believe it.

A man stuck his head in the office doorway. "Excuse me," he said to Parchomenko. He looked straight at Krivitsky. "You know that amateur signal at a hundred and forty-five megahertz?" Krivitsky nodded. "It is not from an amateur," the man in the doorway said.

"How do you know this?" demanded Parchomenko.

"It is encrypted," said the man. Both Parchomenko's and Krivitsky's eyebrows went up in surprise.

CHAPTER 4

—·—·—·—

Trask staggered backward involuntarily, then slipped and fell in the snow. His eyes quickly scanned the front of the building looking for any signs of activity. He looked up at the second- and third-floor windows and saw no lights or movement of any kind. There was a light in the main entrance, but no signs of movement beyond. His gaze flitted over to the entrance at the back of the loading dock at the other end of the building. No movement. Nothing. Panic began to rise up within him, but he forced it down.

Was everyone in the building dead? That was ridiculous, he thought, but he couldn't deny that there were bodies inside the building. He had to check out the main entrance. The security office was a little way down the hall to the right. He could tell them what was happening and then wash his hands of the whole thing.

Trask got to his feet with some effort and cautiously approached the main entrance with its bright red double doors. He looked in one corner of the window in the door and noted with relief that the entrance was empty. As he was about to yank the door open, he felt someone's presence behind him. He whirled about and saw an inordinately large Air Force Air Policeman standing directly behind him.

"What's the problem?" said the AP. He had condescension in his voice. The military man was extremely young

34

and arrogant, or so it seemed to the older engineer. Trask pointed to the side door, which was still held open by the completely snow-covered body.

"That guy is dead," he said simply. The AP kept his eyes on Trask while turning his head, then finally shifted his gaze in the direction of the doorway. The action conveyed distrust in Trask's simple declaration. The snow abated a bit, allowing the AP to see the open door with the body on the ground. The AP squinted, then looked back at Trask. There was less arrogance on his face.

"How did he get there?" the AP asked with some suspicion.

Trask shrugged. "Don't know."

The AP glanced over Trask's person and appeared somewhat satisfied that he didn't have a weapon on him. He glanced into the main entrance in indecision whether to check out Trask's story first or deposit him with other security forces. He made up his mind quickly.

"All right. Let's go," he said with all the authority he could muster and tried to grab Trask's arm to lead him into the building.

"Wait a minute," said Trask. "I'm not sure the building's safe to enter."

The AP screwed up his face in disbelief. *"What?"*

Trask's voice grew shaky as he explained. "There's bodies in the entrance hallway." He again pointed to the side door.

The AP's face became serious. He let Trask's arm go and then stepped back away from him. He gestured toward the side door. "Let's go check it out. Stay in front of me."

Trask turned in the direction of the side door and realized that his legs felt like rubber. He trod through the accumulating snow and stopped ten feet short of the doorway. The AP caught up with him and circled around so that he was between the door and Trask. He glanced at the form in the doorway and back at Trask. The man was still on his side and obviously dead. The AP looked back at the body, then looked into the building. He stared for a moment in disbelief, then turned back to Trask with fear on his face. He quickly unsnapped his holster, fumbled a bit, and then pulled out an automatic.

"I want some answers and I want them now!" He grasped the gun with both hands and pointed it at Trask's head.

Trask gestured in frustration. "I don't have any answers! I just walked up here and found this guy lying there!" he replied. His head began to throb.

"Where were you coming from?" asked the AP. The gun never wavered.

Trask hesitated and inadvertently created the illusion of trying to conceal something. "I was coming from one of the buildings down near the old airstrip—"

"What the hell were you doing there?" interrupted the AP.

Trask hesitated again. This is bad, he thought. I hope this kid doesn't go off the deep end and start blasting away. "I got drunk last night," explained Trask. He could see that the AP hadn't expected so direct an answer.

"Listen, we had better find out if the rest of the building is all right," said Trask in an effort to distract the young man from his suspicions.

The AP wasn't deterred immediately. "What's your job here?" he asked.

"I'm a field service engineer. I help maintain the radar," replied Trask. The automatic seemed to become less ominous as it became obvious to Trask that the AP was adding things up. A flicker of recognition crossed his face, and he lowered the weapon, to Trask's relief. He kept it pointed at him, however. "Your name?"

"Frank Trask." The AP thought about that for a moment, and with the next question Trask figured that he was largely out of trouble.

"What could do something like this?" The AP gestured to the body in the doorway. There was a tinge of fear in his voice.

Trask shook his head in frustration. "I don't know." He pointed to the body. "He doesn't appear gunshot." Trask hesitated. "Maybe the food or water? I didn't have any last night."

The AP shook his head. "I had both," he said simply.

Trask thought for a minute. "Gas?" he asked.

The AP shot him a look that said he agreed with the possibility. "Let's see if we can look through the window of the security office," he offered. Trask readily agreed.

Together they made their way through the mounting snow back toward the window to the Air Force Security office. It was easy to see the contents of the brightly lit room. Three prostrate figures were immediately evident. Trask could hear the AP suck in his breath in reaction to the grisly sight. They both backed up a few steps, then looked at one another.

"I've got a gas mask in the six-by," he said to Trask, using the peculiar air force nickname for a pickup truck. The engineer nodded, then looked back at the security office window. The AP started off on a run to his vehicle, which was parked around the left wing of the building.

He returned a minute later with the gas mask in one hand and an M16 in the other. He was gasping for breath by the time he stopped in front of Trask. The AP put the M16 between his legs, pulled off the hood of his parka, and put on the mask, then picked up the M16, pulled back the cocking bar and was ready. He glanced at Trask and hesitated. The AP pulled out his automatic and threw it to Trask, then lifted his mask enough to speak.

"I sure hope you're not the guy who did this." He didn't smile. He was gone in a second through the main entrance.

I have to hand it to him, thought Trask. He's got guts. He examined the automatic. It was one of the standard 9-mm Berettas that the U.S. military used for sidearms. He took off what he thought was the safety and squatted below the security office window to wait for the return of the AP.

The AP. Trask didn't even know the young man's name.

What the hell was going on around here? he thought. What about the rest of the island? *Was everyone else dead?* What was the AP running into inside the building? He forced his mind to stop the useless exercise of asking questions that he had no way of answering. Trask was determined to settle down and patiently wait for his young ally to return. His eyes wandered across the space between the two side wings that jutted out from the front of the building.

His gaze was drawn to what he thought was a shadow near the edge of the right wing. He looked idly at it through the continuing snow, and saw that it would disappear behind a surge of snow that would decrease visibility to a few feet, then it would reappear as the snow waned. Trask thought the shape of the shadow changed once or twice, but he wasn't sure. He suddenly realized that it was impossible to have a shadow there—no object was around to block the light. The engineer slowly rose to his feet while trying to discern any movement of the shadow through the driving snow. Was someone there? His mind ran on with more impossible questions.

He had just made up his mind to investigate when the AP came stumbling out of the main entrance. The young man yanked off his gas mask with a shaking hand. Trask saw that his face was white with terror. His voice wavered with fear.

"*All dead,*" he gasped. "Every one of them."

Trask's jaw dropped. "The whole building?" asked Trask.

The AP nodded his head furiously. "Must have been gas. No gunshot wounds, or stab wounds, or any blood at all!" The young airman was out of breath.

Trask reached out and grabbed him by the arm. "We've got to find out who's left and what's going on," commanded the engineer. "Come on."

He began to drag the AP in the direction of the shadow he had seen. If someone were there, he might know what was going on . . . or the man belonging to the shadow might try to kill them also. He hefted the automatic and decided he would at least get a few shots at the bastards before they got him. Trask looked at the AP and saw that he was still in shock at the horror that was hidden within the building.

"Come on," he repeated. The young man began to stumble after him.

Trask squinted in the direction of the shadow. With a sudden lessening of snow, he saw that the shape had disappeared. They reached the corner of the side wing, and

Trask slowed to a stop with the AP obediently stopping behind him. Trask's heart pounded with the exertion of running through the snow and with the fear that was rapidly coursing through him. He peered around the corner as the wind gusted, then abated, and he saw a figure running away from the building and toward one of the vehicles that was parked on the side of the building.

"Look!" shouted Trask. The AP raised his eyes and seemed to snap out of the state he was in. He immediately raised his M16 in an attempt to shoot the fleeing figure.

"Stop!" yelled Trask to the young airman and shoved the rifle barrel aside. "We have to capture him to find out what's happening!"

The fugitive got to a vehicle, climbed in and sped away from the building. Trask and the AP ran over to the left wing of the building, jumped into the young man's six-by and started the engine. The AP shoved it into gear, gunned the motor, and raced down the road after the rapidly disappearing vehicle.

CHAPTER 5

The island of Shemya lies approximately forty miles due east of the island of Attu at the tip of the Aleutians. Shemya is mostly covered with tall grass and tundra and it has a relatively smooth coastline on its southern coast, while its northern coastline is irregular and highlighted by steep cliffs. Its beaches are composed of black sand, a sign of previous volcanic activity, and for this reason Shemya is sometimes called the "Black Pearl of the Aleutians."

The island is small by any measure, approximately only two by four miles; however, during World War II some forty thousand personnel were crammed onto the island. An airstrip had been built on the southwestern corner of the island, and it had seen tremendous use in those days for the bombing of Japan, but had since fallen into disrepair; the runway had a fairly wide crack running across a portion of it, the calling card from a previous earthquake.

North of the old airstrip lies a curved portion of the coastline which forms a natural harbor; however, the anchorage can be used only during the summer months due to the inclement weather during the rest of the year. The interior of the island is marked by small lakes and ponds around which man has set a network of roads, some paved, the rest only dirt. Along the southern coastline is the airstrip with its attendant hangars and buildings that are devoted to housing Detachment 1, Sixth Strategic Wing, one of the

Strategic Air Command's reconnaissance groups. This group, which flies RC-135 aircraft, known as COBRA BALL, had received some limited notoriety during the KAL 007 incident some years ago. The Soviets had claimed that the KAL airliner was acting in concert with a COBRA BALL aircraft that had been operating in an area adjacent to the Kamchatka Peninsula, and they had used this as an excuse for shooting down the Korean airliner.

The northeastern end of the island is the home of the now unused White Alice, the troposcatter communications link marked by its peculiar curved bedspring-type antennas. This station was shut down a few years ago leaving only the satellite terminal for radio communication with the United States and the hub of U.S. defense activity, NORAD.

The northwestern central section of Shemya contains Building 600, the living quarters for the island's personnel, and within a few miles of Building 600 lies the old diesel power plant with its multitude of fuel tanks nearby. South of the fuel dump a nuclear power plant was built during the waning years of President Sargent's first term, and the diesel power plant was relegated to backup status. The northern coast also was the location for a now obsolete radar installation which was the predecessor to the COBRA DANE radar.

COBRA DANE sits on the extreme northwestern coast of Shemya high up on the cliffs overlooking the beach. The steel building, which houses the radar, has its "working side" pointed toward the Kamchatka Peninsula, the site of the Russian Federation's test range. This side of the building is flat and tilted backward so that the phased array antenna which covers the face of the building has the optimum pointing angle. The multistory building was upgraded, along with the radar and its attendant computers and displays, at the same time the nuclear power plant was installed to greatly increase the electrical power capability on the island.

The COBRA DANE radar has a 99 percent probability of detecting a baseball-sized object at a range of two thousand nautical miles, and in its spacetrack mode it has a range of twenty-five thousand miles. It can track two hundred objects at ranges exceeding one thousand miles.

It was in the COBRA DANE radar building in the early hours of Christmas morning that Lieutenant Colonel Alan Driscoll sat unmoving with his head lying on the desk. The unnerving quiet of the Space Surveillance Operations Center suddenly closed in on him and forced him to lift his head from the table. He looked about wildly while noisily sucking air into his lungs in an effort to alleviate the silence, then looked up at the situation screen to see if anything had changed. Nothing had. The United States was still bathed in white. His eyes moved upwards and he found himself staring at the part of the display representing Russia. It was untouched.

He looked for a while and patiently waited for his mind to form a conclusion. Russia was untouched. The radar could certainly track missiles going in either direction, so why . . . His mind froze. He came to the only conclusion he could. *No American ICBMs had impacted on Russia!*

He gasped and sat up straight in the chair while his mind raced. What was happening at this moment in the Kremlin and in Washington? His eyes involuntarily shifted to the East Coast of the United States. It was almost completely bathed in white. Washington had ceased to exist. What of the American president? Had he reached safety in time? Was he in the Airborne Command Post? Or had some obscure general taken over the reins of government?

He shook his head as if to clear it and tried to put the questions out of his mind. Thoughts of his wife suddenly swept in to fill the void. He hadn't thought about her for the last few days in the rush caused by the rapidly worsening relations with Russia. His gaze flicked immediately to where he imagined Kansas to be on the situation screen. Solid white. His mouth flew open in surprise.

It wasn't supposed to matter. He was SVRR, the Sluzhba Vneshnei Razvedki Rossiy, the Russian Foreign Intelligence Service, known by the shortened initials SVR, the most highly trained and sophisticated of all the intelligence agencies on the planet. He was the most elite of the elite, a sleeper, or a mole, in the service of the SVR. His years of training and indoctrination were swept away as he slowly got out of his chair and stood in front of the screen. He raised his fists in fury.

"*No!*" he screamed in a long, drawn-out wail.

Driscoll wasn't supposed to fall in love with her, or even to care for her; she was just part of his cover, another aspect to the acting he was continuously doing, but he hadn't realized that she would mean so much to him in the end. He was suddenly glad that they didn't have any children, even though she had wanted them. He had always demurred—his superiors would not have liked it. Another gasp escaped him, and he became weak at the thought of losing her. He staggered backwards until he reached the chair, and then he sat down heavily.

After he had reviewed and updated the plan to take over the island, he would have figured out some plan to get her to safety. He would have looked for telltale signs of the impending attack and then told her to take a trip to someplace safe. Where? Australia, maybe. His mind went limp. They had given him no time, the attack had come right on the heels of the completion of his training. He wanted to weep again in the memory of his lost wife, but he found that he could not. He began to feel guilty. Surely his wife was worth a few tears. With a force of will he drove his thoughts in a new direction.

The sudden collapse of communism in 1991 had left him and his kind wondering if their deactivation was imminent. The attempted coup in the same year had raised hopes, but it was quickly crushed and their hope had died with it. The KGB was broken up into five different ministries, and even though the SVR had retained most of its foreign intelligence assets, their morale had hit rock bottom. They all awaited the deactivation order. But none came. Driscoll was determined to obey the last orders given him, which was a takeover of the island in the event of a nuclear attack.

The events of the past two weeks had brought his emotions and anxiety to a fever pitch. First the successful coup by elements of the GRU and the former KGB, then a hardliner was installed as president. Threats were hurled at the United States and its allies. The massive Russian army moved to its borders, and the world teetered on the brink of war. Those were the signs that told Driscoll to get ready just in case of a nuclear attack. A few hours ago the attack had become reality for Driscoll and his small band of SVR sleepers.

Russia had won a massive victory; it was obvious by the huge, quietly unblinking screen in front of him. A thought suddenly was upon him. The screen used a data link from NORAD to form part of the display, the part that showed the effect on Russia. If NORAD had ceased to function, then his situation screen wouldn't show the true situation in Russia, so perhaps it was almost totally destroyed also. He broke out into a cold sweat at the thought of nowhere to go, no civilization in which he could perform any function. His whole raison d'être was to help ensure the Motherland's victory over the West. If Russia were destroyed in the process, then his actions and his life were meaningless.

The phone rang. It wasn't the one with the continuous ring but another on the table between the two consoles. He looked at it for a moment with a sense of detachment. Who could possibly want anything now? He picked up the receiver. It was one of his men at the satellite terminal who breathlessly asked Driscoll about the status of the war. Driscoll briefly informed him. His man was elated.

"By the way, Mike, is NORAD still operating?" Driscoll held his breath.

"Judging by some of the messages we've found here, NORAD, or part of it at least, is still functional. They keep asking for confirmation of data." The man laughed. "We all know why, don't we?" He laughed again, this time louder and more prolonged. Driscoll grunted. That was certainly understandable, he thought.

"How about the situation channel?" asked Driscoll. He waited anxiously as the man had one of his subordinates check the status of the comm link.

"It's okay, and still receiving NORAD data," was the final reply. Driscoll let his breath out all at once, and then let out a sigh of relief. Russia was still whole. He hung up the phone after exchanging a few congratulatory words and leaned back in his chair.

What would life be like now that the United States had essentially ceased to exist? He thought for a while, then gave it up. He couldn't imagine, he had been away from Russia for too long. He counted the years and found that it had been twenty years since he had left the KGB training camps for his submarine ride to American shores. They had smuggled him ashore at a remote part of Washington State, and he had journeyed to a prearranged spot to pick up his new identity and contact his control agent.

The plan was simple and almost foolproof. The KGB had selected a candidate for the Air Force Academy who was from an orphanage, thereby eliminating messy family relations. The candidate was intercepted en route and murdered, his body completely destroyed in an acid bath. All identification and personal effects were transferred to him and he continued on his way. The first time he was fingerprinted was at the academy, and the only check done on the fingerprints was to see if they existed in the FBI files, which, of course, they didn't.

Driscoll never went back to the orphanage nor corresponded with anyone there and thereby eliminated detection from that source. There was always the possibility that someone from that particular orphanage would cross paths with Driscoll, and therefore a team of KGB agents were assigned to trace the movements of the relatively few people who might recognize that he was not the real Driscoll. In an FBI crunch in the mid-1980s, the number of available KGB agents in the United States went down drastically, so the KGB, with its usual extremely crude thoroughness, murdered as many of the people from the orphanage who could recognize Driscoll as they could without giving the whole operation away.

Driscoll didn't know about it until several years later during an extremely rare meeting with his control agent. His control mentioned it in a rather offhand manner and laughingly noted that Driscoll owed his life to some obscure members of KGB Department Eight, the murder and assassination group. Driscoll was shocked, despite the fact that he had been trained to do the exact same thing if required.

It bothered him for a while, but time gradually made him forget, and he helped it along with generous doses of rationalizations about his exalted calling in the name of socialism.

Driscoll mused a bit about how he would be received back in the mother country. He would be one of the most heroic figures in the history of Russia. He tilted his head back and laughed. He would have the cream of everything: cars, houses, women . . .

He cut the thought short. He started thinking about the immediate situation on the island and began to worry about survivors. They might have to fight some unknown number of people before the amphibious force picked them up. Of course they had an ace in the hole, they always did.

They hadn't expected a lot of opposition, but in case it became significant they had a "trailer" agent, someone who got in with the opposition at the onset of the operation and therefore was in a position to betray them at any time. It was a brilliant idea derived from the famous "Trust" in post–World War I Russia. Felix Dzerzhinsky, who headed the notorious Cheka, the secret police ancestor of the KGB, came up with the idea of creating an opposition group to the Bolsheviks and populating it with his own people. Western democracies funneled vast sums of money into the Trust, believing that the Trust was opposed to Stalin and the Bolsheviks. Dzerzhinsky merely took the money and used it for his own purposes, namely the undermining of the Western democracies themselves. It was simple, yet brilliant.

He thought about their "trailer" agent and worried a bit. Curious person, he thought. So intelligent, so young, so . . .

An alarm went off. Driscoll's gaze flew to the situation screen. A few seconds later, the board began to light up with the same pointed symbols at the top of the screen he had seen earlier. He drew air into his lungs with a sharp noise as he saw the symbols begin to move toward the bottom of the screen.

A second launch!

Driscoll's jaw went slack at the thought of what the United States was like at the moment and momentarily racked his brain at what Russia would want to destroy with a second launch. NORAD, certainly. The rest of the cities? He looked down at the map of the United States and scoured the few areas that were not coated white. Nothing of any consequence, he thought. The Kremlin leadership must have thought it was necessary, or else they would not have added to the already extremely high level of radiation that the first launch probably had produced. The Russians didn't want to increase the possibility that a fallout-laden cloud would disgorge its contents on their homeland unless it was absolutely essential.

He looked at some of the numbers on the only remaining console and grunted. They're hitting some of the same places, he thought. Standard operating procedure. If at first you don't succeed . . . He didn't bother to finish the old saying. His gaze ran over the symbols on the situation screen again and a thought suddenly struck him. His blood ran cold and he fought to shake it off. The thought kept recurring as he examined the situation screen and the numbers on the console. Couldn't be, he thought. Try as he might, he couldn't seem to convince himself, and he slowly became obsessed with finding the answer.

1145 HOURS MOUNTAIN TIME, 25 DECEMBER
NORAD COMMAND HEADQUARTERS
CHEYENNE MOUNTAIN, COLORADO

General Mark Deneen pulled open the large drawer that was under the conference room table. In the drawer were the phones that could, if he wanted to, connect him to the president and other members of the National Command Authority. The phones, all of them white and not the red ones that people imagine, were angled upward in an inverted *V* shape in order to face people seated on either side of the drawer, thereby making it easier to use them. He picked up a handset and pushed a button on his intercom. Communications came back immediately.

"Have you gotten a hold of Shemya yet?" asked Deneen. He impatiently waited for an answer as he stared at the terminal in front of him that was recessed into the conference room table top. The terminal, one of three in the conference room table, showed the global situation and the enormous number of reentry vehicles that various radars were reporting headed their way. The area in the far west, however, was blank. No targets were being reported from the COBRA DANE radar on Shemya.

"Not yet, sir. They're not answering," was the answer.

Deneen quickly hung up and rose from his desk in the glassed-in room that overlooked the operator area and the rows of consoles in the command post. He hurriedly went out the door to the right of the glass wall that separated the conference room from the console area and descended the few steps to the console level. The command post was buzzing with the details of war: impact points, damage assessments, and estimated casualties. The voices had gotten past the early stages of panic and desperation and were now tense and wavering due to the emotional exhaustion of the situation.

The stench of vomit was in the air. Someone had gotten sick. This thing wasn't going well, he thought. First Shemya goes silent, then the command post crew starts crapping out.

Deneen got over to the console where his deputy was standing and put his hand on his back to let him know he was there. His subordinate turned and looked at Deneen.

"Fred, what's the situation with Shemya?" asked Deneen in a low voice.

"No answer, General. We're getting nothing but spacetrack data when we should be getting incoming RVs. Looks like they blew it, sir," said Brigadier General Fred Knight.

Deneen shook his head. "I wouldn't want to be in Commander 16 SURS shoes after this is all over."

Knight agreed. "He's got some answering to do."

Deneen jerked a thumb over his shoulder. "Join me in the battle station."

Knight nodded and followed the Commander in Chief, United States Space Command, back to the conference room overlooking the hectic console operators. General Deneen asked his battle staff, the contingent of officers that occupied the room where he "fought" the war, to leave them alone for a few minutes. They all looked surprised and a bit put out. Deneen shut the office door behind them, leaving him and his deputy alone. He looked very troubled to General Knight.

"You know, Fred, I recommended against all this," said Deneen.

"I know," replied Knight, and lowered his gaze to the floor.

"You know what's going through their minds right now, don't you?" said Deneen, his voice rising as he gestured to the floor below.

"They're wondering if their families have survived the war, or will survive it," said Knight through a grimace.

"You're damn right! That's a hell kind of a thing to put people through! They're so emotionally distraught that we've got people vomiting out there!" said Deneen through clenched teeth.

"Orders—" began Knight.

"Orders from idiots!" snapped Deneen. "We wanted a drill with prior warning just to run the people through their paces. That wasn't good enough. They wanted to take certain isolated locations and see what our people would do without a warning that it was a drill. Then some damn joker kept adding details about the world situation and fed it to our people as if it was the real thing! They were real cute! They only picked locations where they could control access to the news media like the BMEWS sites and Shemya in the Aleutians, and our own headquarters after we went on alert and restricted everyone in this damn mountain!"

Knight nodded ruefully. BMEWS, or Ballistic Missile Early Warning System, had locations in some of the most remote locations in the world. Clear, Alaska; Thule, Greenland; and Fylingdales Moor in England were easily isolated so that the Pentagon experimenters could feed their people a couple of weeks of made-up news. Shemya and NORAD headquarters were thrown in as an afterthought.

"It was to be all so realistic," said Deneen. "Start days ahead of the launch exercise with a turnaround of the relations between us and Russia. Throw in a coup by hard-liners and some missing nuclear warheads. Then in a short period have the hard-liners throw threats at us, and we all march to the brink of nuclear war. All so realistic. Too realistic!'' Deneen leaned closer to Knight, who could hear the general's teeth grind together.

"What happens when they find out it's all just a drill?" asked Deneen in sudden despair. "Our people will never be the same again. The emotion of what they think is a real nuclear war is just too much to endure. They'll never forgive us."

Knight shook his head in commiseration with his boss, then had a sudden thought. "Except maybe the people in 16 SURS on Shemya. I'll betcha they never knew there was a drill at all."

CHAPTER 6

Trask squinted to see through the windshield of the truck
as they rumbled down the road. Their vision was obscured
by the almost solid white world outside the vehicle, and
their breath, which came in rapid pulses of vapor, quickly
condensed on the inside of the glass, thereby adding to their
visibility problems. Trask wiped the inside of the windshield, as did the AP, and after a few seconds of concentration, they both spotted the truck they were chasing.

Trask glanced over at his companion and noted that he
had seen the vehicle also. The AP was driving with clear
abandon as they alternately raced and skidded down the
road that led away from Building 600 and toward the eastern end of the island of Shemya. They began to gain on
the fleeing vehicle until the fugitive skillfully negotiated an
embryonic snowdrift, but the AP plowed directly into it
with no evasive action at all. The vehicle slewed sideways
and almost went off the road and into the tundra. Trask
gave the AP an annoyed looked but refrained from saying
anything. He didn't want to distract the young man from
resuming the chase.

"They should be plowing these roads by now," said the
airman. "Where the hell is everybody?" he added in frustration. Trask shook his head in response.

The AP floored the accelerator, causing the wheels to
spin, and cranked the steering wheel around to straighten

out the vehicle. The rear wheels suddenly bit in, and they shot down the road in pursuit of the rapidly disappearing vehicle.

Trask and the AP made up some of the lost ground as they neared a fork in the road where it curved left to avoid an empty quarry, humorously labeled the "Grand Canyon" by the island's occupants. The wind kicked up just at that moment, and the resulting surge of snow completely obscured the roadway. The lead vehicle's speed never slowed as the visibility went to zero. Its driver had not anticipated the curve, and the vehicle went straight off the road through a drainage ditch, slammed through a guard rail and up a small slope. The driver managed to stop the vehicle just before it plummeted over the edge of the quarry. The vehicle's front tires were left to dangle over the edge in free space.

Trask caught a fleeting glimpse of the truck as it went off the road and yelled to the AP to stop. The young man slowed the vehicle and stopped on the road at the point nearest where the first vehicle disappeared. They leaped from the cab and started up the gradual slope to the lip of the quarry.

"Remember, we want to capture him. We won't find out anything if you kill him," yelled Trask over the fury of the wind. The AP looked at Trask for a moment, then nodded in agreement. Trask wondered how much longer the young airman would take orders from him.

They slowed as they caught sight of the stranded vehicle fifty yards beyond. Its engine had stalled, and its driver was desperately trying to restart it. Trask and the AP started off on a dead run and tried to approach the vehicle in the driver's blind spot, which was in between the areas viewed by the two rearview mirrors.

As they approached, they raised their weapons in readiness and slowed to a walk. They circled the vehicle cautiously and slowly approached the driver's side. The hysterical cranking of the engine by the driver was producing no results. The engine fell dormant as the driver gave up.

Trask knelt and pointed the automatic at the door. The

AP took up a standing position behind Trask and put the barrel of the M16 chest high. Together they waited for the driver to exit the vehicle. A few seconds later, the door was flung open and the occupant jumped out.

"Hold it!" yelled Trask. The driver jumped a bit, then whirled about to face Trask and the AP. The driver's hood fell back, exposing a cascade of hair which contained various shades of color, from dark brown to pure blond, and which was driven back from her face by the ruthless wind.

"Lieutenant Gain!" exclaimed Trask as he immediately recognized her. She was far and away the best-looking female on the island. He did a supposedly objective mental review of her physical attributes when she first arrived a week ago. Her nose was a bit too large and pointed, and her eyes were set too close together. She also didn't have a terrifically large chest, but all of these supposed shortcomings were easily overlooked—and most often were, especially on an island with hundreds of men and less than twenty women. Altogether she was a stunning woman.

The initial fear on her face faded a bit as she reacted to the surprise of the two men confronting her. Trask and the AP were still suspicious.

"Why were you running from us?" asked Trask sharply. She seemed to relax slightly at the question. Her voice still shook a bit when she spoke.

"I've just come from the satellite ground terminal. . . ." Her voice trailed off. She swallowed and started again.

"They're all dead," she said finally. The two men lowered their weapons and gaped at her in amazement.

"I was going to report for the morning watch, and when I got there I thought I heard gunfire coming from inside the building. I looked in one of the windows, and there were bodies all over." She stopped with tears in her eyes. She blinked a few times.

"I started back to Building Six Hundred, and when I saw you in front of the building with a gun in your hand, I just thought . . ." She stopped again.

Trask stood up. "Everyone's dead in Building Six Hundred," he said. Her eyes grew wide and her mouth dropped open in surprise. "It looks like someone is trying to take over this island," he concluded. "Let's get in out of this weather."

Trask glanced over the edge of the quarry before they started back to the waiting vehicle on the road. It was at least a hundred-foot drop, and had she gone over the edge, she never would have survived. He took a deep breath to calm his nerves and ran after the other two.

It began to be tough going as the snow was starting to accumulate heavily in spots. They reached the truck, and the AP and Lieutenant Gain climbed into the front seat with Trask getting into the back seat. The young airman started the engine and turned the heater up full blast. Trask had been out in the weather for quite some time now and enjoyed the respite from the cold. They introduced each other and Trask found that Lieutenant Gain's first name was Ellen and that the AP was Airman First Class Rick Elverson. The amenities over, Trask's mind began to race to find the explanation for the incredible situation they were facing.

"Let's add a few things up," he began. "Everyone's dead in Building Six Hundred and there is no sign of who did it." He looked at Elverson for confirmation. The young man nodded.

Trask continued. "If you heard gunshots at the satellite terminal, then whoever is doing this must still be there. They probably used gas in Building Six Hundred. Why not use gas at the satellite ground station? Why shoot everybody?"

"Maybe they need to use the satellite terminal, but they didn't need Building Six Hundred," offered Lieutenant Gain. Trask leaped on the idea. It made sense. The satellite terminal was the island's only communication link to the outside world. If someone wanted to take over the island, the comm installation would be extremely important. Building 600 was the living quarters for everyone on the island— it would be nothing but trouble to a small force with orders to seize the island.

"Yes, they would have to control communications," he mused. He looked quickly at Lieutenant Gain. "You slept in Building Six Hundred last night?" She nodded. "You were reporting to the satellite terminal for the morning watch?" Trask asked the lieutenant. She nodded again.

"And you?" he asked the young AP.

"Just got off the night shift at the operations center at the airstrip," Elverson replied.

Trask shook his head in wonder. "All three of us were in transit. It happened while all three of us were on the road. A few minutes either way and we'd all be dead."

The trio fell silent as they considered their close brush with death. The wind drummed at the sides of the truck and the snow piled up around the vehicle in a frenzy of wintertime activity.

"Why?" asked Lieutenant Gain suddenly. "What possible reason could there be to murder everyone on the island?"

She gave Trask an imploring look. The AP joined the young lieutenant in questioning Trask with his eyes.

The engineer shook his head to say that he had no answers. "Sabotage? But by whom?" he asked.

"SVR?" offered Elverson. Trask and Gain gave him a quizzical look. "You know," he explained, "the former KGB?"

Trask gave him a second glance, then looked at Lieutenant Gain. "Are there KGB on the island?" asked Trask, not really expecting an answer.

The lieutenant shrugged. "Could be, I guess," she replied.

Elverson changed the subject. "We'd better get to shelter before we get stuck out here," he said. The other two nodded in agreement.

"Where could we go that's safe?" asked Trask. He thought for a while, then snapped his fingers. "The old power plant," he said with finality.

"Yes," said Lieutenant Gain. "It's not manned, except during alerts, but it's maintained just in case something happens with the nuclear plant. Whoever is trying to take over the island maybe wouldn't bother with it, especially if they were a small force."

"Let's go," said Trask to the AP. The young airman deliberately looked at Lieutenant Gain, but she had already turned and was looking out the side window. She had a look of shocked desperation on her face as she struggled to control the panic rising within her. Trask grimaced at the thought of what had just happened on the island. He looked at Elverson, who seemed to be hesitating, and caught a glimpse of a change of expression on his face as he turned back around. Trask stared at the back of his head for a few seconds in puzzlement. What was that all about, he thought. Lust? At a time like this? He shrugged it off.

Elverson put the truck in gear and with some difficulty turned the vehicle around to head toward the old power plant. The wheels spun, then dug in, and the truck lurched off down the road. They rode in silence, each with their own thoughts about the fantastic events of the morning. Elverson cursed once or twice as he attempted to get around a snowdrift, but otherwise they kept their silence until the old power plant loomed in front of them. The unremitting snowstorm alternately hid and then revealed the structures and their attendant fuel tanks in the distance.

"We had better be careful," advised Trask. "We ought to peek in a few windows before we go barging in there."

The AP gave him an annoyed look. "What are you? Some kind of nervous Nellie?"

It was Trask's turn to be annoyed. "We've survived this far by pure luck. I know from experience that luck doesn't take you too far," was his sarcastic reply.

The AP smiled in amusement at the older engineer's caution. "We don't have too many worries with this." He hefted the M16. Trask was about to reply, but Lieutenant Gain cut him off.

"Let's go. We have to find out who's left alive. There might be a working phone inside," she replied. Trask hadn't thought of that. They could phone around and assess the damage to the installation's population. They might even be able to figure out who had killed most of their co-workers.

They got out of the truck and began to circle around to approach the building from a side that had no windows. They struggled through the mounting snow with the young airman in the lead and paused only once to momentarily hide behind a parked vehicle. They then sprinted the few yards remaining to the building and pressed themselves against the wall. Elverson slid along the wall until he came upon a window, then cautiously peeked in. Trask noted with some satisfaction that the young airman was following his suggestions anyway despite his recent bravado.

"Nothing," he said in a voice barely heard above the wind. He slid to the next window with Trask following him with the same result. No lights, no activity. Elverson motioned to the door and indicated that he was going to enter. Trask nodded.

The young AP paused and inhaled deeply, then jerked open the door and leaped inside. Trask stayed outside and peered around the corner into the doorway. His eyes quickly scanned what he could see of the interior of the building. There were a few offices near the exterior walls of the building and beyond that sat the massive diesel generators that formed the backup power for the island. There was no sign of life, no movement of any kind.

It became obvious that the building was empty of life and they walked slowly into the gloomy interior.

"Strange," mumbled Lieutenant Gain. "I would have thought someone would be here with the heightened alert of the past few days."

Trask grunted in agreement. The latest communiqué stated that, due to unrest in Russia, the recent coup by hardliners, and the loss or "misplacement" of several nuclear weapons in the former Soviet Union, the United States had gone from a relatively normal Defense Condition 5, or DEFCON 5, to a higher alert status of DEFCON 4. The lower the DEFCON number, the higher the alert status. DEFCON 1, the highest state of readiness, meant war had already broken out. The change of alert status was also used sometimes as a signal of resolve by the United States to the Russians. As far as Shemya Air Force Base was concerned, more personnel were assigned to the twenty-four-hour-a-day watches that manned the radar on the island and steps were taken to insure uninterrupted operation of the radar. Maintenance personnel were on immediate call day or night.

"Let's try the phones," said Trask. He made for one of the offices with Lieutenant Gain close on his heels. Elverson stayed in the open area with a watchful eye on the corners and recesses of the building. Trask boldly walked into the open doorway of the nearest office and immediately saw an empty desk with a telephone on it. He hoped that it was still operational. After pulling up a chair, he sat down at the desk and placed a hand on the phone. He glanced up at Lieutenant Gain, who was standing in front of the desk.

"I guess there's no point in calling Building Six Hundred or the satellite terminal," he said.

She compressed her lips into a straight line. "Try the airport," she said. He nodded. He searched briefly for a telephone book and quickly found the number. He picked up the receiver, dialed the number and held his breath. The phone was answered halfway through the first ring.

"Yes."

The answer was tense, but not panic-stricken, not at all what Trask had expected. He suddenly realized he was at a loss for words.

"Listen. I've got a problem . . ." he began.

"Everything went all right at the radar building, didn't it?" the voice interrupted.

"I've just come from Building Six Hundred and everyone is dead there." Trask's voice almost cracked under the strain. His statement was greeted with silence.

"Who is this?"

"It doesn't matter. Somebody's got to check out Building Six Hundred," persisted Trask. I have a bad feeling about this, he thought.

"Yes? . . . Well, look, we'll get someone out there right away." The voice hesitated. "Where are you calling from?"

Trask thought furiously. "I'm in the radar building." He hung up. Elverson had joined them in the office during Trask's conversation. Trask looked up at both of them.

"They've got the airport also," he said.

CHAPTER 7

━ ∙ ━ ∙ ━ ∙ ━

0930 HOURS, 25 DECEMBER
SHEMYA ISLAND

Trask looked first at Elverson, then at Lieutenant Gain. "I guess it's obvious someone has taken over the island," said the engineer.

"What about the radar building?" asked Lieutenant Gain.

Trask gestured to the phone. "He asked me if everything went all right at the radar building. He must have thought I was someone else. I think we have to assume that the radar building was taken over also." Trask shook his head in frustration. "The question is: Why?"

Gain's expression grew more serious and depressed. "Are these the opening shots of World War Three?" she asked.

Trask gave her a sharp glance. "Unfortunately, that's the only explanation that makes sense," he said, his voice tinged with despair.

"So, what do we do about it?" asked Elverson. He looked at Trask and seemed to pointedly ignore the female lieutenant.

"We try to stop them," replied Trask. "But we only have two weapons and we're probably outnumbered ten or fifteen to one. So, we need help." He looked at Lieutenant Gain. She returned his gaze with a questioning look.

"That's where you come in, Lieutenant," said Trask.

"You said you were in comm, and we've got to send a message."

She was surprised at the suggestion and tried to talk the older engineer out of it. "I heard gunfire at the satellite terminal. That means they've got it," she objected.

Trask was undeterred. "Maybe we could sneak in and send a message?"

Ellen rolled her eyes around. "Don't you think they'll keep the satellite station manned twenty-four hours a day?"

"What about White Alice?" he asked, referring to the island's high-frequency troposcatter link.

"That was shut down a few years ago," she said.

"Could we get it running?" asked Trask. "Did they remove all the equipment?"

"I don't know," she said in a thoughtful tone, then shook her head. "But they probably cut the power to the building. Besides, there's got to be somebody listening on that frequency to do any good, and with White Alice stations all over the arctic being shut down . . ." She shrugged and left the rest unsaid.

Trask had to concede the point. He sat for a minute in thought, then stood and looked Lieutenant Gain in the eye. "That still doesn't change anything. We've got to send a message. The air force has got to know what's happening here."

She hesitated, then finally nodded in agreement. "Yes, but how?"

Trask shrugged, looked at the floor and rubbed his chin while another thought struck him. "Of course, we might be the least of their worries," he mumbled.

"Why do you say that?" asked Elverson.

Trask glanced at the young AP and shrugged again as if to say that his statement was obvious. "If this is World War Three, then U.S. forces are probably trying to repel a massive attack on our bases worldwide by the Russians. A little action like this would be down in the noise. The president is probably desperately trying to figure out how not to use his tactical nuclear weapons and at the same time to stop the Russian attack."

"Oh," said Elverson in a dull manner which did nothing to convince Trask that he understood the situation.

"C'mon, let's send that message," said Trask after a moment. The other two looked skeptical. "We've got to check out the satellite terminal at least," said Trask. "If the place looks like an SVR convention, then we'll forget it."

The other two reluctantly nodded, and they all walked through the office doorway and into the generator area with Elverson leading the way. They reached the door to the building and cautiously peered into the still-raging storm outside.

"I still don't understand why no one's here," said Trask. "During any alert this place is always manned in case something happens to the nuclear power plant." He shook his head in puzzlement.

Elverson peered out the doorway again and then motioned the other two to follow him. They went through the doorway and into the fury of the storm while the wind whipped at them and threatened to invade the warm security of their parkas. All three of them pulled their parkas more tightly around their bodies in an attempt to stem the advance of the arctic wind and staggered in the direction of their vehicle. They momentarily lost sight of their truck, but pressed on with determination and resighted their vehicle after a minute of furious snowfall. They reached the truck, and after brushing the snow from the windows, they gratefully climbed in and resumed their former positions: Elverson behind the wheel, Gain in the front seat on the passenger side, and Trask in the back seat.

Elverson started the vehicle only after several tries and then rather irritably slammed it into gear.

"Wait a minute!" said Lieutenant Gain as she stared out the window. Trask followed her gaze and at first didn't see anything but blinding snow, but as the snowfall momentarily lifted, he saw an object in the distance.

It was a truck wheel, seemingly suspended in midair. Its appearance totally disoriented him—the wheel was horizontal to the ground and appeared to have nothing around it. Trask grabbed the M16 and flipped off the safety. Lieutenant Gain and Trask jumped from the truck simultaneously and left Elverson to wonder what was going on.

As they approached the wheel, Trask's disorientation faded and he realized that the "suspended" wheel was an optical illusion. The wheel was attached to a truck that was lying on its side. Snow had drifted around the truck and obscured most of it, except for the front wheel, which gave the appearance of hanging in midair. They went around to the top part of the truck and stumbled over something half hidden in the snow. It was a dead body. The man had been shot several times in the chest and side.

Trask suddenly felt concern for Lieutenant Gain and glanced quickly at her to gauge her reaction. She stood with her eyes fixed on the corpse. Based on her subdued reaction, he guessed she would be all right. He went over to the truck and immediately noticed that all the windows were smashed with only a small piece of the windshield still left in one corner of the frame, and even that had a bullet hole through it. He inhaled quickly and peered into the interior of the truck's passenger compartment. He was unprepared for the carnage within. His eyes grew wide and he quickly looked away. Bullets had smashed virtually everything inside the truck, including the three occupants.

Trask staggered backward a bit, then recovered and walked back to Lieutenant Gain, who turned and looked at Trask. She had an ashen complexion.

"Let's go," said Trask in as gruff a manner as he could muster. He grabbed her arm and turned her away from the truck. She gave little resistance.

"What about them?" She gestured back over her shoulder.

Trask shook his head. "You don't want to know." He glanced sideways at her and marveled at her composure. She's a tough number, he thought.

"Are they the crew for the power station?" she asked.

"Probably."

They trudged toward Elverson and their truck without speaking, until she suddenly stopped and broke the silence. "I don't believe this is happening. *How could this be happening?*" she exclaimed in frustration.

"I don't know," he said, and sighed. He looked at Ellen again.

Her face suddenly changed with the determined grim lines dissolving into desperation and fear. Trask's heart went out to the young woman next to him, and he fervently wished that he could somehow undo the morning's events. For her sake, not mine, he thought. She has her whole life ahead of her—she ought to be given a chance to live it.

Ellen looked at him, her blue eyes locked with his in an unspoken plea for help.

"You okay?" he asked in a tone unique to him for its tenderness. She nodded and blinked her eyes quickly a few times.

He smiled at her. "Let's go send a message," he said.

Trask took a step, then froze. He sensed a presence in the storm beyond and suddenly looked about wildly as the wind whipped the snow into a frenzy around him. Trask flipped back the hood of his parka in a frantic motion and brought his M16 up in front of him. Ellen took a few steps past him, then stopped to give him a quizzical look.

"What's the matter?" she shouted over the wind.

He waved to her to be quiet and continued to brave the elements to stare into the wind and snow. His pulse began to pound as he slowly moved toward a small swell in the ground which seemed to be the center of the presence. The wind drove the snow into his face and eyes and all but took his breath away. He leaned into the wind and crouched low to the ground to present the smallest target possible.

Trask reached the swell as the storm lowered his visibility to something less than ten feet, and he slowly began his way around to the other side. He stared into the snow until his eyes watered. Blinking furiously, he refused to give in to the storm.

Trask was on top of him before he knew it.

"Don't shoot! *Don't shoot!*" said a voice in the snowfall.

Trask squinted into the snow in the general direction of the voice and after a few seconds made out the outline of a man. The stranger had his hands outstretched in an unthinking effort to fend off the ominous figure with the automatic weapon.

Trask took a few steps closer while keeping the M16 pointed directly at the stranger. He looked into the man's face—he was obviously terrified.

"Who are you?" asked Trask as the wind nearly swept his words away.

"Harry Vaughan, I'm Harry Vaughan," the man jabbered. *"Don't shoot!"* He took a step toward Trask out of anxiety, but the engineer stepped back quickly.

"Hands on your head!" yelled Trask.

The man was mortified. *"NO!* I didn't mean . . ."

"Hands on your head, damn it!"

He quickly complied.

Trask stepped up to him and patted the obvious places on his person where he might conceal a weapon.

"Don't kill me! Please . . . Oh, God!"

Trask finished his search and stepped back satisfied that he had no weapons on him. Vaughan jammed his eyes shut and prepared for the worst. Trask almost laughed.

"Put your hands down, Harry. I'm not going to kill you," he said in a relaxed voice.

Vaughan opened his eyes and stared at Trask with hope beginning to build on his face. He lifted his hands off the top of his head and nervously waited for Trask's reaction. The engineer smiled.

"C'mon, let's get to the truck," Trask shouted over the storm. Vaughan dropped his arms and with a sigh of relief and a look of gratitude to Trask, he began to move in the direction of the truck. He suddenly thought of something and held up his hand.

"Wait!" he said. He reached back into the snow, and his sudden movement caused Trask to bring his M16 to bear on Vaughan once again. Vaughan pulled a flight bag out of the deepening snow and turned back toward Trask to continue his journey, but stopped when he saw Trask's weapon pointed at him. Trask grabbed the bag and quickly searched it for any weapons. There were none.

"Just being careful," said Trask as he gave the bag back

to Vaughan. Vaughan nodded and calmed down as Trask lowered his weapon.

He started to move and then abruptly stopped upon seeing another figure step in front of him. He glanced back at Trask, his face riddled with fear once again.

Ellen Gain glanced from Vaughan to Trask and back again. She looked surprised.

"I searched him," Trask explained simply.

"Let's get back to the truck," Ellen shouted over the wind.

Vaughan glanced back and forth between them and relaxed a bit. Trask and Gain pointed in the direction he should proceed, and he complied by lowering his head and trudging off into the storm.

They made their way back to the truck and Elverson, who was surprised at the newcomer. They quickly filled Elverson in. He looked Vaughan over with some suspicion, but the man's appearance was so disarming that Elverson satisfied himself for the moment with little more than a cursory glance. Vaughan was young, but small and lightweight in stature. He had thick, wire-framed glasses and a thinning head of blond hair. He was the stereotype of a bookworm.

When Elverson was told of the murdered men in the truck, he didn't seem surprised at all, which Trask thought was curious.

Elverson felt Trask's reaction and thought he should say something. "Well, they've killed everyone else on the island. Why not the power plant crew also?"

Trask shrugged. Perfectly true, he thought.

They got back into the truck with Elverson and Vaughan in the front and Trask and Gain in the rear seat, and they all quickly fell silent. Vaughan looked around nervously. All eyes were on him.

"Can we trust him?" asked Elverson as if Vaughan wasn't there.

"We don't know anything about him," said Ellen.

"What do you do on Shemya?" asked Trask.

Vaughan looked quickly from one to another. "I worked in Personnel," he said. Then, when no one reacted, he said,

"You know, I handled personnel records." He continued to look from one to another as his anxiety increased.

"So, how come you're still alive?" asked Trask.

Vaughan opened his mouth to speak, but no sound issued forth. He finally shrugged. "I don't know!" he said in a voice bordering on panic.

"Where were you just before we picked you up?" asked Elverson.

"I was hiding from those ... those murderers." He looked at Trask. "I thought you were one of them," he added apologetically.

"What were you doing out here in the first place?" asked Ellen Gain. "There's no personnel records in the middle of a snowstorm."

"I ... I was going to the power plant."

"Why?" The word was flung at him by Elverson.

Vaughan looked at him with fear on his face. "I had a friend at the power plant. John Masters. We play ... used to play chess. . . ."

"You went out in the middle of a snowstorm on Christmas morning just to play chess?" asked Elverson incredulously.

"Yes! I knew John was at the plant because of the alert, and when he's there he doesn't have much to do so we ... play chess." He ended it lamely.

"That's so stupid, it's probably true," said Trask.

Vaughan looked at the engineer and brightened a bit. "Yes, it's stupid," agreed Vaughan.

Elverson picked up Vaughan's bag, gave him a dirty look, and unzipped it. He turned it upside down and dumped the contents on the front seat between them. A miniature chess board with pieces and a book on chess were prominent among the articles on the seat.

"I used to supply the board and pieces," said Vaughan in a hopeful tone.

"Looks like we can trust you, Harry," said Trask with a smile as Elverson disgustedly began to return the articles to Vaughan's bag.

Harry Vaughan let out one more sigh of relief.

They all faced forward and prepared to leave when they

heard a truck motor over the whine of the wind. After a few seconds the truck lurched into view. It screeched to a halt and four men carrying automatic weapons jumped out. Inexplicably, they didn't notice the truck with the four of them in it, and they ran immediately over to the power plant building.

This was their first look at the force that had taken over the island. They seemed to be ordinary air force personnel and they carried M16s, but their actions clearly indicated that they were after Trask and his companions. This greatly surprised Trask, who had been expecting Russians in full combat gear. He immediately thought of the man on the phone who had spoken perfect, colloquial, Americanized English. Russian moles, must be.

He snapped out of his thoughts and saw that the others were staring in surprise at the small party which was swarming over the building they had just left.

"Let's get the hell out of here!" shouted Trask.

Elverson jumped, then responded by gunning the engine and taking off at a high rate of speed down the road. The men at the power plant looked up at the noise and quickly ran to their truck to give chase. They faded from view as Elverson flung the truck around a curve in the road.

"How did they know we were here?" asked Lieutenant Gain.

Trask didn't answer and Elverson only cursed at the condition of the road. The road straightened and after a few moments the pursuing truck swung into view and began to slowly gain on them. Trask grabbed the M16 and gave the automatic to Lieutenant Gain.

"You know how to use that?" he asked almost calmly.

She nodded. Trask glanced through the rear window at their pursuers and saw that two men were leaning out the side windows and pointing their weapons toward them.

"Get down!" yelled Trask and pulled Gain down on the seat. He threw his body over hers.

A second later, a blast of gunfire slammed into the truck, shattering the rear window and splintering the windshield, and spraying them with small pieces of glass. Elverson lifted his head enough to peek over the dashboard in time to see another curve in the road. He whipped the truck around the bend and the rear end broke out into a skid. He turned the steering wheel in the opposite direction, the rear snapped around in line with the road, then he straightened the wheel and stomped on the accelerator. The truck leaped forward as Trask sat up and looked to see if Lieutenant Gain was all right. She sat up and shook the glass from her as a thoroughly whitened Vaughan peeked over the front seat. Trask glanced out the back window.

"Get them when they round the curve!" he shouted.

Gain nodded and pulled back on the slide of the automatic to pump a bullet into the chamber. She cupped her left hand, placed the butt of the automatic in it and pointed it rearward. Trask pulled back on the cocking bar and put the M16 on fully automatic. He shoved the barrel through the now completely open rear window and waited for the pursuing truck to reappear around the curve. Trask fought to keep aim at the point where he thought the pursuing truck would become visible as their truck bounced and skidded along the road.

The truck suddenly appeared in a skid similar to what Elverson had done in the same curve, and the men hanging out the side windows had to hang on for their lives. Trask steadied the M16 and pressed the trigger. The weapon kicked at his shoulder, and a second later he heard the explosive thump of Gain's automatic.

The pursuing truck swerved, then straightened, as their attackers took aim at the fleeing vehicle. Trask saw small dots of fire erupt from the barrels of their weapons as he desperately kept his finger on the trigger.

Gain's weapon spoke rapidly as she and Trask kept up a furious rate of fire. Their combined fire finally met the truck with devastating results. One of the pursuers' weapons fell silent and Trask saw it fall away from the vehicle and bounce off the road. At the same time, the windshield shattered, and the truck suddenly swerved sharply to the right. The other man stopped firing and grabbed on to the door to keep from being thrown away from the truck as it flew off the road. It continued on for twenty yards and then flipped over in the tundra. The truck slid, bouncing and slewing on the uneven ground, until some unseen spark ignited the gas tank. With a thump of displaced air, flames enveloped the vehicle and its occupants.

Trask started to breathe again as he watched the snow-storm gradually close in around the burning vehicle. Elverson slowed the truck from breakneck speed to something more reasonable and looked around at Trask.

"Where did you learn to shoot like that?" he asked.

Trask couldn't help feeling elation. "Vietnam," he said, and looked at Lieutenant Gain. She had a clear look of relief on her face.

"Yes," she said in agreement with Elverson. "Nice shooting."

"I feel sick," said Vaughan.

"You didn't do so bad yourself," replied Trask to Lieu-tenant Gain, and ignored Vaughan's plight.

She gave him a strained, lopsided smile. Trask almost laughed. They had struck back against their attackers, and he couldn't help but feel a surge of pride and excitement.

"Vietnam, huh. Did you see much combat?" asked El-verson.

Memories invaded Trask's mind. "Not much. I went on a few patrols, but that was all. Hell, I was a cook." He was getting good at shoving his thoughts aside.

"A cook," said Lieutenant Gain matter-of-factly, and then smiled and shook her head.

They lapsed into silence as the heady aftermath of their initial combat began to wane. Trask's thoughts turned to the next step. Nothing had changed except maybe they had evened the odds a little. They should still concentrate on sending a message. Trask looked about for landmarks to determine their location and found that they happened to be headed toward White Alice. Elverson slowed the vehicle as if in response to Trask's unspoken wish.

"We're getting close to White Alice," Elverson ex-plained.

"We've got to approach the building carefully. They could be waiting for us," said Lieutenant Gain.

"I would bet they don't have anyone there, but let's go past it anyway, then we can swing around and get back toward the satellite station," said Trask. The road to White Alice led off from the main road forming a rough semicircle and ending up on the main road again a half mile down the road. By following the semicircular road and then heading back in their original direction, they would avoid the crash site of their pursuers and any possible survivors.

They rumbled on for half an hour, slipping and sliding along the unplowed roads as Elverson pushed the truck's speed as high as he dared. They spotted the low-slung satellite terminal building first with the white antenna radome hidden from them by the snowfall until they were on top of the building itself. They slid into an adjoining parking lot and stopped the truck behind some parked vehicles.

"Are you sure this is a good idea?" asked Vaughan. He apparently didn't like the idea of tackling a building that was most likely full of the killers who had taken over the island.

"There's no other way," replied Trask in a curt tone of voice. He offered the M16 to Elverson. "Maybe you should take this," he said. "And I'll take the automatic," continued Trask. "That'll leave Lieutenant Gain free to send the message."

Trask glanced at Vaughan, whose eyes had grown as big as dinner plates.

"You'll stay out of the way, won't you?" asked Trask. He didn't expect an answer. Vaughan swallowed, then nervously nodded.

They all got out of the truck and ran over to two parked vehicles in front of the squat building which housed the communications equipment. The storm surged and the satellite terminal faded from view. Trask hoped the low visibility would continue until they got up to the communications building.

They started off at a run toward the building, but the storm and the accumulated snow quickly reduced their pace to a fast walk. Trask's head started to pound with the exertion, and the effects of his hangover began to reassert themselves on his system. The older man was gasping for breath by the time they were halfway to the building. He looked at the younger people next to him and saw that they were only breathing deeply, and he regretted his alcoholic activities for the thousandth time in an hour.

Elverson got to the building first and pressed himself against the outside wall. Trask followed with Lieutenant Gain and Harry Vaughan close behind him. They looked at the few windows in the building in search of activity, but there seemed to be none. A light issued from one of them, but that was the only indication that the building might be occupied.

Elverson ran up to the outside doorway, twisted the knob, and flung the door back. He leaped through the doorway just as Trask came up behind him. The two of them went down a short hallway to the door to the comm room. Elverson quickly threw the door open and ran inside. Two men seated at consoles looked up in surprise at the sound of the intrusion. One man opened his mouth to say something, but Elverson cut him off with a burst from the M16. The man took the blast in the chest and flew backward to land at the feet of the second console operator. Elverson adjusted his aim toward the second man and pulled the trigger. Nothing happened. The M16 was empty.

The console operator leaped sideways in the direction of an M16 that was lying on a table in a far corner of the room. Trask shoved Elverson aside and fired a wild shot into the wall. The man reached the M16 and whirled around, cocking the weapon as he moved. Trask hit the floor and rolled to one side. Elverson threw himself in the opposite direction.

The console operator fired a short burst, missing both of them, while Trask got the automatic leveled at the trunk of the man's body. A fraction of a second later, the man had corrected his aim, but Trask fired before he could pull the trigger. The bullet slammed into the man's shoulder and spun him around. He continued the rest of the way around on his own until he faced Trask again. He lifted the M16 with one hand to point it at the engineer.

Trask fired again. The impact of the bullet entering the man's chest drove him backwards and caused the burst of fire from the M16 to hit the wall behind Trask. The console operator hit the floor, rolled over and was still. Trask quickly looked over at the first console operator, but his mangled body was quiet and lying in an ever widening pool of blood.

Trask discovered he was holding his breath, and he let it out with an explosive gasp. He dropped his head until his chin touched the floor, then he rolled over and stared at the ceiling. He waited for his heart to stop pounding, then gave up and propped himself up on one elbow. Elverson was seated in an upright position clutching the empty M16 with a petrified look on his face. His eyes left the scene of the carnage and wandered over to Trask. Elverson's chest heaved as he took a deep breath.

"Shit," Trask said simply.

Lieutenant Gain was suddenly next to him and gave him an almost frantic look. "Are you all right?!"

Trask grunted and struggled to get up. "I guess I'm okay."

He stood and wobbled a bit and then leaned on Lieutenant Gain. Trask lifted his right hand and looked at the automatic he was still holding. The slide had locked in its rearmost position, a sign that the gun was empty.

"Next time we do this, we've got to reload these damn things before we go into action," he gasped.

Incredibly, they had forgotten to reload their weapons after their battle with the truck on the road. Trask had virtually emptied the magazine of Elverson's M16, with the result that Elverson had only one short burst left. Lieutenant Gain had fired twelve shots, leaving only three for Trask.

Trask sighed again to calm his pounding heart, then shoved the automatic into the pocket of his parka. He looked at the two men they had just killed. More Americans. He gestured to the now empty consoles.

"You had better get to it before somebody else shows up," he said to Lieutenant Gain.

She nodded quickly, then gave him a relieved-you're-all-right look. She went over, sat down at one of the consoles and immediately got to work.

Harry Vaughan peeked into the still-open doorway and his eyes seemed even bigger than before.

"C'mon, Harry, it's all right," said Trask.

Vaughan stepped inside, then seemed to wobble as he caught sight of the two bodies on the floor. He put his hand over his mouth in shock at the grisly scene, and Trask began to wonder if their bespectacled companion might faint. Vaughan took a few deep breaths and went over to stare out the door.

Trask turned away and went over to pick up two M16s, then glanced in Elverson's direction and caught the young AP staring at Lieutenant Gain with an expression approaching jealousy.

Idiot, thought Trask. He nearly gets us all killed by not reloading his M16, and then he finds time to be jealous. There are more important things to worry about, like surviving this disastrous situation we're in. Elverson stood and Trask handed him one of the captured M16s.

"This one is fully loaded," he said sarcastically.

Elverson stared at Trask in obvious annoyance. "You didn't load the automatic either, Pops, so what are you bitching about," was his retort.

Trask bristled, but forced himself to calm down. The young man had a point. He let it pass. Trask picked up a clip belt from the floor and threw it over his shoulder.

"Let's keep an eye out, shall we?" he said to Elverson while gesturing toward the door. The young AP grunted and nodded. They moved out the door and up the hallway, with Elverson taking the outside doorway while Trask went over to a window.

"What the devil's going on here?" mumbled Lieutenant Gain as she stared at the console. She looked up. "Frank, come over here for a minute, will you?" she shouted loudly enough for Trask and Elverson to hear.

Trask turned and caught Elverson's look of annoyance at her use of Trask's first name, then went back down the hall and into the comm room. He walked over to stand beside her as she pointed to the display on the screen.

"They're using NORAD's channel, but they're transmitting something from disk, not operational data from the radar," she explained.

"Can you display what they're transmitting?" he asked.

She nodded and typed in a command on the keyboard.

The display changed and Trask recognized it almost immediately.

"That's spacetracking data." He scratched his head. "Are you sure they're getting this from disk?"

"Yes, I'm certain," she replied.

"That doesn't make any sense," he mused. "Why send NORAD old spacetrack data instead of current radar data?" He thought for a moment. "I don't suppose the status display could be wrong," he said.

She shook her head vehemently. "This system was just completely checked a few days ago."

"Can you override it and send NORAD a message?"

She shrugged. "I think so."

"Better make it fast before someone shows up," replied Trask, then he went up the hall and back over to the window to scan the outside area.

Ellen Gain, with a furtive look over her shoulder to make sure the others were outside and that Vaughan wasn't looking, reached behind the terminal and located the brightness adjustment. She quickly turned it down to obliterate what was to be displayed on the screen. With another glance around the room, she began to type furiously.

After a minute of observing the snowstorm, Trask walked back to the comm room to stand over Ellen Gain. She looked up.

"Damn CRT went down," she explained.

Trask frowned, then heard a noise up the hall. He leaned out the comm room doorway and saw Elverson's anxious face.

"We've got company!" Elverson shouted.

"Damn!" said Trask. He ran up the hall with Vaughan following him and looked out the doorway into the snowstorm beyond just in time to see a vehicle come to a stop. He left Elverson crouching in the doorway and hurriedly went back to the window. Vaughan backed away from the doorway as if it had the plague. He was white with fear. Trask flipped the light switch off and opened the window. He pulled back the cocking bar on the M16 and shoved the barrel out into the weather.

Several men had jumped out of the truck and were cautiously rounding one of the parked vehicles. Trask decided to wait until they were in the open before firing. He looked away from the window and started to tell Elverson to hold his fire when he heard the staccato cracking of Elverson's M16.

The men jumped behind the truck as Elverson's burst reduced the glass in the truck to splinters. Trask groaned in frustration and began to fire around the truck to keep their attackers pinned down. The men went around the other side of the truck and began to return fire toward the doorway.

Elverson rolled into the hallway as gunfire shot the doorway to pieces. He shouted for another clip and Trask threw him one. Vaughan hit the floor and stretched out flat while still clutching his flight bag. Trask peered back through the window and saw two men aiming at him. He quickly yanked his head back down as a burst of gunfire smashed through the window and slammed into the wall on the other side of the room.

Elverson jumped to his feet and ran down the hallway with Vaughan running past him in terrified flight. Trask backed his way down the hall, keeping his M16 pointed at the door. He saw a form pass across the threshold, and he pulled the trigger, sending a burst into the frame of the outside door. Vaughan and Elverson reached the comm room and ran inside to temporary safety. Trask fired another quick burst toward the door, then turned and ran for the comm room.

He just turned the corner into the room when gunfire from the SVR agents slammed into the wall near the door. Trask let out a gasp at his near escape and hurriedly looked about the room for some means to escape. Trask looked over at Ellen and was horrified to see her still seated at the console, bravely trying to send a message. With the sounds of enemy agents' footsteps just outside the room, he leaped over to her side and pulled her to the floor as a blast of gunfire passed through the comm room doorway and demolished the two consoles above them.

"Is there another exit to this place?" he shouted in her

ear as Elverson sprayed the doorway with lead. She thought quickly, then nodded.

She crawled past the destroyed equipment to a doorway that led to another part of the building. Trask immediately followed, then looked back to see Elverson and Vaughan literally on his heels.

They crawled through the doorway and found themselves in the comparative safety of the transmitter room. They heard more gunfire batter the room they had just left as they followed Ellen around the transmitters to a door that led to the outside. She grabbed the handle and opened it a crack, then peered out and pronounced it safe. In a second she was through the doorway and outside the building. Trask and Elverson followed and the three of them immediately spotted a snow-covered vehicle.

They ran for it with Trask praying that there were keys inside. They opened the driver's side door and eagerly looked inside. No keys. Trask feverishly racked his brain; he had seen a toolbox somewhere in the building, the kind used by electricians. He turned and began to run back toward the building, but Ellen desperately grabbed him by the arm.

"Frank, *NO!*" she yelled over the wind.

There was no time to explain. He shoved her away and ran back to the doorway they had just left. As he leaped through it, he half expected to get a burst from an M16, but there was no one. Trask raced around the transmitter room, spotted the toolbox and nearly flew over to it with a prayer on his lips. He flipped it open and saw that his prayer was answered. Wire and wire cutters were right on top.

A rattle of gunfire floated to him from another part of the building as he raced to the door with the tools. They were very close now. He ran back to the truck waving the precious wire in his hand as Elverson gave him a look of enlightenment and Ellen and Vaughan looked mystified.

"I wasn't a juvenile delinquent for nothing," he gasped, and flung open the hood. He immediately got to work while the others nervously kept watch for the reappearance of their assailants.

"Get in!" shouted Trask two minutes later.

The others leaped into the truck as Trask touched two bare wires together. The truck coughed into life. An instant later Trask shoved it into gear and took off down the road.

Their assailants made their way through the building and only spotted the fleeing vehicle after it had a good head start. They fired a few futile shots after the rapidly disappearing truck, but they were off the mark.

CHAPTER 8

Colonel Andrei Sobchak looked over the short message from his colleagues at the Federal Agency for Government Communications and Information. An intelligence-gathering ship in the Aleutians had intercepted signals coming from Shemya Air Force Base, the most interesting of which was the signal from the COBRA DANE radar. The signal characteristics had changed abruptly at 1727 Greenwich Mean Time. The conclusion of the signals experts was that the radar had gone from spacetrack mode, used for tracking objects in orbit, to early warning mode, which is used for tracking suborbital flights coming over the North Pole, which would be an ICBM attack from Russia. The time listed would coincide with the start of the drill the Americans were having to test their strategic readiness. Common procedure now was to inform the other side of such drills so that military moves would not be misinterpreted as preparations for an actual attack.

Even though the United States and the remnants of the former Soviet Union had excellent relations, the warrior class within each had a lingering distrust of the other. Nuclear warheads were being destroyed at a very slow pace in Russia while the Russians and the Americans haggled over the level of aid from the Western democracies to the newly formed Eastern democracies. The "let's not blow it now" syndrome had permeated the West, and when drills were scheduled, the military was careful to inform its Russian counterparts.

Sobchak smiled to himself with the knowledge that he knew more about the American strategic drill than most of the people involved in the drill itself. His smile lingered as he looked over the final note of an encrypted signal in an amateur ham band that the *Kursograf* had also intercepted. So the Americans were going to encrypted base radio, but why in an amateur band?

Colonel Sobchak looked up at a knock at his office door. "Come in," he said loudly, expecting to see his secretary. Instead a stiff officer in a colonel's uniform walked in and stood in front of his desk. The look on his face told Sobchak that this wasn't a social call.

"Colonel Sobchak, I am Colonel Parchomenko from Government Communications," the visitor began.

Sobchak glanced at the bottom of the page in front of him. "Yes, Colonel, I was just reading your memo—"

"The signal in the ham band . . ." began Parchomenko. Sobchak could hear his voice shake. "It is encrypted—"

Sobchak grew impatient. He had already gotten to the end of the memo. "Yes, yes," he interrupted. He picked up the memo to show his visitor that he knew all about it. The look on Parchomenko's face made him pause.

Parchomenko passed a shaking hand over his face. "I came here to tell you myself. I didn't trust the phones," he mumbled almost to himself.

Sobchak gave the secure phone on his desk half a glance. He fixed his eyes on Parchomenko. "Yes?" The single word was more of a command than a question.

Parchomenko hesitated. Sobchak sensed his visitor's reluctance and knew that something was very wrong.

"The signal is encrypted with one of our codes," said Parchomenko, then he exhaled in a long sigh.

"What? How can that be? Wait a minute. Codes are codes the world over. How can you tell it's one of ours?" asked Sobchak.

Parchomenko waved his hand as if to dismiss the question. "The Americans and we set up our cryptographic gear in different ways. The chances of the Americans having the same code we do is extremely small."

"Still, it could happen," countered Sobchak.

"It did *not* happen," replied Parchomenko irritably. "It is our code, one designated for the SVR." The SVR was responsible for the "illegals," the agents who are smuggled into a country unknown to the target country's intelligence service.

Sobchak whirled and stabbed a button on his phone. He picked up the handset and waited a few seconds, then he spoke quickly. "Colonel General Tofimov, I believe we have a problem."

2035 HOURS, 25 DECEMBER
SHEMYA ISLAND'S SOUTHERN COAST

Frank Trask peered through the dirty window of the trailer at the slowing snowstorm outside. The snow had accumulated to a foot in most places and had gone to more than that around the edges of buildings and in several random places in the area. The storm had abated somewhat with a resulting improvement in visibility even though night had fallen several hours ago. Trask scanned what little he could see of the road in the glow caused by the fallen snow. They had escaped their encounter with the island saboteurs and were taking refuge in some unused trailers which had been used as temporary living quarters near the southeastern tip of the island. Trask turned from the window and let out a sigh. He was tired, deathly tired, and his head had begun to throb from his alcoholic excesses the night before.

"Merry Christmas," he mumbled to no one in particular. He looked at Ellen Gain. She gave him a depressed look and then stared at the floor. He shifted his gaze to Vaughan. The young man looked more tired than scared.

"Well, I guess we've lost them for the time being," offered Trask.

"They'll get us eventually," replied Elverson. No one argued the point.

Trask lowered himself into a dilapidated chair and rubbed his face. "Let's sum up the situation," he began wearily. "We know that someone has taken control of most of the island. We've found bodies almost everywhere we've gone, so we also know that these guys are playing for keeps. They're as ruthless as hell." He hesitated. "And we know that they're Americans," he said quietly.

"They look like Americans and talk like them, but not necessarily Americans," corrected Lieutenant Gain. Trask nodded and readily conceded the point.

"Who then?" asked Vaughan.

Ellen Gain shrugged. "Russians, maybe," she replied.

"Certainly the SVR is ruthless enough, especially if they used to be KGB, but why would they want to take over Shemya?" asked Trask. "This is a direct act of war with the United States. We'll have to retaliate in some manner and the Russians know that, so why would they take such a drastic step as trying to take over a sensitive spot such as this place?"

"All that talk over the last two weeks of a coup by hardliners in Russia. Maybe they've reverted back to the Cold War. The news reports said they were beginning to build up troops on the Ukraine border. Maybe they invaded Europe," said Gain. She hesitated and her face took on a look of desperation and fear.

They sat in silence for a few minutes as they digested the implications of her statement. Trask looked intently at Ellen as a new thought struck him.

"You said that the people who took over the satellite station were playing something from memory over the channel to NORAD," he said.

"Yes, you looked at that and said it was spacetracking data," she replied.

Trask nodded thoughtfully. "Now, why were they doing that?" He backed up a bit mentally. "We've got a Russian takeover of the island with a war pending, or maybe already started in Europe. And they're not sending current radar data, but they're playing old stuff from memory." Trask stopped, expecting some kind of conclusion to pop up in his mind, but there was nothing forthcoming. He shook his head in confusion.

"Their reason for the takeover must be to disable the radar," said Ellen.

"Yes, but to murder hundreds of people to do it?" replied Trask. He thought for a bit and a glimmer of an idea began to run through his mind. "Wait a minute, now. Suppose they didn't care, because they were already at war with us. . . ." His thought evaporated.

"What bothers me is that it wouldn't last long," said Ellen. "They couldn't hope to hold out for a long time; we would just invade the place and take it back."

"Suppose they didn't need it for a long time. . . . Oh, my God!" gasped Trask. The conclusion hit him with the force of a cannon shell. The others looked at him questioningly.

"One of the purposes of the radar is for early warning of a Russian ICBM launch against the United States," said Trask. "They're playing old data back to NORAD to fool them into thinking that there is no launch when there really *is* a launch!"

Gain and Elverson screwed up their faces in disbelief.

Trask persisted. "Don't you see? The Russians launch their missiles, but the radar on Shemya indicates that everything is normal. The president doesn't launch on warning because maybe, just maybe, everything's okay. That means that they can catch all our ICBMs in their silos and wipe them out!"

Ellen was unconvinced. "But we have satellites to warn of a Russian launch."

"Maybe something has happened to the satellites that we don't know about, especially if we're already at war," replied Trask.

"That's true enough," said Ellen thoughtfully. "One of the scenarios for the beginning of World War Three is that it'll begin in space with the Russians trying to destroy some of our satellites, especially the ones that give us early warning of ICBM launches."

"But that's a dead giveaway of a launch by the Russians. If they blinded us like that, we'd launch first with a preemptive strike," objected Elverson. The remark surprised

Trask, who studied Elverson intently for the first time. He felt some sort of undercurrent in the young airman, but he couldn't find the words to describe it. Perhaps it was his imagination. Trask decided to put off thinking about it until later.

"If you were the president of the United States," Trask began, "and some sensors told you that warheads were heading toward the United States, but other sensors, like the COBRA DANE radar, told you just the opposite, that everything was okay, then that would make you hesitate to launch a retaliatory strike. Maybe that's what they wanted—to make the president hesitate to launch until their first strike hit and took out all our ICBMs. Then what's happening to us would make sense. In order to do that, they would have to take over the island, then play old spacecraft tracking data back to NORAD instead of what was really coming from the radar's computer, which would be data showing the launch of Russian ICBMs."

The implications of Trask's theory began to sink into all of them as they sat in silence for several minutes. Trask looked at the floor, then put his head in his hands. He sat like that until Ellen's voice broke the silence.

"You mean to tell us that the United States has been . . . *destroyed?*"

Her voice was quiet and steady but betrayed a great desperation. Trask lifted his head and looked at her with sympathy. She was young and had a lot to live for, in contrast to his own personal situation. He clenched his teeth together and nodded in response to her question.

She locked her eyes to his as she searched for something, he didn't know what. He looked back to convince her of the sincerity of his conclusions, then went back to staring at the floor. There was another long pause.

Elverson finally spoke. "Do you really believe that?"

Trask nodded, then shrugged. "What other explanation is there?"

There was a gasp from Ellen. The others quickly looked at her. She had her hand to her mouth and had a faraway look on her face.

"You're right!" she exclaimed as she shifted her gaze

to Trask. "When I was near the satellite terminal, I could hear the loudspeaker. They were calling a change in SAC alert status. They went from COCKED PISTOL to ROUNDHOUSE! That's virtually the same as DEFCON 1!"

She sat with her mouth open in shock. Trask stared at her as the panic and fear of a real nuclear war began to pass through him. He had been unconsciously hoping that one of the others would somehow prove him wrong. Instead Ellen Gain had come up with something to prove him right.

The four of them looked at each other in absolute despair until Ellen got up and turned her back on the others. She stood like that for several minutes as Vaughan, Elverson, and Trask gazed at nothing in particular. Trask struggled with his emotions as he fought to stifle thoughts of what might have happened to people he knew and loved in the United States. What was it like back there? He thought of the movies he had seen depicting the horrible aftermath of nuclear war and a shiver arose from deep within him. Could it be like what was portrayed in the movies? He thought for a bit. Probably not, he concluded. It was probably much worse. They remained in silence for a while. He jumped a bit as Elverson spoke.

"So where does that leave us?" Elverson asked of no one in particular.

Trask shook his head. "In hell, I guess," he replied in a hoarse voice. He instantly tried to revise his statement. "Well, we've got to survive, that's for sure. We might be some of the few human beings left on this planet who haven't been exposed to large doses of radiation."

Ellen turned around. Her eyes looked wet. When she spoke her voice was husky with emotion. "The radiation will get us eventually, won't it?"

Trask again shook his head, but this time he was more emphatic and hopeful. "Not necessarily. It all depends on whether it rains before it gets here or not. A lot of it could fall to earth before the radiation cloud gets around to this part of the world."

He suddenly thought of the Kamchatka Peninsula, where the Russians conduct missile tests and had several secret bases. The United States would certainly hit that area with a number of nuclear weapons in a general strategic exchange and Shemya was only a few hundred miles away. A cold feeling started to invade his insides. He shook off the thought and hoped the others wouldn't think of it.

"Our first problem is dealing with the killers on this island," he said in an effort to distract the others from the disastrous world situation.

"If they are SVR, then the Russians will probably send in a team to evacuate the island after the war is over," said Trask.

Elverson interrupted. "That is, if they're able. Russia could be destroyed also."

"Or maybe they won't bother with such a small group of people . . ." began Trask.

"Oh, they'll bother all right. These guys are superheroes to them," responded Elverson. He sounded very certain. Another incongruous remark, thought Trask. How could he be so sure? He mentally shrugged off the remark as a certain amount of immaturity.

"The bottom line is that we're stuck on the island for an unknown length of time and with an unknown number of people who are trying to kill us," said Trask. "I think our best course is to stay out of their way until either the Russians pick them up or they leave by themselves."

"They could fly out if any of them could pilot a plane," offered Ellen. Trask nodded.

"That would get them out of our hair pretty quickly," agreed Elverson.

"I don't suppose either of you know how to pilot a plane," asked Trask. Vaughan and Elverson shook their heads. Trask caught their reaction, then glanced at Ellen. She, on the other hand, was not shaking her head.

"I doubt if I could fly an RC-135," she mumbled.

Trask was surprised. "But you *can* fly a plane?" he asked.

She looked at him briefly. "I washed out of flight school, but I did learn to fly some prop stuff."

Vaughan perked up at that point. "Maybe we can fly out of here!" he said, stating the obvious.

"Not that many prop planes on the island, if any at all," she replied. Their enthusiasm faded.

"What about the boats?" asked Trask.

"Maybe, but not until the weather clears," Ellen replied. "We probably have a phase one weather alert and a sea state five out there. The boats we have will never make it with that kind of weather."

"Looks like we're stuck here for at least a couple of months, if we can't find a prop plane," mumbled Vaughan in a depressed manner.

Trask looked at Ellen, who had gotten very quiet and seemed to be lost in thought for a moment. She suddenly snapped her fingers. "I've got it!" They all looked at her in surprise. She gave the others an excited look.

"The base commander flew in his Piper Warrior a few days ago, and I know he didn't fly it back out again! It must still be here!"

"You can fly something like that?" asked Trask in surprise and elation. She nodded vigorously.

Trask began to think furiously. They had to get around the SVR in the airport operations building, or else they would never reach the airplane. All the SVR groups on the island were probably connected by radio, and the group that was holding the airport could probably call for reinforcements. How long before they got there? There was no way of telling. Once exposed and the SVR in the airport knew what they were up to, they would have to move very fast, very fast indeed.

He glanced at Ellen as her face suddenly sagged with disappointment.

"What's the matter?" he asked.

She shook her head. "It won't work. The runway is full of snow," she replied.

Her words shocked and depressed him, and he felt as if all his energy was drained from him. He resolved not to give up the idea. "We'll just have to plow the runway. That's all."

"That's all?" asked Elverson in a sarcastic tone.

"They must have a snowplow around the airport somewhere," retorted Trask.

"And what will the SVR be doing while you're plowing the runway?" asked Elverson.

"Maybe they'll think it was ordered by one of them," offered Ellen, not too hopefully.

"That's ridiculous," replied Elverson.

"Once we're in the air, they can't do anything to us," said Trask.

"It's getting in the air that bothers me," said Elverson.

"It's either that or eventually getting caught and murdered by the Russians," replied Trask. "I say let's give it a try."

He looked at Ellen for support. She thought for a moment, but in the end she didn't disappoint him. She nodded. They both looked at Elverson. He shook his head.

"This is stupid," he said, but he seemed resigned to the attempt.

"All right, we should go now for the best chance at surprise," said Trask, then he stopped as he noticed a sour look on Ellen's face.

"I can't fly at night," she stated simply.

Trask sighed with exaggerated patience and tried again. "Then we'll try it during daylight." He looked at Elverson. The young man reluctantly nodded. Trask looked at Ellen, and she seemed almost as reluctant but nodded anyway.

They lapsed into silence for a while as the realities of their immediate situation began to press in on them. Fatigue was beginning to weigh heavily on Trask and his stomach began to growl with lack of food. He hadn't thought of food at all with his hangover and the fantastic events of the day to distract him. He knew that they would have to attend to that detail tomorrow at the latest if they were to survive. He wondered if the SVR had thought to control the food supply, or even poison it, and shuddered at the thought.

He stood and looked out the window once more into the gloom of arctic night. The snow had tapered off greatly from what it had been at the height of the storm, and the visibility was improved commensurately except for the almost complete darkness. Night could be a problem.

"I guess we'll have to set up some sort of watches, so that they don't surprise us," Trask said, thinking out loud.

Elverson moved in his seat. "I'll take the first watch," he said, and looked at his watch. He looked at Trask. "You'll relieve me at oh-two-hundred?"

Trask nodded quickly. Ellen Gain glanced at them in a sudden movement. "Make it midnight. Then I'll relieve you at oh-four-hundred." Both men looked at her in surprise, then they both nodded. They had forgotten to include Lieutenant Gain in their watch coverage.

Instinctively they all looked at Harry Vaughan. He suddenly seemed ill at ease.

"Well . . . I'll take a watch too," he said reluctantly.

"Why don't you sleep tonight? Tomorrow night you can stand a watch," said Ellen Gain. He looked at her and nodded gratefully.

Elverson headed for the door. "I'll get into one of the other trailers to get a better view of the road," he said.

Trask nodded. "Good idea," he said.

Elverson gave Ellen a lingering look before leaving, which set Trask to thinking about some of Elverson's inconsistent behavior. Ellen didn't seem to notice and cringed at the icy blast from the door as Elverson exited the trailer. Trask decided again to postpone his analysis of Elverson's actions to a later moment when he wasn't so tired.

He looked at Vaughan. "You'd better pick out one of the other trailers," said Trask. "We can't all fit in the same bed."

Vaughan returned the look and became very animated. "Yes! Yes, you're right!" he said, and disappeared in the midst of another icy blast from the doorway.

Trask went over to the bed in one corner of the room and sat down. He got up after a minute and searched the closet for a blanket, found two of them and threw them on the bed.

"I'll get you set up here, and then I'll pick out a trailer of my own." He stopped and became thoughtful. "I don't believe what's happened today. Maybe we'll wake up tomorrow and it'll all be a dream," he said in a low voice. He heard a muffled sound and looked quickly in Ellen's direction. She was standing with her back to him, but she was bent over slightly and her shoulders were shaking.

Trask quickly went over to her, put his hands on her shoulders and gently turned her around. She responded by gripping the front of his shirt tightly and burying her face in his chest. He tried to soothe her by telling her that they were still alive and they still had hope. He tried to put as much hope into his voice as he could muster, but he wasn't convinced himself. His efforts were to no avail, and all he could do was to hold her tightly to provide some sort of reassurance.

Trask closed his eyes and immediately the scent of her hair and the feeling of her body next to his were upon him. He buried his face in her hair and his heart went out to her in her misery. His own life flitted across his memory, and he realized over again that when he came to Shemya he really had nothing to live for. He was just going through the motions and doing a bad job at that.

The feeling rushed in at him all at once and didn't give him a chance for reflection or argument. Someone like Ellen would make life worth living. Not just someone like Ellen. *Ellen. Only Ellen.* He felt his emotions slipping away and struggled against them. It was ridiculous. She was young enough to be his daughter. Well, almost. He felt himself slipping again. Then she did him in.

"Oh God, Frank. *Hold me!*" she sobbed.

He encircled her in an even tighter embrace and quite unwillingly began to think of all the things that lovers do that they would never be able to do. Her shaking started to abate, and after a few minutes she lifted her head from his chest.

"I'm sorry," she said while wiping her eyes and managing half a smile. He half smiled back and nodded to tell her that it was all right. She stayed encircled by his arms.

"It was just too much to think about. I guess I just had to let it out somehow," she said apologetically.

He looked at her intently. She was so young and vulnerable, and seemed emotionally dependent upon him for strength in this most disastrous of situations. It had been a long time since anyone had been dependent upon him for anything. He continued to look at her until she lifted her eyes to his. A tear rolled unheeded down her cheek. He slowly moved his face closer to hers and half expected her to pull away, but instead she lifted her lips so that they met his.

She felt cold and her kiss trembled at first but grew more steady as the passion in him rose to a level he had not experienced in many years. She kissed him back with mounting excitement until when their lips finally parted she was breathless.

"We shouldn't be doing this," he said while not really believing it.

Her face changed as her passion and desperation were forced down and her professional side resurfaced. Trask pulled her close once again, but Ellen put her hands on his chest and gently kept him a short distance away.

"You're right. We shouldn't be doing this," she said slowly.

Trask cursed himself under his breath. His desire for her wouldn't diminish for quite a while. He only wanted her.

Ellen extricated herself from Trask's embrace and seemed embarrassed. "I hope . . . you don't think . . ." She left the rest unsaid.

Trask grimaced and replied, "Forget what I think. What matters is that we survive this mess."

Ellen nodded absentmindedly and went over to the bed. She lay down fully clothed and pulled one of the blankets over her, then gave Trask a quick look. He moved toward the door.

"Sleep tight," he mumbled, but he couldn't keep the disappointment out of his voice. When he put his hand on the doorknob, Ellen spoke in a low voice.

"Frank."

He turned and looked at her.

"Don't go," she whispered.

CHAPTER 9

Harry Vaughan crouched just below the windowsill and listened with his eyes closed. He detected one or two muffled noises from the direction of the trailer that he had just left and thought that it must be Trask and Gain settling down for the night. He strained his ears to hear something in the direction of Elverson's trailer, but he could hear nothing. He opened his eyes and gazed into the dark emptiness surrounding him in his own trailer. The light that was reflected from the snow outside cast a subdued glow within and was sufficient to make out most of the details inside the trailer.

He suddenly yawned. It stuck with him until his eyes watered and made him shake his head in surprise. He took a deep breath and his insides fluttered a little. His anxiety hadn't decreased that much, and yet he was yawning. The human body was a funny thing, he thought. He peeked through the dirty glass of the only window in the trailer and stared for a few minutes, then finally came to the conclusion that nothing was moving outside. The wind kicked up now and then and created the illusion of continuing snowfall, but after a few moments the wind would back down again, and the flurry of snowflakes would settle to the ground.

He yawned again and this time fatigue suffused his body, making his extremities feel like concrete. Interesting, he thought, a few hours ago he was afraid for his life. There was no fatigue in him then, but now all his body wanted was sleep. Vaughan resolved that he would get none for quite a while.

He thought of the young Air Policeman, Elverson. There was something irrational about him, and it scared Vaughan. Vaughan was a lover of chess, of the orderly, the logical, the predictable, and there was something about Elverson that was the opposite of those qualities. Perhaps he feared that Elverson, if left to his own devices, would kill him without any hard evidence to prove that he was one of the island's killers. He shook Elverson from his mind.

His thoughts ran immediately to Trask and his seeming leadership of the situation. He wondered how long that would last, probably as long as Elverson and Gain wanted it to. Trask seemed tough, though reasonable—there shouldn't be any trouble from that quarter. Trask wouldn't pull the trigger unless he had good reason, and Vaughan would give him none. He sensed an undercurrent in Trask, though, a hint of sadness or regret.

He thought of Ellen Gain, how attractive she was and how she ignored him almost completely. He didn't mind, though; indeed, if it was the other way around, he would be quite flustered and embarrassed. It was plain that she was attracted to Trask—she seemed to sense the pain within him and wanted to soothe it any way she could. He suddenly smiled. He wondered what they were doing right at the moment. Quite a woman; he had never seen any woman so cool under fire as she had been. The picture of Ellen firing the automatic out the rear window of the truck passed through his mind and he marveled at her composure. She worried him a little, though. Might she be convinced by an irrational Elverson? He mentally shrugged. There was always Trask to fall back on.

Vaughan strained the limits of his hearing once again, but he heard nothing except the whistle of the wind in the small cracks around the door where the weather stripping had rotted away. He tried to filter out the wind and concentrate on other sounds but found it impossible. The sounds of his companions were masked by the wind, or were below his threshold of hearing.

He looked out the window once again and tried to see the trailers on either side but found that he would have to lean out the window to see in either direction. Vaughan gathered his courage and decided his journey had better begin soon or he would run the risk of being detected, or maybe he would just plain run out of time. He tried to gauge the distance he would have to walk; it was difficult to judge because he had never been in this corner of the island before, and with snow-covered roads . . . He revisited his previous decision to walk instead of taking the truck. Elverson or Trask had the keys, and it would be almost impossible to get them. Even if he could, the noise of the engine would almost surely alert them to his departure. If he was going to get there at all, he would have to walk.

Vaughan went to the door and opened it a crack to listen to the outside world. The wind had picked up a bit and howled around the corners of the trailers as it rearranged the snow into graceful curves of white. He stepped out onto the catwalk that lay between the trailers and listened intently for any sound other than the smooth wind. The wind assailed him and the metal frames of his glasses seemed to bite into his face with an unrelenting cold. He reached for the hood on his parka but then decided against it so that he would have nothing to impede his hearing.

Vaughan took a step to test the surface of the catwalk and was satisfied at the nonsound of his footstep. After closing the door, he took another, quicker step, which made a crunching noise on the wooden catwalk. He froze at the noise, which was barely heard over the wind, and strained his hearing to the limit. Vaughan waited several agonizing minutes as he tried to decide whether anyone inside the trailers could have heard the footstep.

Waiting and listening could be more dangerous than moving, he thought. His heart began to pound as he took several steps toward the end of the catwalk and worried over the real and imagined noise of each step. He peeked around the corner of the trailers and suddenly wondered how he was to get away undetected. Elverson was on watch to his right, and Trask and Gain were to his left and possibly asleep, although a casual glance out the window and . . . He refused to think about the possibilities.

On the other hand, Elverson was alert and would probably shoot him without hesitation. But the road he needed to take was directly in front of Elverson. Another road led out of the trailer camp at right angles to the first road, but it represented a longer and more arduous route to his destination.

Well, it was a pretty clear-cut decision, he thought. He didn't want a blast from an M16 in his back. It was the longer road or nothing at all. Vaughan turned left and got down on his hands and knees in order to crawl past the trailer containing Trask and Gain. With his heart in his throat, he wiggled through the snow toward the occupied trailer. As he crawled past the catwalk, he became almost paralyzed with the vision of Trask waiting for him in the shadows with a loaded M16. His memory of Trask's automatic weapon with the gaping hole at the end of its barrel passed over him in a wave of terror. The merest whim of the man behind it could deal death to him in the blink of an eye.

Vaughan scrambled past the catwalk in a rush and imagined he made quite a bit of noise doing it. He got to his feet and quickly got past the last of the trailers. The young man struggled his way down the unplowed road while looking back every few seconds. He could detect no movement—the trailers looked unoccupied, and he made sure that he was out of the line of sight of Elverson. After a minute or two, the trailers themselves were out of sight as he looked back, and he began to breathe easier.

He strained his eyes to decipher what was ahead and didn't have much success in the almost zero visibility. It was all he could do to keep on the road and not wander off into the middle of the tundra. If that happened, he would lose his bearings completely and could wander until dawn. He thought the road led to somewhere near the airport and he decided to bear to the right every chance he could, at least until he thought he was headed in the right direction for his destination.

Would there be patrols at night? Would he run into other survivors? Would he make it back in time? He slogged along the road and felt that he had a distorted notion of the passage of time. A glance at his watch told him that he had been on the road for only half an hour. He quickened his pace anyway, the shorter the amount of time he was away, the less chance he would be detected. If he was caught, it would be extremely difficult to explain his absence. It could mean his death sentence.

He looked to his left at the subdued glow in the sky to the south and could see one or two of the airport buildings outlined against the horizon. There would most likely be people in the air ops building, which was the main airport building and contained the air traffic controllers. He briefly wondered what kind of silhouette he made against the snow. No matter, he decided after a while, they wouldn't shoot at something that far away. Or would they? He gave the airport a nervous glance and tried to get his mind on something else.

Vaughan knew if he kept the airport to his left, the road would swing around until the ops building was almost directly behind him. At that point another road on the left would join with the road he was already on. Then he would know that he would be headed in approximately the right direction and could navigate by other landmarks at that point. The key was to stay on the road and not wander off; he had no wish to struggle through the tundra.

In a few moments he came to the point where the ops building was directly behind him as he faced the road, and he immediately began to strain his eyes to find a road which joined up on his left. On cue, the undulations in the undisturbed snow announced a road that came from the left. He knew now where he was. His destination lay about a mile farther along the road he was on. Vaughan grunted in satisfaction and continued to slog along as the road curved gently to the right.

He glanced back in the direction of the trailers and saw nothing but darkness, and then let his gaze sweep around to detect any activity on the island. He inhaled quickly as he spotted a glow off to his right. He stopped, pushed the

hood on his parka back and squinted in the direction of the
low-level light. It was moving in the direction of the trailers, but he had no idea how far it was from him, or what
it was. The light varied greatly in intensity from a bright
light to total darkness and did so in rapid fashion. Vaughan
thought once that he saw two distinct lights, but just then
a gust of wind blew snow into his face and he had to look
away briefly. When he looked back the light was gone.

Vaughan waited a minute or two for the glow to reappear, then gave up and decided to resume his journey. What
was it? Truck headlights? Why would anyone be moving
around at night? The possibility of the island's conquerors
attacking the trailers suddenly flashed through his mind and
his legs seemed to lose strength and become rubbery. He
didn't like violence—he had seen enough for an entire lifetime. He pushed the thoughts from his mind and with re-
newed vigor pressed on toward his goal.

Vaughan pounded his way through the snow until he
heard the sound of a jet engine. His head flew up and he
stared into the cold night sky. The aircraft could be anywhere by now with its sound just getting to him. Who was
he? Was help on the way? He strained his hearing but could
hear nothing except the increasing wind and the rustle of
snow that was kicked up from time to time.

Scheduled planes would attempt to land on Shemya but
would get no response from the tower unless the island's
captors had come up with some ruse to keep planes away.
That would make sense.

Vaughan lowered his eyes and gazed into the distance.
After a few moments he resumed his journey. After what
seemed to be an eternity, he finally detected a structure
looming in front of him. It was darker than the surrounding
sky and seemed to be the same general shape of the building he wanted. His steps quickened, and after passing by a
small swell in the ground, he saw the light in the front
doorway of Building 600.

Vaughan decided to stop and observe the building for a
few moments to discover if anyone was about. It rapidly
became obvious that the building was deserted, and he

quickly made the decision to complete his mission. It would be a long walk back.

He approached the building and looked through the main entrance. There was no one. To be extra cautious he went over to the security office window and peeked in. The sight of the bodies shocked him even though Trask had told him what had happened to everyone in the building. Trask's theory was that gas had been used, and it certainly seemed plausible. Suppose there were still some pockets of gas around? He had better play it safe.

He stumbled back through the snow to the front parking lot and quickly found a parked truck used by Security. After brushing enough snow off to find the door handle, he yanked the door open and rummaged around in the front seat for a gas mask. He had wondered why security personnel had been issued gas masks in the first place, but he chalked it up to Pentagon paranoia about Russian chemical weapons. Now he was glad they were so paranoid. He found the mask and ran as fast as he could back to the front entrance of the building. After slipping the mask on and praying he had it on right, he entered the building.

The main entrance led immediately to a lengthwise corridor, nicknamed Main Street. Vaughan turned right and noticed two bodies at the far end. He suddenly seemed unable to breathe and staggered a bit until he leaned against the wall. He forced the panic inside him down and continued the few feet remaining to enter the security office. He tried to ignore the bodies that were strewn about the floor, but one man in particular caught his attention. The dead man had his mouth open in a soundless scream and his eyes had rolled up inside his head. Vaughan quickly looked away.

A quick scan of the room and he saw what he had journeyed so far to find. He ran over to the computer terminal in a flash while praying that the computer was still up. He sat down at the terminal and immediately saw that the screen was blank except for the blinking cursor in the upper left-hand corner. Vaughan held his breath and hit the Return key. The computer came back with a prompt to log on.

He let out his breath in an explosive gasp, thought for a moment and began to type.

0200 HOURS, EASTERN STANDARD TIME
26 DECEMBER
FOURTH FLOOR, C RING, THE PENTAGON

The meeting of the Central Imagery Office Executive Committee came to order quickly. The Central Imagery Office, or CIO, is a separate intelligence agency housed in the Pentagon and controls imaging satellites for the entire U.S. intelligence community. The executive committee determined priorities and processed requests for satellite imaging.

Hugh Lynch headed one of the government's newest agencies born from changes due to the Gulf War and the end of the Cold War. The National Reconnaissance Office, run jointly by the air force and the CIA, had, in the administration's and Congress's minds, become bloated, and they were convinced that its multibillion-dollar budget was not cost-effective. NRO's performance during the Gulf War had also come under criticism for what was called inadequate and untimely reconnaissance pictures. As a result, in early 1992, NRO was augmented by the CIO, or Central Imagery Office.

Hugh Lynch, the chairman, looked straight at the air force representative, Lieutenant General David Manning.

"How long has Shemya been out of contact?" asked the director.

"Actually we've had one message on one of the NORAD channels," replied General Manning. "It's pretty cryptic." He shoved the text of the message toward Lynch, who picked it up and read it.

ALPHA, BRAVO, VICTOR, DELTA, SEVEN, ONE, NINE
READER HITS THE SKIDS AFTER GOING TO THE POST.
                                              BLUE FOX

Lynch put the page down and looked blankly at General Manning.

"If I didn't know better," said Manning, "I'd say this was one of our friends from Langley."

Jeff Snyder, the CIA representative, suddenly sat up straight in his chair.

Lynch shrugged. "You'll run it by them, of course," he said as he glanced at the CIA man.

"Do you have any of your people on Shemya?" asked Manning point-blank as he stared at the man from Langley.

"Why would we do something like that?" replied Snyder. "We're not supposed to operate within the United States."

Manning raised his eyebrows at the evasion. "You forget about President Reagan signing the executive order allowing limited CIA operations within the United States." It wasn't a question.

Do we have anyone on Shemya? Snyder resolved to find out. He was relieved when Lynch got back on the subject of the meeting.

"How long since normal transmission from Shemya?" asked the CIO director.

"About fifteen hours now," said the general.

Lynch rubbed his chin. "Any jamming? Russian activity of any kind that would explain this?"

The general shook his head. "No, nothing. There was an AGI in the vicinity during the exercise, but it moved away on a heading back to Petropavlovsk about six hours ago."

"How was that confirmed?" asked Lynch.

"RF-4F recon run made three hours ago from Elmendorf," said Manning, and he produced a folder from within his briefcase. He spread some pictures on the desk in front of them. The attendees leaned forward to get a good look. They were infrared pictures and looked like slightly fuzzy negatives.

"These were taken at altitude"—he pointed at several pictures to one side—"and you can readily see some distinguishing features of the air base." Manning's finger stabbed a bright spot to the left of center of the island. "This is the heat given off by the nuclear reactors on the island. The smaller glow directly north of the cooling tower is the COBRA DANE radar building. A little bit to the east is Building Six Hundred, the living quarters, and next to it to the southeast is Building Six Fifteen, the BAQ.''

His audience squinted to see the two fuzzy dots denoting the heat leakage from the two buildings. One of them noticed another dot in the upper central part of the island.

"What's that?" he asked.

"Unknown at this point," replied Manning. "This location is very near or on a road on the island, but there are no buildings there to give off heat. There should be no heat source there."

They all began to shift their gaze to General Manning to get the punch line. He didn't disappoint them.

"There are some things we don't see," he said, and swept his finger over the bottom part of the photo. "The airstrip should be faintly visible here, but clearly we see nothing."

"And why should the airstrip be visible on infrared?" asked Lynch.

"It doesn't snow very often on Shemya, but it did today," replied Manning. "If the runway was plowed, the tarmac would have picked up some UV even through the clouds. Against the background of a snow cover on the rest of the island, the reradiated heat should have clearly shown up. But it didn't."

The director's eyebrows went up. "Are you saying the runway wasn't plowed?"

Manning nodded. "Next question: Why wasn't it plowed?" Lynch looked at him questioningly. "The situation is the same with the roads," continued Manning. "We should see at least some of them on infrared, but there is nothing. They apparently weren't plowed either."

Lynch looked back down at the pictures. "They made a low-level run as well, I guess."

"Yes," said Manning, "and it does show what appears to be one individual walking on a road in the center of the island. Beyond that, it doesn't provide any more information, except to confirm that no excess heat was being radiated from the runway or the roads." He twisted his mouth to convey frustration. "We didn't get a close-up of the unknown heat source in the middle of the island either."

"So we've got a total breakdown in communications, no plowing going on, and one guy walking down a road. Not riding in a truck, but *walking*," said Lynch. "I don't think I like the implications."

The air force general nodded and waited.

"And now you want a Keyhole run," said Lynch. The general nodded.

"I concur," said Lynch. "Let's talk to our scheduling people to see how quickly we can get some imagery of this situation." The meeting was at an end.

The director gave General Manning a final look. "If I were you, I'd get some people out there right away."

"We've talked to the navy and got some helicopters from a marine unit that is taking cold weather training up there. Company I of the Naval Security Group Activity is standing by on Adak to recon Shemya," Manning replied. "But we have to find out what they might be walking into."

Lieutenant General Manning made a quick exit with Lynch nodding absentmindedly in agreement with the general's remark.

Jeff Snyder picked up the message and reread it. *Reader hits the skids after going to the post*. A nonsense phrase whose individual words meant nothing, but collectively had they some great import? Created by his own people? The message was sent by Blue Fox. One of the Company's agents? For what purpose?

He would have to get this to the Deputy Director for Operations, the DDO, and the Deputy Director for Intelligence, the DDI. The question bothered him.

Do we have CIA personnel on Shemya?

0900 HOURS, LOCAL TIME, 26 DECEMBER
SVR HEADQUARTERS
MOSCOW RING ROAD, MOSCOW

The buzzer went off several times before he pushed the intercom button. "Yes." He hoped he put the right amount of annoyance in the one word.

The duty officer's voice sounded surprised. "Colonel General Tofimov and Colonels Parchomenko and Sobchak to see you, General."

That was surprising. It was the day after Christmas, and even though a lot of the senior officers still adhered to their atheism, they appreciated more than one day off around Christmas. There weren't many people in the building and those people weren't much interested in doing a lot of work. As relations with the Americans improved, their work calmed down considerably. Intelligence was still sorely needed, but the constant near panic induced by Communist paranoia had all but disappeared. He had the day off as well but had come in to the office as much out of habit as anything else.

General Vladimir Iskanderov pushed the intercom button a second time. "Send them in."

The door opened as Iskanderov put the file he was reading into the top drawer of his desk and carefully locked it. The general walked in and sat in the chair opposite the desk while the colonels stood stiffly behind their superiors. Iskanderov raised his bullish, nearly bald head and lifted an eyebrow. His meaning was clear. This had better be important.

"General, we have uncovered a matter of grave concern," began General Tofimov.

"Yes, I can see that," said Iskanderov. "When the deputy chief of the SVR visits me and brings a representative from Signals Intelligence—" He gave Parchomenko an inquiring look. The colonel nodded to confirm the general's statement. "Then things must be very grave indeed."

Tofimov didn't waste words. He handed over a piece of paper which the general read and then reread.

" 'Mission one-four-one Delta is accomplished.' " Iskanderov shrugged and looked at Tofimov.

"That message was intercepted this morning from the American base at Shemya in the Aleutians," said Tofimov. Iskanderov gave him a blank look a hair short of impatience.

"It was encrypted with one of our codes," said Tofimov. "One set aside for our illegals."

General Iskanderov's eyes narrowed. "And what is Mission one-four-one Delta?"

"I don't know yet," was Tofimov's simple reply.

Iskanderov sat back in his chair and reread the message. He suddenly looked at Tofimov and opened his mouth to say something. He stopped as he became aware of the continuing presence of the two colonels. "Wait outside," he said, and the two officers immediately left the office.

"Yevgeny Filippovich," said Iskanderov in a low voice, "I sincerely hope that this Mission one-four-one Delta is not what I think it is."

Tofimov turned more pale than he had been, even though he had a decided lack of color to begin with. "We are checking on it now. But it cannot be! They were all ordered to be removed."

"Yes, the secret protocols that the Americans demanded as a condition for their economic aid," replied Iskanderov. "We pull out our sleepers and they will pull out theirs. The problem has always been the same: How do we know when all of them are out?"

"Yes, Vladimir Fedorovich, and the Americans have the same problem," said Tofimov in an almost sad voice.

"It sounds like we do not know when our own people are out," said Iskanderov in an accusing tone.

Tofimov's mouth opened in indignation, but he was too stunned to say anything.

"Do not worry, Yevgeny Filippovich," said Iskanderov. "This Mission one-four-one Delta must be something else. What could possibly have happened to trigger a takeover of the island?"

CHAPTER 10

━ ∙ ━ ∙ ━ ∙ ━

2130 HOURS, 25 DECEMBER
SHEMYA'S SOUTHERN COAST

Trask lazily looked at the ceiling of the trailer as he luxu-riated in a seldom experienced euphoria. He glanced down at the top of Ellen's head, which appeared as a confusion of blond hair in the murky glow produced by the fallen snow outside. She was lying on her side with her head on his chest, and she hadn't moved for quite a while, thereby giving the impression that she had fallen asleep. He felt a contentment that he had never known, and he began to suspect that the source of his discontent was the world in general. Now that the world was destroyed, he felt a curious relief—he no longer had to contend with a system that had branded him a failure. It was a new start, with new rules.

He lifted his hand and touched Ellen's back through her parka, which she still had on, and his thoughts turned into a hodgepodge of scenes of Ellen's face as he had known her throughout the day. He remembered her firing the au-tomatic out the shattered rear window of the truck; she was tough then. He remembered the look on her face as he held her in his arms. She was a little girl then, and at the same time she was the most desirable woman he had ever known. He had gone over the edge, and he knew it. If they were to start the world over again, then he would do it by her side.

Just then she began to stir and rolled her head upright to peer at him through her tousled hair. He laughed out loud and looked down at her uplifted face. She put her chin on his chest and actually smiled for an instant.

"Thanks . . . for staying," she said. Then she giggled. She covered her face for an instant, then looked back at him. She was more serious this time. "I really did need for you to stay, Frank," she said.

"Yes, I know. You want me close, but not too close," he said as he pulled at her parka.

She wrinkled up her face as if to say "Wise guy," then she got a thoughtful expression on her face and spoke again after a minute or two. "You know what I want?"

"What?"

"I want you to tell me everything will be all right."

"Everything will be all right," he said flippantly.

"Idiot. Not like that!"

He grinned and shrugged as she buried her face in his chest again in mock disgust. She looked up again immediately.

"Do you think we're crazy?" she asked.

"Why?"

"Here we are laughing while the rest of the world is a radioactive ruin." She wasn't smiling. His smile vanished also.

"I guess there is nothing else to do," he replied.

"But *laugh*?"

He shook his head in frustration. They lay quietly for a few minutes, each with their own thoughts.

Trask finally broke the silence. "I don't believe I shot and killed a couple of people today. It's like a nightmare." His voice had a touch of awe in it.

"You were magnificent. I mean, I didn't know what to do. Battling Russian agents is not exactly in Air Force Officers Training School," said Ellen.

"No, you were the magnificent one," protested Trask. "You were pretty cool firing that automatic at that truck."

"No, you were magnificent," she shot back.

"No, you were."

"No, you."

"No, *you*!"

At that point they both collapsed into laughter and

laughed even harder as an outlet for the stress of the situation. Their laughter eventually subsided, and they looked at each other with broad grins.

"Now that we know how we feel about each other . . ." Ellen began in mock seriousness, and stopped as they both started laughing again. Their laughter subsided more quickly this time and gradually their smiles faded.

"Frank, what are we going to do?" She was deadly serious this time.

He put his arm over his forehead and looked at the ceiling again. "We've got to get some food tomorrow sometime, or else the SVR won't have to worry about us at all. We'll all starve to death. Later we just avoid them until they leave. After that, we'll have to get off here to some safe part of the world, someplace that wouldn't have been hit with ICBMs—"

"Like Tahiti," she interrupted with a dreamy remark.

He was surprised and delighted. "Don't tell me you've had that dream too."

She gave him a surprised look and nodded.

"I've often toyed with the idea of dropping out of society," he continued. "And going to some island like Tahiti. Wind and the sun and the surf and all that."

"That's incredible. I've been thinking the same thing." She thought for a minute, then looked at him out of the corner of her eye. "Why would you want to drop out of society? A rich civilian engineer like you."

He grunted in response to her question. "You're kidding, right?" She gave him a look of innocence.

"I'm not exactly a model of the American success story," Trask replied. "It seems like everything I get involved in goes sour. I'm divorced, my parents think I'm a failure, and I . . ." He hesitated.

"What?" she prompted.

Trask shook his head. He had said to himself that he wasn't going to do this. He always disliked people who felt sorry for themselves.

"What?" she repeated.

He looked at her and decided on impulse to admit what

he had been avoiding for many years now. "I drink too much!" he blurted out.

Ellen looked at him for a moment, then lowered her head and burst into smothered laughter. She stopped after a minute and looked at him, then answered his unspoken question.

"I thought you were going to tell me you were gay." She launched into another fit of giggling as he rolled his eyes upward.

"Here I am trying to tell you my life story and you're laughing your ass off!" He was annoyed.

Ellen stopped laughing and slowly sobered up. She felt some sort of explanation was in order.

"I'm sorry," she said. "This whole situation is so monstrous that I guess it just hasn't sunk in yet. People are trying to kill us, the whole world is destroyed . . . I guess if it did sink in, I'd go crazy. My parents, my brothers . . ." She stopped and searched his face for understanding. Trask shifted his gaze to her face and noticed that she had tears in her eyes. He instantly regretted his annoyance of a few minutes ago. Better she should have laughed herself silly than for him to cut her off just to save whatever pride he had left. He wrapped his arms around her and held her tightly. She let out a sigh and wiped her eyes and nestled into his embrace. After a few long minutes she quietly spoke.

"What was Vietnam like?" she asked.

He shrugged. "Boring."

"With a war going on?"

"I was a cook," he replied. "Cooking is boring whether a war is going on or not."

She thought for a moment, then tried again. "You mean you're not a drug-crazed hippie like they say all Vietnam veterans are," she said, tongue in cheek.

Trask chuckled. "I was more like an alcohol-crazed yuppie."

She started into another fit of giggling. After a few moments she tapered off and stopped. She quickly sobered up.

"See any combat?" she asked simply.

He smiled in a moment of rare amusement. People who

have never been in combat always seem fascinated by it, particularly military personnel who seem hung up by the fact that they train for it, but haven't yet experienced it. He was a bit surprised that Ellen seemed to feel that way; he hadn't known any female military personnel to exhibit such feelings. He mentally shrugged it off. Times had changed since he was young. He was probably the only one on the island old enough to be a male chauvinist.

"Yeah. A little," he replied in one of his greater understatements.

Her eyes grew a bit wider as her curiosity deepened. Trask had seen the same reaction in some of the other military personnel on the island. The fact that he had been in Vietnam and had combat experience had totally changed their attitude toward him, from one of condescension to almost reverence. He even had a few of them cover up some of his more embarrassing drinking sprees. Trask owed a few favors.

"Well?" She seemed expectant.

"Well what?" he replied as he pretended to not know what she wanted.

"How was it?" she asked a little more softly.

"Like I said, boring," he said.

She rolled her eyes around with rapidly diminishing patience. "The combat!" she said in a mimic of a growl.

"Oh, the combat. Oh, that was . . ." He stopped and groped for a word as she searched his face with increased anticipation. ". . . not boring," he concluded.

Ellen shut her eyes tightly in mock frustration and began to mumble under her breath. "Men . . . A civilian at that . . . Thinks I'm an idiot . . ."

She rolled over swiftly so that her back was to him. He began to laugh. She rolled back and began to pound his chest in mock fury, causing him to laugh even harder. He calmed down after a few minutes and looked at her with a smile as she gave him a pseudodisgusted look.

"Well?" She tried to have an acid tone to her voice but didn't quite make it.

He smiled again and gave up. "We went through a few

rocket attacks, and I went on a few patrols. That's all; it wasn't much.'' He hesitated. ''Not like some guys.''

His smile vanished. A fleeting dizziness reminiscent of his days in the jungle caught him suddenly. He began to think of those in his unit whose names were inscribed on the black granite wall in Washington, D.C. *So many had died because . . .*

Trask glanced at her quickly. She had seen the change in his expression and had a stricken look on her face. She stammered a bit when she spoke.

''I . . . I'm sorry.'' She started to say something else but couldn't find the words.

He smiled with no humor behind it and sought to reassure her. ''It's okay. Vietnam was nothing compared to what we got ourselves into this time.''

They both lapsed into a depressed silence for a long time. She pressed herself closer to him, and he stroked her hair in an absentminded fashion.

''Frank.''

''Yeah.''

''You make me feel . . . secure. Wanted.''

He kissed her on top of her head. They lay still for several minutes and reveled in the closeness of their bodies to one another. Trask was glad just to be next to her.

''What's a good-looking girl like you doing in a place like this?'' He couldn't resist the cliché.

''You mean why did I join the air force.''

''Yeah.''

''Rebellion, pure and simple,'' she explained. ''I come from a filthy-rich family from Philadelphia's Main Line. And the male members of the family tend to dominate everything and everybody. I didn't like that at all, so I tried to outdo everybody in the family in everything. I managed to get better grades than the boys throughout school, but my parents just wanted me to be a nice quiet Barbie doll. No brains, you know, just a piece of furniture. Well, I had other ideas. I tried to think of the thing that would drive them crazy the most, and I came up with the air force. My parents think the military is just something for the poor masses to endure, and that their family should avoid it at all costs. When I joined, they nearly had a shit fit.''

She stopped to grunt with satisfaction at the memory of her parents' frustration.

''So, you're the great American success story,'' concluded Trask.

She looked him in the eye. ''Yeah.'' Her tone seemed a little sarcastic.

''Don't knock it. It pays the rent,'' he said.

She suddenly picked her head up off his chest and propped herself up on one elbow. ''Tell me about your life. Was it really that bad?''

He gave her a long look, then shifted his gaze up to the ceiling. ''I was never starving, if that's what you mean. I just never made it. You know, never really had any status, always had trouble with anything I ever tried. I didn't do well in school. I graduated in the bottom quarter of the engineering class. I guess you have to be a certain kind of person to be a good engineer, but I could never figure out what it took to really make it in engineering. I bounced from one job to another until I finally wound up here. This is kind of a last chance for me—if I screw this up, I don't know where I'll get another job.''

''Something will turn up, you'll see,'' she replied.

They suddenly looked at each other and realized that they had been talking as if the events of the day had not happened and everything were normal.

''I mean . . . You know what I mean,'' she stammered helplessly.

''Yeah, I know what you mean.''

They lay in depressed silence for a while with Trask's hands playing over Ellen's back. He reached up to massage her shoulders and felt her wince and pull her left shoulder away slightly.

''What happened there?'' he asked with concern in his voice.

Ellen hesitated before answering. *Should I tell him the truth?* ''Oh . . .'' she began. ''Auto accident a few years ago.'' She held her breath. She wasn't a good liar. ''I never did recover fully.'' That was the truth.

"It must've been pretty bad," he replied in an invitation for her to talk about it.

"Yeah." She offered nothing further. He decided to drop it.

They lay quietly until Ellen broke the silence with a question that Trask suspected she had wanted to ask for some time.

"Frank."

He mumbled acknowledgement.

"Are you married?" she asked.

"Divorced."

"I'm sorry to hear that."

"I'm not. She was a bitch."

She thought for a while. "Any kids?"

"Yeah. A boy and a girl, the classic American family."

"What were they like?"

"They were brats, just like their mother." He lapsed into silence. After a minute he squeezed Ellen in an emotional embrace.

"I loved them anyway," he said, his voice breaking.

He began to weep while Ellen attempted to console him.

CHAPTER 11

Fear.

The sight, the sound, the feel of the jungle swirled about him once again, from the dull mist against the dark green background to the stinking, sucking ooze that enveloped his feet.

At nineteen, Frank Trask was the youngest of his unit, the "Charlie Zappers," which was the unofficial name for his particular group of snipers. He had been selected out of many to "volunteer" for this unit and it probably had something to do with the fact that he was the best shot in his company. That coupled with the need for replacement snipers was all the army needed to make him change units. Trask didn't care. It was combat either way. He was terrified to even be in Vietnam, never mind which unit he was in.

The men in his unit would split up into pairs and then slip quietly through the jungle to set up ambushes for the VC or NVA regulars.

Trask was the oddball of the group. Not only was he the youngest, but he was the only draftee and was one of the few men who hadn't been trained in the United States to be a sniper. One of the older men, who was at the advanced age of twenty-one, took Trask under his wing and paired off with him for the younger man's first mission.

It seemed to Trask that they traveled very lightly, with only food, ammo, and, of course, their bolt-action, high-powered rifles complete with long-range sights and starlight scopes for nighttime combat. He would have felt better with a bullet-proof "flak" jacket and the helmet that he had been issued, but the older man had ordered him to leave them behind. Trask had to settle for a camouflage jacket and a bush hat.

Trask saw the wisdom in that decision after only a few miles of their trek through the jungle. His partner was determined to use none of the established jungle trails, and instead he plunged into the densest parts of the undergrowth that he could find. The light load began to weigh more heavily on him with each step he took through the dense, congested world they were traveling in, until after five miles he was gasping for breath. His partner, on the other hand, seemed to glide along, twisting and leaning to adroitly avoid bushes and hanging vines.

Trask began to swing and slap at the insects immediately upon entering the undergrowth and quickly drew a hissed chewing out from his partner. Let the insects have at it, otherwise the noise could draw fire. Black strings of leeches began to suck at his legs, and Trask drew another volley when he began to tear at them in horrified reaction. Trask listened in miserable silence and squirmed at the thought of what the leeches were doing to his bloodstream. He took savage satisfaction after seeing his partner pick up several of the bloodsuckers by wading through a particularly putrid and evil-smelling swamp. When they stopped for a rest, he told his partner of the horrifying parasites. Trask's satisfaction faded when his partner grunted soundlessly and calmly started to remove them. No thanks. Nothing.

Trask looked his partner over in detail for the first time, and squinted to see the man under the camouflage paint and the grime of the jungle. He was only a few years older than Trask, but he easily looked double Trask's age. Was it because he was beginning his third year in-country? What motivated a man to keep re-upping for this kind of combat?

Trask's eyes fell on his partner's forearm where his stripes would normally be. He had a "hard" three up and one down in the soldier's common parlance; officially he was a staff sergeant, "hard" meaning that he was a line combat soldier as opposed to a specialist. Trask felt insignificant with his one puny stripe, and involuntarily touched his sleeve where his rank would have been. Their insignia had been left behind, along with all other uniform devices, and also their keys, wallets, cigarette lighters and pocket change. Anything that could make a sound was rejected, and the sergeant was one of the few who insisted that their dog tags be left behind also, even though they were lined with rubber to prevent them from jingling together. Trask instinctively touched his chest above his heart.

How will they identify my body if I get killed? I'll rot away here forever.

The sergeant eyed him and Trask quickly looked away. His partner stood and slid off into the jungle without a word, leaving Trask to scramble after him.

After three days' travel through the densest jungle, they arrived at their destination and set up an ambush for the VC. At first, Trask wondered why they were stopping; there were no visible differences to their surroundings to warrant a halt. He knew better than to ask the sergeant—Trask had been given strict orders not to talk *at all,* no matter what happened. He caught the sergeant's eye and shrugged while looking about them. His partner replied by pointing off into the jungle, then showed him using hand signals where to set up and even how to sit.

Trask gratefully sat down even though he knew that the insects would have him for supper. The pace had been a horrendous one with the sergeant periodically giving him killing looks in an effort to hurry him along. He looked in the sergeant's direction and barely saw him in the feeble light that filtered down through the foliage. Trask didn't exist for him at the moment; he was staring intently into the jungle.

Trask looked in the direction of the sergeant's gaze and strained his eyes to discern what captured his partner's attention. He gave up after a while and suddenly realized that his body was racing as if he was still struggling his way through the jungle. His heart pounded and his lungs strained at the humid, heavy, decaying atmosphere. He should have calmed down by now, but he realized that as exhaustion waned a new feeling overcame him. *Fear.*

It grabbed at him and seemed to settle in his chest like

a tight band encircling him. Trask inhaled deeply several times but still couldn't shake the feeling of suffocation. He tried to console himself with the thought that he was the ambusher, a "thirteen-cent killer," the name referring to the price of the bullets they used. It was he who would instill fear into the enemy and not the other way around. At least it wasn't supposed to be the other way around. When the VC were waiting to ambush U.S. troops, did they feel as much fear as he did now? Trask tried to convince himself that they did, but eventually wound up believing just the opposite.

He risked some movement to reach up and touch his face, and found that his skin had erupted into a mass of welts and bruises caused by insects and stubborn jungle vines. Glad there's no mirrors in the jungle, he thought, and almost laughed. He didn't want to see what he looked like. Trask settled down for a wait and tried to keep his fear down to manageable proportions.

Four days later, the sergeant suddenly appeared next to him and waved him to his feet. Trask had suffered greatly with the heat and humidity, the insects and the slime, but when the time came to leave, he felt a new surge of energy flow through him. He dragged himself to his feet and stumbled almost happily after the rapidly moving sergeant.

They had gone a few miles when the sergeant suddenly stopped and stared intently off into the distance. Trask followed his gaze once again and this time he saw a break in the jungle, and through it he saw hills with blue skies above them. The sight exhilarated him beyond proportion for such a simple scene, but it was his first look in a week at the world beyond the stinking jungle. It was a beautiful world he had left behind.

The sergeant got his field glasses out and peered through them at some distant object, the nature of which Trask couldn't guess. Maybe he just wanted to look at the "outside" world, thought Trask. It quickly became apparent that the sergeant had other things on his mind. He wordlessly handed Trask the glasses and pointed. Trask obediently raised the binoculars to his eyes and after a moment located what had interested his partner. There, in a clearing on a hillside that seemed halfway around the world, was a company of North Vietnamese regulars. They were completely relaxed and listening with perfect attention to a harangue by a company officer. Trask estimated the distance at about a mile.

The sergeant's voice sounded unnaturally loud in the relatively quiet jungle. Trask jumped and looked at him in surprise. They hadn't spoken in five days.

"Get ready to move fast when I pull the trigger on them." He gestured toward the distant clearing. Trask glanced in the direction of the clearing and then back at the sergeant with mounting surprise.

"That's an impossible shot!" he whispered in a hoarse voice.

"It's about a mile and a half," replied the sergeant, and calmly lifted his rifle to peer through the sight.

Trask shook his head. Their weapons were only effective for a thousand yards at best, but his partner was going to try to hit a target twenty-five hundred yards away. The sergeant looked past the telescopic sight to stare at the foliage between their location and the clearing, and Trask knew he was trying to judge wind strength and direction. The sergeant looked back into the sight and elevated the barrel in a series of steps.

"Keep your eye on that gook officer," said the sergeant in a whisper.

Trask trained his binoculars on the obvious leader of the NVA troops in the clearing. The sergeant's rifle erupted three times. The enemy officer suddenly grabbed at his neck, gave a half twist, and crumpled to the ground. Trask's jaw dropped in astonishment.

"You got him!" he whispered with awe as he watched the officer's men scurry about in shock and confusion. The sergeant took one last look through the sight and gave Trask half a smile of satisfaction.

"They never even heard the shot," he said in a matter-of-fact tone. Trask nodded slowly. That would explain it. A silent bullet from nowhere had just struck down their leader before their very eyes.

Fear. That's what Trask and the sergeant were all about.

Instill fear in the enemy. Demoralize them, make them fear as his own countrymen had feared. The sergeant turned to go, but Trask lingered with the binoculars up to his face and his eyes fixed at the clearing. He could see the fear stamped into the myriad Oriental faces. His partner was a highly successful man; he had accomplished his mission.

The sergeant was nearly out of sight by the time Trask moved to go. He stumbled quickly after his superior, his mind a jumble of thoughts.

They never even heard the shot. The sergeant's words formed a whirlwind in his mind. How can you hate someone who fears you?

Three days later, they were back at their base for a few days' rest which Trask sorely needed. He was mentally, physically, and emotionally drained from his first mission as a sniper. The events of the mission would run and rerun themselves through his mind at night until he finally would drift off into a troubled slumber in the early morning hours. His body began to heal from the insect and leech bites and the scratches from the undergrowth, but his mind felt like a wound had been opened. He shuddered to think about what he would be called upon to do in the remaining twelve months of his tour.

An undercurrent of excitement ran through the camp; it wasn't as if he had overheard anything, but it was the quicker step of the officers and noncoms, the look on their faces, the light in their eyes, that made him sense that something was up.

Most of the men in his unit went to a briefing and then began to quietly prepare for the upcoming mission. Trask and one other man new to the unit were excluded. He was relieved; he had drawn a bye on this one.

The rest of the unit completed preparations and then waited. A day rolled by. Trask stopped paying attention and concentrated on rest and a few letters to home. Late that day, he was summoned to see the company commander. His partner, the sergeant, along with the rest of the company officers were present also. He entered just as the sergeant was stating that despite Trask's inexperience, he would still "do the job."

Trask came to attention in front of the CO's table and saluted as the officers clucked their tongues and put expressions of doubt on their broad, square-jawed faces. The CO looked Trask straight in the eye and briefed him on the mission. Several high-ranking NVA and VC officers were going to meet in the jungle in a few days to draw up plans for an offensive around year's end. The company's mission was to ambush them and kill as many as possible.

Fear. That's what we're all about.

It could shorten the war, the CO added as Trask's expression sagged. At first they were going to take only experienced personnel, but a patrol was overdue and they could no longer wait for them. He was ordered to get ready.

She wasn't supposed to be there. Trask was purposely put in an area where they expected a minimum of trouble. Most of the activity was to happen on the other side of the clearing, but she walked toward him for some unknown reason as Trask held his breath. As she walked into his "fire zone," he felt something akin to panic race through him. He lifted the rifle to the firing position, his blood feeling like gelatin. If she spotted anything now . . .

He had been told that surveillance cannot last indefinitely. After a few days, or in the VC's case, a few hours, a sixth sense warns of trouble. They had been watching the Communist encampment for eight hours now, and Trask supposed that his superiors were waiting for more enemy officers to arrive.

Trask looked at her through the sight and saw that she was relaxed and even had a partial smile on her face. Who was she? General's whore, maybe?

She suddenly slowed her pace and looked about with rapidly mounting alarm. Trask inhaled hysterically and held it.

Fear.

A face! She had seen one of the dirty, round-eyed, square-jawed faces that lined the jungle. Her mouth was opening now; she was inhaling rapidly in preparation for a panic-driven scream.

The choice flashed across Trask's cortex and became

clear to him. Kill her, or she'll scream a warning and possibly get his entire unit wiped out. He shrank back from either option and feverishly tried to come up with a third choice.

Trask lowered the gun barrel until the crosshairs in the sight were centered a few inches in front of her feet. He fired twice with his rifle making a powerful but quiet thumping sound due to the silencer on the barrel. Maybe if he could shock her into silence . . .

Kill! Kill her!

The words formed in his mind from what he knew were the desperate commands of the faces that lined the jungle, but instead he concentrated on raising the rifle so he could see her face in the sight. Her mouth was wide open with her eyes nearly shut.

She screamed.

Trask was vaguely aware of amazement, then sudden movement in the walls of the jungle, and even quicker movement within the huts in the clearing. Panic groped at him and he instinctively sought to undo his mistake.

He pulled the trigger.

The jungle erupted in gunfire and flame just as the hollow-point bullet flew into the woman's open mouth and blew out the back of her head. His eyes locked onto the grisly scene which appeared just inches from his face, until her body fell away and out of view of the telescopic sight.

Trask dropped the rifle. His panic was complete. He ran through the jungle as the world exploded behind him.

Frank Trask awoke with a start and looked wildly about while his heart pounded within him. He waited a minute or two to calm down and noted that everything was as before, Ellen was still in his arms, or rather he was still in hers, and judging by her regular breathing she was asleep. He gently lifted her arm and put it on her leg so that he could get both arms free. He pushed the light button on his watch and saw that it was quarter to twelve. Right on time; he was to relieve Elverson at midnight.

He shook his head to alleviate the grogginess and concluded that he could have slept for a week at least. That would have to wait.

The memory of his dream came flooding back to him, and he risked just letting it happen. Funny, he thought, the first month of his Vietnam tour was crystal clear, but the rest was just a blur. Trask had been quietly transferred out of what remained of his unit and into another company as a cook. To Trask's surprise, there were no accusations of cowardice; perhaps the men who had seen him hesitate had been killed. His unit had taken 90 percent casualties; his partner, the sergeant, didn't make it.

The prevailing opinion of the survivors was that the VC had detected them hours before the woman had appeared in front of Trask. The VC knew with her scream that the Americans would open up on them, so they fired almost simultaneously with the U.S. snipers.

Trask had agonized over the choice he had been given, the woman's life or the lives of his unit, and it was all the more excruciating because it was all for nothing. The VC had known that they were there anyway.

Truth always seemed to sneak up on Trask, but when he saw it, he recognized it immediately. He sometimes flinched, but this time he had the courage to stare it straight in the eye. His failures later in life, his drinking, his divorce, his lack of success in the engineering profession, were all because of his inability to come to terms with what had happened to him years ago in the jungle. Trask had never forgiven himself for his mistake.

Trask had the sharp realization that he had created his own misery and had indulged in an unconscious self-flagellation ever since that unholy incident in the middle of Vietnam. His dreams of an existence in a South Seas paradise had arisen as a result. He shook his head and decided his self-psychoanalysis would have to wait. He had better get moving.

Trask wiggled his way out of bed in an attempt to leave Ellen undisturbed, and in the process pulled the blanket away from her. He looked at her for a moment before covering her, and lingered with a vision of palm trees, blue skies and black sand, and what Ellen might look like in a white string bikini. His dream was never to be. He had found her too late. An earth-shattering war had put survival at a premium, and they would be extremely lucky to be alive after their little war with the SVR.

He tried to be grateful for the moments they already had together, but he wasn't that romantic. He wanted her, now, and for the next hundred years at least.

Trask looked over his weapons and briefly wondered where exactly Elverson was standing watch. He stood over Ellen, thinking nothing, feeling only emotion. He bent down to kiss her and then turned to go.

"Frank."

Her voice was slurred with sleep. He was at her side in an instant.

"Hold me for a minute," she asked. She sat up and he held her in his arms once more, then stepped back and looked at her. He watched her for a minute in silence, then decided to ask about the young AP.

"Did you have any contact with Elverson before today?" he asked.

She shook her head. "I just got to the island last week, so I've never seen him before," she explained.

"I've been on the island for almost eight months and I don't remember ever seeing him," he replied.

"What are you trying to say?"

"I don't know." He shook his head. "How did he know about the SVR, that it succeeded the KGB for foreign intelligence?"

"It was in the newspapers, wasn't it? Are you trying to say he's one of them?" she persisted. He hesitated before answering.

"No, I guess not. He's had plenty of opportunity to kill us both." He stopped and thought for a while. "I don't know. Something just doesn't add up about him," he added.

"Yeah, I know what you mean. He doesn't seem to act like a normal AP," she said. Trask let out a sigh and decided to tell her more about Elverson.

"I caught him looking at you a couple of times in a funny kind of way," he said.

She gave him a lopsided grin. "Some men *do* look at me once in a while," she replied.

"Yeah, but this was different." He couldn't put it into words. Jealousy mixed with regret or something. But that didn't make any sense. He shook the thought from him.

"What do you think of Vaughan?" she asked.

Trask smiled. "He's harmless." She nodded in agreement.

"I've got to go," he said, and turned toward the door. She stopped him with a word.

"Frank." Her voice was low and quiet. He turned and looked at her. She hesitated. She wanted to tell him something but couldn't seem to find the words. Her face was extremely serious. She finally shook her head.

"Be careful," she said after a moment.

Trask knew it wasn't what she wanted to say, but he pretended that it was. He nodded and pulled the automatic from his pocket along with a couple of clips he had retrieved from the truck.

"Here, you might need this," he said as he handed them to Ellen. He then left the trailer in search of Elverson.

Once outside, the bitter arctic cold assailed him and he huddled deep within his parka to save as much warmth as possible. He found the trailer that would give him the best view of the road and cautiously entered it. He didn't want Elverson to shoot him by mistake, but Elverson wasn't there. Trask tried the trailer next to it with the same result.

With mounting alarm he tried all the trailers, one by one, and found them all vacant. Both Elverson and Vaughan were nowhere to be found.

CHAPTER 12

Lieutenant Colonel Alan Driscoll rolled his head to one side and gradually became aware that he was sitting in a chair with his head resting on a table in front of him. He opened one eye and patiently waited for it to focus on something. When his eye finally brought an object into focus, he saw that it was his hand, but it had a greenish glow and was surrounded by blackness. He groaned and heaved his head to an upright position without really thinking about it. His ensuing disorientation made him instinctively run through a half dozen possible locations to explain his whereabouts. A flash of panic ran through him, and then it all came flooding back to him.

Shemya. COBRA DANE radar. War.

Driscoll's eyes were automatically attracted to the light that was emanating from the computer terminal on the table next to him. He looked into the greenish glow and had trouble focusing his eyes again. He shifted his gaze to the surrounding room and peered into the blackness and saw only a handful of pilot lights that glowed red, green and amber from various pieces of equipment. The room lights had automatically shut down for some reason. He concentrated on the closest red pilot light and waited until the light went from a fuzzy ball to a sharp pinpoint of light. After taking a deep breath, he lethargically looked back at the terminal.

His program had terminated, and the computer was patiently waiting for the next input. Every few minutes the computer would send out a new prompt on the screen along with a beep to jog the user into providing it something to do. Driscoll let a prompt go by, then decided to see if his program had worked. He shook his head to clear it and instinctively looked at his watch. It was late at night. How long had he slept? He wasn't certain.

He typed in a few code words and got invalid command indications back. He finally typed in the correct code word and cursed for the thousandth time the fact that the code word didn't appear on the screen as he typed it. It was supposed to be a security measure so that no one could look over his shoulder and memorize it, and then later have unauthorized access to the secrets within the massive computer that formed the heart of the radar.

The screen changed under his direction, and he saw that his program hadn't worked. He had to break a seven-digit code word to access the file he needed. This was a fairly simple problem and he came up with a number sequence program to test all possible combinations of the number. The problem was that, after two tries at the number, the system locked out any further tries until the lockout timed out. Then two more tries could be attempted. This would have taken weeks if he hadn't defeated the lockout, but it was to no avail. In the end it hadn't worked. The computer system had stored all the attempts to break its internal security and flashed a warning message on the console. There were ten million combinations of a seven-digit number and the screen showed ten million attempts . . . with no successes.

He groaned and looked at an adjacent wall. He was in the Computer Room and on the other side of the wall was the Operations Center. He thought of all the bodies lying forever still within that room. His mouth felt dry, and he automatically licked his lips. He was going to need some food and drink before long. He suddenly realized how quiet it was in the Computer Room with just the low-level whirring of fans in some of the equipment. His thoughts ran over the events of yesterday and stopped at one significant point. The cold feeling he had gotten when he had seen the second launch on the screen quickly returned. It was a piece of evidence that led him to conclude the worst. The last piece of evidence that he needed was on the computer.

He ran his fingers through his hair in a brief impulsive gesture. What was next? Did he really have to come up with a program to try all combinations and permutations of letters? Let's see, that's twenty-six to the seventh power. His mind stopped. That would take months. Suppose it was a combination of letters and numbers. That would take an astronomical number of tries to break into that file.

Driscoll's mind raced. The squadron commander was probably dead, and the password gone along with him. People typically derived computer passwords from personal data, such as birth dates or their children's names. There was no hope of finding the squadron commander's birth date without a search of the personnel files. He decided to try to exhaust the other possibilities before getting the squadron commander's file. After racking his brain for the commander's children's names, he tried them forward and backward, and then he tried acronyms made from combinations of their names. None worked. He added the squadron commander's wife's name and continued for a few minutes. Nothing.

Driscoll leaned back in the chair and looked at the console screen with disgust. It was no use; there were just too many combinations. Colonel Jenkins had put something on the computer that he didn't want anyone else to know, even Driscoll himself, the deputy squadron commander. The frustrating part was that he was only one step from finding Jenkins's secret. That data was put there only a few days ago, thought Driscoll. His feeling of dread deepened as he realized that this would line up perfectly with what he had previously feared.

A thought suddenly struck him. Jenkins and he had had a conversation recently about least known facts of people's private lives. It had centered on the maiden name of a person's mother-in-law. Virtually no one knew this information, except family members, because information of that kind was never recorded in any personnel file. Driscoll strained his memory to recall the name. Jenkins had mentioned it, and Driscoll had mentally noted that it was an Italian name. He rubbed his face and got up to walk around the room in an effort to aid his memory.

It suddenly came to mind after his third circuit of the room. Rinaldi. Her name was Rinaldi. He leaped over to the console, wrote the name on a piece of paper and typed it in the computer. When it didn't work, he wrote it backwards to make sure of the sequence of letters, and then with trembling fingers, he typed it into the computer. The suspense was almost unbearable as he saw the screen change and come up with the status he was looking for.

He gasped as he read the screen's unbelievable contents. He jammed his eyes shut, reopened them and reread the screen. *It couldn't be!*

All of this was a drill! *Only a drill!*

CHAPTER 13

General Vladimir Fedorovich Iskanderov thundered down the hallway in the old building known as the Lubyanka. The drab tan interior made an attempt at sophistication with its dark wood wainscoting, but the seediness of the building seemed to penetrate everyone who entered it. The decay seemed to get worse as Iskanderov reached a stairway and descended into the depths of the basement.

Iskanderov didn't notice the state of disrepair of the building—it was all second nature to him. He had spent a large portion of his life within the Lubyanka's walls. Only one thought obsessed him. *What was Mission 141 Delta?*

The search had taken the last frantic four hours with the misplaced files on old sleeper missions finally being located in the Lubyanka's notorious basement. Many a political opponent of past Russian leaders had been tortured and killed in that very same locale. Iskanderov had not thought of anything else but Mission 141 Delta since he had found out about the message intercepted from the *Kursograf*. He intended to stay on the job until the crisis was over. But when would that be?

It had been quite a while since he had slept on the sofa in his office. The last time was the attempted coup during August of 1991. He had stayed at his post and fed information to the then new Russian president, Boris Yeltsin, in return for which Yeltsin had let him keep his job after the collapse of the Soviet Union.

Iskanderov came out of the stairwell huffing and puffing and immediately saw two of his men down the hallway waving him to them. Only a minute ago, he had gotten their phone call that they had found a large cache of files on sleeper missions. It would take some time to go through all the files, but Iskanderov decided not to wait. He could look through a file just as well as one of his subordinates.

Iskanderov got to the door of the room and saw that only a fraction of the safes that lined the walls were open, and there were ten men who were laboriously going over a file each. He had to speed things up.

"Give me your attention," Iskanderov commanded. They all, without exception, looked up at him. "When the file is found, you will not read it. You will give it directly to me and only me. Is that understood?"

All his men nodded or indicated verbally that they understood and then got back to work. Iskanderov glanced at the man conducting the search.

"Open two of them for me. I will search for it myself," the general said. The search organizer raised his eyebrows in surprise but said nothing as he complied with the SVR chief's orders.

Iskanderov pulled out several files from the wall safe and began pouring over the first few pages of each of them in turn. He could see out of the corner of his eye that his man leading the search also pulled out some files and began to scrutinize them. Iskanderov's example had impressed upon the man how urgent the search was.

An array of sleeper missions passed by Iskanderov's eyes during the next hour. Sabotage missions dominated, although some seemed particularly extreme, such as one whose purpose was to blow up skyscrapers in New York City. Some carefully placed charges at the bases of the buildings and they would come tumbling down.

Relics of the past, thought Iskanderov. The American aid that has kept Russia afloat the past few years was with strict stipulations. Pull out your agents along with all the sleepers, the Americans had demanded, or no aid. The Russians, the moderate ones at least, shrugged to themselves and said, Why not? The Americans were no longer enemies or even rivals. They were becoming more and more friendly as the years went on. The Russians complied over the bitter objections of the still-lingering Communist and ultranationalist hard-liners.

But how well did we comply? Did the blundering bureaucracy over which I have control pull out *all* our sleepers? Did this American strategic readiness drill trigger a forgotten Russian sleeper mission? Iskanderov's mind froze with that thought.

"Uh, General," said someone tentatively. Iskanderov's head whirled in his direction. "This could be it," said a man seated two tables away. He closed the file and held it up. All eyes fell on him. It seemed they were all holding their breath. The man got up and hurriedly handed the file over to Iskanderov. The general's hand trembled as he took the file.

Iskanderov gave him a long look, opened the file, and began to read. He was vaguely aware that all eyes were now on him. The name, "Mission 141 Delta," was at the top of the page with a sign-off section below it. He flipped the page and the section titled "Purpose" was at the top. Iskanderov didn't read it at first. Instead he faced the small crowd in the room.

"Thank you, gentlemen. You must all leave the room now," he said quietly. They all got up and shuffled out and closed the door behind them. Iskanderov went back to the dreaded paragraph. His eyes refused to focus on the letters, as if they were warning him that he wouldn't like what he would see. He forced his eyes along the letters and commanded himself to understand them.

PURPOSE: *In the event of nuclear hostilities and when a strategic rocket launch is imminent, the KGB company assigned will take control of Shemya Air Force Base. They will, if at all possible, prevent early warning data from the COBRA DANE radar from reaching NORAD Command Post in Cheyenne Mountain. Spacetracking data will be substituted.*

The early warning radar data would detail trajectories of incoming Soviet rockets and provide the American military data for defensive measures. Other sensors, such as BMEWS and DSP, might show a launch by Soviet rockets, but with the COBRA DANE radar showing nothing but a peaceful set of space-tracking data, doubt will be created in the mind of American leaders as to the reliability of what their other sensors are telling them. This will cause a delay until the launch is confirmed, thereby making it impossible for the Americans to launch on warning. Their land-based missiles will then all be destroyed by our initial attack. This mission shall be coordinated with similar missions at Clear, Alaska; Thule, Greenland; Fylingdales Moor, England; and Nurrungar, Australia, which are, respectively, the BMEWS sites and the ground station for the American DSP early warning satellite over the Soviet Union.

Iskanderov's blood ran cold. *How many Americans had died in the past twenty-four hours?* All because one sleeper mission hadn't been deactivated.

". . . and so, comrades, now you know as much as I do," intoned Iskanderov. Silence fell in the briefing room as each participant either stared at Iskanderov or examined the green felt top of the long tapering table at which they were seated. They totally ignored Iskanderov's use of "comrades" as a form of address. That style had gone the way of the Soviet Union. Old habits were hard to break, however, and some of the more senior people had frequent lapses. The quiet continued, interrupted only by a few throat clearings, until the chief of the GRU, the head of Russian military intelligence, spoke up.

"So, we had all their early warning facilities covered by sleeper missions," said General Boris Tolstiakov in a thoughtful tone. "Very interesting." Iskanderov could almost hear the wheels of Tolstiakov's mind whir about. Tolstiakov was one of the old-time intelligence officers. He had even served as a teenager in the Great Patriotic War, the Russian term for World War II. Everyone suspected him of being a hard-liner, but no one knew for sure. The politicians suspected also, but he was so good at his job that no one wanted to get rid of him.

"Yes, not that it matters now," replied the SVR chief. "All have been deactivated in accordance with the secret protocol accompanying the aid from the Americans."

"Except for the one on Shemya Island," said Tolstiakov. The wheels were still going full speed.

Iskanderov gave a rueful nod. "The mission was to kill—*kill,* mind you—everyone on the island. We are victims of our own ruthlessness. When the Americans discover—and they will discover it—who perpetrated this atrocity, they will want revenge. Cutoff of their aid to us will be the kindest thing they will do."

"Do they know yet?" asked Tolstiakov.

Iskanderov shrugged. "We won't know that for a while yet."

"Then there might be time to get someone in there to cover it up," said Tolstiakov.

Iskanderov's jaw went slack with surprise. "Just what are you suggesting?" asked Iskanderov.

"A Spetsnaz team can get in there and make it look like an accident," said Tolstiakov.

Iskanderov looked at him as if he were insane. "And how would you do that?"

Tolstiakov looked at Iskanderov. "How was this team supposed to kill hundreds of people on this island?"

Iskanderov in turn looked at his technical expert, who was a few seats away.

"Poison gas for the most part. But a few had to be shot," replied the expert.

Tolstiakov's mind raced. "Do the Americans have any biological or chemical munitions on Shemya?"

"Unknown. We will check," said Iskanderov. He saw one of his aides make a note.

"Yes, we will check as well," mumbled Tolstiakov as he sat lost in thought for a moment.

Iskanderov caught on. The Spetsnaz team would tamper with the chemical warfare stock to make it appear that it had leaked and wiped out Shemya's occupants. It would look like an accident caused by the Americans themselves. He hated to admit it, but the head of the GRU had the beginnings of a good plan. An instant later, Iskanderov knew the plan wouldn't work.

"The Americans will most likely discover the Spetsnaz team, and they'll be convinced that we are responsible," said Iskanderov. "They'll be twice as angry with us."

Tolstiakov's face lit up. "Then we'll tell them everything. That we sent the team to cover the incident up."

"What! Have you lost your mind? What kind of insanity is this?" shouted Iskanderov.

"And then we'll tell the Americans why we are trying so desperately to cover it all up," continued Tolstiakov as if the outburst from Iskanderov had never happened. "To avoid the cutoff of economic aid to our country. Everyone knows that if that happened there would be starvation, riots in the streets, a total breakdown of civil order. Those elections showed the world that the nationalists and Communists aren't finished yet. A coup by hard-liners would be inevitable. *And a return to the Cold War.*"

The SVR representatives gaped in disbelief at the GRU chief. General Boris Tolstiakov was known throughout the Russian intelligence community for his wild ideas, and in the past some of them had bordered on brilliance, but Iskanderov had become convinced that the man had gone insane.

Tolstiakov saw the look on their faces and glanced at his aide. His subordinate's face wasn't much different. He turned back to the SVR men.

"Look, all we have to do is make up a story that a coup is being planned by—we'll get some of these nationalists who like to shoot off their mouths and threaten other countries—and we'll say that they're just waiting for the right opportunity. A cutoff of aid from the Americans will give them that opportunity. Who knows? Maybe the Americans will help us cover it up."

"I think we'll have to continue this discussion in private," said Iskanderov. He turned to his aides and nodded to them as if to reassure them that everything was all right.

The GRU chief would do his best to convince him that his plan was workable, and he, the SVR chief, must resist him. Iskanderov knew where it would all end—in the lap of Russia's president. Would the president agree with Tolstiakov? Nothing was certain these days.

Iskanderov couldn't shake the feeling of dread that passed over him.

General Boris Tolstiakov settled back into the cushions of his Chaika limousine and watched his aide, Colonel Yuri Solov'yev, take the seat next to him. He gave a curt word to the driver to get moving, and they started off on the short trip to the old Khodinka airfield, the site of the GRU's headquarters.

Tolstiakov eyed his young aide. "You are wondering what we had to talk about so long in private, eh, Yuri Georgievich?" He could see the colonel was upset. "I basically convinced our SVR friend that the plan would work," continued the GRU chief.

"This whole situation is so hideous. How could we have let this happen?" said his aide.

"Do not forget that it was the SVR's sleepers who did this thing, not ours. But we might have to sweep up after them," said Tolstiakov quietly. He eyed his aide again, this time with curiosity. "What do you think of my plan?"

Solov'yev shook his head and looked at the floor of the car. "It's all happening too fast. It's too much to assimilate."

Tolstiakov nodded and seemed satisfied at the nonanswer. But sometimes, he thought, one has to move very quickly indeed to achieve one's goals. They rode in silence for a while until his aide finally spoke.

"We know that the Americans do not have chemical or biological munitions on Shemya," said the colonel. It was apparent to Tolstiakov that his aide had been turning the plan over in his mind. That was good. The GRU chief would need some special help to bring this thing off.

"Yes, I remember the briefing two weeks ago," stated Tolstiakov flatly.

"Then why—"

"The SVR doesn't know that. If there are too many obstacles in the way of our plan initially, then our friend Iskanderov of the SVR would be very reluctant to go along. When he finds out that there are no chemical or biological munitions on Shemya, then it will be too late to back out. By then we will have enlisted the aid of the Americans in covering up the whole situation." Tolstiakov leaned back and closed his eyes. It was a sign to his aide that he didn't want to be engaged in conversation.

Yes, he thought, the help of the Americans was essential. It would allow his Spetsnaz team to get onto the island to complete their mission. In the midst of this disaster, there was opportunity.

2000 HOURS, 26 DECEMBER
PETROPAVLOVSK, ON THE KAMCHATKA PENINSULA

Colonel Ivan Sysoyev stared at the orders which his communications aide had brought him. The message was designated to be read only by him, and so he had labored for thirty minutes to decode it with his own personal codebook. He read it and reread it with mounting surprise and consternation.

Sysoyev squirmed in his chair, his stiff Russian marine infantry uniform making flexing noises with his movement. Sysoyev was definitely not marine infantry; the uniform was a cover for his real function.

Colonel Sysoyev led a Spetsnaz naval brigade stationed at Petropavlovsk, the large Russian naval base on the Kamchatka Peninsula, located less than a thousand miles from the Aleutian chain. His brigade had a headquarters company, a midget submarine group, two battalions of frogmen, a parachute battalion, a signals company, and other supporting units.

Sysoyev was ordered to embark on a fast Akula-class submarine for a trip to the Aleutians. He was to personally lead the mission with thirty of his best men, most of them combat swimmers, or frogmen. He was to take the men from his staff company, a secret organization within the

Spetsnaz brigade composed of only professional soldiers and dedicated to sabotage and assassinating enemy leaders.

Sysoyev frowned. This was the type of orders he would expect if they were at war with the United States, but they were farther from that than at any time in this century.

He read the orders again, but they gave no clue as to the real purpose of the mission. Was this training? He hoped so. He continued frowning as he read the peculiar list of extra equipment he was to take with him. A half a dozen video cameras and a large supply of videotape headed the list, with a number of 35-mm still cameras also listed. He was also ordered to take anyone in his brigade who could pilot American aircraft or helicopters. Unusual indeed.

Some of the Spetsnaz standard procedures were being changed for this mission as well. He was not to shoot his wounded as they had been trained to do, but he was ordered to bring out all of his men, even the bodies of anyone who would be killed.

Sysoyev examined the message header once again. It was straight from the GRU leadership in Moscow, direct to him with no intervening organizations listed and no copies to other commands. Just as if we were at war, he thought again. The thought unsettled him.

He hit the intercom buzzer to his second in command as he got to the part at the end of the message which was not so unusual. Further orders would be given to him en route to the Aleutians.

Perhaps then he would find out what this was all about.

2245 HOURS, 26 DECEMBER
U.S.S. NEW YORK CITY, SSN 696

Sonarman Don Frederick stared at the sonar display above him and watched mesmerized at the slow advance of the million green dots down the screen. Called the "waterfall," the display showed passive acoustic signals 360 degrees around the boat. He currently had the display programmed to show the acoustic data in three different time frames. The top screen on the display showed the last thirty seconds, the middle screen showed the last two minutes, and the bottom screen displayed data greater than two minutes old.

Frederick's eyes were riveted on the top screen to the left—some of the green dots seemed to be coalescing into a brighter green line. It wasn't pretty, but a line was definitely there and it was nearly horizontal.

"Sonar Supe! I have a new high bearing rate contact, designation Sierra Two Zero, bearing three-one-zero. Preliminary classification: submerged hostile!" said the sonarman loudly. A line on the display in a sea of green dots meant a contact. He rolled his tracking ball to put a cursor above the ragged line on the display in front of him. This pointed a hydrophone in the direction of the contact and allowed him to hear along that line of bearing. The sonar supervisor, a chief petty officer behind Frederick who was responsible for the operation of the sonar group, picked up a microphone and informed the OOD in the conn.

Captain Ed Stanley was out of the conning station and at Frederick's side a heartbeat later. He eyeballed the display and noted the true bearing of the contact. *New York City*'s heading was almost heading due north and the contact was heading quickly to the east, judging by the rapid advance of the line on the display from left to right. The captain picked up a microphone and pressed the talk button.

"Conn, man battle stations, come to course zero-eight-zero. Make your depth one hundred and fifty feet," ordered the captain, then he proceeded the few yards from the sonar shack back to the conn as the alarm was sounded throughout the boat. The crew scrambled to their general quarters stations.

It was a guess as to the contact's heading, but Stanley knew from experience that he would come close. The captain felt his boat tilt as his crew got to the ordered heading. He studied the waterfall repeater in the conn which was set to display the same thing that Frederick was seeing. The line on the display stopped its rapid movement to the right and gradually straightened to a nearly vertical advance down the display. Captain Stanley raised his eyebrows in semisurprise at the accuracy of his guess of the contact's course. He was getting good at this. They were now proceeding on the same heading as the contact.

Stanley gazed at the center window of the display, which showed acoustic data stored over the last two minutes. The contact's original bearing was in a straight line with Petropavlovsk, home to Russia's Pacific submarine fleet. Relations with Russia couldn't be better these days and much of the tension that accompanied these missions had disappeared. Still, the U.S. Navy kept an eye on the Russian navy, and vice versa. Each side called it good training, but they all knew that there was a significant threat capability on the other side—if the politicians ever wanted to use it. Anybody with nuclear capability was going to be constantly watched, and anybody with both nuclear and submarine capabilities was going to be an obsession.

"Conn, sonar. Sierra Two Zero speed is three-five knots," said the sonar supervisor over the intercom.

Captain Stanley picked up a microphone. "Sonar, conn aye."

Stanley's XO spoke up at the captain's elbow. "He's going like a bat out of hell, sir."

"Sierra Two Zero has been redesignated Master Five," said a phone talker. The contact had been confirmed hostile.

Stanley nodded and whirled to his other officers. "Let's crank it up. Go to flank speed." He got a crisp aye, aye and the order was relayed. Stanley could feel the boat surge under his feet. The *New York City* could only do about thirty-two knots, but he was trying to counter the tactic used by the Russians to go flat out to attempt to shake their American trackers, then settle down and go to their "real" course to get to their operating area. If the *New York City* could maintain passive sonar contact until the Russian sub slowed down, then his boat could take its time catching up.

"Conn, sonar. Akula-class signature, Captain," said the sonar supervisor with some surprise in his voice.

Now that was unusual, thought Stanley. Most of the contacts out of Petropavlovsk were older subs, and judging by their actions, they were on training missions. This contact had all the earmarks of an old Cold War operational mission.

Captain Stanley watched the sharply defined line on the sonar display gradually grow ragged as the Akula opened up the distance between them. The line would ultimately turn into a jungle of green dots that would blend into the background noise.

In an hour they would lose contact.

CHAPTER 14

The meager light played tricks on Trask's mind as he strained his eyes to see as far down the road as possible. At one point he was certain that an army of Russian troops was heading down the road toward him until he looked away for a few seconds, then looked back. They disappeared in the mists at the limit of his vision.

Where the hell were Elverson and Vaughan? The question ran around and around in his mind. He thought of Ellen. She was safe only two doors down and probably asleep by now. Thoughts of their intimate conversation ran through his mind and he reveled in her desire to keep him close by. Was it real? Did she really need him as much as she seemed to? Or was it just a reaction to yesterday's horrible events? Couldn't be, he thought. She alternated between being vulnerable and being hard as stone. When she was hard, he marveled at her strength. But when she was vulnerable, he had provided what men have always provided to women in similar circumstances. Strength and security. He thought for a moment, then grew a little embarrassed. She had provided the same to him in his time of need. What had she wanted to tell him as he was leaving?

He shook the thoughts from him and concentrated on the road which stretched in front of the trailer he occupied. The Russians would come down that road to get them and he had to be alert.

Where the hell was Vaughan?
Where the hell was Elverson?

He thought he saw some movement at the edge of the road and looked away for a few seconds prior to confirming their presence. He looked back as his heart began to pound. The figure was certainly there and moving rapidly toward Trask's trailer. He strained his eyes to identify the person, but the parka effectively covered the face. It could be anyone.

Trask backed away from the window and picked up his M16. He pulled the cocking bar back and waited with the barrel pointed toward the door. He peeked out the window once more and noted with some relief that there was only one person, but that person evidently had intentions of entering the trailer. He prayed that it was either Elverson or Vaughan.

The outer door was opened with no obvious attempt at caution, and the figure was through the small alcove and opening the inner door in an instant. A heartbeat later, he was in the trailer with Trask.

"Hold it!" Trask growled. The intruder froze with his back to the engineer.

"Drop the weapon," said Trask. The person didn't comply but instead took on a posture of impatience.

"Damn, don't get so melodramatic. It's me, you shithead," replied Elverson.

Trask breathed a sigh of relief, although he was irritated at the young man's casual attitude. "Where the hell were you?" he demanded.

Elverson turned around to face Trask, then gestured toward the door. "I thought I saw something out there and went to investigate—"

"That was pretty dumb, don't you think?" interrupted Trask. He kept the barrel pointed at the AP.

"You're an asshole," retorted Elverson. He completely ignored Trask's M16 and flopped in a chair.

Trask lowered the weapon and mentally gave up. There was just no controlling the young man short of shooting him. He certainly wouldn't do that; he desperately needed him in their fight with the SVR. He considered telling him that Vaughan was missing but then decided not to. Vaughan would probably have a perfectly good explanation for his absence, and there was no sense in getting Elverson excited about it.

"Hell, I'm tired," said Elverson.

"So, go to sleep," replied Trask.

Elverson looked at him and nodded and got up to go back outside. Trask suddenly realized that he was going to go back to Ellen's trailer and had a sense of dread.

"You can sleep here," said Trask simply.

Elverson gave him a glance and seemed to know exactly what was bothering Trask. "It's more comfortable back there."

The remark seemed ominous to the older man, but he felt helpless to counteract it. He searched for some logic to dissuade Elverson from going back to Ellen's trailer.

"If something happens, I'm going to need you pretty fast," said Trask. He held his breath for Elverson's reaction.

The AP grunted and half smiled in the darkness. "Fire a few shots. I'll be here."

He was out the door before Trask could say another word.

Elverson entered the trailer and quietly closed the door. His eyes scanned the darkness, and as they gradually became accustomed to the deeper gloom inside the trailer, he spotted Ellen Gain lying still on the bed. She appeared to be asleep. He briefly wondered what went on between her and Trask and then gave up. He'd never find that out. Lust began to build up in him as he lingered over the mental vision of Ellen's golden hair mingled with the snowflakes when they had first seen her. Of course she would want him—he was young and strong, better looking too than the much older engineer. He had his future to think of, he couldn't share her with Trask.

He crossed the room in two steps and stood over her as she lay on the bed. After a few seconds she rolled over and looked up at him.

"Go to sleep," she ordered.

"Go to sleep in the same room with a babe like you?" he said, with his voice rising at the end of his statement in order to make it a question. She didn't answer.

"By the way, what did you and Trask do while I was gone?" he asked. To Ellen's surprise, he seemed jealous.

"That's none of your damn business, Airman. Go to sleep. That's an order." She growled the last sentence. She rolled over and pretended to ignore him.

"You can't order me around anymore, bitch," he said in a fury, and grabbed her by the shoulders to pull her to her feet. "There is no more air force—" He cut his tirade short as he felt a lump of steel up against his stomach. He saw the venom in her eyes, then glanced down and saw she had the automatic in her hand. It was cocked and she had the muzzle stuck in his solar plexus.

"That's an order," she repeated quietly.

Lieutenant Ellen Gain lay shivering in the dark. Her thoughts were on the recent past, her confrontation with Elverson all but forgotten with the young AP sleeping in another trailer. The wall behind her exploded for the millionth time since her encounter with Vulcher during the past summer. She again felt the thud of the bullet entering her left shoulder and experienced the dizziness and shooting pain before falling unconscious to the floor.

In the intervening months she had recovered from her wounds and was sent to Shemya to follow Vulcher. She had contacted the relatively large contingent of CIA undercover agents that had been sent to Shemya previously to ferret out the infamous SVR mole. They had integrated her with their surveillance teams around the island which were in the process of gathering information on the large number of people that had been transferred to Shemya since the summer.

That was a week ago. Now all of her colleagues were dead. It had been a miracle that she hadn't joined them.

Where was Vulcher now? The question ran around in her mind. He must be part of the SVR crew that took over the island, but who was he? Everyone was suspect, even Trask, as much as she liked and needed him. He seemed to symbolize a new life, someone who would step in and change her life forever. But she wouldn't be fooled. Vulcher could be anyone, even Vaughan, as unlikely as that might be.

If she was any kind of agent, she thought, she would have shot Vulcher instead of letting him shoot her and kill her partner. Instead neither she nor her partner had even gotten off a shot. Her blood ran cold. Vulcher seemed an appropriate name indeed. However, it would be different if they ever met again, she resolved grimly.

What was the expression Vulcher had used? *Va fun qulo?* One of the CIA's agents of Italian heritage had provided the origin of the unusual expression. It was a mispronunciation of *Va affangulo,* which was a particularly vulgar saying in Italian meaning, literally, Go do it in the ass. The Italians pronounce it with a silent letter *o* on the end and effectively cut off the last syllable.

How had a Russian SVR sleeper agent picked up a strange expression like that? Ellen mentally shrugged. Maybe his SVR instructor in American culture had given that to him as one of the eccentric things they were provided with—things that everyone picks up during the course of life in the United States that don't really fit into one's past. His instructor might have even taught him to mispronounce it as well to give an authentic flavor to an epithet picked up by association with Italian-Americans. The mispronunciation would persist, because the expression would never be seen in print.

It was a distinctive idiosyncrasy, but it was nearly useless as an identifier. That sort of expression probably wasn't used often, and on an island with hundreds of people, it would have been pure luck to have been around to hear the expression used.

But all that was changed. If she had any guts, she would find all the SVR agents on the island and kill every one of them, thereby disposing of Vulcher once and for all. He had murdered her partner, Tom McCue, and had put a bullet into her. She wouldn't rest until he was in custody, or preferably dead. The fact was that she didn't have any guts—she was scared to death of the SVR and especially of Vulcher himself.

She shook uncontrollably and groaned out loud. She was as much cold as she was afraid. She needed Trask back here again. He seemed to give her strength. In an ironic twist, the dissolute, aging, alcohol-soaked engineer, who spent his life running away from responsibilities through a series of excuses, was the one who made her feel strong. He was the one who made her feel like a woman instead of like a chess piece, a hunk of wood or ivory that was pushed around, and maybe ultimately sacrificed, by the world's power brokers.

What a hell of a place to find someone like that, she thought. What a hell of a situation to be in. Maybe I'm just as much of a zero as Trask, she thought. Maybe that's why I need him so much. Only he's not a zero. On a scale of one to ten, he pegged the needle on the high side today. Where did he get the courage to do the things he did today after a lifetime of running away? Do I have that kind of courage?

The question hit her again and wouldn't leave her alone. *Where was Vulcher?*

Trask scanned the road for the thousandth time, then leaned back from the window and rubbed his eyes, and vainly tried to prevent the rising storm within him. A numbing fear caught him as he thought of what they were doing and the chances they were taking. They could very easily, and probably would, get killed. The only reason they were all still alive was dumb luck, if one could call that a reason, and that was due to run out at any time. It would happen suddenly. His head would stop a bullet when he was least expecting it.

He inhaled quickly, but he failed to relieve his quivering insides. He wanted to run, to hide, to get far away from the people who would try to kill him. Above all, he wanted a drink; he wanted several; he wanted to lose himself in an uncaring alcoholic stupor, so he could fend off the pain and quivering within him. He gritted his teeth and tried to ride out the fury of his physiological cravings, but the feelings persisted until he cried out in agony.

Why me? Why does this have to happen to me? Why couldn't I have remained as I was? Safe, no commitments, no responsibilities. I didn't have to stand up and be counted; I'd have a few drinks and be fine.

The fire within him hit a peak and his insides felt as if they would rip apart, leaving him bloody and dying. He gasped for breath and jammed his eyes shut as he began to roll in agony on the floor. A tear or two escaped his desperately shut eyes, but Trask ignored them as he squeezed his head in his hands in an external effort to distract him from his internal suffering.

The turmoil seemed to subside, and he was left with an increasing feeling of helplessness and exhaustion. He felt like weeping but directed his thoughts to Ellen as an antidote. He had lied to her about his time in Vietnam and felt a bit guilty as a result, but he consoled himself by thinking that it wasn't really lying if he hadn't told her everything. If they ever got out of this mess, he would tell her all. Maybe then the dreams would stop.

Trask considered that even though he had come to the realization that the incident in Vietnam had been at the root of his failures, he still would have his "little moments" like the one he had just endured. It would be a long road back, but he felt he finally had the means to do it. He had Ellen.

He thought over her sometime dependence on him. He couldn't fail her; he would never forgive himself if he did.

Trask thought of the other woman who had been in his life, his ex-wife. Curiously, she had never engendered that kind of feeling in him all the years that he had known her.

He didn't react immediately to the sound as it suddenly dissipated the peculiar unheard rushing noise that only absolute silence generates.

It was the sound of muffled footsteps. They were very close and in a few seconds they were up to the alcove outer door. Trask's hands shook as he cocked the M16 and pointed it at the inner door. The outer door opened and closed, he heard the stamping of feet, then Ellen came through shaking the snow from her legs. She saw Trask's M16 at the ready and stopped.

"You don't take any chances, do you?" she said.

He quickly lowered the weapon and hoped she hadn't noticed it shaking. "You never know who might be coming through the door," he replied. He was glad to see her. She was obviously all right.

A strange look passed over her face and suddenly she began to shake. He was next to her in a second.

"What is it?" he asked.

She compressed her lips into a line and shook her head.

"Was it Elverson?" He had a demanding tone to his voice.

She couldn't tell him what really bothered her, so she nodded quickly, then told him of her encounter with the young AP. He grew steadily more angry as she went on with a brief summary of the incident.

"... so now I think he's asleep, in one of the other trailers," she concluded. She saw Trask's anger and hugged him in an attempt to lessen its fury.

"I ought to kill that bastard," he said, and ground his teeth.

"You can't do that. I know you. Besides, nothing happened," she said, and almost smiled.

"If he touches you again, I'll kill him," said Trask through a grimace.

"No matter what he's like, we need him to survive," she objected. She was silent for a while, then she gave a forced chuckle. "The gun wasn't loaded, but I wasn't going to tell him that," she said with a lopsided smile. He wasn't listening.

His anger lessened somewhat to the point that he began to feel fear at the prospect of fighting the younger man to protect Ellen. His thoughts went on for a few moments until he decided that Ellen was worth it. There are few things or people worth dying for, but Ellen was certainly one of them.

Trask calmed down and flopped on a chair as she began looking out the window. He wearily recounted the fact that Elverson hadn't been there when he went on watch and told her of their conversation when Elverson finally showed up.

"I wonder what he was doing out there," she mused.

He thought for a minute. "I couldn't find Harry Vaughan either," he said.

She looked up quickly. "Really?" She was surprised.

He nodded, then laughed. "He was probably out taking a leak or something," he said. She rolled her eyes and shook her head in mock disgust at his remark.

Trask leaned back in the chair and nestled his head on the top cushion. It smelled a bit from dirt and sweat, but he ignored it as waves of fatigue swept over him. He closed his eyes and faded into a deep sleep.

When he next opened his eyes, the first vestiges of light from the new day were beginning to penetrate the trailer's window. He yawned and Ellen turned around from her post at the window.

"Thank God you're awake," she said.

He became alarmed. "Why? What happened?"

She gave him her now familiar lopsided smile. "I thought your snoring was going to wake the dead." Trask shook his head and smiled. He seemed refreshed and tried to remember if he had been dreaming. He felt relief; his unconscious hours were a blank.

They sat in silence for a few minutes until a thought struck him and suddenly rejuvenated him with a new surge of energy.

"C'mon, let's take a walk," he said mysteriously.

"Where are we going?" she asked.

He didn't answer but was out the door while she was in mid-sentence. She ran to catch up as he boldly strode up the road that he had seen Elverson walk down only a few hours before. He located Elverson's footprints in the snow and began to backtrack them to see exactly where they went. They traced them over a small rise to where the road flattened out. Trask glanced over his shoulder. The trailers were obscured from view due to the rise that they had traveled over. He grunted and continued to backtrack Elverson's footprints, then suddenly stopped as Ellen asked him what he was doing. He pointed to a mishmash of disturbed snow.

"Look at that! He met someone up here!" he said with certainty.

Trask looked at the snow and back at her, then back and forth once more. There appeared to be tire tracks in addition to the ones they made when they went down the road, and with a little imagination they saw several sets of footprints. The footprints they had been tracking led up to the other marks in the snow. The conclusion seemed inescapable. His blood ran cold. If Elverson really was an enemy agent, he could have killed them at any time.

"I think our young friend bears watching," said Trask with exaggerated formality. "If not outright execution," he added. He looked at Ellen. She seemed frightened.

"That dirty bastard, he—" began Trask.

"Sssh!" she hissed at him.

They both listened intently as the silence surrounding them suddenly seemed oppressive. Trask finally heard indistinct sounds muffled by the snow. He looked at Ellen with alarm and she returned his look.

"Someone's coming!" she said in a loud whisper.

Trask glanced wildly about for some form of cover as he heard the sounds rapidly approach. There was no cover, at least not of the conventional kind. Trask glanced in the direction of the rise beyond which were the trailers. It was too far—they'd never make it in time. He made a quick decision and grabbed Ellen's arm to drag her off the road. She hesitated only an instant, then ran along beside him.

"Quick! Lie down!" he said. She complied but had no idea what he was up to.

Trask scooped up an armful of snow and piled it on top of her. He smoothed it out a bit, then laid down and started to work on himself. He worked until the truck came into view, then he abruptly stopped so that the truck's occupants would not detect any motion on the side of the road. To his chagrin the truck slowed, then stopped at the point where they had seen the extra set of tire tracks.

Trask whispered to Ellen to keep still, then moved his

head slightly to get a better look at the truck. He didn't like what he saw. Two men got out of the truck and walked partway down the road toward the trailers. They seemed to Trask to be looking for something or somebody, and they were both armed with M16s. Trask risked some movement to bring his M16 up to a ready position. He pulled back the cocking bar in an agonizingly slow motion to keep it as quiet as possible.

A firefight here and they were both dead, he thought. The two men waited for a while, then turned and walked up the road until they stood only a few feet from where Trask and Ellen lay. One man stood with his back to them, but the other stood facing them and paused to light a cigarette. Trask could feel his heart begin to pound and worried if the noise would be heard by the two men standing so close nearby. The one man finished lighting his cigarette and flicked the used match in their direction and briefly glanced over to see it fall on the snow. Trask stopped breathing. He closed his eyes and said a fervent prayer for deliverance. The two men began to chat.

"When do you think the others will show up?" said one of them.

"Who the hell knows? This whole operation has been hurry up and wait. By the way, whose idea was this?" said the other.

The other man grunted. "Probably Driscoll's."

"Did you hear what happened at the satellite ground sta—" He suddenly stopped talking.

Trask opened his eyes.

One of the men was looking directly at Ellen with an astonished expression on his face.

Trask's heart felt as if it were grabbed by a huge hand.

"Lieutenant Ga—"

The man's exclamation was interrupted by an explosive sound next to Trask. He pulled the trigger on his M16, then realized that Ellen had fired her automatic. Trask's M16 erupted with a lethal stream of lead aimed at one man's back. Ellen's bullet hit the first man in the chest and drove him backward into the middle of the road. Trask's burst knocked the second man on top of the first. The bodies bounced as they hit the road, and then they were suddenly still. Trask stared at them for a few seconds until he was distracted by the tremendous pounding of his heart. He gulped a few deep breaths in order to settle his body down.

He glanced at Ellen. Her face was white with shock and fear. He heard the truck start and his heart leaped into his throat. There was a third man in the truck!

The driver didn't bother to turn the truck around but shoved it into reverse gear and floored the accelerator. Trask lifted his M16 and fired at the rapidly moving vehicle. His aim was wild and the burst went into the tundra beyond the road. Trask leaped to his feet.

"Come on! We've got to stop him!" he yelled to Ellen.

Trask ran out to the middle of the road, took better aim and fired once again. Most of his bullets missed, but one or two hit the windshield on the passenger's side and shattered it. The vehicle kept moving despite the flying glass and skidded around a turn in the road and out of sight.

"Damn!" shouted Trask.

He considered running after the vehicle but quickly decided that the distance to the bend in the road was too far to be practical. By the time he got there, the driver would have turned the truck around and would be far down the road. He looked around wildly for Ellen. She was standing in the road, a little behind him and looking at the bodies of the two enemy agents they had killed moments before. Her face was ashen in hue and she had her lips compressed together in anguish.

Trask stared at the bodies for a few seconds and suddenly realized that he felt nothing at their deaths. He shook himself back into action and grabbed Ellen's arm.

"Let's go before our friend brings back some of his buddies," he said to Ellen, and led her off down the road at a run.

In a few minutes they were at the trailers and saw with surprise a wild-eyed Harry Vaughan standing at the end of one of the catwalks.

"What happened?" he asked in a shaky voice.

"Tell you later. Let's get out of here!" shouted Trask.

Elverson stuck his head out a trailer door. His face had an unmistakable question on it.

"C'mon, let's go!" shouted Trask.

Elverson and Vaughan joined them and together they all ran toward the truck.

CHAPTER 15

— ▪ — ▪ — ▪ —

Hugh Lynch, director of the Central Imagery Office, settled down in the center chair before the large TV screen on one wall of the room.

The screen was on and showed two logos, the one for the CIO in the right foreground and the large circular emblem of the Pentagon with its striking American bald eagle in the center in the background. An assistant dimmed the lights.

"Keyhole imagery in ten seconds," stated another man who had earphones and a slim microphone an inch from his lips.

The Pentagon and CIO emblems disappeared and were replaced by a noise-filled screen. That lasted five seconds and then the noisy screen was replaced by a dark screen. Tension in the room heightened. They were now seeing in real time, after some delay for propagation from the source satellite to a relay satellite and then down to Fort Belvoir, Virginia, what the orbiting satellite was "seeing."

"We have focused in on the location on Shemya that is most likely to have people around it, Building Six Hundred, where most people live," said a technical assistant. "We got lucky. We should have clear skies over Shemya, which is something that doesn't happen very often. It is just about dawn there, and most of the entrances and exits of Building

Six Hundred face south and slightly east, so we should have sunlight on that side of the building.''

An image appeared as he was talking and the attendees squirmed a bit in their seats in anticipation.

"We have image lock," intoned the man with the headset.

The picture showed the blurred outline of a structure shaped like two *H*'s on top of one another, with the inside *H* superimposed on the horizontal bar of the outside *H*. Lynch strained his eyes to detect motion, then just as he decided that it was a still picture, the screen changed slightly. The screen was being updated about every five seconds.

"We've got about a minute and a half before we get almost directly overhead," said the technical assistant. "Right now we're about five hundred miles away at an approximate elevation angle of thirty degrees. The ground track of the satellite will run a bit to the east of the island, and we're approaching it from the southwest." He turned to the man with the headset on. "Resolution enhancement?"

The man nodded and spoke a few words into the microphone. Lynch waited for the next update on the screen to see if anything earthshaking would reveal itself. He decided nothing really had changed, only the viewing angle, then he glanced at the rest of the audience. In addition to General David Manning and his aide, there were several air force officers and two photo interpreters from NPIC, the National Photographic Interpretation Center. Their eyes were glued to the screen. In their hands were hurriedly prepared documents, called imagery interpretation keys, which showed in the form of sketches what the various structures on the island of Shemya would look like from space.

At the fifth update the picture changed dramatically. With interpolation within the pixels that make up the screen and with contrast enhancement, the shape of the building became startlingly clear. Windows and doors were easily visible, as were cars and trucks that were parked in the lot in front of the building. Everyone in the room leaned forward to get a closer look.

"Parking lot hasn't been cleared of snow, and there's snow over every vehicle, including their windows," said one of the guys from NPIC.

"Looks like we've got tire tracks leading away from the building," said the other NPIC representative. He leaned forward even farther. "But nothing else."

General Manning spoke up. "Can we see in any of the windows?" he asked as he squinted at the screen.

"Hmmm, doubt it," mumbled an NPIC interpreter. "We'll get closer as we pass over, but then we'll be at too high an angle. Sunlight will reflect off the windows as well, making it damn near impossible."

The other NPIC interpreter eyed the trail of vapor coming from a vent on the building's roof. "The building still has heat." The words seemed to hang in the air. No one could conclude anything from that simple fact. At least not yet. These pictures would be gone over in much greater detail later on.

"How is this building heated?" asked General Manning.

One of the photo interpreters glanced at some notes. "Waste hot water from the nuclear power plant."

"So the nuclear plant is unaffected?" asked the general.

"Hard to say," replied the CIO director, Hugh Lynch. They all had to be very careful not to jump to conclusions. Losing contact with an air force base was serious business. Any rescue team sent in would face unknown dangers, and the distinct lack of normal activity on the island raised the possibility that the island's inhabitants might all have been struck down by some calamity. Lynch tried but could not fight off a rapidly increasing chill that ran through him.

"Any ELINT?" asked General Manning suddenly. One of his aides jumped to a secure phone and dialed a number.

The advanced KH-11, which was the satellite generating the images of Shemya, carried, along with its optical equipment, radio receivers which provided electronic intelligence, or ELINT, on any ground transmitters within range.

General Manning thought perhaps some clue of Shemya's fate might be had from any radio emissions from the island.

The general's aide looked up from the phone. "COBRA DANE is radiating and is in early warning mode. Satellite ground station transmitters appear to be off-line. No other emissions."

"The whole damn island is dead," muttered the general. He didn't know how close to the truth he was.

An NPIC photo interpreter suddenly sucked in his breath. Manning gave him a quick glance. The other photo interpreter jerked himself upright as his eyes locked onto a portion of the screen. They both had seen something significant.

"What is it?" asked Director Lynch and General Manning simultaneously.

"Right side, inside front wing where it joins the main building," said the first NPIC man, and pointed to the screen. The other NPIC representative busily gave the man with the headset instructions to zoom in on that section of the image. The corner of the building filled the screen after the next update.

"Resolution!" commanded the first NPIC man. After several seconds the man with the headset shook his head. This was the best the satellite could do.

After a while General Manning shook his head. The image seemed to be too blurry to make out. He turned to the NPIC men. "What do you think it is?" he asked.

"Open door," said one of them simply.

"It's being held open by something at the bottom," said the other photo interpreter. They both squinted.

Manning peered at the blurred image. Something clicked in his mind. He could now make out the open door and the lump at the base of the door. His eyes followed the outline of the form on the ground. And then *that* clicked in his mind. It looked like a . . .

"It's a body," said one of the photo interpreters.

"Snow covered. He's been there quite a while, several hours at least." The photo interpreter, his eyes wide in amazement, turned to General Manning.

"That man is dead," he said.

NATIONAL SECURITY AGENCY
FORT MEADE, MARYLAND

The quick reaction directive was clear. Any communications intercepted from Russian installations on the Kamchatka Peninsula, the Komandorski Islands, or far western Siberia was to be scanned by the computer for anything pertaining to Shemya Air Force Base in the Aleutians. Any AGI, an intelligence collection ship, activity in that part of the world would be examined as well.

Merle Travis stared at the screen in front of him. What was going on now? Why did a directive like that come through? Normally the directives would concern foreign bases, and not just those suspected of being enemies of the United States. NSA kept an eye—or an ear?—on friendly countries as well.

But one of our own bases? Well, he decided after a while, it still was the Russians that they were intercepting. It was just information about Shemya that they were keying on. Maybe that wasn't so unusual.

He settled down and began to type, and in half an hour he had the array of Cray computers set up to pick off any references to Shemya or its location. He also set the computers to detect messages with known sets of encryption codes, such as the ones from Petropavlovsk, that had been broken earlier or the ones used by the Russian subs home-ported there.

Travis typed in the final command to start the computers off on their search and leaned back to look into the glassed-in room containing the set of Cray computers. Contrary to what is always shown in the technically inaccurate movies and TV series, computers have very few flashing lights and don't make any noise at all, except perhaps the quiet drumming of the cooling fans. The Crays were no exception. They just sat there—and when they didn't work, there were no flashes of sparks, no explosions. They just sat there as quiet as ever.

Cold too. The glassed-in room was chilly by human standards, but that was necessary to keep the electronics from overheating. The computer itself was a series of panels about five feet tall that were joined at their edges to form the spokes of an imagined wheel when viewed from the top. That configuration reduced signal path delays within the computer, which was critical to increasing the speed of the computations. That and the utilization of parallel processing, the use of several processors to work on a piece of a puzzle simultaneously, had pushed the processing speed to undreamed-of levels.

And all that was at his fingertips. Travis had a fleeting wish that he could use this massive computing power to see if he could win the state lottery. Let's see, he thought, if I put all past history of the lottery into the computer . . . What would that give me? A histogram, or probability that the first digit would most likely be a certain number, the second digit would most likely be a certain number, and so on for each digit. But he could get that information from the newspaper. He shook his head. Bad idea.

The phone next to the computer terminal rang. He picked it up. "Travis here."

"Merle, this is Joe Peck from Codes. I've got a Priority One directive to break all codes ASAP in the western Siberia, Kamchatka Peninsula area, including the Aleutians. I've got some of them done. You want a partial dump now?"

Travis nodded to himself. "Yeah, might as well. This one looks pretty hot."

"Okay, here it comes."

Travis glanced at a terminal halfway across the room and saw the screen change as the new encryption code parameters were sent over the LAN, the Local Area Network, into the separate computer that fed data to the Cray computers. The screen rolled for about thirty seconds with a list of all the files that were transferred.

When the screen stopped rolling Travis said, "Okay, Joe, I've got 'em. Thanks." He hung up.

The new codes would be automatically fed into the Crays as they swept through the masses of data collected by U.S. intelligence assets. Encrypted data would be unencrypted and the resulting clear messages would be searched for the

keywords that Travis had put into the computers. Every bit
of data that was intercepted by intelligence agencies wasn't
processed immediately. The massive flow of incoming messages from satellites, ground-based interceptors, and sometimes from human intelligence was stored but typically only
searched by specific request from intelligence agencies.
One notable exception was message traffic to and from the
various embassies in the world. The CIA *always* wanted
that stuff. Negotiations of any kind were always a lot easier
with that kind of intelligence.

Travis was trained to look for unusual patterns in the
intercepted data, such as frequency of transmission of a
particular message, unusual times of transmission, and so
on. So when his screen began to fill with data identifying
messages that needed further decryption, his job suddenly
got more interesting. There were five messages from Petropavlovsk that evidently had at least one more level of
encryption. He involuntarily glanced at the computer terminal across the room. It was busy dumping code parameters into the Cray computers.

The screen on the code computer changed as another set
of code parameters came across the LAN from Joe Peck.
Travis settled back for a wait until all the codes were sent
to the Crays. Ten minutes later, the five messages needing
further decryption were reduced to one. The status line indicated that two codes were used on the message already.
Three levels of encryption? thought Travis. Not unheard of,
but unusual. Especially since the Soviet Union collapsed.
What use does anyone have for secrets these days?

The thought stopped him short. If there were no secrets,
there would be no need for the NSA. It would be the un-
employment line for him and thousands like him. He shook
the thought from him and got to work. The only unusual
message was the one with at least three levels of encryption. Might as well start there. He picked up the phone and
dialed the number for the codes group. Joe Peck answered.

''Joe, did you dump all the code parameters to me yet?''
asked Travis.

"Yeah, Merle, you got them all," replied Peck. There was a question in his voice, however.

"Looks like you've got one more to do. There's one message that's already gone through two codes and it's still encrypted."

"Huh, that's something," said Peck. He seemed to get lost in thought. Travis knew he was already deciding how to set up his array of computers to break the code. "Well, send it to me and I'll see what I can do," he said after a moment.

"Right," said Travis, who was already typing in the instructions to send the message over the LAN to Peck. He hung up the phone, finished sending the message and sat back to read some of the translated intercepted messages from the Russians at Petropavlovsk. Most of it was boring beyond imagination. Requisitions for toilet paper, food, medicine, furniture, snow shovels filled the screen. Couldn't be much there. Nothing that looked like radar data. They encrypt this shit? he asked himself.

He typed in commands to display any data that might be connected to radars. One message came up that talked about pulse repetition rates, power spectra, effective isotropic radiated power, and antenna beam angles. Yes, thought Travis, this is it. They're talking about the COBRA DANE radar on Shemya. Probably this message originated from a Russian intelligence-gathering ship, he thought.

The message icon on Travis's screen began to flash on and off, telling him that someone, probably Joe Peck, was sending him a message by computer. He got the message on the screen and read it.

TO: *Merle*
FROM: *Joe*
SUBJECT: *Message number 9452378CXZ*
  This was encrypted with three levels of codes, the outer one belonging to Petropavlovsk. The second level code is the same as one identified as belonging to the Kursograf, *a Russian AGI in the Aleutians. The inner code has unknown origin, but it has the same*

> *characteristics as some of the codes belonging to known Russian sleepers.*
>   *Message reads as follows:*
>   *Mission 141 Delta is accomplished.*

Travis got a sudden cold feeling. Russian sleeper agents had apparently sent a message from somewhere in the Aleutians to the Russian intelligence ship, which then relayed it to Petropavlovsk. They in turn relayed it to Moscow, and on each step along the way it picked up another level of encryption.

One question went around and around in Travis's mind as he dialed the number that would make all hell break loose. *What was Mission 141 Delta?*

KIEV, UKRAINE

Douglas Carr stared out the car window with the flash message still on his mind. The message as much as said to drop everything else and do nothing but the task detailed in the text of the message. Someone at Langley had done their homework on this one. The message contained the contact's name, his home address, his work address, a detailed description, and several photographs. Someone desperately wanted information from Dimitri Yanklovin.

The car ran over some particularly rough bumps which bounced Carr and his assistant, Pat McLaughlin, around in the back seat. It was unusual for Carr, as CIA chief of station, Kiev, to go see a contact with a foreign intelligence service. *Formerly* with a foreign intelligence service, corrected Carr. Yanklovin had retired from the KGB at about the time the Soviet Union had crumbled and Ukraine had become an independent nation. The former spook had settled in his apartment overlooking the Dnieper River, and immediately attracted agents from the American intelligence services and many other intelligence agencies around the globe. None of them had ever gotten much from him, though. Carr had been told that at one point there had been a waiting line outside his apartment. They all had a laugh over that.

The message that Carr had received was no laughing matter, though. The Company wanted answers and wanted them fast. Carr gave McLaughlin a sideways glance. The big Irishman wasn't known as a thug. He just looked like one. Carr hoped Yanklovin would get the idea without resorting to anything physical. The message had said to get the answers *by any means necessary*. That left Carr with a bad feeling about the whole thing. What could be that urgent after the collapse of the Soviet Union? The Russians and the Ukrainians and the whole damn bunch of them were our friends now, weren't they? But he knew from his own profession that the surveillance never slackened. Some of the urgency was gone, but they still had to constantly monitor things in Russia and all the nations of the former Soviet Union. There were too many factions vying for power, and too many nuclear weapons still around to relax their vigil.

Another set of prodigious bumps jolted his mind back to what he was seeing out the car's window. They had just pulled onto the bridge over the Dnieper River. Carr's eyes wandered to the street that ran parallel to the river and to the apartment buildings that lined the street. Yanklovin's apartment was behind one of the myriad windows that faced the river. Carr had the sudden thought that it would be easy to find Yanklovin's apartment. Just look for the line of intelligence officers outside waiting to get in. He couldn't resist a smile.

The car got past the bridge and immediately turned left onto the first street after the bridge. They traveled a bare hundred yards and slowed to a stop.

The driver pointed to a door. "Here we are, Mr. Carr," he said.

Pat McLaughlin got out on the right side and Carr got out the left side on the street. They met outside the door and glanced at each other.

"Third floor," said McLaughlin. Carr nodded and they both entered the building and proceeded up the stairs. They went halfway down a corridor and knocked at Yanklovin's door.

Partway through the third knock, the door was opened

by an ugly, thick-faced woman of indeterminate age. Couldn't be a mistress, thought Carr, unless Yanklovin has vision problems. Carr settled on housekeeper as the woman's function. She didn't say a word but just stood staring at the two of them.

"We're looking for Dimitri Yanklovin. We're from the American chancery," said Carr in English. He knew the woman probably wouldn't understand him, but he didn't want her to think that they were SVR or GRU. Both he and McLaughlin could speak Russian fluently.

Her eyes looked him over, then flicked to the big Irishman standing a little to Carr's right and behind him. She turned her head toward the inside of the apartment and spoke something guttural which both Americans couldn't understand. After a few seconds the door was opened wider by a man. Carr and McLaughlin recognized him immediately from the photo sent to them with the message from Langley.

"Mr. Yanklovin, my name is Douglas Carr and this is Pat McLaughlin," said Carr as he jerked a thumb over his shoulder at his companion. Yanklovin relaxed a bit but became more suspicious at the same time. "We're from the American chancery, and we'd like to talk to you for a few minutes."

Yanklovin stared at them for a few seconds, then his face softened in resignation. "Yes, it is okay," he said with a heavy accent.

The woman seemed to lose all interest in the two Americans and quickly disappeared into another room as Yanklovin led the two over to a sofa. He sat in a chair while the two Americans settled in the sofa. It wasn't all that comfortable, decided Carr.

Yanklovin pointed to Carr. "I have seen your picture before." He pointed to McLaughlin. "Not him though."

Carr got right to the point. "We have an urgent request. Do you know anything about an SVR sleeper action called Mission one-four-one Delta?"

Yanklovin looked at the Americans with a practiced impassive air. "How did you come by the mission name?"

Still grubbing for details? thought Carr. Even though

you're retired and living in what has become another country? The information, if he could get it from Carr, might be worth a favor or two from the still-powerful SVR.

"I couldn't tell you even if I knew. Of all people, you know that," replied Carr.

Yanklovin stared for a few seconds, then nodded slowly. "Just so," he said simply. "Why is this so important?"

Carr compressed his lips. "It just is, that's all."

Yanklovin lowered his head and stared at the floor for what seemed like an eternity. "Ah, yes. Assistant Chief of Station, Warsaw. Perhaps 1990?"

It was all a game to him. Carr wanted to grab him by the throat to wring all the gamesmanship out of him so he could get his information and get the hell out of here. He had to hand it to Yanklovin, though. He had a damn fine memory.

"Mission one-four-one Delta?" said Carr with his eyebrows raised in a gentle reminder.

"And how do you know that I know anything about this?" asked the former KGB agent.

Carr was running out of patience. "We know that you were in the First Chief Directorate, Directorate S. You made it your whole damned career. Please, for God's sake, tell us what you know."

"And what am I offered for this?" asked Yanklovin.

Carr was prepared for this. He handed a small black book to Yanklovin. "One million American dollars in a numbered account in Zurich."

Yanklovin's mouth dropped open. He took the book with trembling hands and stared at the number printed on the first page. His eyes teared for a moment, and he blinked them quickly. He slowly closed the book and carefully placed it in his pants pocket. He sat lost in thought.

Yanklovin's head suddenly shot upright and the blood drained from his face. "My God! Is there now a problem with one of your air force bases?"

CHAPTER 16

Trask gazed out the back window of the truck and watched the trailers disappear in the distance as Elverson flung the vehicle along the unplowed road. He turned around and began to study his companions and attempted to come to some conclusion regarding each of them. The only one he was sure of was Ellen; he was in love with her, but he felt certain that there were no mysteries about her, unlike the other two.

He was suddenly filled with dread. A silent prayer passed his lips that they both would survive this ordeal and somehow escape to live a few years together. He tore his eyes from her and stared at the floor. That would only happen if he concentrated on the problems at hand and started solving them. No one was going to do it for him.

Trask lifted his eyes and stared at the back of Elverson's head. There was a real puzzle, he thought. Most APs, especially the ones in the forward areas, like Shemya, had a great deal of discipline ingrained into them by the training they received. As a result they were rather deferential to authority and readily accepted orders from their superior officers. Elverson was not like that at all. Trask would have expected that he would have accepted Lieutenant Gain's authority, but it was evident that he did not, especially after the incident last night.

Trask mulled over Ellen's recounting of the incident and

164

began to feel sick to his stomach. At least Ellen had handled him well—he couldn't seem to handle the young airman at all. Elverson just didn't take him seriously. Self-pity again, he thought with disgust. Hadn't he had enough of that? Self-pity would do no good, not if he and Ellen were to survive.

His gaze fell on Harry Vaughan, who was bouncing along beside him in the back seat of the truck. There was another mystery, thought Trask. Was he really as harmless as he looked? Trask mentally shrugged. There was no telling, but maybe he should stir the pot a little to see what developed. He fingered his M16 and quietly checked to see that it was loaded. This was getting to be a very dangerous game.

Elverson asked what had happened on the road above the trailers as he rapidly glanced between Ellen, the road ahead, and Trask via the rearview mirror. Trask succinctly summed up their encounter, including their killing of two enemy agents, and then studied Elverson's reaction. The AP gave a low whistle and began to regard Trask with a mixture of curiosity and appreciation.

"Where are we headed?" asked Elverson in an abrupt change of subject.

"There should be some buildings dead ahead. We ought to hole up in them until we figure out where to look for that plane so we can get the hell out of here," answered Trask.

No one objected, and after a moment or two, Elverson nodded. Ten minutes later, the buildings could be seen down the road in the early morning light. Elverson grunted and pointed.

Trask nodded. "Yeah, that's it. Maybe we can hide the truck in one of them too."

"What about the tracks in the snow?" asked Ellen.

Trask groaned. He hadn't thought about that. His mind raced.

"Maybe we could put the truck in one building, and then we could hide in another," offered Harry Vaughan.

"What good would that do?" asked Ellen.

"The tire tracks would lead up to the building that the

truck was in, and they would probably check that out first. That would give us time to sneak away," he replied.

"How would we get away with no truck?" snorted Elverson.

"We couldn't get away, but it would give us a chance to ambush them," said Trask. "They wouldn't expect gunfire from a different building. We might be able to take them by surprise."

Ellen shrugged, but the expression on her face conveyed the impression that the scheme could work. Elverson frowned a bit but didn't object.

"Okay, let's try it," said Trask. Vaughan smiled slightly and gave Trask a friendly look. Trask pretended that he didn't notice and began to study the buildings they were rapidly approaching to pick the most suitable one for sheltering the truck.

The buildings were run down as evidenced by the weather-worn wood and the dirty windows and looked as if they hadn't been used for a decade or more. Trask gave a nervous scan of the area—they were very close to the airport and he hoped that the SVR weren't too alert at this hour of the morning.

"Head for that one," Ellen commanded Elverson. "It looks like a garage."

All eyes shifted in the direction she was pointing, and they all concluded that that particular building was the best one to house the truck. It had a wide door in the front that was obviously for some kind of vehicles, and it seemed to be in good condition. Elverson obediently headed for it.

They jumped out of the truck after pulling up in front of the building, and while Ellen and Trask searched the horizon for any movement, Elverson rummaged around in the truck for chain cutters to defeat the padlock on the door. He gave up after a few minutes and wound up using the butt of his M16 to smash the wood around the hasp that secured the door. Trask worried about the noise, but it was better than if Elverson had shot the door free.

Elverson pushed the door open, pulled the truck into the building and quickly shut the door. They all looked about and soon found a suitable building to hide in. After trooping through the snow and smashing a window, they gained entry. Inside there were a few dilapidated chairs and a not-so-steady table. One by one they chose a chair or a spot in the room to just stand, and Trask decided to place himself as strategically as possible for what he was about to do. He went over to the table and tested it to see if it would take his weight, then decided to only partially sit on it while keeping one foot on the floor. He maneuvered his M16 so that it didn't seem obvious that it was pointing somewhere between Elverson and Vaughan. He laid it on one thigh and held it casually in one hand while slowly slipping the safety off. He decided he had better start before he lost his nerve.

"We've got another problem," Trask stated flatly.

They all looked at him with curiosity; Elverson's look was mixed with arrogance, and Vaughan seemed extremely nervous.

"The SVR knows every step we make," he said, and let it sink in for a few moments. They seemed skeptical, even Ellen. "Think about it," Trask continued. "We're at the old power plant, right? The next thing you know the SVR shows up. At the satellite ground terminal and at the trailers, they show up there too."

"What are you trying to say, Frank?" asked Ellen.

He didn't answer immediately but instead looked at each one of them in turn. They waited expectantly.

"One of us is a traitor," said Trask in a steady voice.

Elverson screwed up his mouth in disgust as Vaughan's eyes grew wide, and Ellen patiently waited for Trask to go on. He deliberately stared at Elverson.

"When I went to relieve you on watch last night, you weren't in the trailer," said Trask.

"I already told you about that," replied the young AP heatedly. "I heard something and went to investigate." His eyes searched Trask in a fever and quickly centered on the engineer's automatic weapon. He immediately figured out where it was pointing and why. He flicked his eyes toward his own weapon that he had parked up against the wall next to him. Trask saw the rapid eye motion and swiftly brought his M16 to the firing position.

"Forget it!" he said sharply.

Elverson sucked in his breath and kept his hands away from the M16 next to him.

"Ellen, get his weapon!" ordered Trask. Ellen complied after some gyrations to keep out of the line of fire, then looked at him with a doubt-ridden expression on her face.

"Frank, are you sure you know what you're doing?" she asked.

Trask chose to ignore her and continued his cross-examination of Elverson. "We followed your tracks in the snow back up the hill, and they met up with other tracks, footprints, and tire tracks. Now, I want to know who you met up there."

Elverson shook his head and was clearly scared but didn't seem to be panicking. "I didn't meet anybody. I told you I heard a noise and went to investigate, but when I got there no one was there. I didn't see any tracks, but it was dark—they might have been there, but I didn't see them."

"*You're lying!*" said Trask.

"Frank, those tracks could have been made at two different times," interjected Ellen in a calm voice.

The obvious flaw that Ellen pointed out in Trask's reasoning hit the engineer like a lightning bolt. He had assumed, without realizing it, that the two sets of tracks had been made at the same time, which meant that Elverson had met the opposition, which implied further that Elverson *was* the opposition. If the two sets of tracks were made at different times, then his whole line of reasoning fell apart. He resisted it anyway.

"He's a Russian, I know it!" said Trask.

"Why?" asked Ellen sharply. "Because you want him to be?"

Trask shifted his gaze from Elverson to give Ellen a shocked look. Did he really want Elverson to be an SVR agent so that he could have an excuse to eliminate the competition for Ellen? The question ran around and around in his mind until he became very confused. He slowly lowered the M16 and Elverson and Ellen breathed a sigh of relief.

"Boy, Pops, you really had me worried for a minute," said Elverson.

Trask gave him a dirty look. "We still have the same

problem as before. One of us is tipping our location to the SVR," repeated Trask in a weary tone. He shifted his gaze to Harry Vaughan, who seemed mortified that anyone would even pay attention to him.

"Where were you last night?" asked Trask.

Elverson's eyebrows went up in surprise. "He wasn't in the trailers the whole time?" he asked.

Trask grimaced. "He was nowhere around when I went to relieve you on watch."

All eyes turned to Vaughan, and the three of them impatiently awaited his explanation. He looked from one to another with an expression bordering on panic. "Well, I ... I—"

"Damn it, where were you?" shouted Elverson.

Vaughan cringed and stopped stammering long enough to blurt out a sentence. "I went for a walk." His eyes continually flicked from Elverson to Trask to Gain and back again in a desperate search for an indication that someone believed him.

"Where?" asked Trask.

Vaughan held his hands out with his palms up to convey the difficulty in answering the question. "I ... I don't know. I just walked."

"He's lying," stated Elverson flatly.

"The SVR is crawling all over the island, we almost get killed a couple of times, and you just take a walk in the bitter cold at night just for the hell of it?" asked Trask in an incredulous tone.

"I ..." started Vaughan, then stopped in frustration.

"How could he have tipped off the Russians as to where we were?" asked Ellen.

"When we picked him up, he could have just gotten done killing everyone in that truck we found near the old power plant," said Elverson. "And he could have taken a walk to alert them last night."

"That's ridiculous," objected Vaughan in a panic.

Trask mulled Elverson's accusations over in his mind and resisted it. Vaughan seemed so harmless.

"What about at the satellite terminal?" asked Trask.

Elverson shrugged. "I don't know. Did he pick up the phone?"

"No, no, that's not true!" said Vaughan.

Elverson suddenly grabbed for Vaughan's flight bag, which was lying by his side on the floor. "It can't hurt to search this one more time," he said with an air of expectancy.

Trask studied Vaughan's face as Elverson searched his bag again. Vaughan was clearly worried but didn't seem to object to his bag's being searched.

"Whoa! What's this?" said Elverson as he felt the lining of one side of the flight bag. He pulled a knife out of his pocket and quickly cut the lining so that he could remove the object. He held up a small metallic box and shot Vaughan a look filled with venom. "What's this?" he asked again.

"I don't know! I never saw it before!" shouted Vaughan in a frenzy. Elverson looked at the object once again, then tossed it to Trask.

"You're the engineer, Trask. What is it?" asked the AP.

Trask looked it over. It was a small metal box, about half the size of a pack of cigarettes, and it had a stubby piece of tubular metal sticking out the top. Trask shook his head slowly.

"It looks like a transmitter," he replied.

U.S.S. *NEW YORK CITY*

"Captain, conn."

The intercom was insistent. Captain Ed Stanley struggled to awake after a few hours of fitful rest. He had just fallen into a deep sleep when the intercom jarred him awake. He fingered the talk lever.

"Captain, aye," he mumbled, his mouth lethargic with interrupted sleep.

"Captain, we've picked up Master Five," replied the OOD.

That bolted him awake. "I'll be right there," answered Stanley.

Stanley had left strict orders to be informed if they had

any other contacts that appeared to be Master Five, their Russian Akula-class sub contact out of Petropavlovsk. He dressed in a hurry, bypassing his socks, and put his feet into slippers instead. Stanley hurried down to the sonar shack.

Sonarman Don Frederick looked up as Stanley leaned over his shoulder. Doesn't this guy ever sleep? thought Stanley. He was awake and on duty when I turned in. I wake up a few hours later, and he's still on duty. I'll have to talk to the division officer about that. I have to make sure that the crew is well rested. Even so, I'm damn glad to have him. He's one of the best sonarmen in the fleet.

Frederick pointed to the waterfall. It showed a ragged line almost straight down the display. The *New York City* was on the same course and was matching the contact's speed.

"Signature?" asked Stanley.

"Master Five confirmed," replied Frederick.

The captain nodded. "Speed?" asked Stanley.

"Twenty-five knots," said Frederick.

Stanley nodded again. "Good work." He patted Frederick on the shoulder and got a quick smile in return. Stanley went out of the sonar shack and into the conn.

"Master Five course?" he asked the OOD.

"Zero-four-two, sir," replied the junior officer.

Stanley went over to the charts, located his boat's position and plotted the contact's course from their position. The line intersected an island in the Aleutians. Stanley squinted at the small print on the chart.

Master Five was headed toward Shemya.

CHAPTER 17

— · — · — · —

Trask was flabbergasted. The evidence was irrefutable. They all stood in silence for a few moments, Ellen with her mouth open in surprise, Elverson staring hard at Trask, Trask looking at Harry Vaughan, and the slight young man gaping at all of them with his eyes wider than they had ever been. Vaughan sputtered a bit before he got the words out.

"I . . . I never saw that before in my life! That's not mine!" he blurted.

"There's your traitor, Trask," said Elverson through clenched teeth.

Ellen managed to get her mouth closed to ask a question. "Are you sure it's a transmitter, Frank?"

Trask shrugged and looked at her. "I don't know what else it would be."

"But it's not mine!" shouted Vaughan.

"Shut up!" growled Elverson.

Vaughan shot the young AP a look of total fear, then managed to tear his eyes away to look at Trask. "Trask, I've got to talk to you," pleaded Vaughan.

"I don't see any keying switch," mumbled Trask. He ignored Vaughan as he turned the device over in his hands. "It's certainly not for voice, there's no microphone."

"Trask . . ." pleaded Vaughan.

"I told you to shut up!" said Elverson.

"Maybe it's a beacon," suggested Ellen.

Trask glanced at her and nodded. "The perfect homing device," he said with a twist of his mouth.

"Trask, *for God's sake*—" began Vaughan.

Elverson stepped up to Vaughan and punched him in the face. The smaller man flew backwards, hit the wall and sagged to the floor. Blood appeared on his lower lip and began to slowly run down his chin. Elverson went up to him and drew back his foot to kick him, but Ellen's sharp command stopped him.

"Elverson, stop it!" she ordered. The airman looked around at the lieutenant, ground his teeth, and backed up a step from Vaughan.

Trask hefted the miniature transmitter and gave Vaughan a sharp look. "Let's theorize a bit," Trask began. "Let's say the Russians want to take over a U.S. military installation, like Shemya. So, they get a bunch of moles to kill everybody on the island. But they're not so sure that they'll get everyone, because maybe they don't have a whole lot of people available—after all, good moles don't grow on trees." He gave them a twisted grin, then continued.

"So they reason that groups of survivors might spring up, and with all the weapons floating around, they could be quite dangerous. Then they get a brilliant idea. One of the moles will pretend to be one of the survivors and will be in a position to betray them at any time. Only another problem comes up. Communications. The mole might not get the chance to pick up a phone, or call on a walkie-talkie, or whatever, to tell his friends where the survivors are located. So they solve it by hiding a small homing device among his personal effects."

"Very subtle, very simple," concluded Ellen.

Trask nodded, then looked at Vaughan. "You screwed up when you took that walk last night," he said.

Vaughan was beside himself with frustration. "No! You've got it all wrong! I took that walk—"

"We know why you took that walk," interrupted Elverson. "To tell your friends how many of us there were."

"*NO!*" shouted Vaughan.

"The question is: What are we going to do with him?" asked Trask.

Elverson spoke up right away. "That's simple. We kill him."

Trask gave Elverson a disgusted look while Vaughan nearly choked with panic.

"Please, let me explain!" begged Vaughan.

"All right, explain," said Ellen.

Vaughan swallowed a few times and took a deep breath to settle his insides. He began to talk in a shaky voice. "I went to Building Six Hundred last night."

"Building Six Hundred? What the hell for?" interrupted Elverson. Ellen gave him a warning look.

"I . . . I didn't remember Elverson in the incoming processing, but I did remember Lieutenant Gain. It was only a week ago. So I went to look up their personnel records. . . ."

"*What?*" shouted Elverson.

Trask shook his head. Vaughan's story was ridiculous. "Building Six Hundred is full of gas that killed everybody there, you couldn't have gotten in," stated Trask flatly.

"I got a gas mask," replied Vaughan.

"Let's just kill this bastard and get the hell out of here," said Elverson.

Trask looked at Ellen and she mirrored his own feelings exactly. Anger, hatred, disappointment flooded her face. That made it unanimous. Vaughan had convinced no one.

"Let's tie him up until we figure out what to do with him," said Ellen in a weary tone.

Elverson took the cue and secured Vaughan's wrists with a length of cord taken from a pile of trash in one corner of the room. He also tied Vaughan's wrists to the trunk of his body.

"We still should kill this bastard," said Elverson as he gestured toward Vaughan.

Trask shook his head immediately. He just couldn't bring himself to kill in cold blood no matter what the crime. "Let's just leave him here," he said.

"We're bringing him with us," said Ellen with authority in her voice.

"Why?" asked Trask. "He'll only get in the way and might even sabotage our attempt to escape."

Ellen turned to him and gave him a cool look. Trask was surprised at the sudden change in her attitude.

"He could be valuable to tell our intelligence people how the SVR operates," she said in a low voice.

Trask shook his head and finally gave up, even though he believed there weren't any intelligence forces left. Another question popped into his mind, but Ellen had the answer before he could articulate it.

"After we find the plane, we'll try Adak first," said Ellen. "With max fuel we'll make it. The Piper Warrior has a range of about six hundred to seven hundred miles. If Adak's hit, then we'll put it down anywhere we can. We won't have enough fuel to go anywhere else."

Trask went over to a window and searched the horizon for activity. It seemed that they were the only survivors left in the world. Was this his last day to be alive? His insides fluttered, and he felt the desire for a drink rush up within him. He wanted everything to stop, he wanted the SVR to disappear, he wanted Vaughan and Elverson to disappear, he wanted Shemya to disappear. He only wanted Ellen . . . and a drink. He shook his head to clear it but still felt muddled. . . . And miles to go before we sleep, he thought. A quotation from somewhere, he wasn't sure where.

Ellen walked up and stood next to him, and gazed out the window. Well, I have my answer, she thought. I had asked myself if I had the guts to go after Vulcher. So much for my guts. Or the lack thereof. Leaving this terrible place is too much of a temptation. What I should do is grab Vaughan and strangle the life out of him until he tells me where Vulcher is. But how do I describe someone I've never seen to Vaughan? Vaughan wouldn't know anyone by a CIA code name. Maybe it would be a useless exercise anyway.

The SVR agents they had shot near the trailers had mentioned 16 SURS Deputy Commander Driscoll as the head man. Was he Vulcher? Where could she find Driscoll now? She almost changed her mind and decided to stay to take revenge on the SVR, but fear raged through her at the prospect. She would swallow her pride and leave, and hope she got to safety.

Ellen turned to Trask. He didn't look at her but sensed her next to him. She was all business.

"We can start searching for the plane in those buildings over there," she said as she pointed to a set of newer structures about two hundred yards away. Trask nodded.

They silently got ready and after taking a second look around to insure that no enemy agents were in sight, they left with Elverson shoving Vaughan out the door first. Trask took a last look at Vaughan's things from his flight bag and absentmindedly picked up a notebook. The rest were innocuous things, of no value to anyone, including intelligence people.

Once outside, they began to walk toward the buildings that Ellen had indicated. They had unanimously agreed to forgo the use of the truck due to its noise and the inability to see where the roads were, even though nothing was said by anyone. Elverson, Vaughan, and Gain headed for the other buildings while Trask walked back toward the building that housed the truck. Ellen turned and gave him an inquiring look.

"The transmitter," he said as he held it up. "We don't want to take it with us. They might be able to trace the signal—use it like a homing device. Let them trace it to here. We'll be long gone."

She nodded quickly, and Trask put it on a windowsill so that it would transmit a good, clean signal unimpeded by the metal of the truck, and then ran out to rejoin the others.

The new buildings were arranged in the form of a small complex, much like a cul-de-sac in a residential area. Over half the buildings were small hangars and most were empty except for one that had RC-135s in it. Trask, upon discovering these aircraft, had turned to Ellen with a hopeful look on his face. She just shook her head.

They finished searching the set of buildings and gave an anxious look in the direction of the next set of buildings and hangars. These were much closer to the airport operations building and carried a correspondingly greater risk of detection. They collectively summoned up their courage and set off for the hangars while giving the ops building in the distance a nervous glance every few seconds.

Their hopes began to fade as the first two hangars they searched yielded nothing. They hit paydirt on the third. A Piper Warrior in top-notch condition greeted their eyes as they entered the building. It was a small single-engine aircraft with seats for the pilot and three passengers.

Ellen ran over and immediately climbed in. In a second she was out again, with an excited look on her face. "The keys are still in it! I don't believe it!"

Trask went over to the plane and grinned up at her. "I guess we must live right," he said, then laughed as he realized the total inaccuracy of his statement. Ellen went back inside the plane and began her preflight check.

"Now all we need is a snowplow," muttered Trask as he looked around the hangar. He found a window right away and went over to it.

Judging by the arrangement of the buildings nearby, he reasoned that they were on a spur off a taxi lane that ran parallel to the main runway. Where would the snowplows be? His eyes scanned the area—there wasn't a whole lot to look at, only a few scattered geometric shapes sticking up above ground, which marked the hangars that were within his field of vision.

A building off to his left caught his attention. It seemed more like a garage than a hangar. A definite possibility, he thought. He called Elverson over. Trask indicated the building and said that he was going over to have a look. Elverson shrugged and gave him a dull stare. Trask shook his head. Such enthusiasm, he thought.

Trask looked at Vaughan, who was sitting near the door of the building. His face reflected extreme dejection, but his previous panic seemed to have subsided to manageable proportions. He glanced up briefly and caught Trask's eye. The young man tilted his head quickly to one side in the universal beckoning gesture. Trask looked away, then back again, and finally gave in to Vaughan's plaintive look. He strolled over and stood above him.

Vaughan glanced beyond Trask to see where Elverson

was. Satisfied that he was in no immediate danger from the young AP, he began to speak in a whisper.

"Trask," he said, "I found something. . . ." He peered over at Elverson and grew agitated. Trask glanced over his shoulder and saw that Elverson was starting to walk toward them.

"Elverson's records—" started Vaughan, but Elverson drowned him out.

"What's this shithead telling you?" asked Elverson in a loud voice as he walked up to them.

Trask shook his head. "Nothing important," he replied.

"What was it?" asked the AP, who looked inquiringly from Vaughan to Trask and back again.

Trask decided to ignore him and started to look over his M16. It was fully loaded. He cocked it again to be sure and put on the safety. No sense having the weapon go off due to a slip in the snow or some other mistake. He glanced at Vaughan, who had given up his attempt to talk to Trask out of fear of Elverson. Trask shook his head slowly. Vaughan just wouldn't stop lying.

Trask went back to Ellen, who was still excitedly checking out the aircraft.

"There's not a lot of fuel left, Frank," she said in an out-of-breath tone. "Adak is out of the question. It'll be Attu or nothing. I hope Attu's okay."

Trask nodded. "At least we'll be away from here." He glanced over his shoulder at the window. "There's a building nearby that might have some snowplows. I'm going to check it out. If it does have one, then I'll start plowing right away. I don't want to risk having to come back here."

"You only have to do a third of the runway, you know," she said. "This thing will take off in a hell of a lot less distance than one of the big jets."

Trask nodded again. "I'll plow right up to the door so you can taxi out of here. You'd better be ready. They might be shooting at me by then."

She nodded and gave him a worried look. "Be careful," she said.

Trask saw movement out of the corner of his eye and a sense of alarm flashed through him. He whirled and stared out a window at the other end of the hangar and immediately saw movement in the distance. He squinted and realized that there were several armed men around the building where they had left the truck . . . and the homing device!

"We've got company!" he said in a low, tense voice.

Ellen was next to him in a second. "Looks like your guess was right, Frank, about the homing device," she said in an equally tense voice. "I hope that building you found has a snowplow."

"We've still got a few minutes, but that's about all," he said. "They'll be over here when they find the tracks in the snow. I'd better get moving." She nodded.

He left by one of the side doors and headed straight for the building. He had relatively easy going until he left the paved portion of the ground and started to cross the tundra. He waded his way through the snow across the short stretch of spongy, uneven ground, and all the while he expected a burst of gunfire from one of the now silent buildings, or from the party they had seen at the other building. Fortunately the hangar blocked their view of him, so he wouldn't be seen until he was plowing the runway.

Thirty seconds later, he was at the edge of the building and peeking into the huge open doorway that eliminated one whole wall of the structure. A row of snowplows, with their huge V-shaped blades sticking out in front, gave the illusion of a fleet of battleships at sea.

One was slightly out in front of the row and was more snow covered than the rest. It somehow invited him, and he felt drawn to it. After a nervous glance around, he made his way toward it and hesitated behind the bulk of every snowplow in line. He climbed up to the cab and suddenly noticed the bulletholes in the windshield and the red stains on the rear window and back of the seat. His eyes instantly went to the body which had fallen over and was lying lengthwise on the seat. The air around him seemed incredibly still.

Trask swallowed once and began to search for the ignition keys. He found them soon enough. They were clenched in the dead man's fist. Trask inhaled quickly, then pried them loose and nervously stuck them into the ignition. He glanced at the body once again and decided to remove the dead man before continuing. After wrestling the body to the ground, he returned to the cab and got behind the wheel. He pushed down on the clutch pedal, gave another glance around, and held his breath as he turned the key.

The revving of the engine seemed unnaturally loud to him, and he began to sweat as the truck refused to start. The engine suddenly began to rumble on its own, but Trask pressed lightly on the accelerator anyway to keep the engine running. He took a deep breath to settle his insides and shoved the truck in gear. No sense in waiting, he thought, they'll hear the engine noise and get some people to investigate on the double.

He moved out of the garage and gunned the engine for all it was worth. The truck had chains on its wheels, multiwheel drive and every sort of traction aid he could have hoped for, but he still seemed to be crawling along. He made a right and tried to keep on what he thought were the paved portions of the ground as the snow flew on either side of him in a frenzy before the onslaught of the huge V-shaped nose of the truck. He got out to what he thought was the taxi lane and turned left to get to the end of the main runway. He squirmed around in the seat to look behind him at the hangar where Ellen and the others were hiding. All seemed quiet. He hoped that Ellen would only start the airplane's engine when he returned to the hangar area.

He reached the end of the runway, whirled the snowplow around and mashed his foot to the floor. The truck lurched ahead reluctantly and soon his vision was totally obscured by flying snow. How wide a path did he have to make? He never thought to ask Ellen. Once up and once back would have to do. He wouldn't have any more time than that, if he had that much.

The truck groaned and scraped along at an agonizingly slow pace and Trask held his breath waiting for the first sounds of gunfire.

CHAPTER 18

Douglas Meyers had been trying for several hours to put together a briefing on the Shemya incident for his boss, the deputy director of Central Intelligence. As the deputy director for operations, Meyers had a crucial role in the crisis. One of his department's agents, Blue Fox, was on Shemya and had sent that cryptic message over an unauthorized channel. He had the words memorized.

ALPHA, BRAVO, VICTOR, DELTA, SEVEN, ONE, NINE
READER HITS THE SKIDS AFTER GOING TO THE POST.
BLUE FOX

The meaning of the message was derived from its entirety, not from a decoding of each letter or word. The phrases were memorized in case a code book was unavailable. Blue Fox had probably picked one from memory that most closely fit the situation. The message's meaning was: *Heavy enemy agent activity. Company agent requests assistance.*

The problem with the phrases was that tone and especially urgency were missing from the meaning. The Company had tried to make up for that with more phrases, but that just exacerbated the problem of memorizing a larger number of phrases. Blue Fox could have been under great

181

duress and just picked a phrase that came to mind. That kind of thing happened all the time.

Meyers grunted and smiled to himself. Blue Fox. His agent's code name was taken from the only indigenous animal species on Shemya, the blue fox. He briefly wondered what his agent was doing at the moment. Meyers could, if he probed his organization deeply enough, find out the identity of Blue Fox, but there would be no point to it—the information would do him no good whatsoever. It might even hinder the decision process. Meyers didn't have to know the identity of the agent, but he did have to know the capability of Blue Fox, in case this agent would have to depart from his or her charted course of action.

Meyers reviewed the file on Blue Fox in his mind. Just before the coup attempt in the then Soviet Union during August 1991, a defector had revealed that a Russian sleeper agent had been smuggled into the United States from Canada. Due to the covert nature of the defector—the Russians thought that he had been killed in an accident—the CIA elected to attempt to find the sleeper, code-named Vulcher, themselves rather than turn the effort over to the FBI. Blue Fox had been assigned and had trailed the sleeper for several years while never knowing his real identity or what he looked like.

Then the accommodation with the Russians occurred and sleeper teams all over the United States were being deactivated. Blue Fox had eventually caught up with Vulcher just as he was to be deactivated. But then something had gone wrong.

Blue Fox had been in on that horrendous shootout when the SVR control agent was killed and Meyers had lost a valuable agent, both killed by Vulcher. Now they had a renegade SVR agent on their hands who was also probably in control of his former control agent's network. The identity of the remainder of the network was still a mystery. The SVR stonewalled on all the CIA requests for details. They had wanted to take Blue Fox, in light of the agent's wounds, off the case, but the agent would have none of it and had insisted to be kept in charge. And then Blue Fox followed Vulcher to Shemya.

Meyers sighed and let his eyes randomly wander over the desk top. What did Blue Fox mean by "heavy enemy agent activity"? If Blue Fox needed help, then he or she wouldn't have long to wait. Two helicopters with marines had just lifted off for Shemya from Adak Naval Station, farther up the Aleutian chain. In a few hours they would have results from that survey team and know the fate of Shemya.

Meyers turned his thoughts back to his briefing and soon was totally engrossed in preparing his presentation. There was a noise at the door to his office. Meyers looked up in irritation as one of his subordinates burst into his office. His assistant was holding a piece of paper in his hand and had a concerned look on his face. The man stopped in front of Meyers's desk and leaned over with his hands on the desk top. The paper must be the text of the message they were all waiting for from the chief of station, Kiev. The DDO had the feeling the news wasn't good. His subordinate took a deep breath to settle himself before speaking.

"Well, we've found out what Mission one-four-one Delta is," said Meyers's assistant.

NATIONAL MILITARY COMMAND CENTER
THE PENTAGON

General Gerald Brumbaugh had just settled down into his watch routine as command duty officer when one of the myriad phones on his desk rang. The ring itself didn't give away any urgency—it was the same ring he had heard in countless other similar situations. The phone was color-coded black, thereby conveying the heavy significance of the person on the other end of the line. Brumbaugh raised his eyebrows and hurriedly picked up the receiver.

"CDO, General Brum—" he began to say.

"General, this is the deputy director of operations for the CIA. Has the marine force from Adak lifted off for Shemya yet?" said Meyers in a hastened tone.

Brumbaugh had just finished his ongoing watch briefing from the off-going command duty officer. The situation on Shemya was the chief topic of the briefing.

"Yes, they lifted off about three hours ago," said Brumbaugh.

"General, you've got to recall them immediately," said Meyers in a loud voice.

Brumbaugh waited for an explanation. After a few seconds he said, "I presume you're going to tell me why."

"General, they could be flying into a trap," said Meyers.

TWENTY MILES SOUTHEAST OF SHEMYA

The two CH-53E Super Stallion helicopters flew just under the cloud cover of 250 feet as they raced over the North Pacific toward their rendezvous with Shemya Island. Half an hour ago, they had flown over Buldir Island, which they used as a navigation point, and the helicopter crews knew that their destination lay only eighty miles to the northwest. The lack of any TACAN signals from Shemya complicated their navigation problem, and the crews breathed a sigh of relief when sighting Buldir Island. The ten marines in each helicopter began to get ready.

Captain Bob Supplee, United States Marine Corps, looked over his men and silently shook his head. He knew when he joined the corps to expect the unexpected, but this had taken him by surprise. His unit was the Naval Security Group Activity, called Company I, based on Adak and involved in fleet communications, and he had only thirty-seven troopers in the unit. The helicopters had been borrowed from a marine unit that was taking cold weather training in Alaska.

His thoughts turned to the Christmas season, the smell of the Christmas tree, and the delight in the eyes of his two-year-old son as he played with his toys. He saved thoughts of his wife for quiet moments when he could linger over them and savor them as long as possible. Captain Supplee hadn't had a quiet moment since he was ordered on this survey mission to Shemya.

What would they find on this island the size of a pinhead in the middle of nowhere? He knew that communications with the island had been interrupted, and that some calamity might have struck the island's occupants. Other than that, he, and everyone else at Adak Naval Air Station, knew nothing.

He glanced at his watch. ETA in about two minutes. If the weather was clear, they would have been able to see the island on the horizon. As it was, they would come upon the island suddenly, a fact that further contributed to Supplee's discomfort. He looked over his men again. They were sitting on canvas seats along the side walls and all looked expectantly at their company commander. Rather than shout over the drumming of the rotor blades, Supplee held up two fingers to indicate how much time they had left.

Supplee stood and stretched, then leaned through the doorway to the flight deck where the three-man crew was seated. The copilot was trying to raise the Shemya operations building without success.

"Shemya Tower, this is Black Gang. We are two helicopter aircraft from Adak Naval Air Station. We are approaching you from the southeast. Request clearance to land. Over." He tried a few more times, then gave Supplee a shrug.

The flight engineer saw Supplee in the doorway and pointed to the fuel gauge. It showed that they had less than half remaining. The tanks had been topped off just before they lifted off. Before they left Adak, the crew had said that if they couldn't get fuel on Shemya, then it would be a one-way trip. The fuel gauge confirmed it. More discomfort, thought Supplee.

Suddenly the island of Shemya burst into view. The ceiling was higher over the island, about eight hundred feet, and it allowed an almost unbroken view of the entire island. The nearness of the island gave Supplee a chill, but he shook it off.

"There's a hopeful sign," said the copilot. He pointed to the end of the runway nearest them. "They're starting to plow it."

Supplee craned his neck to see the large snowplow throwing two huge plumes of snow to each side as it barreled down the runway. The snowplow seemed in a hurry. Another strange aspect to this situation, he thought.

"Captain, shall we wait until they get part of the runway clear?" asked the copilot.

Supplee shook his head. "Negative. We go in as planned." The copilot nodded and radioed the decision to the other helo.

Supplee's eyes automatically went to the airstrip that was outlined by different levels of snow among the drifts. The plan was to set down as close as they could to the operations building, which doubled as the airfield tower. Normally the marines would jump into the snow with their gear, then move several yards away and huddle over their gear, an "ahkio huddle," named after the ahkio sleds they used. They would link up their arms to protect themselves from the whiteout and the icy blast from the helicopter rotors, then move off when their leader gave them the sign. With a thumbs-up sign from the team leader, the helicopter would take off.

Not knowing what to expect, Supplee had modified the procedure to establish a defensive perimeter immediately around the helicopter after he and his men exited the helo via the rear loading ramp. They would then quickly take up positions around the building and proceed to check it out. The other helicopter would fly cover for them.

Supplee turned to his men. He shouted over the rotor noise for his men to take unloading positions.

Trask gradually drew abreast of the operations building, which was beyond the runway across a narrow stretch of tundra at one end of the plane parking strip, and he stared at the windows through the cloud of snow that was kicked up by the plow to see if anyone had noticed him. It was a ridiculous thought. If they were awake, they would have seen him by now. Could they be sleeping? Even more ridiculous. Why hadn't they fired on him? Maybe Ellen was right, maybe they thought that someone had ordered the plowing of the runway. Maybe they thought Driscoll ordered it done and hadn't told them. They would be checking now, lifting the phone . . .

Trask thought he saw the flash of a face in one of the windows and instantly decided to turn the plow around to widen the path on his way back to the hangar. The truck slewed about as he kept his foot to the floor, but he finally got it straightened out and back on the path he had just beaten through the snow. It wasn't the straightest path he had ever seen, but he thought it straight enough for Ellen to get them airborne. He glanced back at the tower and still didn't see any activity.

Trask's thoughts turned to the enemy party that was at the other building. Certainly they had heard and seen the snowplow by now and were coming to investigate. He cursed the apparent slowness of the huge lumbering truck and pounded on the steering wheel in frustration. He glanced wildly about and still didn't detect any activity.

He eventually reached the end of the runway after what seemed to be an interminable length of time and threw the snowplow into a violent left-hand turn. The truck went wide in the turn until he finally straightened it out. He looked behind him and saw that there were two narrow paths instead of one wide lane. He hoped Ellen could get through it to the main runway. There was no turning back; it was probably only a matter of seconds before the SVR tried to stop him.

Trask rumbled down the taxi lane and past the garage, and started to forge a new path from the garage to the hangar that Ellen and the others were in. A new thought struck him and his heart sank. He would have to plow in the reverse direction from the hangar to the garage in order to get a wide enough lane in the snow for the plane. That meant that he would only be able to get into the plane at the garage. More delay. He bit his lip and tried to push the accelerator farther down into the floor.

The thrumming sound of helicopter rotors suddenly filled the air, penetrating through the roar of the truck's engine. Trask squirmed around in the seat to see where it was coming from.

Captain Supplee's helicopter slowed its descent as it approached the ops building. The aircraft fuselage was oriented at an angle to the building, so that Supplee could watch the building for activity out a side window and also have the rear loading ramp away from the building. After they landed, his men could unload with the body of the helicopter between them and the building. It would shield them from any weapons fire.

The aircraft was one hundred feet off the ground when Supplee spotted movement at the far edge of the building. He wasn't alarmed until a man walked into full view. He carried on his shoulder a contraption that looked like a bazooka. It was a boxlike enclosure which had a five-foot-long, round tube sticking out the back. Supplee recognized it immediately.

Stinger!

Supplee turned to shout a warning just as an elongated flash came from the stubby front barrel of the weapon. Supplee had just enough time to leap to the other side of the cabin when the missile hit. The missile covered its short flight distance in less than two seconds and homed in on the large turbine exhaust pod on the side of the helicopter nearest the ops building. The warhead exploded, shattering the entire right side of the helicopter and taking five of the seven rotor blades with it.

The helicopter, with half the marines inside it already dead, rolled to its right and dropped like a stone. The two remaining rotor blades flailed away at the air in a futile attempt to keep the aircraft aloft. The helicopter slammed into the parking area tarmac at an awkward angle and nearly rolled completely over from one side to the other. The rotors hacked themselves to pieces as they struck the unyielding asphalt.

The helicopter lay on its top with fumes from its fuel gathering about it, enshrouding it in imminent danger. Miraculously, Captain Supplee and two others crawled away from the wreckage in a frenzy driven by panic. The fumes ignited with a thump, and the fuel tanks exploded a second later, dousing one of Supplee's survivors with flaming JP-5.

A chill ran through Trask as he saw the two huge helicopters approach the ops building. The sides of the helicopters had "U.S. Marines" painted on them. *The Marines are landing!* The thrill that that expression gave him was indescribable. The U.S. Marines were the finest fighting force on the face of the earth, and it was they who were coming to help him.

Trask slowed the snowplow to a crawl as he watched the lead helicopter approach the parking area in front of the ops building. The aircraft suddenly exploded and dropped to the earth, the thunderous sound rolling across the frozen land unimpeded until it reached Trask. He gaped at it for a moment, his mind stopped at the horror that lay before him.

His mind suddenly clicked into gear, and he whirled around to face the roadway while his right foot slammed the accelerator pedal to the floor. *How many marines had just died?*

Supplee squirmed around in the two feet of snow on the tarmac and managed to put out the flames that had engulfed his man. He had to use only his right arm—his left arm was numb. He looked about in terror. Most of his men had died in the last ten seconds. The helicopter wreckage was totally involved in flames—no one else had gotten out except the three of them. The intense heat quickly melted the wet snow with the resulting water boiling near the wreckage.

Supplee looked over the man he had just saved from the flames. He was obviously in shock and wouldn't last long in that condition. Supplee got to his hands and knees and gasped as pain shot through his left arm. Must be broken, he thought. He put his left hand in a pocket of the winter weather gear he was wearing, and began to slide across the ground toward the other survivor.

In a few seconds he was there, giving words of encouragement to his man, who was in agony. The man kept his legs unnaturally still and Supplee immediately saw that both his legs were broken.

The thumping noise of helicopter rotor blades came through the roar of the flaming wreck beside him. Supplee looked up and saw the second helicopter heading toward the open ocean away from the ops building. The marine captain knew they weren't running away but just maneuvering out to approach the island from a different angle. One thought hit him immediately. *No chaff! No flares! No decoys!* They had departed in a hurry—they didn't have time to load them. And now my men are paying the price, he thought, and savagely bit his lip.

A frenzied rushing sound off to his left made him turn his head, but the burning wreckage blocked his view. When he turned back to the other helicopter, he saw a fragile trail of smoke rapidly approach the Super Stallion. He instantly knew what it was, the horror of it seemingly crushing his chest.

The second helo was out over the water and making a turn to approach the island from the northeast when the missile hit. The missile seemed to go through the aircraft, taking a big chunk of the helo with it. There was a brief explosion engulfing the fuselage in smoke and flame. The helicopter with ten of Supplee's precious men was transformed into a ball of flame with a tail section protruding from it. The whole mass wobbled out of control and fell to the sea. The thirty-thousand-pound helicopter hit the thirty-degree water and immediately sank, dragging the few survivors of the explosion with it.

The enormous splash in the distance told Supplee that his men were gone.

CHAPTER 19

As Trask approached the hangar, he noticed that the massive door was open with the plane's propeller whirring and sending up a small cloud of dust within. Trask instinctively glanced in the direction of the other building, where they had left their truck, and his heart froze. Some of the SVR party were pointing in his direction, while others were running back toward their truck. In less than a minute they would be headed in his direction.

He pulled up next to the open hangar door and whirled the truck in a U-turn while Ellen gunned the engine to bring the plane out. Trask followed his path back toward the garage with Ellen anxiously keeping the plane only a few feet behind him. He pulled up to the garage and leaped out of the snowplow while it was still moving and ran breathlessly toward the slowly moving plane. He looked back the way they had come and saw that the SVR truck was headed toward them at a high rate of speed and was terrifyingly close. Trask put out every ounce of energy he had left and sprinted the remaining few yards faster than he thought possible.

Trask leaped onto the wing and got a hold of the leading edge to hang on. Ellen gunned the engine, and the plane jerked ahead, causing Trask to loosen his grip and almost fall off. He got a good grip on the door handle, adjusted for the increasing wind and pulled the door open. Trask hopped into the seat next to Ellen and glanced at Elverson and Vaughan in the rear. He looked toward Ellen, and, with the enemy truck visible in his peripheral vision through the side window, he watched her grimace as she tried to get as much speed out of the plane as possible. A glance out the window at the rapidly moving truck told him that it would be close, very close. It was all up to Ellen now.

A shadow seemed to pass over them. They all instinctively glanced up and saw the marine helicopter race out to sea and meet its quick death at the hands of another Stinger missile.

"Marines!" gasped Trask, who was out of breath. "That's two that got shot down! They're launching missiles from somewhere."

Ellen gaped at him uncomprehendingly. "Maybe we should stop if they're coming to rescue us."

"No! We've got no choice now! Keep going!" wheezed Trask. He glanced to the rear. "They'll be on us in a second!"

Ellen swallowed hard and jammed the throttle forward.

The U.S. Marines had always been, in Trask's mind, the ultimate fighting force, the best in the world. When he had first seen the word *Marines* on the sides of the helicopters, he thought that no one could stop them from being rescued. The U.S. Marines were invincible, weren't they? The phrase "The Marines have landed" carried a myriad of thoughts and emotions along with it. Reassurance that everything would be all right and a much needed boost in a man's gut were only two of the reactions that the phrase engendered. Hope had blazed brightly, but briefly.

As high as Trask's emotions were knowing that marines were going to land, that is how low they fell when he saw both helicopters go down in flames. If these enemy agents could defeat the invincible so easily, then what chance did he and the others have? A kid, a woman, and a drunk would try to do something the U.S. Marines couldn't do. He gave Ellen a sideways glance. He didn't know about the kid or especially the drunk, but this was some kind of woman.

They were on the taxi lane with the pursuing truck driving on a road that was behind them and at a right angle to the lane. The truck hit a snowdrift and slowed perceptibly. Hope shot up in them as they approached the end of the taxi lane and made the right turn to get to the main runway.

Ellen saw the plowed lane split into two narrow ones and her mouth dropped open.

"What the hell is this?" she said. The plane slowed a bit.

"Don't ask! Just gun it!" shouted Trask.

Ellen complied and the plane picked up speed. "I hope we don't snap the landing gear!" she shouted over the engine noise.

Trask glanced to the rear and saw the truck pop out of the snowdrift and rapidly pick up speed. The truck left the road and began to bounce over the tundra in an effort to cut them off. The plane hit the snow and suddenly slowed as Ellen worked the rudder to keep a more or less straight heading, then picked up speed as Ellen got them past Trask's abortive turn. She swung the Warrior around and gave it all the throttle it would take.

"I hope it's warmed up enough! We could stall!" she shouted.

"Got no choice!" yelled Trask, and he looked out the window on his side to see that their pursuers were just crossing the taxi lane at a right angle and were evidently trying to get in front of them to prevent their takeoff. He judged their own speed and his heart went into his throat. He and his companions wouldn't make it.

Trask looked wildly about. He had left his M16 in the snowplow! He found Ellen's under the seat and got ready for a gunfight when the truck would cut them off. Ellen never slowed but continued to pick up speed as she nervously eyed the truck on its collision course with them. The truck crossed the taxi lane and hit the short stretch of tundra next to the main runway.

Trask's mind froze in a desperate prayer as he simultaneously felt the lift building on the wings and saw the truck bounce over the unpaved ground. *Please God . . .*

The response to his prayer was faster and surer than he could have imagined. The truck bounced, slewed around and skidded to a stop. In a flash of realization Trask knew that their pursuers were stuck in the snow.

He experienced a second of exultation until he saw that they were rapidly approaching the end of his plowed path.

If they hit the snow at this speed . . . He left the thought unfinished and shot a look at Ellen. She was grim-faced and going for broke.

The plane lifted a bit into the air and seemed too tentative, then bounced on the ground and swooped into the air with authority, only a few feet in front of the rest of the unplowed runway.

They were airborne! He gave a shout of exultation and looked at Ellen with admiration. She had done it! Ellen let out a sigh with raised eyebrows and then grinned. Trask grinned back and looked out his window at the truck that was rapidly falling below them as they gained altitude. His gaze swept over the terrain past the burning helicopter wreckage and the ops building until his brain registered a flash of warning. His eyes darted back to the building as he quickly recognized the danger. There was a man on the side of the ops building pointing a shoulder-fired missile launcher at them! That was how the marine helicopters were shot down!

He could only sit and gape at him—he felt totally helpless. An idea hit him like a thunderbolt. Stingers were heat seekers—if he had a heat source, he could possibly decoy the missile. He rummaged around the cabin in a frenzy for anything he could use.

"What's the matter?" asked Ellen over the engine noise. He could only grunt in return.

Trask spotted a flash of red near his feet. It was a sign with the word *Emergency* over a small compartment. He ripped open the door and reached inside. His hand closed around a flare gun. He tore it from its mounting and took out one of only two flares that were in the compartment. He broke open the gun and loaded the cylindrical flare into the breech of the pistol and snapped it shut. Trask yanked open the small rectangular window and turned to Ellen, who was looking at him as if he had lost his mind.

"Throttle back when I tell you!" he shouted.

Ellen shook her head. "Why?"

"Stinger!" The one word from Trask snapped Ellen almost to attention. She nodded furiously in instant agreement with him.

Trask squirmed around in the seat and stuck the flare gun through the small opening. He looked back at the enemy agent who had the Stinger on his shoulder. Trask extended his right arm with the flare gun in his hand as far as he could and suddenly wondered how he should fire it at the missile. Fire it straight at the missile or fire it behind the plane? Or maybe straight up?

A second later he saw a puff of smoke and the missile fly away from the launcher. It flew toward them at a horrifying speed. He made an instant decision and fired the flare straight at the nose of the missile. The flare shot out away from the plane.

"Now!" yelled Trask at the top of his voice. Ellen immediately yanked back on the throttle. The aircraft slowed quickly as Trask watched the trajectory of the flare curve behind the plane and toward the ground. Trask kept his eyes riveted on the missile.

The aircraft's stall warning alarm went off. Someone behind him said, "Oh, shit!"

Trask held his breath as the missile bore on straight at them, then suddenly curved toward the flare. The missile fell harmlessly below and behind them, seduced by Trask's improvised heat source. He let his breath out in an explosive gasp. He grabbed Ellen by the arm. "Go! Go!"

Ellen shoved the throttles forward and the plane picked up speed. The alarm shut off and everyone breathed easier.

Trask stared back at the agents on the ground and his mind froze. He now saw a second man behind the first with something that looked like a long tube in his hands. It was another missile! They were reloading the launcher! A second missile would be headed toward them in seconds!

"Another Stinger!" yelled Trask as he reached down for the second flare. He tried to yank it out of the compartment but caught the edge of the flare cartridge on the compartment lip and it popped out of his hand. The cartridge rolled out of sight under his seat. Trask tore off his seat belt and was after it in a second.

* * *

Captain Supplee quickly got past the shock of seeing his men die in the second helicopter. Fury filled him and he searched for a way to get back at the island's killers.

The sound of a small plane's engine a moment ago had been lost amid the crackling of the flames that were rapidly consuming the helicopter wreckage. The aircraft had taken off on the runway to his left but was completely ignored by Supplee in the confusion and shock of the attack on his men. He had no idea who was on the plane and, at the moment, didn't care.

Supplee slid along the ground, ignoring the intense pain that shot through his left arm, and got around the fiery wreckage that moments before had been a proud U.S. Marine helicopter with ten of his men aboard. He reached inside his white outer weather gear and unsnapped the holster on his right side. Supplee withdrew the automatic and attempted to point it past the wreckage of the helicopter in the direction of the enemy agent.

Supplee's hand shook as he tried to steady the barrel in the enemy agent's direction. The pistol felt like a ton of lead—his hand wavered and fell. He sighed in exhaustion and started to look around for something to prop up his hand so he could fire at this enemy agent who had so quickly murdered virtually all of his men.

Supplee scrambled over nearer to the wreckage and plucked a ragged piece of sheet metal from the inferno. Out of the corner of his eye, he could see the agent launch the first missile; its intended target was beyond Supplee's vision. He didn't care who was the target—he saw only a chance to take revenge on the person who had killed his men without warning.

Supplee glanced up just as a gust of wind blew a cloud of snow into the air. When the snow settled down, Supplee could see two agents, one with the launcher on his shoulder, and one with a launch tube with a missile inside it in his hands ready to reload the launcher. Supplee got the hot piece of metal into position in front of him, with the surrounding snow rapidly melting and causing curls of steam that were immediately carried away by the freshening wind.

He propped his wrist on the top edge, but the metal edge was sharp and it immediately cut through his glove and into his flesh.

Supplee ignored the pain in his right hand and steadied the sights on the agent with the launcher. He lined up the fluorescent dots on the front and back sights and began firing, the weapon jumping with each shot. The first two shots missed, the third hit the missile launcher, the fourth smashed into the agent's face, and the fifth hit him in the left shoulder.

Supplee grimly slammed his wrist back down on the sharp metal and kept firing as he swept his aim across the second agent's body. After again missing twice, Supplee put three slugs in succession into the second agent's chest. Supplee fired twice more, almost by habit, but both bullets missed everything.

Trask expected the missile any second, and time seemed to slow down for him as he frantically searched under the seat for the flare. His hand finally closed around it, and he struggled to get back up in his seat. After what seemed like an eternity, he got upright again and quickly reloaded the flare gun.

Trask again stuck the flare gun out the window and pointed it toward the ground. His eyes finally focused on the two agents with their Stinger launcher, but incredibly, they were lying on the ground!

What had happened? Trask's mind raced. Someone or something had taken them out. He yanked his arm back inside the cabin and slammed the window shut. Trask was about to congratulate himself for escaping the island when he caught movement in his peripheral vision. His eyes flicked over to the truck that had been pursuing them. Enemy agents were now standing next to the vehicle and were pointing automatic weapons at Trask's fleeing aircraft.

Flashes of fire erupted from the tips of their weapons and he heard dull cracking over the roar of the plane's engine. In a few seconds we'll be away, he thought. They won't be able to touch us.

A few other sounds made it to him and he disregarded

them one by one, until one sound seemed to be in perfect rhythm with the muzzle flashes. A split second later he knew that bullets were smashing into the aircraft.

Trask froze with fear. He sat helpless and could do nothing as he lived in terror of the bullet that would smash into him and take his life. Things began to happen rapidly.

A burst from the men below hit the side of the aircraft with a horrifying rapidity of sound like the ripping of a large canvas. There seemed to be an explosion of sound behind him. Vaughan grunted in pain.

The window on Trask's right side took most of the blast, sending bullet fragments into his face and body.

Ellen screamed.

Trask recoiled violently from the blast and held his head below the dashboard to keep it out of danger and away from the wind. He slowly took stock by passing his hands over his face and letting the pain register in his mind. He had several cuts on his face, but otherwise he was all right. After cautiously opening his eyes, he found that his left eye could open only halfway due to a piece of metal stuck in his eyebrow. With shaking hands he pulled it out and pressed down with his fingers to stop the bleeding.

Elverson leaned over Vaughan and pointed his M16 out the smashed window and opened up on the men on the ground.

Trask suddenly realized he couldn't hear the plane's engine. The only sound between the cracking of Elverson's M16 was the wind whistling past the rapidly slowing aircraft. Elverson's weapon fell silent as he also realized the plane's engine had stopped. Trask looked at Ellen in shock.

"What is it?" screamed Trask.

She kept looking forward and had fear in her normally beautiful features. She shook her head. "They might have hit a fuel line or maybe it stalled—I don't know!" she said.

"Start it!" yelled Elverson from the rear seat.

"*I CAN'T!*" She was nearly crying.

Trask's breath came in short gasps as he looked about in desperation. He stared up ahead and saw nothing but small lakes and he began to panic. They couldn't land there! They had to go beyond the lakes! He strained his eyes but couldn't make out the terrain past the lakes. Beyond them was the leading edge of a rapidly moving snowstorm that was going to sweep the island. It was on him in a flash.

"The old airport!" he shouted. "We've got to make it to the old airport!"

Ellen shook her head. "Not enough airspeed!" she shouted.

"We'll make it!" said Trask hopefully.

The plane's upward momentum slowed and stopped, and the plane began to glide downwards, slowly at first, then with ever increasing speed. Ellen suppressed the panic within her and took one hand off the yoke to hit the starter. The prop turned over rapidly as Ellen pumped the starter, but the engine remained silent. It was no use.

"Must be a fuel line," she yelled over the increasing noise of the wind.

Trask saw that they were out over the lakes, but they were descending at a very rapid rate. How long could they stay in the air?

The old runway appeared at the edge of the mist in the distance. It wasn't in line with the new airport runway—the old runway was at a 45 degree angle to the new one.

"You'll have to make a turn to the left," he yelled to Ellen.

She shook her head. "Not enough altitude."

"Try it anyway."

She shook her head a second time. "What about the snow on the runway?"

"It'll cushion our landing," replied Trask.

"We'll flip over!" she shouted.

Trask fixed his eyes on the old runway and held the rapidly rising ground at the edge of his vision. They were low, too low, and he knew they were not going to make it.

The last lake rolled by on their left and the abandoned buildings and hangars of the old airstrip were directly in front of them. Ellen tried her best to keep enough altitude above the buildings and they nearly cleared the buildings.

The landing gear hit the peak of the roof of one building and canted the wings over at an awkward angle. The land-

ing struts snapped off, leaving the rest of the aircraft to
continue on until the tip of the lowest wing hit the snow
on the runway. The wing immediately slowed down, with
the rest of the plane swinging around violently, resulting in
an end-for-end whirling motion of the entire aircraft.

The plane destroyed itself quickly with deafening rend-
ing and crashing sounds. Trask heard the cockpit disinte-
grate around him as the white-covered ground rushed up at
him from an unexpected angle and he lost consciousness.

CHAPTER 20

Captain Bob Supplee groaned and heaved himself up on his knees and right hand; his left hand was still in his pocket. His left arm hurt ferociously, and the pain in his right wrist was beginning to get to him as well. So, he thought, I've taken out two of the enemy, whoever they are, after losing twenty of my men. He snorted in disgust. What the hell kind of ratio is that?

He jerked himself upright and waited until the shooting pain in his broken arm subsided a bit, then made the supreme effort to get himself on his feet. He stood and swayed for a moment and thought he was going to fall, but then the dizziness gradually diminished and he took his first hard look around.

The small plane had disappeared into the wall of an advancing storm that was now sweeping the western end of the island. Who were they? Survivors of some attack? Is that why the men with the Stinger wanted to shoot them down? And who were those killers? He had heard some small arms fire—like multiple M16s—from close by. Had someone else tried to shoot down the plane? Supplee shook his head and looked down the runway again.

The fuzzy white edge of the storm headed toward him at about thirty miles an hour. In a minute or two it'll be here, Supplee thought, and I won't be able to see shit. The wind picked up at that moment and sent a cloud of already fallen snow blasting by him. I have to get my men to shelter. Can't leave them out here during a blizzard. How will I transport them? And where is there shelter?

"Got to get moving," he groaned out loud to himself. Suddenly voices came to him from behind the burning helicopter wreckage. Supplee dropped to a crouch and held his automatic out in front of him. He glanced at the weapon he still held in his right hand. How many shots left? The magazine held fifteen rounds and he had used quite a few just to kill the two men with the Stinger launcher. He searched his waist for another clip, but there was none. The force of the crash had shredded his clothes and scattered his extra sidearm clips.

He looked about in a panic. The man with the broken legs had a bag of grenades that were to be used with a grenade launcher—if only he could find one. Supplee got the grenade bag from his wounded man and scrambled about searching the debris from the helicopter while simultaneously keeping an eye out for the owners of the voices. He started to circle the wreckage on his knees and his right hand until he glimpsed the back of three men. He stopped and quickly retreated. The men were fortunately headed around the other side of the helicopter wreckage to determine the fate of the Stinger crew.

It won't be long before they put two and two together and come looking for me, thought Supplee. He moved forward cautiously and knelt on something under the snow. He brushed the snow aside and couldn't believe his luck when he saw it was the sought-after grenade launcher. The grenade launcher looked like a sawed-off shotgun with a very large bore. Supplee quickly got as much snow out of the barrel as possible, broke open the breech, and loaded it with a grenade from the bag.

Supplee snapped the grenade launcher shut and settled down on his back in the snow to keep as low a profile as possible. He dug the stock of the grenade launcher into the snow and held it with his right hand while propping the barrel up on his right knee. If anyone looked in his direction they might think that he was just another lump of debris from the wreckage.

He took a careful look around and spotted a truck to his right near the eastern end of the runway. Okay, he thought, that answers the question of transportation. The only thing was that the damn truck was out in the open, and he'd get cut down in a second by the three men who were on the other side of the wreckage.

Supplee suddenly was hit with the thought that the men might go around the wreckage and see his two wounded men on the other side. These killers would shoot them without a second thought. He began to inch sideways to his right to see if he could spot the three men again. He slid about ten feet when the men suddenly came into view. They were running directly at him!

Supplee didn't hesitate. He squeezed the trigger of the grenade launcher and the weapon jumped into life, sending a grenade in the enemy's direction. He immediately put it between his knees and put another round into the breech of the grenade launcher with his one good hand. Then he got set to send another grenade in their direction.

The men, who hadn't seen Supplee yet, spotted the movement in the snow beyond and began to point in the marine's direction when the first grenade went off behind them. One man fell dying, but the other two hit the ground and brought their M16s up to fire.

Supplee raised the barrel a fraction and launched a second grenade in their direction, then rolled frantically to his left. He screamed out loud as he rolled on top of his broken left arm, then gritted his teeth and kept rolling until he was on his back again. Seconds later he could hear the staccato cracking of the M16s as they opened up on him. Several bullets whizzed by his right ear just before the thump of the second grenade shook the ground underneath him.

The blizzard finally reached him and hit with a vengeance, reducing visibility to zero.

1530 HOURS, EASTERN STANDARD TIME, 26 DECEMBER CIA HEADQUARTERS, LANGLEY, VIRGINIA

Douglas Meyers irritably picked up the phone. He had just gotten done his briefing for the DCI on the Shemya business and was working on organizing the people who would work the list of action items that resulted, when he was interrupted by the phone.

"DDO," he said into the handset.

"Sir, we have a Russian General Vladimir Fedorovich Iskanderov on the line for you. Voice print analysis confirms his identity," said an anonymous voice from the communications department.

Meyers instantly forgot about the briefing action items. "Yes, put him on immediately." Meyers heard a click and a buzz that went away a second later to be replaced by low-level background noise.

"Douglas Meyers?" asked a heavily accented voice.

"Yes. General Iskanderov?"

"*Da*. What we will discuss should be for our ears only," said Iskanderov in near-perfect English.

"I agree, General," replied Meyers. He poised a finger over a red button on the box below his phone. "I'm going to scramble . . . now." Meyers pushed the button, which lit a red pilot light with the word *scrambled* below it. The background noise changed in tone and lowered in volume somewhat. When Iskanderov talked, he sounded farther away than normal.

"Douglas, you must understand that we know about the situation on Shemya," said Iskanderov.

"Really? How—"

"Let us not play games with each other. The time for that is past. We must work together now and solve this terrible problem," said Iskanderov quickly.

"Why would you want to help us solve one of our problems? Don't you have enough of your own?" asked Meyers facetiously.

"This problem is a Russian problem!" snapped Iskanderov, his patience waning.

"Just how is tha—"

"These are Russian agents that have taken over Shemya!" thundered Iskanderov.

Meyers's mouth popped open in surprise. The director of the SVR was admitting the failure of his organization. The time for playing games really *was* past. Iskanderov went on in an effort to get in an apology quickly.

"This was an undeactivated sleeper team that thought your drill was a real attack. This was a terrible mistake, you must know that. Should this get out, the consequences would be devastating," continued the Russian general.

"For who? The United States or the Russian government?" said Meyers. He couldn't keep the sarcasm out of his voice.

"There are elements of the old hard-line Communist structure left in Russia and, among certain segments of the population, they enjoy a great popularity. Along with these ultranationalists, who want to put the Soviet Union back together again, they form a formidable political force. We saw that during the recent elections in December of 1993," Iskanderov stated flatly. "Should aid from the United States be cut off, the resulting chaos would give them the opportunity to take over once again. That would mean a return to the Cold War."

"What the hell is this, General? You're blackmailing us after attacking one of our air force bases? Are you nuts?" Meyers's temper was just barely in check.

"No! Douglas, listen to me!" implored Iskanderov. "What would the American people's reaction be to this situation? They would demand a cutoff of aid to Russia—"

It was Meyers's turn to interrupt. "Just who or what are these hard-line elements you're talking about? You've got to be more specific, General."

"The Nationalists may form a coalition with some of the old Communists. You've seen the demonstrations in Moscow. You know that they enjoy great popularity with the military and many of the people," said Iskanderov.

"Are you telling me they're strong enough to seize power?" Meyers shot back. The only group showing those tendencies was the GRU, he thought. Now *that* might be believable.

"Yes, we believe so. I—"

"Then you've got to give us something more to go on than that," said Meyers. He was giving Iskanderov a hard time, but he got a cold feeling. Iskanderov knew his people better than anyone, including the CIA. *Especially* the CIA, he added.

"We will gather the required information and I will get back to you," said Iskanderov in a resigned tone.

"And you'll give us all the details of this Mission one-four-one Delta?" Meyers bit his tongue at the slip. He hadn't wanted to let the SVR know that the CIA had information on the mission.

There was a hesitation on the line. Meyers was sure Iskanderov had caught Meyers's mistake. Now the general knew that their communications system had a leak. He might have suspected, but to have it confirmed by a high CIA official was something else. Meyers felt like banging his head on his desk.

"It will be done," said Iskanderov in a low voice.

John Goldblum, the director of Central Intelligence, was coming to the close of his fifteen-minute review of a National Security Council briefing held just an hour ago.

"So it's been decided that we'll keep the lid on this thing for the moment. This General Iskanderov could be right about another coup attempt. The feeling in the White House and in the Pentagon is that we've backed off in our defense posture so much by this time that we can't afford to have a resurgence of the old Soviet threat. We're going to play it by ear, but we should prepare plans for a cover story."

Meyers nodded absentmindedly. He had expected this. "I've got an idea. The marines are preparing to hit Shemya again with a much larger force after losing contact with their first two helicopters. We should delay them until we can get some of our own people up there to control things. We might also think about keeping the marine contingent as small as possible. If we do have to cover up and make it stick for a long time, then the least number of people that know about this, the better."

Goldblum nodded. "Agreed. I'll get back to the Security Council with the recommendation." He turned as if to dismiss Meyers, then he turned back again with a thoughtful expression on his face. "Our agent on Shemya—any word?"

Meyers shook his head. "No, sir. Nothing other than that one message." His thoughts ran on.

Where was Blue Fox? Was their agent still alive?

CHAPTER 21

The world came back to Trask slowly as he felt the mists retreat from his senses and the normal sensations begin to return. The mists would part briefly, allowing him a glimpse of consciousness, then close in again as if reluctant to allow him more than a glimmer of the outside world. Sensations hit him one at a time, a glimpse of cold, of whiteness, and then through a myriad of other feelings until finally one above all rushed in at him and took his breath away. Pain.

He gasped and groped for air, and it felt as if he were hanging upside down, although he still had no certain idea of his exact orientation. He was torn between his desire to breathe and his reluctance to inhale, as that might increase his already overbearing pain. His breath finally came in short, quick gasps as a sort of compromise between the two competing desires. As he inhaled, he felt a sort of furriness in his mouth and it seemed to threaten to smother him, but then, just as quickly, it was gone and replaced by a feeling of wetness. Snow, he thought dully.

After gathering his courage, he managed to get his eyes open for a brief instant and then spent the next several minutes analyzing what he had seen. To his left was darkness which gradually grew less intense as he analyzed from left to right until he reached a fuzzy, wavy line which seemed to separate something close to him from something far away. Past the fuzzy line was a dull, gray nothingness. He realized with some surprise that he was lying on his left side in the snow.

Trask opened his eyes again and confirmed the vision, and then concentrated on breathing more regularly as he began to come to terms with the pain that ran throughout his body. He felt brave enough to roll onto his back in order to ease some of the pain emanating from his left side, and he accomplished it with surprising facility. Maybe I'm not hurt as badly as I feel, he thought. Hope sprang up within him, but he still looked about as much as he could before he decided to move any farther. He couldn't see anything, just the dull gray sky and the thick snowfall.

Trask rolled over onto his stomach and gasped as unexpected pain shot through his left side. After the pain subsided, he looked up and saw the remains of the airplane with a wide track in the snow that led up to him. He decided that he must have been thrown out of the aircraft and that he slid twenty yards to his present location. He refocused his attention on the aircraft. There was a small fire near the rear of the wreckage, but it didn't seem anxious to spread to the rest of the remains. Trask breathed a sigh and allowed a thought to run unimpeded across his mind. Ellen had said that there wasn't much fuel left in the plane.

Ellen!

A surge of energy ran through him generated by desperation at the thought of what might have happened to Ellen. He managed to scramble to his feet, and he began to stagger in the general direction of the smashed aircraft. He spotted a lump in the snow which looked like a body and headed toward it. It began to move before he got close to it, and, from the moaning that emanated from it, he knew that it was Elverson.

With some effort he redirected his course back toward the plane while his eyes hungrily searched the wreckage for a hint of Ellen's body. Trask got to the right side of what used to be the fuselage and peered into a huge hole that had been ripped into the skin of the aircraft and was greeted with a grisly sight. Harry Vaughan lay in the bottom of a pile of debris in the interior of the plane. Trask's eyes ran over his body and stopped in horror when his gaze reached where Vaughan's head used to be. Something had penetrated the left side of his head with great force and had scattered flesh and bone over the inside of the airplane.

Trask staggered back a few paces and averted his eyes as his stomach churned. Desperation grew within him as a horrifying picture of Ellen in the same state as Vaughan ran through his mind. His head flew up as he heard a sob, but he couldn't place the direction. He began to circle the plane and hope grew in him that Ellen might have been spared Vaughan's fate.

Trask got to the other side of the wreckage just in time to see Ellen walk haltingly away from the plane. She slipped and fell in the snow, tried to get to her feet, then gave up and lay still. He was beside her in a second.

"Ellen, are you all right?" he asked with a shaking voice.

She rolled over and looked at him with relief suffusing her face. She nodded and seemed about to cry. He hugged her as tears welled up in him. He had almost lost her. She gave him a wry smile.

"Now you know why I washed out of flight school," she said in a frail voice.

He smiled and shook his head. "It's not your fault." She grunted but didn't seem to accept his statement.

Trask helped her to her feet and they both paused to look at the wrecked aircraft.

"It's a miracle we're still alive," Ellen mumbled.

Trask nodded in agreement, then gave her a sharp look. "Vaughan didn't make it," he said simply. She looked at him in surprise and seemed at a loss for words.

"Somehow he just didn't . . ." She let it trail off. Trask nodded again. He knew what she wanted to say. Vaughan didn't seem like an enemy agent. He had wanted to tell Trask something. Now that he was gone, Trask wished he had listened. Whatever he had wanted to say had died with him.

Trask shook off the feeling. Vaughan was an SVR spy, wasn't he? The transmitter in his bag proved that.

Ellen looked at him. "Elverson?" she asked.

"He's on the other side, and he was moving the last I saw of him," replied Trask.

On cue, Elverson came walking around to their side of the aircraft while shaking his head to clear it. He didn't say anything, just nodded to them. He looked about as if suddenly noticing that there were only three of them.

"Where's Vaughan?" he asked in a hoarse voice.

"He's dead," said Trask.

Elverson nodded as if he had already known. "Yeah, he took a couple of bullets from the guys on the ground. No big loss. Serves him right, the bastard."

Trask looked at Ellen but didn't reply.

He looked about and saw that they had hit the old runway at the wrong angle and had almost flown across it instead of down its length. The plane had piled up on one side of the runway near some abandoned buildings. The wind began to stiffen, driving the dense snowfall into their faces. Trask immediately thought that their first priority was to seek shelter and recover somewhat, then they would have to make plans to continue their flight from the SVR on the island.

Trask squinted up into the dull gray sky and wondered how long they would have lasted in the air with this kind of weather. Would they have gone down in the water? They could have survived only a minute or two with the temperature of the water near freezing. He shook the thoughts from him.

"Let's get the weapons and get to one of those buildings over there," he said as he gestured toward a row of dilapidated structures. The other two nodded in agreement.

Trask began to move, then gasped in pain at the effort and grabbed Ellen for support.

She held up his right side and gave him a look of concern. "Are you okay?"

"I'll be all right in a second," he mumbled. He waited for the pain to subside and glumly wondered if he had any broken ribs. He gingerly took a deep breath and derived some satisfaction from the general absence of pain as he inhaled. Movement of his left arm and leg caused the greatest pain, but it seemed to lessen the more he moved the affected limbs.

They moved over to the wreckage and began a quick search for any surviving weapons, finding the two M16s without much effort. They looked about for the automatic until Ellen suddenly remembered and sheepishly pulled it from her pocket. In silent agreement they turned and headed toward the nearest building. Trask and Ellen limped slightly while Elverson seemed unaffected by the plane crash. They forced their way into the building by breaking a window and slowly filed in out of the worsening weather.

Trask and Ellen slid to the floor as Elverson took up a post by an unbroken window. Trask passed his hand over his face and was surprised at the number of lumps and tender spots present. He had taken quite a beating. His thoughts were weary and depressed as he took stock of their situation.

They were on the western end of the island with no food or water and in a readily identifiable location. The SVR could find them very easily, if they wanted to take the trouble. They had no transportation, and on foot they were as good as dead. Darkness would arrive in a few hours, at about four o'clock, and on top of all that, the air outside was turning into a wall of white as another snowstorm ravaged the island.

On the plus side, they were still alive and not badly injured from the crash compared to what could have happened, even though Trask felt that he couldn't do the hundred-yard dash in much under an hour. They were lucky and unlucky at the same time.

He thought over their weapons situation—they were lucky there, even though they had lost some ammunition. They had a total of three clips for two M16s, while Ellen had only one extra clip for the automatic. If they got into a firefight with an SVR force of any size at all, then it wouldn't last long, and he knew what the result would be. Still, it could be worse, he thought. At least they had some weapons.

Trask glanced over at Ellen. She sat with her head resting against the wall and her eyes closed, and she seemed totally exhausted. He shook his head in admiration. She had been magnificent under fire. A person could search a whole lifetime and not find half the woman she was. He suddenly felt desperation—they had to survive this.

The hideous sight of Harry Vaughan suddenly intruded into his thoughts, and he squirmed in discomfort. He found himself wondering how Vaughan's head had been smashed the way it had. Probably a fuselage rib had broken loose and had impaled him. He studied the mental picture of the inside of the wreckage that he had formed in his mind and came to the conclusion that it couldn't have been a piece of metal like a rib, because there weren't any in the immediate vicinity of Vaughan's body. Elverson had mentioned that Vaughan got hit by the enemy agents on the ground. That was it then.

He pulled off his gloves and tried to warm his hands by blowing on them, then he shoved them into his pockets. His right hand hit a small notebook, which he immediately pulled from his pocket in an effort to remember where he had gotten it. It came to him after a minute. It was Harry Vaughan's notebook—he had picked it up from the floor after Elverson had searched Vaughan's flight bag. He opened it and began to idly thumb through it. The first half of the notebook was filled with notes on chess written in an excruciatingly neat hand; the second half was empty. Would the SVR have thought to add this kind of detail to one of their agents' personal effects? He shrugged. Could be.

Trask thumbed through it again quickly and noted one entry that seemed different from the others. It was the last entry in the book and the handwriting was not as neat as the rest. He read it and his mind raced furiously with memories. The names of each of them were listed with a notation of their start date on the island. Ellen's was very recent and he recognized his own, but next to Elverson's name, Vaughan had noted in bold capital letters that there was a basic problem in his record. A scribbled notation, even less legible than the hurried entry and very uncharacteristic of Vaughan's otherwise meticulous script, appeared next to the note. Trask squinted and seemed to make out the name of Schwarzkopf with the letters *H* and *S* next to it. A high school named after the famous general of the Gulf War? Trask shrugged. Could be. A school could do worse than naming it after the legendary officer. A lot worse.

Some numbers were scratched below the name and Trask could make out 1990. So Elverson graduated from Schwarzkopf High School in 1990. So what? No problem there. He sat and thought for a moment. How could that be a problem?

The answer hit him like a cannon shell. The Gulf War began in 1991! The American public didn't even know General Schwarzkopf existed in 1990! Trask's blood ran cold. *Was that what Vaughan had tried to tell him?*

Could it be that Vaughan wasn't the traitor but Elverson was? On the other hand, they had found the homing device in Vaughan's flight bag, and he had been missing during the night. But what of Vaughan's story? He claimed that he had gone to Building 600 to check up on their personnel records, because he wasn't sure who they were. Would he have thought to write something in his notebook to convince the rest of them his trip at night was legitimate? Possibly. He would want to have some sort of backup if he really was an agent and if he got caught. The high school could have been named for the general before the Gulf War. It was possible. Or it could be a different Schwarzkopf altogether.

Would the SVR make a mistake like that? Possibly they had come up with the school, then adjusted the graduation date to fit Elverson's age. And then they didn't go back to check when the school got its name. That was possible also. There was no way to know for sure.

Trask shook his head and took a hard look at Elverson. He seemed relaxed enough. Vaughan hadn't seemed like an enemy agent and Elverson didn't seem like an AP, but then again the SVR wouldn't exactly pick somebody with a thick Russian accent for a mission like this one. No, Vaughan was the agent, and a very good one at that. He had come to a rather sickening end, thought Trask, and recalled someone directly behind him moaning in pain for a few seconds immediately after the burst of fire hit the side of the plane. Must've been Vaughan. Maybe he had taken a bullet then, just as Elverson had said, but it couldn't have split his head open, or else he wouldn't have been moaning. That had to have happened later.

Realization rushed in at him suddenly, and in a flash of insight he knew how Harry Vaughan had died.

Supplee's breath came in ragged gasps as he stared into the air turned solid white by the driving blizzard. He had heard the grenade go off, then there was nothing, no sound, no gunfire. Nothing.

Repeat. *Repeat.*

Supplee propped the grenade launcher up on his right knee again at the same angle as before and pointed it a bit more to the left to compensate for the increased wind.

The whirl of snow directly in front of him darkened with a rapidly moving shape. Supplee stiffened with alarm. The enemy agent suddenly became visible as if he had just stepped through a door in the wall of snow around him. He was wounded, with blood streaming down his face, but he was running at near top speed toward the wounded marine captain.

They spotted each other simultaneously, with Supplee having a split second's worth of warning over the agent. The man slowed almost to a stop and brought his M16 up to firing position. Supplee was flat on his back with his grenade launcher pointed skyward. He dropped his knee to the ground to lower the grenade launcher barrel and fired the grenade point-blank at his attacker.

The agent's eyes grew wide as the stubby wide-bore barrel swung down in his direction. He didn't have his M16 pointed directly at the marine yet, and he instinctively knew the marine would get off the first shot. The agent gave up trying to get a shot at the marine and began to duck as Supplee shot a grenade straight at him.

The marine captain dropped the launcher and rolled up on his right hand and knees as the grenade streaked past the agent's right ear. The agent hit the deck, then stuck his head up to see it land thirty yards behind him. He stuck his head down into the snow and waited for the detonation.

Supplee scrambled back around the still-burning wreckage of the helicopter and groped in his right pocket for his
sidearm. His hand closed around the butt of the automatic
just as the grenade went off in the distance. Too far to have
taken out that enemy agent, he thought. He'll be on me in
a flash. Supplee yanked on the automatic and got it halfway
out of his pocket, then got the front sight caught on the
inside fabric.

The agent came charging out of the snowfall with his
M16 in front of him. He spotted Supplee and swung his
weapon up to fire. Supplee flopped on his left side in a
panic, ignoring the shooting pain from his broken arm, and
shoved the gun back into the depths of his pocket. Then he
pointed the automatic, and his pocket as well, at his attacker. The marine opened fire, shredding his pocket in a
frenzied attempt to get in the first shot. The agent got his
M16 barrel around and swung it a bit too far before he
opened fire. The snow kicked up a foot to Supplee's right
as the agent emptied half a clip in a second.

Supplee fired three rounds before the automatic fell
empty. All three found their mark. One hit the onrushing
man in the hip, and the other two pounded into his chest.
He suddenly stood straight up, his forward flight now
halted, and hesitated a moment before collapsing straight
downward amid the snow on the ground only a yard from
Supplee's feet.

Supplee held his gun hand up in an attempt to cover his
assailant, but then he began to shudder violently as the pain
in his left arm roared through his body. He rolled to his
right and lay flat on his back as he gasped for breath while
waiting for the pain to subside. Had he gotten all three of
them? Were there any more of the enemy around? Who the
hell *were* the enemy?

After ten minutes, the pain subsided to manageable proportions and he decided to rouse himself to see if he could
answer some of the questions that plagued him. He struggled to a sitting position and stared at the body that lay at
his feet. To his surprise he found that the man was still
alive—he was letting out moaning sounds that were quickly

swept away by the storm. The snow was accumulating rapidly; his attacker already had a coating of white over him.

Supplee slid over to him and got around to face him squarely. This was his first close look at one of his men's killers. The man was breathing in quick gasps with his eyes closed. He looked every inch an American—just another American.

"Who the hell are you people? Why did you shoot us down?" Supplee shouted angrily over the wind and snow.

The man opened his eyes and stared at Supplee. Then he grunted almost in amusement. "Don't you know? I'm sure you could guess," he replied in a hoarse voice.

"Who? Damn it! Tell me! Are you terrorists?" asked Supplee.

"Terrorists?" He shook his head and started to laugh until his body was racked with pain. He made a terrible gurgling sound like a wet cough. "We're the *Komitet*. You know. They used to call us the KGB."

"Russians? You're Russians?" asked Supplee incredulously. The man nodded slowly. "But why?" asked Supplee. "Why would you do something like this? We're not at war with you!"

The man gave half a smile. "Are you sure? What's the United States like these last two days?"

"What the hell are you talking about?" yelled Supplee. "There's nothing wrong with the United States. You lousy bastard! You murdered all my men for nothing!"

Supplee struggled over to the agent's M16 lying a few feet away in the snow. He picked it up and popped the clip out. About ten rounds left, that'll be just enough, Supplee thought grimly. He slammed the clip back in and pulled back on the cocking bar. He checked to see that it was on full automatic and that the safety was off.

Supplee got himself on his feet with a vengeance. He staggered over to the wounded man and stood over him. He took the barrel of the weapon and jammed it in the man's neck. His finger slid toward the trigger.

Supplee stood for a full minute pressing the cold barrel into the man's flesh with his finger resting heavily on the trigger. He swayed with the gusts of wind that drove the snow at him as his mind reeled with what he wanted to do to the helpless man below him. The man never said a word—he had expected that he would be shot. Supplee lowered the weapon in a rush. No, he thought. Not like this. Maybe they could do something like that, but I couldn't.

Supplee staggered back a couple of steps and thought about the two survivors from his helicopter. If they didn't die from their wounds, then the snowstorm would freeze them to death. He had to get them to shelter, and he had to do it fast. He shouldered the M16, then began to stagger in the direction of the truck that he had seen at the edge of the runway. Transportation was what he needed—he certainly couldn't drag anyone anywhere in his current condition.

What shall I do with this Russian agent? The answer came to him quickly. Do nothing. Just leave him there. He won't last long in this weather with his wounds. That settled, Supplee tried to quicken his gait toward the truck. His foot hit something in the rapidly mounting snow. Supplee bent down painfully and picked up the grenade launcher. He resolved instantly to take it with him. It had been the difference between life and death before, and it might prove to be the same again.

He spotted the bag of grenades, which was almost covered by the snow, and dragged it along with him. Grenade launchers are no good without something to launch. Supplee looked about to reorient himself, then trudged off in the assumed direction of the truck. The snow alternately swirled around him or drove horizontally at his back as he grimly tried to keep a swift pace toward his destination. The sharp wind actually helped him and seemed to keep him propped up and moving with its intense intermittent gusts.

Supplee staggered down the taxi lane, then struggled through the tundra to where the truck had become stuck at the edge of the runway. A dark shadow turned into the outlines of the truck, and Supplee gasped a prayer of thanks. The wind let up for a brief second, and he heard the engine running. Buoyed by his stroke of luck, he dragged himself over to the door in a few quick steps and yanked the door open. A wave of blessed heat came at him. Even the heater was on! He mumbled another prayer of thanks and threw the weapons and grenades on the front seat. He slid in behind the wheel and clumsily closed the door with his right hand.

The heat flowed into his body, soothing it and making him feel the exhaustion in him. No rest yet, he thought. Not until my men are safe. A new thought struck him that he could still be attacked at any time. There might be more Russian agents on their way to investigate the gunfire and explosions. He paused to reload the grenade launcher; he had no clips for the automatic that was left dangling out of the shredded bottom of his pocket, or for the M16. The half a clip left in the M16 and the grenades would have to be enough.

Supplee put the truck in gear and pressed on the accelerator pedal. His heart sank when the rear wheels began to spin. He rocked the truck back and forth by alternating between forward and reverse gear until the truck broke free and slowly began to roll down the runway.

He got to the point where a small lane went at a right angle from the runway and led to the parking area in front of the ops building. He turned the truck to the right and rumbled along the lane for a few minutes until he pulled alongside his men. The man with the broken legs was crying out in agony. The other was still. Supplee checked him out first and found to his surprise that he was still alive. He judged that the man wouldn't last long unless he got him some medical attention quickly.

Supplee dragged him over to the truck and, after several minutes of struggle, got him into the back seat. He propped him up to one side to leave room for the other man. Supplee went over to the other man and examined his legs. Both were broken below the knees and both were compound fractures. The man tried to shout something over the wind and pointed with a shaking hand to his left. Supplee followed the direction and spotted a medical kit half hidden in the snow. His man had known it was there but couldn't get to it.

Supplee shouted to him to hang on and scrambled to get the kit. He withdrew an antitetanus syringe and injected it into his man. Then he got out another syringe and injected him with a painkiller. There were no splints in the kit, and Supplee searched for some substitutes. He found some pieces of wood about a foot long and some duct tape in the back of the truck. He straightened the man's legs as well as he could with one hand and taped the pieces of wood to each leg. His man didn't cry out as before, and Supplee knew that the painkiller had taken effect.

The marine captain grabbed his man by the collar and dragged him over to the truck. After many more minutes of struggle, he had him safely in the back seat. Supplee was about to get into the front seat when he heard a cracking sound in the distance. A bullet slammed into the windshield, sending pieces of glass over the interior of the truck.

Supplee dropped behind the truck and cautiously peered around the left fender to see where the fire was coming from. Another crack. The ops building! Supplee got to the driver's side door and slid along the front seat to get to his grenade launcher. Another bullet hit the windshield, putting a hole in it without shattering the entire window, and sprayed him with fine pieces of glass. He yanked the grenade launcher after him as he slid out the door and along the left side of the truck.

Supplee propped the launcher on the fender of the truck and pointed it in the direction of the ops building. He heard another crack, but with the snowstorm still driving all around him, his visibility was near zero. He wondered how his attacker could see through the storm.

The wind and snow lifted briefly and Supplee could make out a set of windows about twenty feet above ground. He judged wind and elevation and squeezed off a round. The weapon gave off its peculiar thunking noise and sent a grenade arcing toward the building. The grenade hit the side of the building and exploded five feet below the window. Supplee quickly shoved another grenade into the breech and readjusted his angle. He sent another grenade toward the building, this time to explode a foot below the window.

The gunfire from the building, which was sporadic individual shots, turned immediately to the rattling sound of an M16 on full automatic. Supplee dropped behind the truck and worked another grenade into the chamber as bullets smashed into the truck and flew inches over his head. The gunfire suddenly ceased. He's reloading, thought Supplee.

He leaped to his feet and carefully aimed the launcher. The next grenade went neatly through one of the windows. The grenade went off with a muffled thump mixed with the sound of shattering glass. Supplee put two more grenades into the windows and listened to the explosions wreak havoc inside the building. He waited a while for the gunfire to reoccur, but there were only the sounds of the storm streaking down the runway.

Supplee knew he should go and check out his attacker to see if the grenades had done their job, but he didn't have the strength. He staggered back to the truck and got in the front seat. He turned around and looked over his men. The man with the broken legs was unconscious but all right. The man with the burns, who had been in shock, had two bullet holes in his face. Supplee checked his carotid artery with a shaking hand. His man was dead.

He slowly let out his breath in frustration and anger. Only he and one man still survived. What was all this about? The Russians take over one of our bases for no reason? His thoughts were swept away by pain. His left arm began to throb terribly. He probed it gingerly with his right hand and found that it was extremely swollen. He pulled two syringes out of the medical kit and gave himself an antitetanus shot and a painkiller.

Supplee let himself go as the painkiller deadened his agony and the truck's heater warmed him. The still-running engine vibrated the cab of the truck slightly, and it felt to Supplee like a massage. Exhaustion caught up to him and he slipped into unconsciousness.

CHAPTER 22

━ ･ ━ ･ ━ ･ ━

Major Ken Rickman, United States Marine Corps, squinted into the wind to see the helicopter sway to a rough landing. Orders had come through that delayed his departure until this second party could arrive. He was annoyed at it all—he desperately wanted to find out what had happened to twenty of Adak's Company I and their company commander, Captain Bob Supplee, who was also one of his best friends. Instead he had to wait for some people from Elmendorf to join him.

The helo landed with a bump and he ran to the side door to greet them. Maybe if he went to them, he could speed things up and get his people moving. He heard his name being called over the furious wind. He turned just as he reached the helicopter door and saw his exec waving for him to return to the operations building that sat near the intersection of the two runways.

Rickman glanced at the helicopter—the occupants made no move to open the door—then ran back to where his exec was standing.

"What's up, Mark?" he asked as he got in out of the building storm.

His exec held up a handset. "NMCC," he said with his eyebrows raised. "Air Force General Manning."

Rickman was suitably impressed. It was a call from the

National Military Command Center in the Pentagon. He pressed the handset to his ear and plugged up his other ear with his finger.

"Yes, sir, Major Rickman, Marine Corps, here."

"Major, has the other party gotten there yet?"

"Yes, sir. They just landed," replied Rickman.

"Good. What I am about to tell you is top secret. Share this only with the people you absolutely have to. Is that understood, Major?" asked Manning.

"Yes, sir. It is understood," replied Rickman as the hair began to stand up on the back of his neck. Now what?

"Intelligence believes that Shemya has been taken over by a hostile force, possibly a renegade group of Russian sleeper agents. Your orders are to secure the island, by force if necessary," said Manning.

Rickman grew a bit dizzy at the information—Russian sleeper agents?—but then his mind kicked in. He needed to know more.

"General, if they've taken the island, then they'll have access to all the weapons in Shemya's arsenal," said Rickman, his mind racing. "I need to know what they've got up there. Also how many agents are we talking about, sir? I need to know what we're up against."

"We are attempting to get that information from PACAF and CIA now, but it probably won't be here before you lift off," replied Manning. "Stay in touch and we'll get it to you."

"General, what about backup? I've got two hundred and forty-six marines and a couple of F-18s flying cover," said Rickman. The question alone implied that it wasn't enough.

Manning hesitated, then his voice came over the satellite link in a low, somber tone. "As of the moment, Major, you're it."

They both fell silent as the impending operation hung over them like a sword. What am I going into? Rickman's thoughts turned toward his men. What did Captain Supplee and his men go into? Were they still alive?

"The other party, General, what's their mission?" asked Rickman.

"You needn't concern yourself with them," said Man-

ning. "Their mission is highly classified and you are not
to speculate about them to your people. They will accomplish their mission independent of your people, but you will
render all assistance necessary if requested. Is that understood, Major?"

"Yes, sir. It is," replied Rickman.

"Understand, Major, that you will report only to me,"
ordered Manning in his most authoritative voice. "Everyone else is out of the loop. NMCC will control this thing,
no one else. I think you can guess why."

"Aye, aye, sir," said Rickman in a subdued voice. Yeah,
I can guess why, he thought. This whole damned thing will
have to be covered up. The other group from Elmendorf is
the cover-up committee. Relations with the Russians have
to be preserved. Damn the Russians!

"That is all, Major. Good luck," said Manning.

"Thank you, sir," said Rickman, and hung up. He turned
to his exec.

"This ain't a drill, is it?" asked Captain Marcus Bryan.

"No, it ain't," replied Rickman, imitating his exec's
tone. "We're the lucky ones to be taking cold weather
training at this time. Let's get this show on the road," he
said, and strode out of the building and into the wind. A
few snowflakes hit his face, the harbinger of an imminent
storm. Terrific, he thought. Flying helicopters in a blizzard
just makes my day.

The thunder of the two F-18s as they went to afterburn-
ers down at one end of the runway seemed to part the wind
with a fury. Rickman gazed into the distance and watched
the aircraft on their takeoff run down runway 5-23, which
ran roughly east-west. Rickman was near the western end
of the runway and his helicopters were lined up on the 18-
36 runway, which ran north-south. The fighter aircraft blew
by him at over one hundred knots and lifted off smartly a
few seconds later. He watched them until they became just
four dots of flame as they disappeared into the mist.

Rickman walked over to the helicopter carrying the
"other group." At least I should introduce myself, he
grumbled to himself. The side door opened and a middle-

aged man got out. He looked fit and very capable. He extended a hand in friendship.

"Craig Scanlon," he said, and shook the marine's hand. "Major Rickman, I guess."

It wasn't a question and Scanlon wasn't particularly guessing either, thought Rickman. Scanlon was dressed in white and wasn't carrying any external weapons. Who was this guy? CIA maybe. Or some old colonel in the Delta Force?

They exchanged amenities without exchanging any real information. They parted and Rickman walked over to his group of seven helicopters crammed with his men. He had gotten a look at the men inside Scanlon's helicopter. They also were dressed in white—de rigueur in arctic combat—and they carried weapons. They had AKMs, the direct descendant of the Russian AK47.

They also had something else—medical kits, the big metal kind with a large blood-red cross on the front. Every other man had one. Rickman shook his head in puzzlement. Russian weapons and a lot of medical kits.

Too many medical kits.

1000 HOURS, 27 DECEMBER
OFF SHEMYA'S SOUTHERN COAST
ABOARD THE ADMIRAL CHARKIN

Captain First Rank Vasily Makeyev looked over his sonar operator's shoulder at the display in front of them. Was an American submarine hiding just out of range of his sensors?

His sonar operator shook his head in frustration. "It's gone now, sir."

Makeyev exhaled as he straightened. The display had indicated that something might be to the south of them, but he had seen many indications such as these in the past. When they were investigated, they all proved to be false contacts, except one several years ago. That one exception had shaken him when it had occurred, and still, he admitted, shook him to this day. The realization that an American submarine had been stalking them, listening to them, and could have sunk them at any time, was shattering, especially when he and his crew had realized that they couldn't hear the American boat.

Makeyev summed up the situation in his mind. His Akula-class boat was very quiet, but it had a steel hull which made it vulnerable to detection by magnetic anomaly detectors, or MAD, which are carried by the American Orion antisub aircraft. Still, it would be dumb luck for an Orion to detect them without first knowing their general location. His greatest threat would be if they had picked up an American sub on their tail as they left Petropavlovsk. If a Los Angeles– or Sturgeon-class attack submarine was out there, then he stood a very good chance of being detected.

And then what? The United States and Russia weren't at war, but the *Admiral Charkin* was inside U.S. territorial waters. The Americans might shoot first and ask questions later. If they knew what he and his passengers were up to, they would certainly attack him.

Makeyev went over to the diving officer. "Make your depth twenty meters." The diving officer moved to comply.

Makeyev went down a ladder to the deck below and made his way to the outside hatch just aft of the submarine's superstructure. A group of thirty men were lined up down the corridor awaiting the departure order. They all wore thick wet suits which gave them a fat ungainly appearance. The bags they carried contained white parkas along with food, first aid kits, and, of course, their weapons. Makeyev made his way to the front of the line and their leader, GRU Colonel Ivan Sysoyev.

"You and your men are ready, Colonel?" asked Makeyev.

"Yes. How close are we to shore, Captain?" asked Sysoyev.

"Approximately five hundred meters."

Sysoyev beamed. "Excellent, Captain. That gives us an easy time getting to shore. *Spasiba!*"

Makeyev nodded modestly. The plan was to let the Spetsnaz team out underwater to lessen their chance of detection. The team would float to the surface and inflate rubber boats to get to Shemya's shoreline. While on the rubber boats, the team would change out of their wet suits and into the heavy clothes and parkas they all had. Makeyev would have to surface to retrieve the team on the return trip, a fact that had him worried.

A nearby intercom speaker jumped into life.

"Captain, we are at the ordered depth," said the diving officer. Makeyev acknowledged the information, then turned to the GRU officer.

"I wish you Godspeed, Colonel," said Makeyev.

The colonel's eyebrows flew up in surprise at Makeyev's use of the Western expression. The flourishing of democracy in Russia has had an effect on all of us, he thought. His face broke into a broad smile and he shook Makeyev's hand.

Colonel Sysoyev turned and started up the ladder to the hatch above. Now I will find out what has really happened on this desolate American island, he thought.

And carry out those startling orders he had been given by the leaders of the GRU during the journey from Petropavlovsk.

U.S.S. NEW YORK CITY, SSN 696

"Conn, Sonar. Master Five has stopped dead in the water," said the sonar supervisor in a hushed voice over the intercom.

Captain Ed Stanley glanced over to the screen called the waterfall. It showed constant bearing rate as the green line swept across the screen. The *New York City* was passing by the contact to the south.

"All stop," he said quietly to the OOD. The OOD repeated the order. "Rig ship for silent running," ordered Stanley. He looked at the waterfall again. The green line had stopped its sideways travel and was now running vertically down the screen, indicating constant bearing, but was fading rapidly into a jumble of green dots as the engine and screw noise from the Russian boat disappeared.

"Sonar, Conn. Any transients?" asked the OOD over the intercom.

Sonarman Don Frederick knew that question was coming

and was already straining his ears to detect any sound that would give away the activities of the Akula to the north.

"Loud transients, on Master Five bearing," he said suddenly as his hands flew up to his earphones. The sonar supervisor relayed Frederick's remarks to the conn.

"Sonar, Conn aye. Any ID on the sounds?" came the OOD's voice over the intercom.

Frederick was ready for the question. "Negative, it's like nothing I've ever heard from an Akula," replied Frederick as he glanced at the sonar supervisor. He listened closely for a moment. "Now we're getting air transients."

"Sonar, this is the captain. Play the recording over the speaker in the Conn," said Stanley.

"Sonar, aye, aye, Captain," said the sonar supervisor, and hit the button to put it on a speaker for the captain's benefit. A series of scraping noises were followed by a clunking noise, then the unmistakable sound of a squeaky hinge mingled with air bubbles.

"What do you make of that?" asked the captain of his XO, who had just joined him.

The XO remained thoughtful for a minute. "You know, it sounds like a boat doing SEAL ops. You remember, Captain, last December when we were trailing the *Pintado* during the exercise. We heard noises something like these when a SEAL team was deployed from a boat while submerged."

"Hatch, then bubbles," mused Stanley. "All right. Periscope depth. Let's take a look."

His crew quickly got the boat to the prescribed depth and raised the periscope. Stanley peered through it and swung around to the Russian boat's bearing. He jacked up the magnification and centered up on some dots on the surface in the distance. He looked disbelieving through the periscope and pulled his head back seemingly to reset his mind, then looked again.

"Men in rubber boats," said Stanley.

"Landing party?" asked his XO in disbelief.

The captain nodded quickly. His mind raced on with a summary of the situation. His boat was still undetected by the sub north of them. This Russian sub had damn near

landed on Shemya and was now sending a landing party
ashore. For what purpose? He should tell the Pentagon
about this, but that would possibly give away his presence
to the Russians. What should he do?

He would wait before transmitting a message, he decided. He had to see what else the Russians were up to.

SHEMYA

Trask awoke with a start and realized he couldn't remember
whether he had been dreaming or not. He sighed with relief—maybe the dreams would stop now that he had, more
or less, confronted what had been bothering him. He
counted Ellen on his side in his constant battle with the
world and shuddered to think what would happen to him
if she wasn't.

Trask glanced at his watch and found that it had been
ruined in the crash. How long had he slept? He looked at
the window. Judging by the light, or the lack thereof, he
thought it was early morning. Vaughan's death came to
mind and the notes in the little man's book, which made
him take a long look at Ellen, then Elverson, both dozing
across the room. He decided he had better keep the knowledge to himself for now until he had more evidence. After
a few moments, he decided that he had better get them
moving. Ellen started to stir and Elverson suddenly sat upright, instantly awake. Oh, to be twenty years younger,
thought Trask wistfully.

"One thing is certain. We've stayed here too long,"
Trask stated firmly. Ellen lazily opened her eyes while Elverson chose to ignore him.

"Why?" she asked.

"The SVR will know exactly where we are, and it won't
take them long to come looking," he replied. "We probably shouldn't have stayed here overnight."

She nodded wearily. "You're right, of course."

Elverson turned around and looked at Trask. "Where are
we going to go in this snow?" he asked, and nodded
slightly toward the outside. The snowstorm which raged

intermittently all night had transformed the world outside their building into swirls of white flakes.

"Best cover in the world," said Trask. Elverson grunted and Trask interpreted the gesture as Elverson's grudging agreement.

"We've got to decide where we're going," said Ellen to Trask.

"We could double back to the trailers. They would never think to look for us there," replied Trask.

Ellen shrugged. "Sounds good, I guess," she said.

"It's a long walk, are you sure you're up to it?" asked Elverson with no real concern in his voice.

Trask nodded. "I'll make it."

Ellen got to her feet. "Let's go then," she said, and moved toward the door. She pulled it open and cringed at the assault of the wind which drove the snow directly at her. She bent over and went outside.

Trask waited for Elverson to go ahead of him and then stepped outside into the teeth of the wind and snow. It didn't register in his mind immediately when he saw the snow kick up in front of him, but then he heard something slap into the side of the building in rapid fashion. The sound of cracking in the distance came a split second later and he knew they were under fire.

"Quick! Back inside!" he shouted over the whine of the wind and then nearly got trampled by a rapidly moving Elverson.

They scrambled inside and looked at each other in shock. The SVR had found them!

"Everyone okay?" asked Trask. The other two nodded.

"Looks like we stayed here a little *too* long," said Ellen as Elverson crawled over to the window. He peered out cautiously and cursed at the snowfall.

"Can't see a damned thing," he mumbled.

"The gunfire must've come from up the hill toward the north," said Trask. "Maybe I can circle around and get behind him."

Elverson redirected his gaze to stare at Trask. "Why should you be the hero?"

Trask looked him in the eye. "Somebody's got to do it."

He looked over to Ellen. "Give me the automatic." She looked at him as if he wasn't serious. "I might need a hidden edge with whoever is up there," he explained. She reluctantly agreed and pulled the automatic and the extra clip from her pocket.

Trask stuffed the pistol in his pocket and went over to a window on the opposite side of the building. He tried to open it, and couldn't, and wound up smashing it to pieces. He glanced back at Elverson.

"Keep 'em busy, will ya?" he said, then climbed through the window. Elverson grunted in reply.

Trask went straight back from the building for a hundred yards in the direction away from the gunfire, then turned and looked back to assess the visibility. He could barely see the building he had just left. Satisfied with that, he started to make the wide circle that would bring him around behind where he thought the sniper was.

The snow closed in around him in a complete whiteout, and he began to worry about losing his sense of direction. He could wander around for hours in a snowstorm this intense. He slowed his pace and stared to his left as he tried to discern where the building was located.

The sudden cracking of Elverson's M16 came to him, and a second later he heard the reply from their attacker. With new bearings he started off with greater vigor.

It was an uphill climb over uneven terrain in a blinding snowstorm, and after a few minutes he had slowed his pace considerably. His sore left leg began to bother him also, and along with a lack of food for the past twenty-four hours, he began to regret his willingness to outflank the sniper. He kept roughly on course by using the intermittent exchange of fire between Elverson and the sniper as a reference point. Trask kept going until he was sure that the sniper was behind him, then he turned left and headed at a right angle to his original path.

The terrain suddenly flattened out and he saw the remnants of recent tire tracks cut into the snow. He made another left turn and slowly went down the road, following the tracks while straining his eyes to detect the first signs of the sniper. A dark spot in the snowstorm formed in front of him, and he cautiously approached it. It took on a familiar outline, and an instant later he recognized it as a truck.

Trask crouched as low as he could and ran up to the rear of the vehicle while suddenly thinking that he had no idea how many people there might be up here. He had assumed that there was only one sniper because they had heard only one weapon being fired. He gritted his teeth and decided that there was no turning back.

He went around to the passenger's side and cautiously peeked through the rear window. He breathed a sigh of relief as he saw that there was no one in the vehicle. A single crack of a rifle nearby made him jump, and he knew that he was very near his quarry. Trask got down on his hands and knees and crawled to the front of the truck. He peered around the right fender and saw the sniper lying in the snow on a small swell in the ground. The sniper had an M16 lying beside him in the snow, but he was presently using a rifle with a telescopic sight on it. Memories leaped at Trask, but with a force of will he suppressed them. He had to keep his mind on the job at hand.

Trask pulled back on the cocking bar of his M16 as silently as he could, flipped it on auto and carefully took aim at a point lower than where the man actually was. When he pulled the trigger, the barrel would lift due to the recoil of the bullets being fired, and the resultant stream of lead would cut across the sniper's body. He hoped it wouldn't be necessary.

"Hold it!" shouted Trask.

The sniper's head went up in surprise. He whirled about to look at Trask.

"Drop it!" shouted Trask.

The sniper didn't hesitate. He pulled his rifle around to bring it to bear on Trask and did it so quickly that Trask barely had time enough to react. Trask pulled the trigger and watched as the bullets stitched a line from the snow on one side of the man's body across to the snow on the other side. The blast left the sniper wiggling in agony and stained the snow with blood. He eventually slowed and stopped except for a reflexive twitch now and then.

Trask closed his eyes and turned his head away. He fought with his emotions for a bit, then decided to get up to check on the sniper's condition. He walked over and looked down at the man who so recently was his enemy and felt pity for the body sprawled out in the snow. With an effort of will, he shook the emotions from him and went back to the truck.

Relief filled him as he saw that the keys were still in the ignition. Right at the moment he had no stomach for searching the body of his victim for the keys to the truck. Curious, he thought, he had felt nothing after having killed a man at the trailers, but now he felt an almost overpowering revulsion to having killed the sniper. *Because I was one?* He shoved the thought from his mind.

A new thought struck him and moved him to action. The sniper was obviously not trying to assault the building containing the three of them, and probably not even trying to kill them, but only trying to keep them there until others reinforced him. That meant that another group of SVR agents was on its way. He had better get moving.

Trask climbed halfway into the truck, then turned and looked at the sniper and jumped back out again. He ran over to the body and picked up the M16 only to see that there was no ammunition clip with it. Trask spotted one half-buried in the snow and retrieved it. It was empty. The sniper had run out and had switched to the high-powered rifle. He picked up the rifle from the snow to check its magazine and saw that only a few cartridges had been expended.

Trask ran back to the truck, got in and threw the rifle on the seat beside him. He thought for a second and lowered his gaze to stare at the rifle next to him. On impulse he took the weapon and shoved it under the seat. Nothing like having an edge, he thought. He pulled the clip from his M16 and noted that it was full except for the few bullets expended in the burst to kill the sniper. He reinserted the clip and put the M16 next to him. He then reached into his pocket for the automatic. One full clip and the one that was in the weapon was half full. Trask sat looking at the automatic and the clips as his mind began to race.

Elverson glanced at Ellen Gain. "That was an M16," he said after hearing the rattle of gunfire in the distance.

She looked at him. "You think it was Trask?" she asked. Elverson shrugged and made no reply.

They both sat crouched next to the open window and peered into the dazzle of white that was the snowstorm, and as they strained their eyes in the direction of the last burst of gunfire, they slowly came to realize that the sniper was missing his rhythm. The muffled roar of a truck engine as it started floated over to them despite the subduing effect of the millions of snowflakes and the whine of the wind.

"Somebody's coming," said Elverson, and brought his M16 up in front of him.

"Hold it. It might be Trask," ordered Ellen.

Elverson cocked his M16 anyway and pushed the barrel out the open window. The sound of the truck engine grew in intensity and after a minute they saw two pinpoints of light that they recognized as the truck headlights. The truck approached the building rapidly and bounced and skidded along the road as its driver pushed it as fast as it would go.

Ellen strained her eyes to see who was driving and was staring at the windshield on the driver's side when she heard a slight movement next to her ear. She whirled and saw Elverson with his finger hard on the trigger. He let the trigger go, and she gave him a furious look. He responded with a surprised but guilty glance. He had pulled the trigger, but the automatic weapon was empty.

"Damn it, Elverson! That could be Trask out there!" She spat the words out, but the airman ignored her as he calmly removed the clip to confirm that it was empty.

The truck screeched to a halt outside the building as Ellen held her breath, and Elverson grimly shoved the clip back into the M16 and thought about a bluff. The door was flung open, Trask came rushing through and gestured to them to immediately follow him.

"Come on! Let's get the hell out of here!" he shouted.

Ellen let out her breath and called his name in a burst of relief. Even Elverson looked relieved.

"What about the sniper?" asked Elverson.

Trask gave him a look and hesitated. "He's dead," Trask finally mumbled. Elverson shot him a look bordering on respect, but Ellen seemed only more relieved.

They quickly left the building and climbed into the truck with Elverson driving, Ellen in the front seat on the passenger's side, and Trask in the rear seat. Trask quickly filled them in on his theory about the imminent reinforcements, and they all agreed that they had better vacate the area immediately. They decided to carry out their original plan and double back to the trailers.

The trio rode down the runway past the still-smoking wreckage of their plane as Trask cautioned Elverson to watch out for the wide crack in the runway which was left over from a decades-old earthquake. Elverson spotted it as a ragged depression in the thick snow and swerved to avoid it. He then picked out the most discernible road off the old airstrip and went onto a side road that would lead them back past the new airport and eventually to the trailers they had once occupied.

Ellen, meanwhile, rummaged in the glove compartment and came up with a pair of binoculars and a full ammo clip which she inserted into Elverson's empty M16. She picked up the binoculars and began to scan for any activity in the distance even though the dense snowfall greatly hampered her efforts.

Trask worried about their imminent trip past the airport but took some comfort in the extremely limited visibility. They pulled onto the road on the southern edge of the island just as the snowfall let up a bit and greatly increased their visibility. Trask stared off to the left along with Ellen, who was using her binoculars, and tried to pick out any activity around the airport operations building. They could only make out the now-dimmed flames from the downed helicopter.

The road initially swung away from the airstrip, ran roughly parallel for a while and then narrowed back toward the runway as it followed the irregular outline of the shore.

The trio's vehicle had just reached the point where the road ran parallel to the runway when Ellen idly glanced out the front window. Elverson was busy staring at the road's snowdrifts, and Trask's eyes were glued out the left windows.

"Stop the truck!" she ordered. Elverson complied.

"What is it?" asked Trask as he looked in the same direction.

"Some people on the beach," she said with a note of surprise in her voice. Trask murmured surprise as well.

"We ought to get up there and see who it is," said Trask. Ellen nodded in agreement.

Trask's eyes scanned the area and his gaze went almost immediately to a group of buildings that were a hundred yards ahead. They were obviously empty and they could be used to provide the needed cover to observe whoever was on the beach. He pointed them out and he and Ellen quickly agreed to sneak up behind them and use them as a vantage point. They also agreed to abandon the truck for the moment so that the engine noise wouldn't give them away.

They all got out of the truck and started off down the road toward the buildings. They circled around to the rear of the buildings but approached them at an angle so that the buildings were constantly between them and the people on the beach. Trask worried that they would be easily seen up against the background of snow that covered the island, but there was nothing to be done about it except to use the buildings as a screen.

Elverson led the way and seemed to easily run through the drifted snow while Ellen followed with Trask lagging in the rear, huffing and puffing all the way. He was totally out of breath when they reached the rear door of one of the buildings. They cautiously entered and made their way through the interior until they reached the side that faced the beach, and upon locating a window, they cautiously peered through the dirty glass.

They saw several rubber boats and thirty men dressed in white. It was a landing party!

Trask looked at Ellen. She had the binoculars from the truck and had them trained toward the beach. She lowered them and looked at Trask with alarm. He took the binoculars from her and gazed at the landing party for a long moment.

"They're Russians," he said simply.

"How do you know?" asked Elverson.

"I know an AK47 when I see one," replied Trask, "The VC had plenty of them in 'Nam. These are probably AKMs, but it's essentially the same as an AK47."

"They must be coming to evacuate their people off the island," Elverson offered.

They stood in silence for a while as they watched the men on the beach scramble to get their rubber boats higher on the snow-covered beach. The boats were large and had outboard motors, and looked very capable of withstanding the arctic seas. The landing party spent several minutes covering the boats with snow to hide them.

"I don't know. Maybe they're here for other reasons," Ellen mused.

"What the hell are you talking about?" asked Elverson.

She ignored him and turned to Trask. "One thing is certain, we must be at war with Russia. And we're the only defense this island's got."

"You're not suggesting that we try to defend the whole island from them?" asked Trask incredulously.

"No, of course not," she replied. "But the most valuable thing on this island to the Russians is the COBRA DANE radar. Knowledge of what that radar can do would be invaluable to them in evaluating other radars that might have survived the nuclear attack. We've got to stop them from getting any secrets out of the radar."

Trask resisted her logic for a few moments; he certainly didn't want another confrontation with the SVR, or with this tough-looking and probably extremely competent landing party. Their successes up until now had been due to surprise and luck, and he had the nagging feeling that both would run out soon. He finally gave in to her point of view and nodded in agreement.

"Okay, if we're going to destroy parts of the radar, then we had better beat them there," he said.

"Yes, you had better get going," was her short reply.

Trask looked at her in surprise. "You're coming with us, aren't you?"

She shook her head as she brought the binoculars up to her eyes once more. "We've also got to send a message to let the air force know what's going on here. They might be able to bomb our friends on the beach there as they're leaving. They probably came by submarine. Maybe whatever's left of the U.S. Navy can sink it if an air strike doesn't work."

Trask was amazed that Ellen was thinking in terms of a continuing war with Russia. He had always thought that the war would last only a few hours, with both sides losing.

"So you two get to the radar building and destroy what you can of the radar, and I'll get back to the satellite communications terminal to try to send a message," she said.

Trask shook his head in indecision. "I don't know. I don't like it. The comm terminal is bound to be crawling with enemy agents."

"Look, I'm not going to get myself killed. If it's lousy with Russians, then I won't go near the place." She was trying to reassure him. Trask felt only slightly better.

"They're starting to split up. We'd better get moving," she said, glancing out the window.

Trask looked toward the beach and counted six groups of five men each who were fanning out in different directions.

"You'd better give me something," said Elverson.

Trask looked at him and pretended to wonder what he meant, then he made a show of noticing that the young man had no weapon. He hesitated and deliberately looked at his M16 and then at Ellen's.

"Ellen's going to need that M16," he said, thereby implying that hers was the only one available. Elverson gave him a steady look. Trask held his breath.

"Then give me the automatic," Elverson said quietly.

Trask made his eyebrows go up in surprise. "Ah yes! The automatic!" he replied and pulled it from his pocket as if he had just remembered it. He gave it to Elverson, who gave the weapon a cursory glance, then shoved it into his pocket.

Trask decided to quickly change the subject. "You had better take the truck," he said to Ellen. She looked at him questioningly.

"The message has to take top priority," he replied. "We can use the other truck we left near the airport. It's probably still there. Or we can steal another snowplow." He gave her a lopsided smile. She nodded. There was a brief silence.

"Maybe I'd better come with you," he said in a low voice.

She shook her head vehemently. "You're the only one who knows the radar and what should be destroyed first."

He was forced to agree with her reasoning once again. She turned to go. Trask grabbed her arm. She looked at him without saying a word while a gamut of emotions ran across her face. He gazed at her and couldn't think what to say. Was this the last time he would see her?

"Be careful," he finally mumbled. She nodded and was suddenly gone.

He stared after her for a few moments, then glanced in Elverson's direction. He expected some sarcastic remark from the young man but saw that he was standing by and looking rather ill at ease. He looked back toward the beach and just caught the remaining groups of white-clad Russians as they moved off the beach and quickly blended in with the snow on the ground. He glanced down at his own olive-drab parka. The Russians didn't miss a trick.

He looked back out the window and saw two groups of men head down the beach road at a dead run toward the eastern end of the island. Two other groups went straight across the road toward the main airport buildings, and the two remaining groups ran westward along the road toward the radar building and the nuclear power plant. They would pass close by the building that Trask and Elverson were in.

Trask and Elverson pressed their backs to the wall on either side of the window and breathlessly waited for the westward-bound groups to pass them by, while Trask said a prayer that Ellen had gotten away in time. The sound of their boots crunching their way through the snow grew in intensity, reached a peak, then gradually faded in the distance.

Trask glanced back out the window and began to breathe normally again. His mind began to race. They would have to avoid the landing party groups by taking the road on the extreme perimeter of the island, which was the long way around to the radar building. Without the truck, they could forget it. The landing party was making good speed even though they were on foot, and they were probably in tip-top shape and hard as a rock, all of them.

He did some mental calculations. They were approximately in the middle of the island. That meant the Russians had about two miles to go to get to the radar building, and they were trotting along at six to eight miles an hour. They would be at the radar building in fifteen to twenty minutes. He looked at Elverson. They didn't have much time.

"Let's go," he said to the young AP, then took a final look out the window.

They got to a doorway and cautiously left the building. They then started off at a fast pace for the building where they had left the truck.

CHAPTER 23

▬ ▪ ▬ ▪ ▬ ▪ ▬

1030 HOURS, 27 DECEMBER
SHEMYA

Craig Scanlon's helicopter touched down in a remote portion of the island near the northern shore. His men immediately swarmed out the loading ramp in the rear of the helicopter and formed a defensive perimeter. Two men went over to some flat terrain and quickly set up a satellite communications terminal. In ten minutes they were in direct communication with CIA headquarters at Langley.

Scanlon looked after his men with satisfaction. All the training was paying off. This SEAL team that was attached to the CIA covert operations staff was quick and competent at their jobs. They were all dressed identically with the arctic white parkas, and they all carried Russian weapons, had Russian ID cards, and almost all spoke Russian fluently. They were dead ringers for a Russian Spetsnaz team.

Scanlon grunted to himself. When the Soviet Union went out of business, their future seemed doomed. They were the odds-on favorite to be cut by the bureaucrats' ax. But they had lingered in limbo, waiting for the inevitable word to retrain to penetrate some other country. Some *enemy* country. The word never came, and they waited with their efficiency slipping by the day. Then came the briefing yesterday, and a sense of satisfaction ran through him that he had thought he would never feel again.

They were in action against the Russians, something they had dreamed of for decades. So what if it was all a mistake?

241

So what if these damn sleepers were hung out to dry by their government? This would probably be the last covert action against the Russians for quite a long time. Unless they became a threat again.

Scanlon stood with his back to the sea and his face into the wind. To his right lay one of their objectives, the CO-BRA DANE radar, which lay enshrouded in the mist of some lingering snowfall. They had other objectives, such as the satellite ground terminal, but none was as important as the radar.

Along with his physical objectives, he was to make contact with the CIA operative on Shemya and evacuate the agent. The Company didn't want a lot of questions about this particular person, and it would be disastrous for the public to discover the agent's real purpose for being on Shemya. He suddenly felt one of his men at his elbow.

"Sir, Snipe's on the radio," said his second in command.

Scanlon nodded and hurried over to the satellite terminal. He took the handset and put it to his ear.

"Raven here," he said into the handset.

"This is Snipe. Mission Option Seven is hereby ordered. Acknowledge."

"Acknowledged that Mission Option Seven is ordered. Anything else, sir?" asked Scanlon.

"That is all. Out."

Scanlon gave the handset back to his radioman and turned to watch his teams disperse across the island according to a preset plan. Then he faced the interior of the island once again. He glanced to his right as the orders direct from the DDO ran through his mind.

The nuclear power plant had just become one of his objectives.

SHEMYA'S AIRPORT

"Black Gang Leader, this is Blue Light Leader, answer up!"

The words seemed to come from inside his body as he struggled to place his whereabouts. The shroud of sleep wasn't easy to cast off, but with a monumental effort, he got his eyes open only to feel dizziness sweep over him.

"Black Gang Leader, this is Blue Light Leader. Damn it, Bob, this is Ken Rickman, answer up!"

Supplee's eyes went open and stayed open at the sound of his friend, Major Ken Rickman. He groaned and attempted to sit upright, but the pain in his racked body prevented him from moving quickly.

"Captain Supplee, report your status."

The voice came from the walkie-talkie he still had clipped on his belt. It was a miracle it still worked, considering the beating he and the radio had taken from the crash. He grabbed the radio with his right hand and pressed the talk lever.

"Blue Light, this is Black Gang—" Supplee let out an oath as the radio slipped out of his hand and fell on the seat.

"This is Blue Light Leader. Nice to hear you're okay, Bob. Now, what happened? Why haven't you called in?" Rickman sounded more than a little annoyed.

"Blue Light, both aircraft shot down. All dead except for me and one other. Both of us wounded. The bad guys have Stingers. I say again, Stingers!" Supplee ran out of breath as the pain in his left arm reasserted itself.

"Roger, Black Gang, copy Stingers," said Rickman, his voice subdued. "Give us your location."

"I'm in a truck on the parking area opposite the ops building near the helicopter wreckage," said Supplee.

"Roger, Black Gang. Give number and capability of enemy," ordered Rickman. He was all business. He'd care for his friend later.

"Number unknown. I took out four or five of them, but there's probably more in the ops building. If I were you, I'd blow the shit out of the ops building before getting anywhere near this place," replied Supplee.

"Roger, understand, Black Gang. We're five miles out and heading your way. Hang on for a few more minutes. Can you get away from the ops building?" replied Rickman.

Supplee suddenly realized that the truck was still running

and the heater was still on. Practically no fuel left, though, he thought as he glanced at the fuel gauge, but the little that was left would do the job.

"Roger, Blue Light, can do," he said into the microphone.

Supplee put the radio down and squirmed around to square himself with the steering wheel. He took a good look around and saw that the storm had largely passed with only a few snowflakes being driven by the still-ferocious wind. Visibility had improved greatly. He could see the ops building and the black streaks that were left from his grenades. If there were any Russians left in that building, they wouldn't last long. Rickman was going to take his suggestion—the ops building didn't have long to live.

Supplee jammed the truck into gear and rumbled off down the taxi strip toward the eastern end of the island. After getting several hundred yards away from the ops building, he swung the truck around so he could watch the fireworks.

He didn't have long to wait. Two laser-guided bombs smashed into the ops building and totally demolished the structure in an instant. Pieces of the building were thrown hundreds of yards into the air, with some of them landing close to Supplee's truck. No worries from anyone in that building, he thought with relief.

A voice came from the radio lying on the seat next to him. "Black Gang, have you in sight. We are thirty seconds from touchdown. We'll send over our corpsmen right away."

Seconds later the sky seemed to be filled with helicopters. All of them had "U.S. Marines" on the fuselage. Supplee almost cried with delight.

Colonel Ivan Sysoyev's head jerked around as noise of the explosion rolled over the island. His eyes busily searched the limit of his visibility for the source of the noise. His group was on the road headed away from the airstrip toward Building 600 where most of the bodies were.

The blast had come from near where they had landed on the eastern end of the island, he concluded, and he thought he saw flames among the residual snowfall from the storm. What was that? His men had no orders to destroy anything, and could only fire if fired upon. How many survivors of this disaster could there be?

He turned to his radio operator. "Get me Alpha Five," he ordered. Alpha Five was the group near the airport. They should be in a position by now to see what was going on, he thought.

"This is Alpha Five," came a voice over the radio. "The airport operations building has just been destroyed by attack aircraft." His man was clearly excited.

The GRU colonel took the microphone from the radio operator. "Did you get it on tape?" asked Sysoyev brusquely as his mind raced with the possibilities.

"Yes, sir, every second of it!" said the voice. "Just a minute—" The voice stopped abruptly. There was a moment's worth of hesitation. When he came back on, his voice was grim. "Helicopters! Seven of them! U.S. Marines are landing!"

The damn Americans were retaking the island! His operational timing was off. The Americans weren't supposed to get back here so soon, he thought. He and his men were supposed to be done and off the island before the Americans attacked.

"How big are the helicopters?" he asked.

"Helicopters are CH-53 Super Stallions. They can hold up to fifty-five troops in each one," said his man at the airport.

Sysoyev did the multiplication in his head in record time. There could be 385 U.S. Marines about to swarm the island. His Spetsnaz team were among the best fighters in the world. They were good, but they weren't that good.

Sysoyev looked about him, now suddenly unsure of what to do. He'd have to get what he could and get out fast. He held the microphone up to his mouth once more.

"Get as much as you can on tape, but stay out of sight."

Lieutenant Ellen Gain gunned the truck's engine for all it was worth as she bounced and slid her way past Building 600, the site of her original encounter with Trask and Elverson. She thought of it briefly but redirected her thoughts to the dangerous course that lay ahead. There probably would be someone at the comm terminal, and he wouldn't be very friendly. She forced herself to think of the mechanics of sending a message and suddenly remembered that both consoles were destroyed in the firefight at the comm center. She chewed her lip over that, and then quickly remembered that there always was a spare console in the transmitter room.

The road swung to the left, and it triggered the memory of her nearly disastrous encounter with the quarry beyond. She had almost taken a nosedive off the edge in the heavy snow. When was that? She was surprised to remember that it was only two days ago. It seemed like a hundred years had passed.

The road straightened, and she mashed her foot to the floor, but then immediately she had to let up due to the drifted snow on the unplowed roads. She snaked her way around the heaviest piles of snow, went around a turn and thought of their first encounter with the SVR. She imagined the truck lying on its side and appearing as a blackened, burned-out hulk. She thought that the weather would have cooled the fire that had raged within, and would have even deposited some snow on the upturned side of the wreckage. And what would be near the wreck? Her mind produced the vision of two partially snow-covered bodies.

She grimly pushed down on the accelerator and tried not to think of any more details of the wreck. The truck shot forward, and after a few moments she realized that the comm terminal was just ahead. She also realized with relief that she wouldn't have to drive past the actual wreck she had been imagining. The truck with its ill-fated occupants was another quarter mile down the road past the satellite ground terminal. She brought the truck to a quick stop when she saw the telltale antennas and shut off the engine.

Gain got out of the truck with the M16 slung over her shoulder and left the door open, rather than risk the noise of closing it. After unslinging her weapon and insuring it was loaded, she started off down the road, then after a hundred yards or so she left the road and trod through the tundra until she spotted a parked vehicle from which she could observe the comm center.

There was no movement of any kind. She tuned her hearing to pick up sound through the wind, but there was nothing. The stillness was unnerving. After ten minutes, she decided she wasn't going to get a better opportunity if she waited all day. She briefly wondered where the landing party was, and suddenly was in a panic to get inside the comm center and send the message before they arrived.

Gain gathered her courage, jumped to her feet and sprinted toward the door of the building. She made it to the door and tried to minimize the sounds of her breathing as she listened briefly for sounds within. She heard nothing. She cautiously opened the door and entered with her M16 out in front. She took the short hallway to the communications room and peered through the doorway.

The bodies of the two SVR agents that Trask and Elverson had killed two days ago were missing. The SVR must have cleaned up, she thought. Her attention went directly to the new console that had been wheeled into place beside the two smashed ones. Where was the SVR? She satisfied herself with the answer that the comm center was no longer needed now that the operation was over. She laid down her weapon and quickly went over to the console. The landing party still might show up here, and with that thought she felt panic rise within her. She didn't have much time.

Sounds floated over to her. The squeak of a floorboard. The rustle of material. The unmistakable sound of a bolt being pulled back.

She looked up in horror.

A white-clad man was standing in the doorway to the transmitter room pointing an automatic weapon at her. A second white-clad man stood next to him.

"Blue Fox, I presume," he said with a smile.

CHAPTER 24

Phil Hatfield lowered his binoculars while keeping his eyes trained on the low-slung building that appeared between the two high rises in downtown Moscow. There was going to be a meeting—he was sure of it—and it was going to happen very soon.

The two other units under his direction had reported that several high-ranking members of the GRU had arrived and had quickly been ushered inside. Their manner had indicated that they did not want to be seen. Hatfield had the feeling, however, that all the participants were not yet there. One to go, he thought, and he'll be a big one.

Hatfield glanced at his partner with an unspoken question. His partner, wearing headphones and listening to his other units, briefly shook his head—nothing yet. Hatfield let his gaze sweep over the equipment that represented the state-of-the-art in surveillance equipment. It was compact—a little more than two suitcases. It had to be small and lightweight as well; they might have to move very quietly and very quickly. Hatfield knew all about that. He had been in enough scrapes in the past.

Feeling began to rise in him as he thought over how the equipment did its job. The equipment was set up as if his superiors didn't trust him. There was no way for him to listen in on what was being said in the target building, not like the previous equipment where he could plug in a headset and see if he could decipher what was going on. He knew he shouldn't feel insulted, after all, the lack of monitoring capability was only a quirk of the equipment's development.

The equipment was originally designed to pick up the electromagnetic fields that all computer systems, especially video terminals, radiate, and then reconstruct the video image that appears on the screens. American engineers had developed the system, but the CIA had found quickly that the Russians just didn't use that many computers for intelligence work, at least not for the juiciest of details, and almost never put any details of their covert operations in a computer. The system had found limited use in Hatfield's section.

His section, code-named Tollgate, had run the gamut of surveillance equipment over the last ten to fifteen years. When he was a new recruit, the state-of-the-art was in planting "bugs"; however, the Russians soon became adept at locating them, and just the act of planting one would place a number of agents in jeopardy. Then came the laser surveillance equipment which bounced a low-strength laser beam off a window and detected the vibrations in the glass that were caused by conversations within. The Russian countermeasure to the laser detector was simple, as all good countermeasures are—they merely put speakers near the windows and played loud martial music to drown out the weak vibrations caused by their conversations.

A CIA expert was called in and quickly devised the ingeniously simple counter-countermeasure of obtaining recordings of the same music played by the Russians and programming the equipment to subtract out the loud music and leave the weak voice vibrations behind.

It worked well for several years until the Russians called in an expert of their own. The Russians quickly switched from martial music to random noise and all efforts by American intelligence to subtract out the noise failed.

The CIA then stumbled across a list of buildings in Moscow and other cities that would be used in the future for high-level intelligence meetings by the GRU. They quickly got some agents in the maintenance business to do work on some of the buildings on the list. To use the newly acquired surveillance equipment, they reasoned that they needed a good antenna inside the buildings, due to the obvious difficulties in getting outside antennas close enough to do any good.

Three relatively good antennas run through every building: telephone lines, electrical power lines, and water pipes. The Russians ripped out all the telephone lines, but left the other two untouched. Hatfield's section installed transducers on both the power lines and the water pipes and transmitted the data, not by conventionally radiating electromagnetic fields—that would have been as easy to detect as a "bug"—but by using the power lines themselves as the transmission medium and sent a low-level, hard-to-detect signal back outside the building. Hatfield's people had only to tap into the power lines in any building within a half mile radius of the target building and they would have a strong enough signal to use.

Only there was nothing to detect. The Russians didn't trust computers with the kind of information that Hatfield needed. Their expert was called in again and this time he brought a CIA surveillance engineer as well. After scratching his head for a month, the engineer noticed some noise outside the frequencies they normally worked with. He modified the equipment to detect these signals and discovered with surprise that he could extract conversations that were being held within the buildings. This occurred only on the water pipe channel and not on the power line channel.

Analysis done at Langley showed that the transducers used in the target buildings were microphonic, meaning that they picked up vibrations in the pipes as well as the weak electrical currents they were originally designed to pick up, and transmitted both as electrical signals. It was a simple matter to change the surveillance equipment to process the "noise" instead of the original signal.

The system was imperfect at best. The effectiveness of the system depended upon the proximity of the conversation to water pipes, with the best clarity realized when conversations were held in the lavatories. Next best were rooms that had water pipes running through them or next to them.

They did get some tantalizing bits now and then that had provided the all-important confirmation of information from other sources that intelligence forces desperately need.

The equipment gave Hatfield the feeling of being on the outside looking in. He didn't have any idea that it was even working except for the disk drive light that blinked on and off when the system dumped its data on a floppy disk. His people would then take the disk to a drop site to transmit the data back to the American embassy. All the analysis was done back at Langley. He had no idea what was going on inside the target building, and he didn't like it.

His partner suddenly pressed the earphones tightly to his ears in an instinctive gesture. Hatfield instantly knew that this was what he had been waiting for. His partner shot him a look loaded with significance. He said only one word, but it was enough to send needles up Hatfield's spine.

"Tolstiakov."

The head man! This was highly unusual, Hatfield thought, as the excitement rose within him. The leader of the GRU *never* would go to these meetings, unless something was being discussed that Tolstiakov didn't want the other members of Russian government to know about. What was happening? What was being said? He couldn't help giving the equipment on the other side of the room a jealous look. His envy gave way to worry. How did he know it was working? He looked over the control settings—everything was right.

The rest of the room seemed to fade as Hatfield found himself staring at the lower left side of the equipment. The red disk drive light blinked on and off in a steady rhythm.

General Vladimir Fedorovich Iskanderov's headache was getting worse. Maybe he was too old for all of this, he decided. When democracy broke out in the former Soviet Union, he was secretly overjoyed and immensely relieved. He had no stomach for confrontations with the nearly invincible United States. He flipped two aspirin into his mouth and worked them to the back of his throat, then he drank quickly from his cup that was filled with lukewarm tea. He wiped the drops on the desk top that fell from his hurried drink away with his sleeve.

"General, GRU Colonel Yuri Georgievich Solov'yev to see you," said a voice over his intercom.

Iskanderov gave the intercom a quick look as the name registered immediately in his mind. Colonel Solov'yev was General Tolstiakov's aide. What would the aide to the GRU chief want with him? Probably just a messenger, he thought. I ought to make him wait. But something told him that whatever this Colonel Solov'yev had to say was important. He had no idea what was happening on Shemya, and he was desperate for the information before the Americans called back. Maybe the colonel brought some word.

Iskanderov pushed the talk lever on the intercom. "Show him in."

The colonel walked in and stood stiffly in front of Iskanderov's desk. The general waved him to a nearby chair. The colonel sat and seemed very ill at ease. Iskanderov stared at him for a moment, then realized he still had the bottle of aspirin in his hand and quickly dropped it into an open drawer. He absentmindedly wiped a few remaining drops of tea off his desk while continuing to look at the increasingly nervous GRU officer.

When it became apparent that Iskanderov was waiting for the colonel to speak, Solov'yev tried the amenities. "Are you feeling all right, General?" He tried to put concern into his voice, but it sounded pretty lame.

Iskanderov ignored the question. "Do you bring me any information from our esteemed General Tolstiakov about this Shemya business?"

Colonel Solov'yev swallowed nervously. "Yes, General. But not the kind you might think." He hesitated and his gaze dropped to play randomly over the floor.

What is this? More surprises? thought Iskanderov.

"General, you know about our plan to cover up this whole affair, and the Spetsnaz team sent to Shemya." Solov'yev hesitated again and Iskanderov had the sudden realization that the GRU colonel was here on his own. Solov'yev's boss, General Tolstiakov, didn't know his aide was here talking with the chief of the SVR. Iskanderov riveted his attention on the young colonel.

"General, there is a plot for the military takeover of the government," said the colonel in a rush. He stopped talking and the words hung heavily between them.

This particular turn of events didn't surprise Iskanderov. There were always some plots floating around, but they never amounted to much. Disgruntled people always seemed to make a spectacle of themselves, especially the ones in the military. That made them easy to spot and take care of. Maybe this young colonel had stumbled upon his first one. Then again, he might be confusing the Shemya plan with a real plot.

Iskanderov grunted. "You mean the one Tolstiakov cooked up for the Americans' benefit, or a real one?"

"A real one, General, I assure you," replied the colonel.

What game was Tolstiakov playing now? Iskanderov's eyes bored in on the hapless colonel.

"I was present at a meeting just an hour ago where the GRU's *real* plan was being discussed," said Solov'yev as his eyes rose to meet the general's. "The Spetsnaz team has not been ordered to cover up the affair. They are carrying cameras to record the whole thing. They will leak this affair to the international press. Some of the SVR sleeper agents will be brought back to serve as witnesses. American aid will be cut off to Russia after the American people see those tapes. Chaos will result. Starvation. Panic in the streets—"

"What does the GRU have to gain in all of this?" interrupted Iskanderov. He was skeptical. Tolstiakov might be a little unstable, but he wasn't crazy.

"It was SVR agents that perpetrated this atrocity on Shemya," said Solov'yev as he held the general's stare. "The GRU will not only move to destroy the SVR, but the army will also impose martial law over the whole country."

Iskanderov's blood ran cold. Tolstiakov had concocted a brilliant plan, one in which he had enlisted the SVR's help. In effect, he was using the SVR to destroy themselves. The breakup of the KGB in 1991 wasn't enough for Tolstiakov—he wanted all foreign intelligence for himself! Fury welled up in Iskanderov, but he forced it down. He needed a clear head for what would come next.

He picked up a phone which Colonel Solov'yev took as a signal to go. The colonel stood and took a step towards the door.

"Sit down, Colonel," growled Iskanderov. "We have some explaining to do to one of this country's best friends." He lifted the handset to his mouth. "Get me Douglas Meyers at Langley immediately."

Meyers dropped the phone back on the hook and immediately picked up another one. He saw his hand shake for the first time in many years. The phone call from Iskanderov had shaken him greatly. But it all could be just a game. The Russians still weren't above pulling a fast one now and then.

"This is the DDO," said Meyers to the person who answered the phone. "I need the latest intercepts from Section D immediately." The man on the other end of the line acknowledged the order and hung up.

Meyers punched another button on his phone and heard it ring. It was picked up on the second ring. "Sam, get in here now," said Meyers. The man acknowledged the command, and Meyers heard the man's chair creak with his sudden movement just before he hung up. Meyers dropped the phone back on the cradle and held his head in his hands.

Iskanderov was very clear on a couple of points. The SVR chief stated flatly that his people could easily handle the GRU conspirators, including General Tolstiakov himself. But the Americans were the ones to stop the Spetsnaz team. Russia couldn't be in the position of sending forces to Shemya to battle its own forces. Someone, somewhere, would find out, and this entire incident would become public. Then the GRU would win in the end. The Spetsnaz team had to be annihilated before they reached Russian territory. Once on Russian soil, Iskanderov couldn't guarantee that the tapes would not fall into the wrong hands. And all that meant that the U.S. Navy had to sink the sub that had brought the Spetsnaz team to Shemya. Could they get forces there that quickly? This game was being played on the edge of disaster.

But was it all true? Or was Iskanderov playing some kind of game? That is what he needed Sam Turner's people for. He needed confirmation of Iskanderov's story.

Turner burst into Meyer's office. "What's up, Doug?" he asked breathlessly.

"What assets do we have on the GRU leadership?" asked Meyers.

"We've got a partial surveillance section, Tollgate, on the top brass in Moscow," began Turner.

"Why not a full one?" snapped Meyers. His mood surprised Turner.

"Wasn't available. We're supposed to get a full one up to speed on—"

"Listen, Sam, I need whatever you've got immediately," said Meyers in a softer tone of voice.

"We've gotten a preliminary report from Tollgate of a high-level meeting of the GRU leadership including Tolstiakov just this morning," replied Turner. "They were going to send it by normal channels, but I'll tell them to send it immediately by the emergency channel if you authorize it."

"Do it," said Meyers.

"Yes sir," replied Turner, and got up to go.

"Sam," said Meyers. Turner stopped in his tracks and glanced over his shoulder. "This intercept is to be DDO Eyes Only," said Meyers.

"Yes sir," said Turner. The only person who would know the contents of the intercept would be Meyers himself.

A half hour later, the phone buzzed softly on Douglas Meyers's desk. He picked it up midway through the first ring. It was Turner.

"Tollgate intercept will be coming up on your screen, sir," said Turner. "Will analysis be needed quickly?"

"I'll let you know. Thank you," said Meyers, and hung up. He turned to his PC and typed in the commands to get the Moscow intercept on the screen. Meyers read in silence for several minutes. The conversation was virtually all there with no gaps, and was 99 percent intelligible, which was unusual for the type of equipment that Tollgate was using. It confirmed Iskanderov's story and Meyers's worst fears. He read to the last word and spun to his set of phones. He knew there should be analysis done to confirm that this was indeed the GRU leadership talking and not some setup from the SVR, but there was no time.

"Get me Raven, and get the NMCC on standby," he ordered the operator.

CHAPTER 25

▬ ▬ ▪ ▬ ▪ ▬ ▪ ▬

Thoughts of his wife floated across Driscoll's mind, and he felt a certain euphoria. He remembered when they first met at an officer's club dance when he was a brand-new second lieutenant. He had always been wary of women due to his special calling in life, but he still belonged to the human race and even his inflexible superiors knew that he needed female companionship.

Suzanne had been warm and tender and had loved him for his own sake and not because of his status in life. She had been initially attracted by the uniform, but that had passed quickly into what society calls a whirlwind romance. She had gotten under his skin, and he hadn't realized a relationship could have such intense feelings. He, at one point, considered telling her the truth about his real beginnings but resisted the temptation as his training took hold. He had settled back and had enjoyed himself with the realization that he didn't have to do anything for his masters for several years yet. They always waited until their sleepers had attained a much higher rank before having them do anything.

It was a wonderful relationship and his wife's presence floated in his mind, until the realization that he would never see her again washed over him like a wave. He had to console himself with the fact that now he knew she was all right, and she would remain so. He thought over the whole situation again, shook his head and almost laughed. What irony!

He heard steps in the hallway and didn't bother to turn around. He would probably get a bullet in the back in the next minute or so. There was only one price for failure as far as his masters were concerned. His face suddenly creased in a maniacal smile. The irony was that he had succeeded beyond his wildest dreams. He rubbed his face in his hands.

"Colonel Driscoll?"

It was a question, and a rather timid one at that. Driscoll turned and peered into the darkness at the figure silhouetted against the ragged doorway of the Operations Room.

"Colonel? Is that you?"

Driscoll delayed a response until he had made out that the man's weapon was dangling by his side. He certainly didn't seem threatening.

"Yeah, it's me," replied Driscoll in a low voice.

The man moved a few steps closer until Driscoll could make out his face. It was one of his men, the youngest one at that.

"I stayed at my post as long as I could." He hesitated. "Then I figured I'd come and find you . . . and see what's next."

Driscoll sighed and nodded.

"It's . . . all over, isn't it?" asked the young man.

"Yeah, it's all over." Driscoll's tone of voice sounded flat.

The young man tried a small smile. "We win?"

Driscoll almost laughed. "Yeah, we won. We won big."

The young man's smile grew into a broad grin. He pulled up a chair and sat down in a position to stare at his superior. "You think we're heroes, sir?"

Driscoll considered telling him; it would remove that stupid grin on his face. He might even break down and cry as Driscoll had done. He couldn't bring himself to do it.

"Yeah, we're heroes all right," said Driscoll, and became more serious.

The young man grew even more excited and was obviously extremely happy. Driscoll attributed that to his youth—he hadn't been away from Russia as long as Driscoll had.

"You had quite a time up here, didn't you, sir." He was looking at the dead strewn around the room.

"Yes, quite a time."

The youth suddenly shifted his gaze to Driscoll and his smile faded. "Are you all right, sir?" There seemed to be genuine concern in his voice.

"I didn't get much sleep the past couple of days," replied Driscoll.

He nodded. "That's understandable. I didn't get much either, sir."

Driscoll stared into the semidarkness in an attempt to fix a name to the young man's face. The glow from the situation screen, especially the lower, totally white portion, provided the most light. The young man turned his face toward the screen and gazed at it for a moment, fascinated by what it represented.

"You're Jensen, aren't you?" asked Driscoll. The young man turned back to look at his senior officer, which shrouded his face in darkness once more.

"Yevgeni Kirilov, Comrade Colonel." He smiled.

Driscoll nodded. There was no longer any reason for pretense. Their mission was over. "You and Sergeant McDonough took out the admin building next door, didn't you?" asked Driscoll.

"Yes, Comrade Colonel. The sergeant was called down to the airport area to hunt for some survivors."

Driscoll nodded. Everyone had left the building to hunt for survivors. He had been alone until now. Driscoll wanted to tell him the "comrade" was no longer necessary. As young as he was, Kirilov still must have been installed in the United States before the Soviet Union went out of business.

Driscoll nodded again. "Well done, Comrade Kirilov," he said, giving in to the old Communist form of address.

"*Spasiba, Tovarisch Polkovnik,*" replied the young man.

They both heard the noise at the same time and jumped from their chairs to look out the ruined doorway and into the corridor beyond. Driscoll's young companion brought up his M16 to a ready position and pointed the barrel toward the doorway. They both strained their ears to pick up any sound that would give away what might be happening out in the corridor, but they heard nothing.

Driscoll heard a rustling behind him and whirled around to see two white-clad men pointing automatic weapons at him from the doorway to the Mission Processing Room. His mouth fell open in surprise and he saw, out of the corner of his eye, that Jensen had started to turn toward the noise as well. While he was in midturn, they heard a voice from the corridor.

"Drop the weapon," it said in heavily accented English.

Jensen was caught midway, and saw that there were two sets of automatic weapons pointed at him, one from the corridor and one from the doorway that led to the Mission Processing Room. He quickly complied with the order. His M16 clattered to the floor.

The white-clad men moved into the room and quickly searched Driscoll and Jensen. After satisfying themselves that there were no other weapons on either of them, they backed away and surprisingly lowered their weapons. One of them stepped forward and stiffly saluted.

"Colonel, I am Colonel Titov, First Commando Unit, Second Attack Brigade. We are here to evacuate you and your people from this island." He spoke with a heavy Russian accent.

Jensen broke out into a broad smile, tilted back his head and laughed.

"Colonel . . ." began Driscoll.

"Let me congratulate you on your outstanding performance on this mission. You will certainly become a hero of the Russian Federation!" said the leader of the group.

Driscoll looked back and forth between the obviously delighted Jensen and the officer in front of him and saw what was coming.

"There is one detail that we must attend to before evacuation," continued the officer as one of his men brought out a medical kit with a large red cross on the front.

They opened it and he saw neat stacks of hypodermic needles within.

"The gas that was used by your people could have affected all of you on this island. Therefore, we must inoculate you against infection."

The officer finished his explanation on an almost lame note. Driscoll looked into his eyes and knew he was lying. So this was how it was to happen. He had been wondering.

Jensen quickly rolled up his sleeve and was injected with the contents of the syringe. Driscoll gave the officer a long look and caused the officer to become ill at ease.

"You understand why you must be inoculated, don't you, Colonel?" he asked.

Driscoll lowered his gaze and nodded wearily. "Yes, I understand," he replied.

They waited patiently for a moment for Driscoll to roll up his sleeve, then when he didn't comply, the officer gestured impatiently to one of his men. The man unbuttoned Driscoll's right shirt cuff and rolled up his sleeve. He quickly injected Driscoll with the contents of the second syringe.

The white-clad men seemed to back away from the two of them and just watch for a moment. Jensen turned to Driscoll in order to say something and nearly fell over in the process. He staggered over to a chair and sat down. He attempted to speak again but found that he was nearly paralyzed. His mouth hung open in astonishment and panic crossed his face. Driscoll felt sorry for the youth. After all, it must have been totally unexpected for him, while Driscoll had known what was coming.

Jensen started to choke and then fell over, writhing on the floor. Driscoll felt panic at the sight and tried to think of his wife to counteract the surge within him. The white-clad men turned and started to slowly file out of the room.

"I don't know why we had to use that shit," complained one of the men. "There's enough people with bullet holes in them already."

Driscoll recognized with surprise that the man's heavy Russian accent was gone.

U.S.S. NEW YORK CITY

Captain Ed Stanley shook his head in consternation. Nothing much seemed to be happening in the direction of their Russian Akula contact for the last several hours. He tapped his sonarman on the shoulder for the tenth time in an hour. Frederick looked at him and slowly shook his head. Stanley had to admire the Russians' discipline, keeping so quiet for so long, but it was unnerving to say the least.

Stanley stared at the waterfall, now just a jumble of dots since their contact had stopped dead in the water, but the American sonar still picked up some noises within the sub's hull. Stanley grew increasingly impatient until he could bear it no longer.

"All right, I've had enough," he said under his breath. Stanley walked the few feet from the sonar shack to the conning station. He turned to the diving officer. "Periscope depth." The diving officer gave him an aye, aye and complied with the order. The boat silently drifted upward to the ordered depth.

"Up periscope," ordered the captain.

The periscope slid upward until the handles were at just the right level for the captain to lean on. He slapped the handles down and pushed the button for the hydraulic assist in order to rotate the periscope tube. Stanley swung around until he was on Master Five's bearing. He centered up on a dot on the horizon, then adjusted magnification to get a decent picture of the contact. Two rubber boats floated on the sea with what appeared to be three men in each boat. Some of the men had white winter gear on, but three of the others had on what appeared to be olive drab parkas. Stanley got the impression that they were some of the island's occupants. Prisoners? In a few moments Stanley saw the Russian sub surface and take the people in the rubber boats aboard.

That was it. He had to tell his superiors. "Chief of the Watch, raise the BRA 34," commanded Stanley.

The chief hit the switches to raise the UHF antenna.

"Send a flash message to Commander SUBRON two, copy to COMSUBPAC," ordered Stanley to the communications yeoman. "Have contact with Akula-class submarine at—give our position—and have confirmed that a landing party of unknown strength has been put ashore on Shemya Island. Part of the landing party has returned to the submarine with three members of the island's crew. Request instructions."

The OOD gave Stanley a concerned look. "The transmission will tip our hand to the Russians, sir."

"I know they'll detect the transmission, but I have no choice. Send it," replied Stanley.

THE ADMIRAL CHARKIN

"Captain! Radio transmission close by!" said the ECM officer over the intercom. Captain First Rank Vasily Makeyev was over to the intercom in a flash. The hours of waiting had gone a long way to completely destroying his composure. This was the first incident during the prolonged wait—it might be something to *act* on. His passengers had just gotten safely aboard, and he was free to maneuver.

"Emergency dive!" ordered Makeyev. Then as the sub slid under the sea, "Bearing."

There was a hesitation of a few moments until the voice again boomed from the intercom. "Almost due south, sir."

"Can you make it more accurate than that?" asked Makeyev.

"No sir, the transmission was at UHF and only for a split second, but it was definitely to our south," replied his officer.

Yes, thought Makeyev, and *not* on the island. This transmission was from an American sub who had tailed the *Admiral Charkin* out of Petropavlovsk, and who lurked out of his boat's listening range.

If the Americans knew what they were up to, he and the *Admiral Charkin* wouldn't have long to live.

U.S.S NEW YORK CITY

Captain Stanley stared at the message and its unbelievable contents just handed to him by the communications officer.

He had never seen orders such as these in all his years in the navy, although in his younger days he used to dream about receiving such orders. And to receive them so quickly! Something was up, some real disaster was brewing. Was the United States at war with Russia? He read it again for the fifth time.

COMMANDING OFFICER'S EYES ONLY

FROM: *National Military Command Center*
TO: *Commanding Officer, USS* New York City, *SSN 696*
SUBJ: *Your Master Five contact*

> The U.S. State of Alaska, specifically the island of Shemya in the Aleutian Islands, has been invaded by forces hostile to the United States. These forces originate from the Russian Federation. Pursuant to this act of war you will take the following action.
>
> 1) You are hereby ordered to attack and sink said contact.
>
> 2) You are authorized to use any conventional means at your disposal, up to and including ramming said contact.
>
> 3) Under no circumstances are you to permit said contact to return to Russian territory.

END

Stanley made an instant decision. "Send a message requesting confirmation of these specific orders from COMSUBRON TWO and COMSUBPAC through special access channels," he said to the communications officer.

The man quickly composed a short message for Stanley's approval. The captain glanced at it and scribbled his initials on it, and the comm officer went away to transmit it immediately.

Several minutes later, Stanley had his confirmation in front of him. He sighed and looked up from the message. He never expected to have to do this, even though he had trained most of his adult life for just this sort of thing.

"Sound general quarters! Battle stations torpedo!" he ordered.

The OOD jumped a bit, but then repeated the orders to

the surprised crew. Then he turned to the captain. "What's up, Captain?"

"We've just been ordered to sink the contact," replied Stanley.

The OOD's mouth dropped open. When he recovered he asked, "Are you sure, sir?"

Stanley nodded and shoved the message into his pocket. "It's from NMCC and it's been confirmed by COMSUB-RON TWO and COMSUBPAC."

The OOD set his mouth into a grim line. "I hope they know what they're doing."

"Yeah," said Stanley disgustedly. "Make tubes one to four ready to fire in all respects. OOD, I have the conn," he said in a voice loud enough for everyone to hear.

"The captain has the conn. The OOD retains the deck," said the OOD.

"Helm, all ahead one third," said Stanley. "Left five degrees rudder. Steady on course three-five-zero. Make your depth one hundred and fifty feet."

Stanley took a step toward the fire control crew. "Fire control and tracking party, I intend to destroy Master Five contact pursuant to orders from the National Command Authority. We will use torpedoes two and four and keep one and three for defensive purposes."

THE ADMIRAL CHARKIN

"I hear screws, bearing one-seven-nine degrees!" shouted one of Makeyev's sonarmen.

"Aspect angle," asked Makeyev. The sonarman listened for a few moments, then apologetically shook his head. The acoustic signal wasn't clear or strong enough to come to a conclusion about how the other sub was pointed.

"Course," asked Makeyev.

The sonarman stared at his equipment for a while. "Three-five-zero degrees."

So, the American was headed to the northwest, perhaps in a bid to cut him off from the central Pacific to the southwest.

"Speed," asked Makeyev.

"Blade count indicates ten knots and increasing," said another man.

"Ahead flank. Depth thirty meters. Course zero-nine-zero degrees," commanded Makeyev over the intercom to the conning station. "Send this message to Colonel Sysoyev before lowering the antenna: I am under attack and must maneuver. Will attempt to reestablish communications in five hours."

Captain Makeyev leaned over the sonarman as his boat rapidly picked up speed. He must lose this American for the mission to succeed.

Colonel Sysoyev was thunderstruck at the message from the *Charkin. Under attack*! Was the entire U.S. military here today? *Reestablish communications in five hours.* What was Makeyev thinking? In five minutes the entire Spetsnaz team could all be dead, if they were detected.

Sysoyev's mind was in turmoil. He had anticipated making a hasty exit after hearing that the marines landed on the other end of the island, but now he and his men were on their own for five hours. Could the *Charkin* lose its attackers, then come back to get Sysoyev's men off the island? That sounded almost impossible. No, not almost. It *was* impossible.

Sysoyev knew that his team would have to get back to Russia on their own devices. His team had a backup plan in case something happened to the submarine. They were to get a plane from those on the island and fly out. He had men on his team that could fly virtually anything. The only trouble was that all the island's aircraft were right where the U.S. Marines had landed minutes ago.

So, thought Sysoyev, I will have my confrontation with the vaunted U.S. Marines after all.

CHAPTER 26

The day seemed to get a bit grayer as Trask saw with a sinking feeling that they were too late. Trask and Elverson had found the truck where they had left it, but they were delayed by the circuitous route necessary to evade the landing party. They had gotten as close to the radar building as they had dared with the truck and then proceeded on foot to a ten-foot bluff that faced the rear of the building. They arrived at their vantage point atop the small hill just in time to see a group of white-clad men enter the door at the base of the building.

Trask cursed his luck and Elverson said nothing. There was nothing to do but wait.

Ten minutes later, the white-clad men exited the building, quickly formed up and started off at a trot in the direction of the northern part of the island. They didn't seem to be carrying anything away with them, which puzzled Trask greatly. They would at least want to carry off the computer disks and tapes which formed the top-secret signal processing and computer instructions to the radar. Trask scratched his head. There also was no one with them. He had originally figured that the landing party's main purpose was to evacuate the SVR team that had taken over the island. Did that mean that the radar building was empty? He shrugged. The only way to find out was to go inside and see for himself. Besides, he reasoned, the landing party might come back for the radar's secrets later, and he wanted an opportunity to get to the radar first and destroy what he could.

He quickly communicated this to Elverson as he eyed the silent, dark building. He hoped it was deserted. "All right, let's go," he ordered.

They both got up and ran the hundred yards to the door at the base of the rear of the building. They pressed themselves to the wall of the building and listened to detect any sound within but heard only the sound of their own breathing, with an occasional gasp from the out-of-shape engineer. Trask took a quick look around—there wasn't any movement anywhere. He looked at Elverson and motioned him inside. Elverson took a deep breath, stuck the automatic out in front of him, pulled the door open and leaped inside. Trask was right behind him.

Once inside they pressed themselves against the wall and waited a few seconds for their eyes to get accustomed to the darker conditions in the interior of the building. They listened for a few moments and heard nothing. Elverson then started to move toward the elevator, but Trask grabbed his arm and motioned to the stairs next to the elevator.

"Not as much noise," he whispered in the young AP's ear. Elverson nodded and started toward the stairs. They proceeded up the stairs and paused at every floor to listen for any sounds that would indicate anyone's presence. They heard nothing.

At the fifth floor Trask told Elverson that this was where the control rooms for the radar were located. Elverson cautiously entered the corridor and immediately saw the bodies that littered the floor and the shattered door that led to the Operations Room. He pursed his lips in a soundless whistle and pointed out the bodies to Trask, who was a step behind him. Trask muttered an oath in a low voice.

They cautiously made their way down the hallway until they reached the door to the Operations Room. Elverson peered into the dimly lit room and detected no activity. He mumbled a syllable or two to Trask and then quickly entered the room. He knelt with the automatic out in front of him in anticipation of any danger, but the room was deathly still and both men began to relax.

Trask entered and surveyed the carnage, shattered equipment, and the still-lit situation screen. The room was familiar to him; he had been privy to its secrets for many months now. Bodies were scattered on the floor, and Trask got the notion of their being considered just so much garbage by the SVR.

Trask glanced at Elverson and saw that the AP was staring at one body in particular. He followed the direction of the young man's gaze and saw an extremely contorted corpse with its mouth open in a soundless scream. He recoiled at the sight and looked back at Elverson, who was clearly astonished. The AP's reaction surprised him; he had expected revulsion, but not the look of surprise that so clearly filled his face. Trask's curiosity rose, and he forced himself to look at the body once more. The man was in an air force lieutenant colonel's uniform, and his face, for all its contortion, looked familiar. He looked a little more closely and noted that there were no marks of violence on him at all, no blood which was clearly visible on most of the rest of the bodies.

"Driscoll," mumbled Elverson. Recognition flashed quickly in Trask's mind, the deputy squadron commander. He suddenly remembered the conversation of the two enemy agents on the road near the trailer. Lieutenant Colonel Driscoll had been their leader.

Elverson leaned over and felt the body. "He's still warm. He's dead less than half an hour," he said in amazement. Trask was also surprised. If Driscoll was an SVR agent, then why did the landing party apparently kill him? And why was Elverson so surprised that Driscoll was dead? Trask had never told him that he had heard Driscoll's name mentioned by two SVR agents. Trask shook his head. So many questions, no answers, and no time to find out.

Trask's gaze swept the room once again and came to rest on the situation screen. The display on the situation screen didn't register in his mind at first, but after a moment or two of staring at it, he suddenly realized what it all meant. The breath caught in his throat for a long moment until his body involuntarily sucked in air with a loud gasping noise.

Elverson looked at him quickly and immediately saw the shocked look on the engineer's face. He turned and also looked at the situation screen, although he saw only the outlines of a map of Russia and a thoroughly whitened United States.

"It's worse than I thought. The United States is completely destroyed and Russia is untouched!" gasped Trask.

Elverson made a few sounds of amazement while gaping at the screen as Trask staggered over to a chair and sat down. He held his head in his hands and thought that he would weep but found that he could not.

How could this have happened? This must mean that the SVR had been successful; the old data must have fooled NORAD into thinking that all was normal when the Russians had actually launched their ICBMs at the United States! He glanced at the screen again. Russia was intact; apparently even the U.S. submarines hadn't launched their missiles. *What the hell was going on? Why hadn't the United States retaliated?*

The answer occurred to him almost immediately and he sat thunderstruck. Perhaps there was no one left to give the command. The Russians would have targeted the National Command Centers as their highest priority, and with an attack of enormous magnitude and no warning, they would very likely succeed in decapitating the nation's war machine.

He sat for several minutes in silence as his feelings hit rock bottom, and then slowly started on the way up again.

"It looks like we lost," he said in a surprisingly steady voice. He got to his feet with new resolve. "I don't know what's survived all that, but they won't get this radar. And then I'm going to take a few of the bastards with me," he said in a voice shaking with emotion.

Trask left Elverson still gaping at the screen and went through the battered doorway into the corridor and headed for the Computer Room. He stormed into the room in a careless explosion of movement and walked quickly over to the disk memory equipment. He was about to remove several disks to destroy them when the display on the system console caught his eye. The display wasn't normal; it was flashing with a warning on it.

******************WARNING!*******************
UNKNOWN PERSONNEL HAVE ATTEMPTED TO
PENETRATE COMPUTER SECURITY 10,000,024
TIMES WITH 1 SUCCESS!
******************WARNING!*******************

What the devil was going on? He momentarily forgot
about the disks and sat down at the console. He typed in
several commands and rapidly got to the innermost level
of computer security for which he was authorized. There
was one level to go, and he needed a seven-digit number
or seven letters to unlock the secrets at that level.

Trask frowned in thought. Who tried over ten million
times to penetrate the highest level of computer security?
Was it Lieutenant Colonel Driscoll? Had he paid for his
knowledge with his life? And why? What could possibly
be so important that someone would expend so much effort
to find out? His curiosity was piqued, but he felt the question was academic. It would take too much time for him to
duplicate the effort to crack the code word, and he didn't
have much time before he thought the landing party would
be back.

He pushed himself away from the console with the in-
tention of going back to the memory equipment, but a piece
of paper under one corner of the terminal caught his eye.
He picked it up and found that it had the name Rinaldi
written normally and also written backwards. His pulse
quickened. He counted the number of letters and saw that
it was the same number as the code word. Could this be
it? The last entry on the page was the name written backwards and he decided to try it that way.

With mounting anticipation he typed in the letters and
then hit the Return key. The screen abruptly changed, and
he was left with a piece of text which he began to read. It
accurately described the events of the last several days beginning with the coup in Russia by hard-liners and some
missing nuclear warheads. Then the hard-liners threw
threats at the United States, and the world watched helplessly as the two countries marched to the brink of nuclear

war. This was old news; the air force had kept everyone on the island informed of the tense events between the United States and Russia. He skipped a lot of it until he came to the part involving Christmas morning. He read the sentence and reread it without realizing it.

Time seemed to slow down as he waited for the impact to reach him. His mind worked at a distance from reality, but in a split second realization rushed in at him. His blood turned to ice and he sat in shock at what was on the screen before him.

0727 25 DECEMBER—DEFCON 1 DRILL TO ASSESS
REACTION TIME, CODE NAME
DRAWN SWORD.
CLASSIFICATION—EXEC MAX, TOP SECRET
* * *

The twin hourglass shapes of the cooling towers of the nuclear power plant peeked through the mist and gloom that seemed to hang over the island. They saw only the tops of the towers, from the middle to the bottom was shrouded in white haze. The towers were to their right, and behind them down the road was the radar building. The five of them ran easily even though they had been running through snow-packed roads for twenty minutes.

The road to the nuclear power plant branched off to the right, and the five white-clad men automatically followed the slight outlines in the snow and the orange-tipped metal rods that lined the road to keep vehicles from wandering off the road during a snowstorm. The leader of the CIA/SEAL team turned and glanced at each one of his men. They were running with little exertion, including their "expert," who had not had the benefit of the training that the rest of the men had received. He had worried about this outsider. They had a very stringent timetable, and there could be no room for error; this was not one of their endless drills but a real mission, one with incalculable consequences.

Lieutenant Commander Herbert Lawser glanced at his watch and tried to think about what was happening with the other groups on the island. The group at the radar building would be just finishing up. He looked at his watch again to be sure. He wasn't used to hands on watches anymore, but he was given a different watch before the mission, and for good reason.

Lawser thought over his nuclear expert again and briefly wondered how he had kept in such good shape. He had always thought that engineers got fat and lazy at their sedentary jobs.

The snowfall had virtually stopped except for some stubborn lingering snowflakes that seemed to fall at intermittent intervals. The wind kicked up the already fallen snow and periodically made it seem as if the snowfall was still a blizzard.

The group slowed as the twelve-foot-high fence, which encircled the nuclear power plant, came into view. The fence seemed even higher due to the four feet of concertina wire that was perched at an angle at the top. The fence banged and rattled in the wind, thereby making the motion detectors that were on each section of the fence totally useless.

The five came to a halt at the gate as their leader played his eyes over the plant. All was quiet. Two men produced large wire cutters and immediately began to cut a man-sized hole in the fencing to one side of the gate. Lawser turned around once again and eyed the "expert." So, he *was* breathing more deeply than the others. A curious feeling of satisfaction ran through him as if he had justified all his years of training.

He turned back around and noted that his men had made short work of the fence. He glanced at his watch again. They were thirty seconds early. The five of them were through the fence in seconds as their leader scanned the peculiar set of buildings once again. The cooling towers and the containment building were unmistakable, but the rest of the buildings blurred together in a jumble. The turbine and auxiliary buildings and several other buildings all could be mistaken for each other; however, the expert stepped up and indicated the building that was their destination.

Lawser nodded and began to double-time toward the en-

trance to the building with his men obediently falling in
behind him. They reached the doorway to the control building in something less than a minute, and two men, with
weapons cocked and ready, flanked the doorway while
Lawser and the unarmed expert stood back. The fifth man
looked briefly at Lawser, who gave him a curt gesture to
proceed. The man shifted his gaze to the door and stepped
up to try the doorknob. He opened the door easily and gave
Lawser a quick, surprised glance over his shoulder. He
leaped inside and a few seconds later, he motioned the rest
of the party to enter.

There was a small entrance that contained a doorway
leading to a stairwell, another door leading to a first-floor
corridor, and an elevator. Lawser motioned two of his men
toward the stairway and he and the others entered the elevator. They went up one floor and stopped, and endured an
excruciatingly long moment before the elevator doors
opened.

The doors opened with a slight rattle and the three of
them stepped into the hallway just in time to see the other
two men step into the hallway from the stairwell. All eyes
went to the guard station. They could see two bodies on
the floor in the gap between the counters. The floor was
stained a dark red. Lawser went past the guard station and
cautiously approached the door to the control room. He put
his ear to the door and listened. There were voices, muffled
and intermittent, and there was definitely more than one
man in the room.

Lawser turned to get his expert and found him at his
elbow. The leader gestured to the control room door security mechanism. The expert nodded and got to work
while the others positioned themselves to rush the doorway.

The expert withdrew a plastic card, much like a credit
card but without the swath of magnetic tape, from within
the folds of his white outer garment. He slid the card
through a slot on the wall to the right of the door, and a
light above the slot went from red to green. The expert
reached over to a small keyboard recessed into the top of
a metal box that hung on the wall next to the slot and

tapped out a series of numbers. The other four men held their breath.

The door hissed open on a surge of compressed air. Lawser jumped into the space beyond the door and leaped to his right. The rest of the party quickly followed and found convenient cover behind control panels and partitions. The white-clad men were in place in a mere three seconds.

The three men in the control room were taken completely by surprise but scrambled for their M16s as the last man in the CIA team took up a position in the control room. The control room personnel jumped into the space between the primary and secondary control panels while furiously wondering about the identity of the intruders. The secondary control panels were taller than the primary control panels, and the control room people were able to peer over the primary panels to get a look at the invaders. There were sounds of bolts being pulled back.

"I am Colonel Lyhatkin, First Commando Unit, Second Attack Brigade," said Lawser in a strong, clear, harshly accented voice. Silence ensued. The CIA/SEAL team leader caught one of the control room men peeking over the primary control panel. He looked straight at the man and spoke again.

"We are here to evacuate you from this island." This time he saw two men peeking over the control panel.

"Put down your weapons," said Lawser in his best Russian accent. "We wish to congratulate you on your incredible achievement for the Motherland!"

Now all three were peeking over the control panel with the first man's entire face visible. Lawser smiled. A look of incredulity filled the three faces. The SEAL team leader stepped out from behind the partition that he was using for cover, lowered his AKM, and tried to assume a nonthreatening posture.

The three men slowly came out from behind the control panel and there was an unmistakable look of relief on their faces.

Lawser stepped forward and extended his right hand.

"Congratulations! The Russian Federation has won a massive victory! You will be heroes of Russia!"

The control room men risked a smile and then broke out into broad grins. Lawser shook each man's hand in turn and the rest of the team did likewise, except for the expert, who was in the background studying the settings of the switches on the massive control panel that covered one end of the room.

"Before we go, we must do one thing first," said Lawser. He looked around and one of his men brought a medical kit over to him. They placed it down on a table in the center of the room. They all stared at the front of the metal case with its large cross in the color of blood.

One of the control room men looked curiously at the expert, who was standing with his arms crossed over his chest. He smiled at the expert, trying to be friendly.

The case was opened and one of the CIA team members removed the first syringe.

The control room man's eyes slid down and centered on a digital watch the expert was wearing. His eyes drifted away, then quickly returned to the wristwatch. "You know, I had a watch just like that. Got it for next to nothing at the Acme food store near where I lived."

The man's expression suddenly turned into puzzlement. The expert turned to look at him and noticed the frozen expression of Lawser in his peripheral vision. Lawser patiently waited for the expert to explain that they have these kinds of watches in Russia now.

The expert's mind raced furiously to come up with an adequate reply. All eyes in the room seemed to be focused on the watch and no one breathed for a moment as their minds were taken up with the implications of an American watch on a Russian commando.

The control room man began to back up slowly as fear replaced the puzzled look on his face. The expert began to panic.

"Wait a minute!" he blurted out in perfect English.

Lawser made an attempt at damage control. "We have many kinds of imported watches now in Russia." No one listened to him.

The air in the control room was deadly still for a fraction of a second as each man's mind reacted to the slip of the tongue by the expert. Then, in an explosion of movement, the control room men leaped for their weapons, and the CIA/SEAL team brought theirs to bear on the fleeing men. A burst from an AKM caught one of the SVR agents in the back and sent him to the floor at the base of the control panel. The expert dove to the floor and began to crawl to relative safety behind a partition. The world above him exploded with automatic weapons' fire.

Three of the CIA group opened up on the two remaining SVR moles. A bullet hit one of the SVR agents and caused him to fire wildly; the blast from his M16 slammed into the floor in front of Lawser's men. The remaining fire from the CIA people struck him in the head and chest, killing him before he hit the floor. The CIA group got behind the panels and partitions they had used previously for cover, just as the remaining mole opened fire from behind the main control panel. He fired a burst, then ducked behind the panel, then rose up and fired another burst.

Lawser waited for several bursts to go by, then with a curt word to his men, he pointed his weapon from behind the partition and took aim. His men did the same. Lawser hoped his timing was right.

The SVR agent pointed his M16 toward them and stuck his head above the control panel. The CIA/SEAL team all fired simultaneously. The resulting blast slammed into the control panel, the panel behind it, and the SVR agent's head. His nearly headless body flew back, hit the secondary control panel and slid to the floor.

The control room was suddenly still. An instant later, an alarm bell went off. Lawser's team cautiously left their cover and began to check out the bodies of the SVR agents. The expert let out a long sigh and stepped from behind a partition into Lawser's baleful stare. The expert swallowed once, then directed his attention to the control panel. It was his ball game now.

His eyes scanned the two control panels and lightly avoided the area covered by blood and brain matter. The alarm lights were up high on the secondary control panel and hadn't been damaged by the gunfire. A quick look at these, and he saw why the alarm bell was on. An LED display suddenly lit up and started to blink with the words REACTOR SCRAM appearing and disappearing once a second.

The gunfire that had hit the control panel had tripped the condensate pumps for the steam turbine. The condenser that converts the used steam from the steam turbine back to water immediately started to fill up. The steam turbine that generates the electricity for the island then automatically tripped off the line. A few seconds later, the reactor was automatically shut down, or SCRAM'd, with the control rods dropping into the core and immediately halting the nuclear reaction.

The expert thought the lights would flicker at least now that the nuclear reactor's steam turbine was off-line, but the light intensity never wavered. He then decided that the diesel generators on the northern coast of the island must be providing backup power to the island.

The expert thought for a moment about the sequence he was supposed to go through and decided that the first part had already been accomplished by the gunfire. He picked up the sequence from where the automatic controls had left off and manually shut down the main feedwater pumps. These pumps fed water into the heat exchanger near the reactor. The water actually took heat from the reactor as it boiled to produce steam, and in the process cooled the reactor. With no feedwater, the reactor temperature would climb rapidly.

The secondary control panel responded with an alarm light winking on. The expert gazed over the bullet-scarred panel and shut down the auxiliary feedwater pumps and then found the switch enclosure for the reactor coolant pump control. He flipped up the cover and turned the handle so that the green light blinked out and a red light came on, indicating the pump had been shut down.

Another alarm went off. The expert calmly flipped the alarm switch, killing the sounds. He thought for a moment, then activated the control to close the feedwater block valves as an extra precaution. He then opened the pressurizer block valve and looked expectantly at the reactor coolant system pressure gauge.

He turned around and looked at his companions. They were all right except for one man who had taken some bullet fragments in the side of his face. Even he wasn't bleeding too badly. His eyes met Lawser's. The accusing look was still there, but he speculated that his anger had abated somewhat upon seeing that none of his men were seriously hurt.

The expert turned back around and glanced at the coolant pressure gauge. The pressure was quite high now with no coolant flow, and, at any moment, the safety valve would trip and dump reactor coolant into the drain tank. A second later, the alarm light went on indicating the safety valve had lifted. He looked at the water level in the pressurizer. It was "solid." He knew that the level would drop as soon as the incredibly hot core turned the water to steam.

"Do you know what you're doing?" someone said.

"Yeah," replied the expert in an absentminded fashion.

The emergency injection pumps came on to fill the core with cooling water, but the expert calmly disabled them. He thought for a second, then also killed the automatic operation of the core flood tanks. A glance at the core temperature gauge showed his success, but at the same time it sent a shiver up his spine. The unbelievably hot nuclear core was no longer receiving any cooling water.

"So, what *are* you doing?" another someone asked.

"Ever hear of the China Syndrome?"

The room fell silent once again.

CHAPTER 27

—·—·—·—

Colonel Sysoyev peered through the binoculars at the seven helicopters that lined the runway and the taxi strip. The U.S. Marines had deployed across the eastern end of the island and were making a sweep of the area. Sysoyev had his Spetsnaz team to the west of the marines about halfway down the runaway in two groups, one on either side of the runway.

The marine commander had left a formidable perimeter defense around his helicopters as well as the airport itself. Machine gun nests dotted the perimeter, and behind them Sysoyev could see light mortar emplacements. His men would have to run the gamut of the defenses to get to any of the hangars to steal a plane. His operational plans hadn't counted on a large force occupying the island.

Sysoyev carefully looked over the scene once again. There were several trucks spread out in between the helicopters, and Sysoyev recognized the trucks as tankers. The Americans were refueling the helicopters. A thought struck him. He turned to one of his technical experts, Viktor Potelin.

"What is the range of the American helicopters fully fueled?" he asked.

Potelin thought for a moment. "Sikorsky CH-53D Super Stallion range fully fueled approximately seventeen hundred kilometers," he recited.

Sysoyev nodded. More than enough to get to the Kamchatka Peninsula. And all his men would fit into one helicopter.

"Can you fly it?" Sysoyev asked his expert.

Potelin immediately nodded. "Yes, Colonel."

That was it then. He had found a way out. He looked over the area again and studied the helicopter closest to them. The Americans could bring two machine guns to bear on his people and the mortars would no doubt open up on them if they charged across the runway.

The runway ran roughly east-west with its southern side parallel to the southern shore of the island. The ground dropped away from the southern edge of the runway and tapered down to the shoreline. Sysoyev could move his men along the southern shoreline until they were opposite the target helicopter. A mad dash across the runway and they could be in the helicopter before the Americans could bring significant forces to bear. But he still needed a diversion.

His men on the northern edge of the runway could attack from the opposite direction while he and his men made the dash to the helicopter. Sysoyev called his men on the other side of the runway over the radio and gave them their orders. Sysoyev made up his mind that after stealing the helicopter, he would land, if he could, and pick them up before heading to the Kamchatka Peninsula.

Sysoyev turned to his aide. The man carried a bag made of special material which was waterproof and ostensibly explosion proof, and which contained all the videotapes made while they were on the island. Sysoyev knew that his superiors considered those tapes much more valuable than him or his men. The bag and its precious contents had to be protected at all costs.

Sysoyev gathered his officers and noncommissioned officers around him and gave them their orders. Silently they filed down the slope away from the edge of the runway and struggled through the tundra toward the shore. They went eastward for approximately five hundred yards and climbed the slope to get to the edge of the runway again.

Captain Bob Supplee squirmed and fought the mild sedative that the corpsman had just injected into him. The medical team had put his left arm in an inflatable splint, and even Supplee had to admit that he felt better than he had in the last twenty-four hours. He had checked on his one other survivor, the man with the broken legs, and satisfied himself that his man would be okay. The man was asleep and thankfully out of pain for the moment.

The corpsman turned to leave the helicopter. "Looks like the war is over for you, Captain."

Supplee grunted an acknowledgment, but the corpsman's words grated on his insides. This "war" would never be over for him. Could he have done something to prevent all his people from getting killed? He knew he would ask himself that question all the rest of his life.

Supplee lay back, intending for the sedative to take control and maybe even doze a little. After a minute he sat up again, unstrapped himself with his right hand and stood unsteadily in the middle of the helicopter cabin. Unsure of what he wanted to do, he wandered over to a side window and gazed out at the desolate landscape of Shemya Island. He was about to walk away from the window when he caught movement out of the corner of his eye. Someone was moving at the edge of the runway.

Sysoyev lay flat on his stomach and peered through the binoculars at the American defenses. He couldn't see his other group, which was lost in the mist on the other side of the runway. Their target helicopter was between them and Sysoyev's other group. The U.S. Marine machine gun nest to the left of the helicopter would respond to his other group's attack. However, there was a curious mound of snow far to the right of the helicopter. He stared at it for a while but couldn't decide whether it was a machine gun nest, a mortar emplacement, or just a mound of snow. His men would have to keep an eye on it as they went across the runway. The snow mound was too far away to hit with grenades, and if he did attack it, then that might alert the American marines of his real intentions. No, he would just have to take a chance.

Supplee squinted and stared into the mist of snow thrown into the air by the increasing wind. The group at the edge of the runway was acting very suspiciously and obviously didn't want to be seen by the marine perimeter defense. He pushed himself away from the window and picked up a spare M16, checked that it was fully loaded and went through the tarp the corpsmen had draped across the helicopter cabin to separate the wounded from the rest of the troops. Supplee staggered down the open loading ramp and out onto the snow-covered runway.

"Sergeant of the Guard!" he shouted. The wind quickly took his words away. No one would hear him if he stayed here. He glanced around in a near panic. There was a sentry post between him and another helicopter and a machine gun nest beyond that. The enemy looked as if it was going to penetrate their defenses between the sentry post and the machine gun nest.

Supplee crouched low and ran as fast as he could to the closest sentry station. The pair on sentry duty were huddled behind their snow-covered sandbags and nearly jumped to attention when they saw Supplee running toward them.

"Get down!" he growled. The two marines complied before they even got upright. Supplee got up next to them and quickly told them the situation in a hushed voice. One of the sentries got on his radio and told the Sergeant of the Guard.

"Open fire when they cross the runway," said Supplee. The other two swallowed hard and got ready.

Sysoyev turned to his radioman and grabbed the microphone. "Alpha One, this is Alpha Leader. Now!"

He had barely said the last word when he heard gunfire from across the runway in the direction of his other group. He looked through the binoculars at the left machine gun nest. They had swung around to face his other group and were returning fire. He shifted his gaze to the snow mound to the right. No response or movement at all. It had to be now.

Sysoyev stood and turned to his men, who were scattered about on the ground. He waved them forward without a sound. They all immediately jumped to their feet, forming a rough semicircle around Sysoyev and the man with the bag of tapes. They charged forward quickly in a crouched position, and in a few seconds they had covered half the distance to the helicopter.

Sysoyev gave the snow mound a worried glance. With nothing occurring there, he looked to his left. The marine machine gun was totally preoccupied with his diversionary attack. He looked straight ahead; only twenty yards to go.

Supplee peeked over the sandbags. "Now! Fire, fire, fire!" He swung his M16 up and rested it on the sandbags. The two sentries did likewise.

Gunfire from Supplee and his men erupted at Sysoyev's team. The marine weapons on full automatic emptied their clips into Sysoyev's charging force. Six men on Sysoyev's right flank grunted and dropped to the ground in agony. Sysoyev caught a glimpse of three muzzle flashes just before he hit the ground. The weapons stopped firing briefly as the marines quickly reloaded. The next barrage from them won't have the weapons on full automatic, thought Sysoyev. Now that we're pinned down, they'll put them on semiautomatic and pick their targets carefully. His team had to move quickly.

He turned and ordered three of his men behind him to concentrate fire on the right. He ordered three men on his left to cover him from any fire from the machine gun nest to the left. Sysoyev grabbed his man Potelin, who would fly the helicopter, and the man with the all-important bag.

"Let's go! Now!" shouted Sysoyev in the men's ears. The Spetsnaz team leader leaped to his feet, dragging his men with him. They charged toward the helicopter with all the speed they could muster.

An enormous explosion rocked the ground behind them, hurling all three of them to the ground. Two of Sysoyev's men who were providing covering fire died instantly. Mortar round, thought Sysoyev groggily.

The Sergeant of the Guard must have gotten the mortars going, thought Supplee as he reloaded, but the marine captain was much slower than the other two men.

"Single shot this time!" he ordered. The two men

flipped their M16s on semiautomatic. All three of them
raised up to fire over the sandbags once again.

Automatic weapons' fire exploded at Sysoyev and his
men from both the right and left as the marine machine gun
whirled around to attack them. The marines on the right
had reloaded and were taking on the Spetsnaz survivors of
the explosion. It became a furious gunfight with Spetsnaz
gunfire slamming into the sandbags surrounding the machine gun to their left and the sandbags around the other
marines to their right. In less than two seconds, the sandbags were shredded and sagging, with bullets sending sand
skipping into the air and creating a cloud around the marines. Two marines in the machine gun nest to Sysoyev's
left were hit by gunfire and dropped behind the remaining
sandbags.

Gunfire from the remaining marines to his left found its
mark and a short burst from the machine gun cut across
three of the men Sysoyev had left behind. They screamed
and fell silent. There were only two men left to cover Sysoyev's dash to the helicopter. They fought on valiantly
against the marines, whose own level of fire diminished
while they reloaded their weapons.

Sysoyev dragged himself and the other two men with
him to their feet. He stared at the open side door of the
helicopter. It seemed like a haven beckoning him to safety.
Only ten yards to go, thought Sysoyev. He shoved his men
in front of him with a burst of strength and charged after
them.

Gunfire chattered from his right from Supplee and his
two marines, who sprayed the trio with lead. Sysoyev took
a slug under his right shoulder blade, just missing his body
armor. The bullet penetrated all the way through his body
and exited from his pectoral muscle. The round slammed
into the inside of his body armor and stopped, lodging itself
between his chest and his bullet-proof vest. The impact
threw him to the left and onto the ground.

The man with the bag of tapes took two rounds in the
bag itself, which shattered some cassettes, then continued
on to strike him in the abdomen. He also was hit in the left
arm, the impact of which turned him around in the opposite

direction. Potelin, the designated pilot, was unscathed and immediately grabbed the man with the tape bag and dragged him to the waiting helicopter door. They had gotten lucky—no one was inside the aircraft. He tossed his wounded comrade inside and with bullets flying around him he scrambled back to get his leader.

"No, leave me!" ordered Sysoyev. Potelin almost turned to go, then had a second thought and turned back around.

"This is one order I won't obey," he shouted over the gunfire, and grabbed Sysoyev. He began to drag the colonel toward the helicopter.

Supplee's two marines rapidly reloaded and swung around to keep up the fire. At the same time Sysoyev's remaining two men opened fire with the resulting blast catching Supplee and his men by surprise. Slugs slammed into both Supplee's marines but missed the captain, who was still trying to reload his weapon. His two companions fell backwards and hit the ground groaning with agony. Supplee stayed down and checked out the men's wounds. Neither appeared fatal. The enemy had this sentry post's range, and he would have to wait for them to try to get up and start moving before he could risk firing around the sandbags again.

The two Spetsnaz men, seeing no return fire from Supplee's position, turned and fired in the direction of the machine gun and kept them pinned down for a few precious seconds. Sysoyev and Potelin made it to the helicopter door and struggled through it. Potelin deposited Sysoyev next to the tape man and crouched in the doorway waving the two remaining men to get in.

The men leaped to their feet and fired bursts both right and left to keep the marines pinned, and sprinted toward the door. They all heard a whistling noise coming from above and behind the helicopter. A split second later, a mortar round exploded ten yards away from the helicopter. Potelin ducked behind the side of the helicopter until the flying debris of asphalt and body parts had died down. He glanced out quickly and knew what he would see. Both men were completely gone. Potelin slammed the door shut and got into the pilot's seat.

He looked out the front windows and saw a lone marine in the snowmound take aim on the helicopter. Supplee fired a short burst which shattered the copilot's windows and mangled the seat, sending pieces of Plexiglas throughout the cabin. He then ducked down to escape any potential return fire. Potelin gave thanks that the marine's aim was slightly off the mark and started the engines, then began hurried preflight checks. He glanced at the engine temperature gauges and noted with burgeoning hope that the engines were already fairly warm.

Several explosions went off to his left. Potelin cringed and glanced out the port-side windows to see the second group of their Spetsnaz team wage a frontal assault on U.S. Marine positions. The pilot instantly knew why the other group was desperately attacking the defending marines. The Spetsnaz team's second in command, who was leading the other group, had seen Sysoyev's group make it to the helicopter and knew they needed several minutes to warm up the engines. He was sacrificing his men so that Sysoyev and the precious tapes could escape.

Potelin anxiously watched the temperature gauge slowly rise as the battle waged around the helicopter. The distinctive sound of the Spetsnaz team's AKMs blended with the rattle of the marines' M16s and M60 machine guns. At irregular intervals grenade explosions were heard, some of them frighteningly close. The AKM sound suddenly diminished with the M16s firing on and on. Potelin knew without looking that the rest of the Spetsnaz team was dead. He could wait no longer.

Potelin grabbed the collective, increased rotor speed, and lifted off in a cloud of kicked-up snow.

Major Ken Rickman ran up to the side of a helicopter to take cover. He grabbed a sergeant who was beside him.

"What's happening? Report!" shouted Rickman over the rotor noise of the hijacked helicopter.

"We were attacked by what looks to be a Spetsnaz team, Major!" shouted the sergeant. "They grabbed a helicopter and are hauling ass!"

Rickman peered around his cover and saw Sysoyev's

helicopter rapidly gaining altitude and heading west. Some of Rickman's men were firing their weapons at the fleeing aircraft.

"Sergeant, you're with me!" ordered Rickman, then he turned to his radioman. "Tell all units to fire on the helicopter that's heading west."

His radioman gave him an aye, aye, sir, but Rickman and the sergeant were already running around the helicopter toward the side of the burned-out ops building. Rickman suddenly stopped near the two snow-covered bodies of the sleepers that Captain Supplee had killed hours before. Supplee had told Rickman about the Stinger, and Rickman knew that only the Stinger would have a chance of bringing the helicopter down.

Rickman hurriedly brushed the snow away from any mound of snow that resembled the weapon, finally finding the missile system on the third try. He quickly hoisted it out of the snow and brushed it off.

"All right, Sergeant. Load!" he ordered. The sergeant attached the launcher tube with a missile inside to the grip-stock assembly that contained the sight, launch controller, and the IFF system. Rickman pointed it toward the rapidly fleeing helicopter. He got a tone as the missile locked on the hot exhaust of the helo and he squeezed the trigger. The missile rocketed away on a trail of flame.

Potelin looked over the control panel of the marine helicopter. All the gauges were normal, except that the engines were still not up to normal temperature, but the marines had filled the fuel tank. He squirmed around in his seat and caught a glimpse of Colonel Sysoyev hovering over the man responsible for the videotapes. He saw the colonel shake his head, then wrestle the tape bag from around his man. He knew the man was dead.

An alarm went off in his headphones. What was it? Potelin looked around in a panic. Fuel pressure? Hydraulic pressure? All seemed normal.

The decoy ejector switch caught his eye. Missile launch? He flipped the switch, sending chaff and flares automatically out the aft end of the aircraft.

The Stinger missile flew toward the helicopter with the infrared signal of the helo's exhaust growing stronger as the missile rapidly closed the distance to its target. Suddenly a stronger infrared source, one of the helo's flares, flew into the view of the missile's sensor. The Stinger missile changed course and went after the hotter source. The missile plunged after the flare and detonated far behind the helicopter.

Potelin heard the explosion and held his breath. His eyes flew over the control panel. All was normal. The alarm in his headphones went away. Potelin exhaled with relief. He looked for the IFF switch and berated himself for not activating both the decoys and the IFF just after liftoff. IFF— or Identification, Friend or Foe—lets U.S. forces know that an aircraft is friendly to avoid losses from friendly fire.

Potelin took a deep breath. He knew he hadn't heard the last from the U.S. Marines.

Major Rickman had the sergeant load another launcher tube on the hand grip portion of the system. He looked through the sight and pointed it toward the now rapidly fading helicopter. But the missile didn't lock to the helicopter exhaust. Instead he got an indication of a friendly IFF.

Rickman shook his head in frustration. The irony of what had happened hit him. When Captain Supplee needed flares to decoy Stingers, he didn't have any. He had left so quickly that there wasn't any time to load them. When Rickman wanted to shoot down a captured helicopter, the flares, that Rickman himself had ordered to be loaded, were used by the Russians to get away.

He stared in the direction of the fleeing helicopter. The helo was too far away by now to effectively engage it. Rickman lowered the Stinger launcher to the ground and turned to look for his radioman. On cue, he came running up to the major and the sergeant.

Rickman took the handset from the radio man. "Redline Leader, this is Blue Light Leader."

Thirty thousand feet over Shemya, two F/A-18s slowly circled the island in a racetrack pattern.

"Blue Light Leader, this is Redline Flight. Over," replied Captain Al Branca, U.S. Marine Corps.

"Redline, this is Blue Light," said Rickman. "Hostile forces escaping in captured helicopter. Imperative you engage and destroy. Acknowledge, over."

"Roger, Blue Light. Give heading of hostile force. Over," replied Branca.

"Heading is approximately two-seven-zero degrees. Over," answered Rickman.

"Roger, Blue Light. We're on our way. Out," said Branca. "Tailgun, this is Maniac. You heard Blue Light. Let's go get him!"

His wingman, nicknamed Tailgun, which was derived from his unfortunate tendency toward flatulence, came back with a "Roger" and they both swung around on the same course as the fleeing helicopter. Branca turned on his radar and quickly found the location of the helicopter. The helo was thirty miles west of Shemya and heading for the Komandorski Islands at 165 knots. Branca did a hurried calculation, then relaxed. At the helicopter's speed, it would take nearly two hours to cover the three hundred miles to the Komandorski Islands. Branca and his wingman had plenty of time to dispose of the target.

Branca took a second look at his radar display. Something must be wrong. He switched to the ground tactical commander's frequency. "Blue Light, this is Redline Flight. Uh, this helicopter is squawking friendly. Over."

"Redline, this is Blue Light. That helicopter has been captured by hostile forces. *Captured*. Do you read? Over," said Rickman testily.

"Blue Light, can you positively confirm that all friendly aircraft are on the ground? Over," replied Branca. No way was he going to shoot at any aircraft with a good IFF without positive confirmation. Not after all the havoc over friendly fire during the Gulf War.

"Redline, I do positively confirm that all friendlies are grounded. Over," said Rickman. His tone revealed that he thought that that statement would be the end of it.

Branca thought for a while. He sighed. "What do I do, Tailgun?" he asked his wingman.

"I'll go with whatever you decide," said his wingman.

Branca squirmed around and gave the other plane a sideways glance. "Gee thanks, Tailgun. I'll do the same for you sometime."

"Don't mention it," said his wingman.

Branca made a decision. "Blue Light, I need confirmation from higher authority before I can release weapons."

Rickman exploded. "God damn it, Redline! I *am* the higher authority! Shoot those bastards down now!"

Branca sighed again and stared at the blinking symbol on the radar display that said that his target was a friendly aircraft. Sixty miles from Shemya, 240 miles from Komandorski, thought Branca absentmindedly. What the hell was going on? Why doesn't anyone tell us anything? We're just the hired guns for the corps. No brains, just killers. How dangerous could this one lone helicopter be? The damn thing could be full of Soviet, whoops, Russian generals and it wouldn't be worth an ice cube in the middle of winter. Orders were orders and Blue Light was in tactical command.

"All right, Tailgun. We've got weapons release. I'll do it. You stay on top. My decision, my shot," said Branca.

"Roger, Maniac," replied his wingman.

Branca rolled inverted and sent his fighter aircraft screaming down out of the sky after the helicopter. He flipped up the striped cover on a front panel switch, then pushed the lever to the on position.

"Master arm on!" he said over the radio.

"Uh, Maniac. Better knock on it. The whole western edge of the radar screen just lit up," said his wingman calmly.

"What have we got?" asked Branca. There was a moment's hesitation.

"Just the whole goddamn Russian air force coming after us!" Tailgun's voice had lost its calm tone. "Splash that mother and let's get the hell out of here!"

"Range and speed, Tailgun," reminded Branca.

"Three hundred fifty miles at five hundred fifty knots," said Tailgun.

Branca looked at his radar display. The helicopter was

just west of Attu Island and perilously close to international waters. Once in international waters did any laws come into play? Branca wasn't sure, but he didn't think the Russians could object to the United States shooting down one of its own helicopters.

"You just keep 'em off my ass. Okay, Tailgun?" said Branca.

"Oh yeah, sure. We must have forty aircraft out there coming at us at damn near Mach one and I'm supposed to keep them off your ass? This Gatling gun I got up here doesn't shoot Sidewinders, ya know. Are you shittin' me? Thanks, Maniac."

Branca almost grinned. "Think nothing of it."

The fleeing helicopter detected the two F/A-18s above and behind it and headed for the deck. Potelin put on all the speed he could muster, but Branca's aircraft caught up quickly.

Branca got the helo within his firing circle and heard the tone in his earphones. He hesitated and glanced at his radar display again. Friendly IFF.

Potelin got an indication that the F/A-18's fire control radar was locked on and quickly turned right with the decoy dispenser automatically ejecting chaff and flares.

Branca thought that maybe, just maybe the helicopter would return and land after hearing that his radar was locked on. However, the helicopter's maneuver gave no doubt of what the helicopter pilot's intentions were. He would make an all-out effort to get to the Komandorski Islands. Branca shook his head in disgust. He would try one last time.

"Blue Light, this is Redline Flight," said Branca. "Radar is locked on to target. I want to hear it one more time, Major."

After ten seconds' delay, Branca heard Major Rickman come back. "Redline Leader, this is Blue Light Leader. This is a direct order, and we are in the face of the enemy. You *will* shoot down that helicopter. Out."

The message was loud and clear. Rickman had just told him in the military's peculiar language that Branca could possibly face a firing squad for disobeying the order. A "direct order in the face of the enemy" was the key phrase.

"Oh, man! What are you waiting for?" shouted Tailgun over the radio. "These guys are coming balls to the wall! Smoke the sucker and let's haul ass!"

Branca still had radar lock despite the helicopter's contortions.

"Okay," he said slowly. "Here it comes." Branca launched a Sidewinder from one of his wingtip missile stations and watched the missile rocket away from him and rapidly close the distance to the helicopter.

The helo was rapidly ejecting flares and chaff but the Sidewinder seemingly took no notice as it ran up on the left side of the helicopter and slammed into the exhaust pod. The explosion ripped the entire side of the helicopter open and sheared off six of the seven rotor blades, sending the aircraft spinning wildly out of control. The helicopter hit the water with a tremendous splash and immediately began to sink, dragging its already dead occupants and the bag of videotapes down to a grave ten thousand feet deep.

Branca pulled up and quickly climbed back to his wingman's altitude to meet the oncoming Russian threat.

Tailgun's obviously relieved voice came over the radio. "They're breaking off and heading for home. Whew! That was close, Maniac!"

Yeah, close, thought Branca. Maybe someday I'll find out what happened here today.

SHEMYA

Captain Bob Supplee settled back down on his rack in the helicopter that was reserved for the wounded. He was dizzy from the combined effects of the sedative that he had taken earlier, painkillers for his broken arm, and exposure from being outside in the extreme weather when he was repelling the Spetsnaz attack.

The attack was over and the marines were checking the bodies of the Russians killed and attending to all the wounded, six marines and two Russians. Miraculously no marines were killed outright by the attack, but the Russians had sustained twenty-five killed, and three had escaped in the helicopter and were now presumed dead.

Supplee glanced out the side window one last time before he lay back. Marines were covering up the Russian bodies with snow. That was puzzling, but he didn't search his mind for any reason for the action. He was too tired.

The helicopter started to fill up with wounded, and Supplee wound up lying next to one of the Russians. He was grievously wounded and unconscious. Supplee wondered if he would make it back to Adak. He stared at the Russian. Did I wound him? Was it one of my slugs that hit him? Am I responsible for his condition?

Here it was again. He was coming face-to-face with the consequences of combat. When he was a green lieutenant during the Gulf War, he and his men had taken a trench from the Iraqis, and he had seen death for the first time. All the dead were Iraqis; none of his men were killed, and only two were wounded.

Now he was facing it again. But this time was different. He had been prepared for the Gulf War through months of training, but this was completely unexpected. He had left Adak on a mission to recon Shemya, not exactly routine, but it had turned into a disaster for his men.

For the first time in his career, he had seen his own men fall and die in combat. That made his experience in the Gulf War diminish in impact until it became almost nothing compared to the events of the past twenty-four hours.

He personally had struck back and had taken out a half dozen or so of the enemy, but it gave him only minimal satisfaction. Nineteen of his men and two helicopter crews were dead, and they would never come back.

Thoughts of his wife and two-year-old son filled his mind, as they had a little over twenty-four hours ago when they were approaching the island. He thought of Christmas, just two days ago, and the smell of the Christmas tree filled his mind as he closed his eyes. This was the first Christmas that his son knew about presents, and he had gotten really excited, ripping open everything he could get his hands on. Supplee and his wife had laughed until they cried over their son's reaction.

Relief that he had survived filled him, and he felt guilty. How would the families of the dead feel when they were told the awful news? There would be many more Christmases with his wife and son, he realized, finally giving in to the relief he felt.

But somehow they would never be the same.

CHAPTER 28

U.S.S. *NEW YORK CITY*

The *New York City*'s XO leaned over the fire control crew and eyed the displays in front of him. "Captain, we have a firing solution."

An intercom spoke up. "Bridge, torpedo room. Tubes one to four are ready to fire in all respects."

The OOD hit the transmit lever on the intercom. "Bridge, aye."

"Ship ready?" asked Stanley.

"Ship ready!" replied the XO.

"Solution ready?" asked Stanley.

"Solution ready and loaded into tubes one through four," replied the XO.

"Weapons ready?" asked Stanley.

"Weapons ready!" answered the weapons officer.

"Select torpedo tube number two. Open outer doors," ordered Stanley.

ADMIRAL CHARKIN

The sonarman sat upright at the groaning and clanking sounds of the *New York City*'s torpedo tube door as it rotated around to line up its opening with the torpedo tube itself. He relayed the situation to the conn.

"Contact is opening outer doors!" said a nervous phone talker.

Captain Makeyev tried to stay calm. "What speed are we making?"

"Thirty knots," came the answer from his second in command.

Makeyev shook his head. It wasn't enough to run away from the American torpedoes. "Can we turn north to go around the island?"

His subordinate looked over their position on a chart. "Yes sir. Course zero-three-zero would keep us clear of the island."

"Left full rudder, come to course zero-three-zero," commanded Makeyev. "Launch decoy aft."

The boat rolled to one side as they went into the quick turn. A noisemaker was shot out a tube to simulate the sounds of the submarine to lure the American acoustic-homing torpedoes away from the real submarine.

Makeyev had another thought. Now that he had left a noise blob behind, it might mask his next move.

"All ahead one third. Right full rudder. Come to course two-two-five," said Makeyev. "Open outer doors on tube number one."

Electricity seemed to flow through the crew. They knew that, in a matter of a minute or two, they would fire a torpedo at the American submarine. The relaying of orders was crisp and loud as the crew's adrenaline level shot up.

The sub rapidly centered up on the ordered course. "Stand by to fire," said Makeyev. "Fire one!"

Makeyev listened to the loud noises of the compressed air as it shoved the torpedo out into the water. His weapon was on its way, but he couldn't stick around to see how successful it would be.

"Right full rudder, come to course zero-three-zero. All ahead flank," said Makeyev. He would get back on his previous course to get around the tip of the island.

U.S.S. NEW YORK CITY

The weapons officer eyed the status panel in front of him. "Outer doors open!"

"Stand by to fire," said Captain Stanley.

The fire control technician, who was seated at the console in front of the weapons officer, grabbed the firing switch and shoved it over to the standby position. "Ready," said the weapons officer.

"Shoot!" ordered Stanley. The fire control tech shoved the handle to the shoot position. This simple action caused a sound resembling the noise of an onrushing freight train to echo throughout the boat. After a clunking sound came the noise of compressed air venting into the interior of the boat. The sudden increase in air pressure made the crew's ears pop.

ADMIRAL CHARKIN

"High-speed screws aft!" said a phone talker to Captain Makeyev.

Makeyev nodded his head slowly as the rest of the crew inhaled quickly. The captain had expected the announcement. The American would probably launch another torpedo, then wait to see the result. With his sudden turn at high speed along with the acoustic decoy, he had left quite a bit of noise for the torpedoes to go after. But they probably wouldn't be fooled for long. The American torpedoes would eventually recognize that his boat was no longer there and go back into search mode. When that happened, Makeyev had to be long gone. If he was really lucky, the torpedo he had launched would destroy the American sub, but realistically he could only hope that it would make the American duck for a while.

The basic plan was to round the southeastern end of the island before the American torpedoes could lock onto his boat. He prayed that it would work.

U.S.S. NEW YORK CITY

"Select torpedo tube number four!" ordered Stanley. "Open outer doors!"

"Outer doors open!" replied the weapons officer after a few moments.

"Stand by to fire!" said Stanley.

"Ready," came the weapons officer's reply as the fire control technician grabbed the firing switch and shoved it into the standby position.

"Shoot!" commanded the captain.

The tech jerked the firing switch to the shoot position and once again the sub's crew was treated to the freight train sounds along with the attendant ear popping. Their second torpedo was on its way.

"I've got good wire on two units!" said the weapons officer. The wire-guided torpedoes were giving good telemetry back to their masters on the submarine.

The XO, who was in contact with sonar via his headphones, spoke up. "Sonar has a normal indication on two units."

The crew fell quiet and listened to the screw noise of the torpedoes conducted through the hull of the submarine. The noise faded as the weapons rapidly ran toward their target.

"Torpedoes two and four enabled," said the weapons officer in a quiet voice. The warheads of both torpedoes were enabled now that they were a safe distance from the *New York City*.

The import of what they were doing began to be felt in the crew and it showed in their manner. They all, including and especially the captain, had somber faces. If and when the torpedoes struck, there would be no cheering, no thrill of victory. They had just fired two highly deadly weapons at the submarine of a supposedly friendly country. Relations with the Russians had never been better, but now with their action what would happen between the two countries? Would this mean war?

"High-speed screws! Bearing zero-four-five!" shouted the XO.

"Torpedo room, cut wires!" ordered Stanley. "Close outer doors on two and four." He needed to maneuver, and he couldn't have wires sticking out of his torpedo tubes. "All ahead flank! Left full rudder, come to course three-one-five!"

Captain Stanley turned to his diving officer. "Let's head for the bottom." He received an aye, aye, then turned to his XO. "Eject acoustic decoy," he ordered.

"Already done, sir," replied the boat's second in command.

Stanley nodded and bit his lower lip as fear crept up within him. The Russian had snapshot a torpedo back along the *New York City*'s torpedoes' line of bearing. It would gain the Russian time to get away.

The whine of the Russian torpedo began to be heard through the hull as tension mounted in the crew. The noise grew in intensity, then seemed to level off. The crew stopped and listened and all murmured a silent prayer that they would evade this submarine's most deadly weapon. The sounds faded slowly as it passed astern, seduced away by the noise decoy and the *New York City*'s quick turn. After an eternity they all heard a faraway detonation. Stanley looked expectantly at the XO.

"Detonation, bearing one-five-five degrees," said the XO in response to information from the sonar shack.

Everyone let out their breath at once—it seemed to Stanley that even the submarine sighed as well. The Russian torpedo had exploded far aft of them.

"Unit status," asked the captain of the XO, who repeated the inquiry into his phone.

The two American torpedoes had gone into search mode and had almost immediately detected the sounds of the acoustic decoy and the disturbed water from the *Charkin*'s quick turn.

"Both units in detect mode!" said the XO to Captain Stanley.

The two torpedoes activated their own sonar and began to accelerate toward the noise source. The crew of the *New York City* held its breath.

The torpedoes didn't get a sonar return from the expected large submarine and switched back into search mode, slowing down in the process.

"Both units are back into search mode!" said the surprised XO.

The torpedoes had lost their contact, thought Stanley, and right at the moment his crew had no idea where the Russian sub was. And he desperately needed to find out.

"All right, let's find him," said Stanley in a quiet voice. "Go active and let's put an end to this."

His crew complied and the sharp sounds of the sonar pulses rang throughout the boat. Stanley looked expectantly at his XO.

After thirty seconds, the XO shook his head. "We lost him, sir."

ADMIRAL CHARKIN

The sonar operator looked wide-eyed at the *Charkin*'s captain. "Explosion bearing two-one-zero degrees," he said in an awed voice. The men around them grew excited. They thought they had destroyed the American sub. Makeyev knew better. American submarines weren't so easily sunk.

"Other sounds? Hull collapsing?" he asked.

The sonar man listened intently for a few moments, then shook his head in disappointment.

"We are circling the island," replied one of his men. "The sound could be blocked by the land."

Makeyev nodded slowly. Could be, but he wasn't going to turn about to find out. He'd follow his original plan and get around the island. He began to feel hopeful. Maybe the American was dead.

The sonar operator suddenly gasped and pulled his earphones from him. He gave Makeyev a devastated look.

"Active sonar," he said as Makeyev's hopes fell.

U.S.S. NEW YORK CITY

Captain Stanley's mind raced. The Russian was nowhere to be found. He couldn't have gotten so far to the south that he was out of range. That left only one other place for him to be—on the other side of the island. Stanley decided to keep his boat at flank speed to race around Shemya, then, when he might be in range of the Russian passive sonar, he would slow down to get as quiet as possible. The two subs would, in effect, be playing "chicken," heading toward each other, hoping to detect the other in time to get off the first shot.

Stanley went over to the intercom. "Torpedo room, re-load tubes two and four." He received an acknowledgment, then he went over to the tracking and control party.

"Tracking and control party," he began formally. "When we round the island we will be heading directly at Master Five. Once we detect its presence, we will snapshot tubes one and three, then two and four."

Faces sagged and the crew grew nervous. They all knew that it was standard procedure to keep some torpedoes in reserve for defensive purposes due to the length of time that it took to reload the torpedo tubes. They also knew that they would get only one shot at the enemy. If they didn't sink Master Five, then they themselves would go to the bottom.

Stanley was nervous as well. The unthinkable had just happened—Russian and American submarines had just traded shots at one another. And the Russians had apparently invaded U.S. territory. What the hell was going on?

Stanley gave the helm orders to change course once he got the word that they were clear of the island's western tip, then he settled back for a few minutes to think over the situation. Would the Russians detect him before he could get off a shot? They could find a trench and head for the bottom. The sea floor around Shemya was pretty ragged, ranging from two hundred meters to three thousand meters or more. The Russian couldn't go that deep, but there was a lot of room for him to maneuver.

"Captain, we've just cleared the island to the east," said his XO.

"Ahead one third, right standard rudder, come to course zero-nine-zero. Make your depth one hundred fifty feet," ordered Stanley. "Rig ship for silent running." Stanley walked over to the waterfall sonar display and stared hard at the area where he expected to detect the Russian sub. He turned to the XO. "Tell sonar to concentrate search from bearing zero-eight-zero to one-zero-zero."

The XO nodded and relayed the order to Sonar. The captain tried to settle down to wait, but it was a useless exercise. His actions in the next few minutes, or even seconds, could determine who would win this most sophisticated of all duels. The winner lived, the loser died.

The green waterfall dots seemed to penetrate his mind as they rolled down the display. One spot seemed to get brighter as several of the random dots lined up into a jagged line.

The XO spoke up. "Transients, bearing zero-eight-five."

That was him, it must be! Turn now, or . . . Stanley waited—and prayed—for the waterfall line to get stronger and brighter.

"Captain, we have Master Five on bearing zero-eight-five!" said the XO. The waterfall line became bright and ran virtually straight down the display. He and the Russian were headed almost directly toward each other.

"Left five degrees rudder," ordered the captain. He had to get heading and speed on the Russian to get a solution. The line on the waterfall display suddenly took off at an extreme angle from the vertical.

"Man, he is haulin' ass," mumbled the XO.

"That's good. Maybe he hasn't heard us yet," replied Stanley in a low voice.

A few moments later the XO spoke up again. "Captain, we have a firing solution!"

"Ship ready?" asked the captain.

"Ship ready!" replied the XO.

"Solution ready?" asked Stanley.

"Solution ready and loaded into tubes one through four," replied the XO.

"Weapons ready?" asked Stanley.

"Weapons ready!" answered the weapons officer.

"Select tubes one and three. Open outer doors," ordered Stanley.

Thirty seconds later. "Outer doors open on tubes one and three!" replied the weapons officer.

"Stand by to fire," said the captain. The fire control technician grabbed the firing switch.

"Shoot," ordered the captain.

ADMIRAL CHARKIN

Captain Makeyev sat lost in thought as his submarine raced around Shemya Island. The remainder of his mission was to return the landing party to Russian soil complete with their videotapes of the situation on Shemya. The party with the SVR agent survivors of the disaster that he had picked up were to serve as live witnesses to lend veracity to the tapes. If forced to, Makeyev would make the command decision to return to Russia without the rest of the landing party. The SVR agents along with the few tapes he now had in his possession would have to suffice.

Makeyev shook his head. He didn't like leaving Russian troops on Shemya, but Colonel Sysoyev would know that that was a possibility, especially if Makeyev's boat was under attack. Sysoyev would have to get away using some other means. He snapped out of his reverie as his second in command approached him.

"Shall we slow down, Captain?" he asked. "We have cleared the island's eastern coast and we're heading north-west."

"Yes, dead slow," said Makeyev. "Let's not give the American an easy time of it. He'll figure out that we're not south of the island after he searches the area for a while. Then he'll come around to search the north coast for us. We must be ready for him."

Makeyev's subordinate nodded and gave the appropriate orders. The submarine's straining machinery began to slow as the engineers backed off on the throttle. The boat seemed to get very quiet until a phone talker nearly jumped a foot off the deck.

"Many high-speed screws, bearing two-six-five degrees!" he shouted to Makeyev.

U.S.S. NEW YORK CITY

"Select tubes two and four. Open outer doors," ordered Stanley.

"Outer doors open on tubes two and four!" replied the weapons officer.

"Stand by to fire," said the captain.

The fire control technician grabbed the firing switch and shoved it to the standby position. "Ready!" said the weapons officer in a loud voice.

"Shoot," ordered the captain.

ADMIRAL CHARKIN

Makeyev gaped at him for a bare second, then began bellowing orders. "Right full rudder! Emergency dive! Launch acoustic decoy!" Would his maneuvering be enough? So, he thought, the American hadn't lingered on the southern side of the island at all. He had anticipated Makeyev's move and had raced around the other side of the island to meet him head-on.

Makeyev's boat tilted downward as they tried to outrace the American torpedoes. The sonar phone talker spoke up again with a wavering voice.

"Sonar estimates three—" He stopped and listened intently. "No, four torpedoes in the water."

Makeyev groaned. Four torpedoes! The American captain must have salvoed all his torpedoes at once when he detected Makeyev's submarine. It was a gamble of the highest sort. If Makeyev could avoid the American torpedoes and return the favor, the American sub would be at a distinct disadvantage. It would take about fifteen minutes for the Americans to reload all of their torpedo tubes.

But could Makeyev avoid the American torpedoes? With four torpedoes in the water Makeyev couldn't even take the chance to snapshot a torpedo back toward the American sub. He would have to maneuver at the limits of his boat's ability. He couldn't outrun the torpedoes, but he might be able to outdive them. He turned to his second in command.

"Bottom?" he asked tersely.

"One thousand meters, Captain," replied the man.

Makeyev nodded. Even his boat couldn't go that deep. At least he had room to maneuver. He gave orders to his diving officer to keep the dive angle to the boat's limit, then nervously watched the depth gauge tick off the ever increasing numbers.

The submarine began to creak and groan as the metal surrounding them flexed under the extreme pressure. Through the hull was heard the faint, ever increasing whine of the onrushing torpedoes.

U.S.S. *NEW YORK CITY*

The weapons officer's hushed voice was the only thing heard in the conn. "Detect. Detect. Acquired." He turned and looked straight at Captain Ed Stanley. "All four torpedoes have acquired the target, Captain."

Stanley nodded, then rubbed his face in his hands. Do all my people feel as sick about this as I do? He turned and walked the ten feet to the sonar consoles. Sonarman Don Frederick looked up as the captain entered and came over to him.

"Master Five is diving at flank speed," said Frederick. "Our units are increasing speed and starting to ping."

So that's what the Russian was up to, thought Stanley. He's hoping the torpedoes will implode before he does. It was a desperate gamble. Diving at flank speed was an open invitation to "losing the bubble," or losing control of the dive. After losing the bubble, subs faced the distinct possibility of never surfacing again. Stanley's heart went out to the unknown Russian captain and his men.

Frederick gave the captain a quick glance. "Transients. Same bearing as our units. I think one of ours imploded."

The intercom came alive. "Sonar. Weapons. Tell the captain that we've lost telemetry on unit number two."

Hope flared within Stanley. He couldn't help it. He *wanted* the Russian to get away. The sonar room got very quiet and Stanley could hear the thudding of his heart. Damn those orders! He held his breath.

"Transients," said Frederick softly. "Multiple detonations." He gave the captain an almost apologetic look. "Sounds of a pressure hull breaking up."

It's over, thought Stanley. I've just killed eighty-five Russian sailors.

SHEMYA'S NORTH COAST

"For you, sir. It's Snipe," said the radioman. Craig Scanlon took the handset from the technician.

"Raven here," he said.

"Your timetable has been cut short," said Douglas Meyers over the satellite link. "NORAD's spacetrack is saying that a SPOT satellite is due over Shemya in about thirty minutes. The news media has gotten wind that something unusual has taken place on Shemya, and they've contracted for satellite pictures of the island. That means you and the Blue Light group have got to clear the area immediately. We cannot afford to have pictures of helicopters all over Shemya. Not yet anyway. Acknowledge."

"Raven acknowledges order to leave immediately," said Scanlon.

"One more thing," said Meyers. He hesitated. Scanlon sensed reluctance in Meyers's manner. "Blue Fox is to be the only survivor."

Scanlon wasn't sure he heard right. "Say again, Snipe."

"Blue Fox is to be the only survivor," repeated Meyers. "We need someone to tell the right story. There's got to be a survivor who'll tell what we need to be told. Get her to Attu somehow. Have her take one of the boats tied up in the cove on the western end of the island. We'll be in touch with Blue Fox after things calm down but long before the rescue parties get there, so that we can get the story straight."

"Sir, I'm not sure we can guarantee that—" began Scanlon.

"But Blue Fox can guarantee it by remaining on the island and taking care of it," said Meyers in a firm voice. "That group that Blue Fox was with sounded dangerous to us. Blue Fox will insure that this group is not a problem. Is that understood?"

There was a long silence from Scanlon as he digested what Meyers was telling him. "I . . . don't think Blue Fox will do it, sir," he finally said.

"Those are orders," replied Meyers in a short tone.

"I still don't think she will comply," said Scanlon. "She seems to have become very friendly with one of the group, some engineer named Trask. Besides, she was never in one of those sections that did that sort of thing."

There was silence on the other end of the line as Meyers thought over what to say. "Are you familiar with Blue Fox's mission on Shemya?" he asked after a long pause.

"Yes, sir. I was fully briefed," replied Scanlon.

"Blue Fox is after a renegade SVR agent, code name Vulcher," said Meyers. "She has ample reason to want him dead. Tell Blue Fox that we know Vulcher's identity. He's this engineer, Trask. We found fingerprints in the house where Blue Fox was wounded and they match Trask's."

"Is this true?" asked Scanlon.

"You know better than to ask me that," said Meyers in a firm tone.

"Yes, sir," replied Scanlon. His mind spun around with Meyers's ambiguous reply. "Anything else?" asked Scanlon.

"No, get moving. Snipe out."

Scanlon gave the handset to his man and issued the recall order for his group. He also told the radioman to inform the marines under Major Rickman that they would have to pull out immediately. The helicopter engine began to warm up as his men all returned and began to file into the aircraft.

Lieutenant Ellen Gain walked up to Scanlon, shielding her face from the snow kicked up by the slowly increasing turbulence of the helo rotors.

"We're leaving immediately," said Scanlon. Ellen turned to get into the helicopter. Scanlon grabbed her arm. "You're staying."

Ellen turned and glared at Scanlon. "What the hell are you talking about?"

Scanlon repeated Meyers's orders to Ellen's increasing horror.

"Well, I just won't do it," retorted Ellen. "Tell Snipe to go to hell!"

Scanlon took a tighter grip on Ellen's arm. "You've been after this guy Vulcher. They know who he is."

Ellen's manner suddenly changed. She studied Scanlon's face intently with the obvious question on her face.

"It's Trask," he said over the rotor noise.

Her mouth dropped open in shock. "I . . . don't believe it!"

Scanlon released her arm and nodded. "They got fingerprints from the house where your partner got killed. They match Trask's."

Ellen staggered back and shook her head to clear it. "Are you saying this just to get me to kill him?"

Scanlon shook his head sadly. "I wish I were." I hope I'm not, he thought hurriedly.

"Trask! How could it be Trask? He never acted like . . ." Her voice trailed off.

"They never do," said Scanlon. He kept talking. "You have to do this! I can't leave one of my men on the island. When he would finish and get to Attu, someone eventually will ask where he came from, and no one, I mean no one, can know about this mission. But you, you're already assigned to the island. No one will ask how you got here."

Ellen shook her head in an uncertain manner. The old fear was back.

"You said you wanted to get at Vulcher," Scanlon shouted over the wind. "Now here's your chance to finish him off."

Ellen opened her mouth to say something, but no words came forth. Her fear was slowly changing, transforming itself into something else, as she thought of her night together with Trask. Rage began to boil up within her at the thought of how she had trusted Trask, and how she had been intimate with him. She had leaned on him in a crucial situation, but it had all been a sham. What would he have done when he was finished with her? They would have found her in a ditch somewhere with a bullet in her back.

Scanlon stepped back. "Blue Fox, you have your orders," he announced formally. He turned and ran to the helicopter, leaving Ellen cringing from the helicopter rotor wash. The door slammed shut and the rotor speed increased rapidly. In a blast of air, the helo lifted.

Ellen Gain stood staring at the aircraft as it turned and

flew out to sea. Orders, always orders. She had never been ordered to kill someone before. But she *had* killed before— the SVR agents in the truck and near the trailers that now seemed so long ago.

Ellen turned and peered into the mist at the western end of the island. Trask and Elverson had said that they were going to the COBRA DANE radar building. Her fear hadn't completely gone away, but she found new resolve mounting in her.

She was going to have her revenge on Vulcher.

CHAPTER 29

The green letters on the terminal slipped out of focus as he fought to maintain consciousness. Trask felt light-headed and terribly weak, as if this horrible revelation had somehow drained all the energy from him. His head swam as the full impact of the words in front of him rushed in on him and twisted his mind until he wanted to scream. He shut his eyes and hung his head, and felt himself go numb over the incredible realization that this nightmare had been created by a strategic drill.

His mind froze with one thought. It was all for nothing! *It was all just a drill!*

He pushed himself upright, tilted his head back and rubbed his face with his hands, symbolically attempting to force feeling back into his mind. He sniffled a bit and dragged his eyes open to read the words on the terminal once more. More questions raged through his mind. How had it happened? How?

He came to only one conclusion. Driscoll had misinterpreted a readiness drill for a real war. He was just as taken in as the rest of the island's personnel. The last several days had been part of the drill, including the "tensions" between Russia and the United States. It was a carefully orchestrated, very realistic exercise, a war game that some obscure general had wanted to play. It was too realistic.

He had a thought and cringed at the irony. The Kremlin was always told in advance whenever they had a drill like this. They knew, but the SVR agents in the field had no idea. Maybe they thought that Driscoll would be informed of every drill in advance, and he normally was. This time was different. How many had died because one man wasn't informed? His mind struggled a bit, then he gave it up.

His thoughts went to Ellen. He should have been happy to find out that the world was still whole and that hundreds of millions had not died, but he wasn't. The society that had made him feel like an outcast and a failure was still intact, and he was likely to lose Ellen back to that same society. When he had thought that the world was destroyed, he felt that he had a second chance, and with a woman like Ellen beside him, he would have prevailed in whatever he did. Now, that was all changed.

He took a deep breath and suddenly his M16 caught his eye. Suicide? He thought it over briefly and rejected it. He didn't have the guts.

He eyed the row of disk equipment and thought that the test targets generated by the computer would continue to cycle around the earth on their elliptical paths until someone purged the targets from the computer. They would recur periodically, and he thought that it was this quirk of the system that had probably tipped off Driscoll that it was a drill.

Trask wondered briefly what Driscoll's thoughts had been, but his mind wandered back to Ellen. Where was she and was she all right? His mind considered the worst and then immediately recoiled from the thought. He shook his head and thought he might begin to weep but found that he didn't have the strength.

He heard a noise behind him. It wasn't exactly a noise but more like the presence of someone behind him who wasn't there before. He turned quickly. It was Elverson, and he had the automatic pointed at Trask's head.

"Somehow you just didn't act like an AP," said Trask with no real surprise in his voice.

"I thought I had you convinced when I killed the radio operator at the satellite ground terminal," replied Elverson.

Trask shook his head in disbelief. "That's what had me fooled. I figured if you were SVR, you wouldn't kill your own men. I still don't know why. You didn't do it just to convince me, did you?"

Elverson smiled and shook his head. "I did it to convince Ellen."

Trask's eyebrows went up in surprise. "I'm afraid I still don't understand," Trask said.

"With the entire world destroyed, we really didn't have any place to go." He smiled. "And the only available woman was Ellen. I knew if she thought I was an enemy agent, then she would never be mine. So I decided to throw in with her and hope you would get killed in a fight with the SVR."

His smile vanished. "I underestimated you," he continued. "You knew that something was wrong, even if you couldn't put your finger on it."

"Thanks for the kind words," said Trask sarcastically, then had another thought. "You framed Vaughan, of course."

Elverson raised his eyebrows and half smiled. "Of course. Admit it, Trask, I had you going there."

Trask didn't react. "You planted the homing device on Vaughan to frame him."

Elverson nodded. "That's right, the first time I searched his flight bag. There was a cut in the lining of the bag. I just slipped it in, and after he handled the bag for a while, the device worked its way to the other end. I had to cut it out of the lining, and that made it look like it was sewn in from the beginning. Another unexpected bit of luck was his walk at night, and having you find out by yourself was even better. You were pretty smart, though. You had it figured out, only you had the wrong guy."

"You contacted the other SVR agents last night at the trailers?" asked Trask.

Elverson nodded again. "I gave them orders not to harm Ellen but to capture us both." A half smile came to Elverson's face. "And they were to kill you and Vaughan. Then Ellen and I were to escape sometime later."

He stopped talking and stood regarding Trask as something of a curiosity. "You know, your first and only big mistake was to give me this." He waved the automatic slightly.

It was Trask's turn to smile. "Are you sure?" he said to Elverson. The young man frowned and eyed the automatic with quickly rising alarm.

He pulled the trigger.

In the instant before the hammer completed its short travel, Trask had the fleeting thought that maybe the young man had gotten wise to his deception. Nothing worse than dying when you're expecting otherwise.

The hammer fell on an empty chamber.

The silence of the shot that never happened closed in around them as Elverson's mouth fell open in amazement. They sat for an instant with both of them staring at the gun in Elverson's hand.

In a blur of activity, they both started to move at once, Elverson to recock the pistol and Trask to reach for his M16. Elverson was finished first and hurriedly pointed the automatic at Trask. The dull click of another failed attempt was lost in the noise Trask made in scraping his weapon along the floor in order to bring it up to a ready position.

Elverson threw the empty gun aside and leaped at the engineer. They collided an instant before Trask could get the weapon lined up with Elverson's body. He pulled the trigger anyway and the resulting burst slammed into the ceiling. They wrestled for a few moments face-to-face with Trask at a disadvantage by being caught in the chair. He tried to throw Elverson straight back away from him, but the young man had all the leverage and had him pinned in the chair with the chair's back jammed up against the computer terminal table.

Trask moved his left hand farther toward the end of the barrel and shoved with all his strength to roll Elverson to one side. Elverson, caught unaware, rolled to Trask's right and fell on the floor but still held on to the M16. Trask half stood and desperately tried to dislodge the young man's hands from the weapon. He twisted the weapon with no success and then finally stomped on Elverson's face. The young man cried out in pain and rolled over on his stomach.

Trask swung the weapon around, pointed it at him and pulled the trigger. Two shots were fired, then the weapon fell silent. The slugs went wild, missing Elverson, who was in the process of getting to his feet. It was Trask's turn to be surprised, and he desperately reached into his coat pocket for a fresh clip. He found one immediately and ejected the empty clip onto the floor. He kicked the chair toward Elverson in an effort to slow him down and jammed the full clip home.

Elverson threw the chair out of the way with a growl and then realized that Trask was only a second or two from having a fully cocked and loaded M16. He instantly estimated the time it would take for him to get to Trask and realized he wouldn't make it. He turned and ran as Trask pulled back on the cocking bar. Trask brought the barrel up just as Elverson went through the doorway out into the corridor.

Trask was after him in a flash and began to worry that Elverson would pick up a weapon and be able to fire back. He got to the doorway and saw Elverson enter the Operations Room. He leaped over to what was left of the doorway and chanced a quick look in only to see Elverson heading toward an M16 that was lying on the floor. Trask jumped inside the room and pointed his weapon at the young man.

"Hold it!" he yelled.

Elverson froze with his hand over the stock of the automatic weapon. He looked up at Trask, who stood with his finger tightening on the trigger. For the first time, Trask saw genuine fear on Elverson's face and decided not to kill him right away. His finger relaxed a bit, and he noticed in the semidarkness that for the first time Elverson was breathing more heavily than he was. A surge of satisfaction ran through him.

"I underestimated you," said Elverson in a breathless voice. "If it wasn't for you . . . Damn you, Trask!"

Trask grinned. "Stand up and put your hands on your head," he commanded.

Elverson began to move slowly while trying to gauge the distance between him and the M16 on the floor.

Trask caught his eye and head movements. "Don't even think about it, Russian."

His finger tightened on the trigger and Elverson's eyes widened in near panic. He shrank back from the M16 on the floor and slowly got to his feet. Only after he was standing with his hands on his head, did Trask begin to relax. He stood unmoving for several minutes until Elverson could stand it no longer.

"What are you going to do?" he finally asked.

"I have a confession to make. I haven't the foggiest," Trask replied with a light tone to his voice.

"How did you know?" asked Elverson.

"I was tipped off by Vaughan's notebook. It was a little more detailed than I would have expected, and there was a notation in it that you graduated from a high school named after General Schwarzkopf. But the graduation date was before the Gulf War, before he became famous and started having schools named for him. I thought that maybe it was an attempt to frame you, but then I remembered Vaughan's body. He had been shot in the head, from the *left* side. If the bullet had come from the SVR agents on the ground, then he would have gotten it from the *right* side."

He stopped and studied Elverson's face. The young AP was miserable.

"You shot him in the plane when you began firing at the men on the ground, didn't you?" stated Trask.

Elverson nodded. "I didn't think you would notice, and I was afraid he might convince you later."

Trask grunted in amusement. "You know, I still didn't know for sure that you were SVR until just now. You might have killed Vaughan anyway."

Elverson looked even more miserable.

"You present quite a problem," Trask continued. "A messy problem at that. I'm sure a lot of people would thank me if I shot you right now."

Bewilderment crossed Elverson's face.

"Why?" He seemed genuinely puzzled. Trask in turn was puzzled at his reaction. He thought for a moment and then had it figured out.

"Oh . . . you don't know. Of course, how could you?" mumbled Trask to himself.

"Know what?" asked Elverson in frustration.

"Here's a real kicker for you, Russian. It was all a drill!" He gestured to the rest of the room.

Elverson looked about wildly, afraid to let Trask's comment sink in. "What was a drill?"

"THAT!" Trask pointed to the situation screen.

Elverson eyeballed the screen and his mouth dropped open in astonishment. It was a few minutes before he composed himself.

"I don't believe it," he stated firmly.

"It's not important that you do," said Trask.

Elverson's eyebrows went up in pleasant surprise as he began to look past Trask toward the doorway of the room. He glanced briefly back at Trask, then toward the door again.

"Well, look who's here," he said in a calm tone.

Trask wasn't buying it. "Oldest trick in the—"

"Drop the gun, Frank," came a familiar voice from behind him.

Trask turned in surprise and saw Ellen holding an automatic in her hands.

She had it pointed at his head.

CHAPTER 30

Trask gaped at the figure silhouetted in the doorway. The weapon Ellen Gain had in her hand never wavered.

"Drop the gun, Frank," she said again softly.

Trask was too amazed to comprehend her words. He looked at her incredulously and turned to look at Elverson, who was highly amused.

"Drop the gun, Frank," she repeated with more firmness in her voice.

Trask looked back at her and blinked his eyes several times as her words began to register in his mind.

"Ellen, wha—"

"NOW!"

Trask's M16 clattered to the floor.

She ordered him to back up and then walked past him to stand between him and the consoles with the situation screen filling the wall behind her.

So, it had come full circle, she thought. She had finally caught up to Vulcher, but not until he had put them through absolute hell. She felt relief—her partner was going to be avenged in a few moments, just as soon as she got the guts to pull the trigger.

"I'm sorry, Frank, that it has to end this way," she began. Trask stared at her form, which was silhouetted against the glow from the silent situation screen. He could hardly believe his ears.

"What the hell are you talking about?" he asked. Elverson took a circuitous route to avoid the line of fire and picked up Trask's M16. He then returned to Ellen's side.

She began to explain to Trask. "They want only the right story to be told about all this. So, I'm to be the only survivor." She stopped talking as if that short statement would explain everything. Elverson gave her a nervous look, then relaxed, assuming that she had just forgotten about him. She gave Elverson a half look and mentally shrugged. Scanlon hadn't mentioned him, and she surely wasn't going to kill him in cold blood. Elverson would have to escape with her.

"So, you're SVR then, just like Elverson," replied Trask. The young AP glanced at Ellen quickly, but she didn't notice it.

She gave him a you-have-a-lot-of-nerve look. "Cut the crap, Trask. You know why you're not going to leave this island."

Trask shrugged his shoulders and held his hands with his palms up to show his puzzlement.

"I work for the counterintelligence department of the CIA. My purpose on Shemya was to try to ferret out moles," she said. "Like you, you son of a bitch."

Trask's mouth flopped open in surprise. "I'm not a mole!" he protested, but it sounded lame. Elverson got increasingly ill at ease.

Ellen slowly shook her head. "I've been following you for years. I'm the one you shot in the house in Pennsylvania last August. And it was my partner that you murdered in the back yard."

Trask managed to close his mouth and recover somewhat. "I'm not who you think I am," he said in a tightly controlled voice. "Who told you I'm an SVR agent?"

"I think you can guess," she replied, but offered no further comment.

"If you're looking for SVR agents, then there's one right next to you," he said, gesturing at Elverson.

Ellen gave Elverson a cursory glance and dismissed Trask's allegation with a shake of her head. "Of course, you'd say anything to get me to change my mind."

Trask's mind raced as his gaze swept the room and the corridor beyond. She saw his eyes searching the area.

"They're gone," she replied. "They had a schedule to keep, you know."

Trask stared into the darkness that surrounded her face. He thought he saw a glimmer of a smile. "Who killed Driscoll?" he asked. "Some of your people?" He had to try to keep her talking.

She nodded, then answered his unspoken question. "They were sent to cover up what happened on this island."

"WHAT?"

She nodded her head again.

"Why?" demanded Trask. "The goddamn Russians started this whole thing by thinking that a drill was the real thing! It's their fault! Why the hell are we covering up for them?"

"Oh, for God's sake, you can forget the act," she said, her patience wearing thin. "I know who you are."

There were a few moments of silence as they stood regarding each other with Trask trying to digest the irony of the fact that Ellen thought that he was one of the enemy while she was standing next to a real SVR agent.

"What kind of story will you tell them?" he asked after a while.

She didn't seem to mind telling all the CIA's dirty little secrets. "The CIA team will make the nuclear power plant melt down. The molten core will eventually hit groundwater and then blow up, spraying radiation all over the island."

"That wouldn't be enough to kill everyone on the island. At least a few would survive," he shot back.

"True," she agreed, "but it will be enough to keep any curiosity seekers away from the island."

"Like the news media?" he asked.

"Exactly. Some other story will be made up to explain how everyone died," she replied.

"It'll never work," said Trask flatly.

"Oh, it'll work," she said with seeming certainty. "They'll have me to tell the whole story."

"You can't stay on the island with all the radiation flying around."

"I have a boat waiting in Alcan Cove on the western coast of Shemya. I'll just take it to Attu," she replied in a curt tone.

"Won't they ask where you got the boat?" asked Trask in a weary tone.

"I have a story for that too. Want to hear it?"

Trask shook his head in disgust. "I don't believe that what we had two nights ago meant nothing to you. I know you weren't acting. We shared—"

"A lot has happened since then," said Ellen. "Forget about that night, Frank."

"I can't forget! And neither can you!" he replied.

"That night was irrelevant," she said. "I didn't know who you were until a few minutes ago."

He was silent for a moment. "What's going to happen now?"

She hesitated, and he thought the darkness surrounding her face took on an uncomfortable air. "You can't leave this island," she finally said. "It's going to be my pleasure to put several bullets into your face."

He felt panic rising in him. He searched her shadow for any sign that she might not really go through with her threat. She seemed nervous but resolute. He glanced at Elverson, who was enjoying the entire scene immensely. The young AP was content to let Ellen run the show for now, especially if she was going to shoot Trask.

"Ellen, it doesn't have to be like this," Trask implored. "We talked about dropping out of society, about just turning around and walking away. We can do that now."

"No, we can't." She seemed more certain than before.

Trask pressed on. "Look, Ellen, we talked about Tahiti and how you had dreamed of just pulling up stakes and going there and lying in the sun and doing nothing. I've had those same dreams. Together, we can make those dreams come true." He spoke earnestly and tried to be as convincing as possible. His life depended upon it.

She considered him for a moment and Trask thought he had her convinced, but she slowly shook her head.

"I've chased you for years and now you want me to run

away with you?'' she replied. ''Are you nuts? You'd put a bullet in my back the first chance you got.''

''No,'' said Trask, shaking his head. ''It won't be me. It'll be the man standing right next to you that'll put a bullet in your back.''

''I've had just about enough,'' said Ellen grimly.

Trask thought furiously for some other approach and glanced in a distracted manner at the console at Ellen's elbow. The DEFCON 4 indication had just changed to DEFCON 3. It suddenly hit him what was going to happen and he quickly made a plan of action. He looked back at Ellen and tried to make his voice as grim as possible.

''You're going to be a loose end after you tell your story,'' said Trask. ''You'll know the truth, and someone, somewhere, won't want to take a chance of your talking someday. So, they'll arrange for an accident to happen. If Elverson doesn't get you, then your boys at the CIA will.''

Her manner changed from calm determination to anger. Trask knew he had made a mistake.

''No!'' she said in an angry voice, ''They're not like that! You're an idiot, Trask, to think you can con me!''

An alarm went off. It was the same panic-inducing sound that Driscoll had heard a little over forty-eight hours before. Ellen and Elverson instinctively looked in the direction of the alarm, then glanced at the situation screen as the entire top of the screen lit up with the test targets that no one had purged from the computer.

Trask didn't hesitate. He grabbed a chair and hurled it in Ellen's direction. It knocked her back and off balance, and provided just enough time for him to get to the doorway and beyond.

Ellen shoved the chair aside and pointed the gun in Trask's direction, getting a bead on his back just before he disappeared around the corner. She hesitated, then wondered why she hadn't pulled the trigger. Ellen lowered the automatic slowly.

Elverson brought the M16 up to bear and fired a burst out the doorway, emptying the clip, but was too late. He exploded in an epithet. *''Va fun qulo!''* The obscene Italian saying electrified the air between them like a thunderbolt.

Ellen's head shot around toward the AP. She stared at him in shock with the mispronounced expression that she had heard months ago roaring through her mind.

"You! It was you all the time!" she screamed. She spun around, bringing the automatic to bear on Elverson. He gaped at her in shock, then fled toward the doorway, his legs pumping frantically.

Elverson got to the doorway, dropping his empty M16 just as Ellen opened fire. She fired the automatic as quickly as she could, pumping out rounds with less than a second between each one. The slugs went wild, spraying the doorway with lead and filling the air around Elverson with hissing metal. He squirmed and slid his way out into the corridor, alternately ducking and jaunting to one side or the other.

Elverson got to the corridor and immediately ran toward the elevators, taking the same route that Trask had taken seconds before. The thundering of Ellen's automatic kept up unabated as she flung lead all over the corridor in an attempt to stop him. Elverson ran in a complete panic. Rounds from Ellen's weapon began to rip along the right side of the corridor, so instead of making a right turn into the elevator as Trask had done, Elverson made a left into the Mission Processing Room.

He got inside and flung himself behind a rack of equipment, his heart pounding and adrenaline flooding his system. He passed his hands quickly over his body, then looked at them. No blood, only the pink flesh of his shaking palms. He couldn't believe it—he wasn't hit . . . yet.

Ellen gaped down the corridor in disbelief. She glanced at the automatic held tightly in her right hand. The slide was locked back in its rearmost position, a sign that the clip was empty. She had emptied a full clip at him and hadn't hit him. Her shock and fury at the deception had cost her accuracy. The next time would be different.

Ellen hit the button that released the clip and let it fall to the floor. She pulled out a full one and slipped it into the automatic. She then thumbed the slide release to let it go forward to its normal position, simultaneously pumping a round into the chamber.

She had almost put a bullet into the man she loved. The thought surprised her and horrified her at the same time. To have almost shot the wrong man was horrifying, to think that she loved Trask was surprising. She resolved to concentrate on Elverson and sort out all those other thoughts later.

Her mind raced with what Elverson might be doing. She knew that Elverson had jumped from the corridor to the Mission Processing Room, which also connected back to the room she was in, the Operations Room. Elverson could be coming up on her rear while she looked down the corridor. She formed an instant plan and looked quickly about the room.

Elverson peered around the equipment rack and saw the doorway to the Operations Room. She might not be aware of the circular nature of these rooms, he thought. If he entered the Operations Room from the room he was in, he could come up behind her and surprise her. He came around the rack quickly and picked his steps with care to avoid the bodies and debris which the gunfight two days ago had left about the floor. He crossed the room as silently as possible and peered into the Operations Room.

Nothing was moving. The bodies were just where they had fallen. Even the chair that Trask had thrown was unmoved from its resting place. Best of all, there was an M16 lying a few feet inside the Operations Room. He took a step inside and silently picked up the weapon that Airman Jensen had dropped a few hours earlier. Elverson took out the clip and saw that it was fully loaded. He quietly reloaded the weapon and cocked it.

Elverson glanced at the bullet-scarred doorway that led to the corridor. The outline of a portion of someone's back was visible through the shattered door that once enclosed the room. The person was crouching down and, although the front part of the person was obscured by the wall, it was evident that the individual was facing down the corridor.

It's Ellen, thought Elverson. He took a quick look around the Ops Room again, then started to tiptoe across the room to get close to the doorway. The chaos of the phoney World

War III on the situation screen went on behind him as more and more portions of the United States were lit up in blobs of white by the test targets. He stopped halfway to the door and brought up his M16. He aimed at the back of the person and hesitated. Goodbye, Ellen. It was nice, but . . .

He opened fire, keeping his finger on the trigger until half a clip was expended. The form twitched and flopped as the impact of the bullets drove it across the corridor.

Elverson moved to the doorway and stared down at the body in front of him. Simultaneously he felt movement behind him. One of the bodies in the Operations Room was moving. The body in front of him that he had shot was that of a man, a man with Ellen's parka wrapped around him. He gaped at the corpse, Ellen's deception forming in his mind.

Elverson whirled about in an explosion of movement. One of the bodies in the Operations Room was standing now and had a gun pointed straight at him. He began to shout, but it was cut off by a gun blast. The first round slammed into Elverson's face just under the left cheekbone, shattering the left side of his face and brain and instantly killing him.

Ellen stood, firing round after round into Elverson's body as it twitched and jerked in the air before thudding to the floor. She stopped after firing ten bullets into him and just stood with the gun extended in front of her. She gasped for breath and her chest heaved with the stress of what she had just done.

Thirty seconds later, her mind began to work again. So, it was all over. Vulcher was dead. Her own people had deliberately tricked her so that she would eliminate Trask. She felt weak at the thought of how close she had come to killing him. And now he thinks that I want to kill him. She shook her head at the irony of the whole situation. What Trask had said about their night together was true. She was in love with him, or maybe she was in love with his dream.

Let him go? No, she resolved vehemently. She would find him and make him understand, and then maybe find out what she was in love with, the man, or his dream, or both. Where would he go? The boat. Ellen looked up and desperately called his name. She flung the automatic aside and ran after him.

Trask got to the bottom of the stairs and glanced through the windows as his mind raced. He desperately needed a weapon and he knew there were none left in the truck that he and Elverson had used. His eyes ran over the parking lot and centered on the vehicle which had been used by Ellen.

The sniper's rifle!

Trask ran over to the truck, jumped in and reached under the seat. His hand closed around the rifle. He straightened up in the seat and reached for the ignition, and suddenly realized that Ellen had the keys. He leaped out and ran back to the small hill at the back of the building. He waited for a few minutes, then saw Ellen appear at the rear doorway of the radar building and look wildly about for him. She called his name a few times, then she quickly got into her truck and sped off.

Trask looked carefully about before moving. He wasn't sure whether Ellen was telling the truth about the CIA team. They could still be around. Where was Elverson? He pondered that for a moment, until something Ellen had said registered in his mind. *I'm to be the only survivor,* she had said.

Trask came to a stunning conclusion. She had murdered Elverson. And she was supposed to murder me as well, thought Trask. All of that business about me being an SVR agent was just a smoke screen—maybe for Elverson's benefit. Maybe to make Elverson relax, so that it would be easier to shoot him later. She did the right thing for the wrong reasons. Her words ran through his mind over and over. *I'm to be the only survivor.*

A Klaxon horn sounded. He had never heard that particular alarm before. It seemed to come from the direction of . . . He suddenly remembered something else Ellen had said. *The reactor would melt down! The Klaxon was the evacuation alarm!*

He jumped to his feet and feverishly tried to estimate how much time he had left before deadly radiation covered the island. He ran back to his truck, started it, and raced off down the road with one thought in mind, to get as far from the island's nuclear power plant as possible.

Fury began to build up within him. She had deceived him all along; her supposed need for him was a sham. The only survivor, she was to be the only survivor. After all they had gone through together!

She would be headed for the cove, he thought coldly, to escape in the boat left for her. He gunned the engine, determined to get there in time to stop her.

His truck weaved and skidded along the road that ran toward the middle of the island. A concrete structure with spots of orange embedded in it that were its windows came up on his left. It had the stillness of death about it, in stark contrast to Trask's furious advance down the road.

Trask flew past Building 600 and its hundreds of bodies entombed within and forever still. He would have experienced the emotionally riveting coldness and stillness of the place were it not for the rage that consumed him.

The road swung sharply to the right toward the western coastline, and Trask took the turn with a furious yank on the steering wheel. The truck slewed around dangerously, then centered up on the road once again as Trask made a quick adjustment. The Klaxon screamed on, getting louder as he approached the nuclear power plant, reminding a dead island that the nuclear core within the still-intact containment building was rapidly turning into a molten mass. Trask raced past the fences surrounding the island's nuclear reactor, and in a few minutes he approached a bluff overlooking the cove.

With the cacophony of the Klaxon urging him on, he got his mind to focus on what had to be done. He decided to stop on the road which led to the cove. The road was on higher ground than the beach, so he could easily pinpoint where Ellen had gone. Most of the road was unplowed and made slow going. He fought the snow to get the truck to the edge of the road near the cove.

He spotted Ellen right away. She had just gotten out of her truck and was walking in the direction of the small cabin cruiser which lay tied up at an equally small pier. He picked up the rifle, and quickly got out of the truck. Trask knelt down at the edge of the road and pumped a bullet into the chamber. He looked through the sight, and her face swung into view as if she were only a foot away. He lowered the barrel and placed the crosshairs in front of her feet.

Fear.

He pulled the trigger.

The snow kicked up in front of her and made her jump even before she heard the shot. She leaped back and looked quickly in the direction of the gunshot with her mouth open in disbelief.

That's what we're all about.

The Klaxon sounded dully in the background of the noises in Trask's mind as he instinctively worked the bolt to pump another round into the chamber. He brought the barrel up and looked through the sight. Ellen was looking about wildly to discover the source of the gunshot until she spotted him above her at the edge of the road. Her eyes widened in astonishment. She stood with her arms extended away from her body in supplication and made no move to escape the next bullet.

The only survivor. She was to be the only survivor.

A bead of sweat ran its course down Trask's forehead as memories of the jungle roared into his consciousness. The jungle, ever present just below the surface of his conscious mind, wrapped itself around him. The frigid air which had bitten into his lungs with cold now contained a rotting scent, a clinging humidity. Insects pecked at him and his feet were immersed in a decaying bog.

The sounds that were in his mind came back to him.

KILL! KILL HER!

The men above him in rank, all of them now long dead, still ordered him into action.

Ellen's face filled the sight. Her mouth began to open until he lost the intersection of the crosshairs in the darkness of her throat.

She let out a long, drawn-out wail. It was his name.

"FRANK!"

EPILOGUE

To: *The Director of Central Intelligence*
From: *DDO*
Subj: *Shemya Incident*

The need was expressed in the Committee's last meeting for a summary of some events concerning the disaster at Shemya AFB in the Aleutians. The pertinent facts are as follows:

- A band of some 15 to 20 SVR moles seized control of Shemya AFB during the early hours of Christmas morning.
- The exact time of takeover is uncertain but seems to correspond closely with the time of the readiness drill which was scheduled for that morning.
- A team led by the CIA landed on Shemya two days later and terminated the SVR moles who had seized the island. They also caused the nuclear reactor to melt down and the resulting explosion spread radiation over the island.
- The Russian Spetsnaz team sent to videotape what happened on the island have all been killed, except for two prisoners taken during the battle near the airport. These two were captured by the marines and thus escaped the Company's team. One died en route to Adak, but the other recovered from his wounds and was interrogated at length,

but we got nothing useful from him. He was secretly repatriated a few months later.

- *All videotapes made of the island by the GRU have been destroyed. The submarine that had ferried the Spetsnaz team to Shemya has been sunk and lies at the bottom of the sea at least 3,000 feet down.*
- *A CIA operative was left on the island to be the one survivor who would tell the story. She was to leave by boat; however, she has never been seen nor heard from since. Her body has not been found.*

These last four items were a result of high-level meetings with CIA, National Security Council, and the Pentagon participating. This action has had several advantages. They are as follows:

- *A possible coup resulting from chaos in Russia, which in turn would have resulted from a cutoff in aid from this country, has been avoided.*
- *This action set up the news media completely. The brilliant idea by SVR General Iskanderov (with our concurrence) to carefully leak the story of biological weapons on Shemya had the effect of satisfying the media after months of questions concerning the cause of the disaster. It gave them exactly what they had expected, a government screw-up.*

The CIA had recommended strenuously against the nuclear reactor meltdown, but higher authorities had deemed it necessary in their panic to do something significant for damage control. This country is currently faced with an enormous cleanup of a strategic base in a formerly pristine area of the Aleutians. Environmentalists are now having the government for breakfast.

To summarize, the coverup of the incident has held up well for several months now. The mop-up party only got on the island after most of the bodies were badly decomposed, and therefore the resulting closed caskets hid the relatively few who died from gunshot wounds.

The man called Elverson brought up some problems, but his body was quickly disposed of. His identity remains a mystery, but it is speculated that he was another SVR agent who had recently come to the island. He may even be the long-sought Vulcher, but there is no confirmation of this. And there probably never will be.

It is clear that the sleeper team's objective was to deceive NORAD into thinking that a Russian strategic launch was not coming when it really was. The drill inadvertently triggered their response. Why this particular sleeper team was never deactivated is a mystery. Even the Russians don't know, or won't tell. It is possible that Vulcher's murder of his control agent caused it somehow, but all records were destroyed by Vulcher's control when he found out that his network was to be deactivated.

The SVR has quietly arrested and disposed of the GRU conspirators and is now engaged in a desperate battle with the GRU for supremacy. The current Russian administration is leaning heavily toward the SVR.

Even though the coverup has held up well, there are some very disturbing problems. Civilian space assets, most notably SPOT and Landsat, have imaged the island for months now, and all this data is in the hands of the news media. We didn't dare try to stop it, or they all would have known that something funny was going on. Scrutiny of this data has led to some embarrassing questions about the destruction of the Operations Building, which, as you know, was destroyed by two F/A-18s. The story—concocted in a hurry by our people—that the marine helicopters had crashed into it, is being picked apart this very minute by the media.

The press has also picked up the fact that one of those F/A-18s shot down a marine helicopter with a friendly IFF. We are interviewing the two pilots now, but suspicion seems to center on Captain Al Branca, who is an idealist and seems to intensely dislike the idea of a coverup.

The personnel on Adak have been quiet about it all, even though there are disturbing reports of nightmares by Marine Captain Robert Supplee. So far he has kept silent about what had actually happened on Shemya. Apparently even his wife doesn't know.

The sinking of a Russian submarine has, thankfully, been kept quiet. The Russians know, of course, but they will never reveal it, and the crew of the U.S.S. New York City has been silent about it thus far.

The coverup could come apart quickly, if anyone else starts to talk about their participation in this situation. The lack of a survivor, to tell the media exactly what we wanted them to know, hurts immensely. If the coverup comes apart, we may well wish that we had trusted the American people with the truth from the beginning. The government may have been able to resist American public opinion and not cut off aid to the Russians.

One last thing. The body of a relatively obscure civilian engineer, named Francis Trask, was never found, even though the island was searched extensively time and time again. That is a total of two bodies never accounted for; the other was the CIA operative code-named Blue Fox (aka Nancy Logan and Lieutenant Ellen Gain, USAF), previously mentioned. Two other bodies were substituted in order to keep their relatives from asking too many questions. The boat that Blue Fox was to use for her escape from the island was also never found, even though an extensive search of the surrounding area was made.

The idea of one of our people possibly on the loose somewhere is a disturbing one, and considerable effort is being expended to find her. This single agent has the potential to blow the lid off the whole affair. Information from her wouldn't be speculation or rumor—she knows almost every inside detail of the

Company's involvement from myself on down. The damage to the organization would be enormous, much greater than in the seventies when the CIA was almost dismantled in the wake of our assassination attempts on foreign leaders.

Finding Blue Fox should not take long. As a surveillance agent, she was never fully trained in assuming new identities as our covert agents are.

For her sake, we had better get there before General Iskanderov's people locate her. The SVR does not want this incident to become public knowledge.

This memo must be destroyed upon reading.
DCI EYES ONLY

The sun warmed his back as he floated in a state between sleep and wakefulness. He rolled over to get some time on his other side and lazily opened his eyes. He lay on a ribbon of black sand that was somehow miraculously stuck between palm trees and the magic blue of the South Pacific. He rolled his eyes to his right and took in the vision.

Ellen lay on the sand next to him, a mirage of beauty in a fantastic land. She had her eyes closed, and her blond hair, which had gotten even lighter since their arrival in Tahiti, blew carelessly in the warm wind. His eyes ran over her body and delighted in how she looked in a white string bikini. It took some convincing to get her to wear it, but she gave in finally, although they had to go to deserted beaches to stem her embarrassment. Now she had a dark tan and looked absolutely ravishing.

Initially he had kept a close eye on her and was careful not to get into any arguments with her. After what had almost happened in the radar building, he didn't want to push his luck. He suspected she was doing the same thing after what he had almost done to her in the cove on the western coast of Shemya. It made for a very peaceful relationship with each of them catering to the other.

She had told him that she had had a chance to shoot him in the back in the radar building, but that she just couldn't do it. He had had the chance to make the same mistake he had made in the jungles of Vietnam. But he had refused to do it.

She had told him that her real name was Nancy Logan, but to him she would always be Ellen. He continued to call her Ellen, and she didn't seem to mind. Maybe the change of name suited her as well, reflecting her rejection of what she was and symbolizing their new life.

And now here they were, probably on the run for the rest of their lives, but they wouldn't run just yet. They would enjoy Tahiti for the moment. He closed his eyes and his mind drifted.

The dull realization filled him that he had absolutely nothing to do, nowhere to go, no one to see about anything.

Trask smiled.

STUART WOODS

The *New York Times* Bestselling Author

GRASS ROOTS
71169-/ $5.99 US/ $6.99 Can

When the nation's most influential senator
succumbs to a stroke, his brilliant chief aide
runs in his stead, tackling scandal, the governor
of Georgia and a white supremacist
organization that would rather see him
dead than in office.

Don't miss these other page-turners from
Stuart Woods

WHITE CARGO   70783-7/ $5.99 US/ $6.99 Can
A father searches for his kidnapped daughter in the
drug-soaked Colombian underworld.

DEEP LIE   70266-5/ $5.99 US/ $6.99 Can
At a secret Baltic submarine base, a renegade Soviet
commander prepares a plan so outrageous that it just
might work.

UNDER THE LAKE   70519-2/ $5.99 US/ $6.99 Can

CHIEFS   70347-5/ $5.99 US/ $6.99 Can

RUN BEFORE THE WIND
                70507-9/ $5.99 US/ $6.99 Can

JAMES ELLROY

BROWN'S REQUIEM　　78741-5/$4.50 US/ $5.50 Can
Join ex-cop and sometimes P.I. Fritz Brown beneath the golden glitter of Tinsel Town...where arson, pay-offs, and porn are all part of the game.

CLANDESTINE　　81141-3/$4.99 US/$5.99 Can
Nominated for an Edgar Award for Best Original Paperback Mystery Novel. A compelling thriller about an ambitious L.A. patrolman caught up in the sex and sleaze of smog city where murder is the dark side of love.

KILLER ON THE ROAD　　89934-5/$4.99 US/$5.99 Can
Enter the horrifying world of a killer whose bloody trail of carnage baffles police from coast to coast and whose only pleasure is to kill...and kill again.

Featuring Lloyd Hopkins

BLOOD ON THE MOON　　69851-X/$4.99 US/$5.99 Can
Lloyd Hopkins is an L.A. cop. Hard, driven, brilliant, he's the man they call in when a murder case looks bad.

BECAUSE THE NIGHT　　70063-8/$4.99 US/$5.99 Can
Detective Sergeant Lloyd Hopkins had a hunch that there was a connection between three bloody bodies and one missing cop...a hunch that would take him to the dark heart of madness...and beyond.